James Street.   James Childers.

TOMORROW WE REAP

Tomorrow We Reap

by

JAMES STREET

&

JAMES CHILDERS

DIAL PRESS INC.   NEW YORK, N. Y.

Printed in the United States of America

for MAURINE and for two MARYS

TOMORROW WE REAP

Chapter one

Bruce Dabney reached over the mantel and took down the old ox horn. He walked slowly to the porch of his house, pointed the horn down the valley and sounded again the call to his people, proclaiming danger and summoning them to council.

From the porch of The House the call rolled down the slope, past The Tree where lay the Dabney dead, those who, a century before, founded this fief in Mississippi's wilderness and named it Lebanon because the forest was so mighty. The ground in which the dead rested was, in many ways, more important than the ground on which the living walked, for the pattern of yesterday was the covenant of the valley today and the pledge of tomorrow. And now this heritage was threatened; so Bruce blew the old horn.

The sire of the Dabney family was weary that winter afternoon of 1893 for, like so many old men of the South, he was drained by the thirty bitter years that Secession bred, the legacy of rebellion.

He ran his hand along his white beard; then scratched a rough lump under the skin of his left hand. He cocked his head, listening to the signal echo through Lebanon, rolling eastward past The Tree, thence across Bogue Homa Creek.

The call scarcely reached the north cut to the valley when Kyd, the wife of Bruce, hurried to the porch, a gentle rebuke on her tongue. She looked quickly at her husband and the rebuke never came, for Kyd Dabney knew by his bearing that Bruce was in no mood to accept it.

"No need of raising a racket, Kyd." He spoke gently. "I've already blown it."

Kyd said, "I knew you were working up to it. And I can't see why." Her black eyes were sharp. "After all, the family will be here for supper. Everybody except Sans." White hair had invaded her black hair above her temples. The years, too, had crept in, but seemed to have taken no toll at all and Kyd never faltered, even when her husband doubted his own ways and wisdom.

She held out her hand, the olive skin firm and without wrinkles, expecting him to surrender the horn to her. He didn't, and she looked up at him accusingly. "Your mother is resting," she said. "I'm afraid you scared her."

"This horn won't scare Mama," Bruce said. "She's heard it too many times."

Nevertheless, he stared at the walls of The House as though looking through them and into the room of his mother, Shellie, now aged and helpless, living in the hazy past which occasionally flashed clear.

He wet his lips and looked down at Kyd and then away. "You go tell somebody to light a fire in the parlor. We'll meet there. And there's no use making a fuss, because I aim to blow it again."

The second call rolled away, down the pike from the north cut to the south cut, down Bogue Homa to the village of New Hebron, past the Dabney store and the Dabney mill, the Free Church and the courthouse. It rolled past the shacks of the Irish and Cajuns and Negroes, descendants of those who, years before, helped the Dabneys establish a refuge for Southern Abolitionists and Unionists, a sanctuary that risked battle with the Confederacy, and lost.

In the conflict of Reconstruction, the Dabneys were defeated again; this time by Yankee carpetbaggers and Southern Bourbons who finally got together and closed a deal that took Union soldiers out of the South and changed the land from a conquered province into a colony, sealing the Negro in a far room of the house still divided.

Then lethargy settled over the valley. The Dabney mill cut enough lumber to serve the people. The Store stocked a few items; but it didn't need many goods because money was as rare in the valley as frost, almost as rare as snow. Lebanon was an agrarian settlement in South Mississippi's piney woods where yesterday was like today, and both were drowsy.

Bruce farmed a few acres and bred mules. The brooding pines

looked down on it all, on the pastoral brotherhood and the poverty, and sighed as though they, tall enough to peer beyond the horizon, saw tomorrow rushing in, heard the shouts of the oncoming hordes:

"Span the bayous! Cut the trees and build the cities! Shove the chimneys to the clouds! Let the smoke write new words for old songs, new music for old ballads!"

The South was shaking herself and, although blows still rained on her bony back, she was crawling out of the slough, working herself and her scrawny children from dawn until dark, weaving and pounding; an oxcart pace, but moving.

The nation was swinging out into the West, a flood tide of expansion, and the tide was eddying South, creeping toward Lebanon, its way made ready by entrepreneurs and exploiters heeding the call of Big Money. They came with railroads around their chests and banks on their backs. They plucked up forests by the roots, bringing an industrial revolution to a people who understood a rifle trigger and a fishing pole, but gaped in awe at the gadgets of progress, then frowned, then scowled.

By 1893, these invaders, probing the South, had completed a railroad through Ellisville, only eight miles north of Lebanon, and a vanguard of timber cruisers and buyers already were in the valley picking up holdings, some by barter, many by purchase of tax claims.

In the village of New Hebron was a rough pine office, newly built, and through its doors moved the agents of the Peninsula Lumber Company, buying all Lebanon land that was for sale and grabbing some that wasn't. With the company agents there came contractors and surveyors, company lawyers and engineers, all crowding into the valley.

There came, too, Mr. G. T. Thrumbull, a widower, to manage the mill that Peninsula was building. His daughter, Ruth Thrumbull, came with him and they found a home site on the east ridge of the valley, then returned to Chicago to prepare plans for their house and to await completion of the mill.

The Peninsula people left their footprints everywhere, occasionally even on the fringes of the Dabney land.

Bruce saw the marks, the threats scarred in the earth, and consulted with Kyd who advised caution. He talked with his sons—Sans and Mingo. Mingo, too, advised caution. Sans urged action.

Thinking of his sons, some of the lethargy left Bruce and he reached for the Dabney horn, calling his folks to his fireside.

Down the pike, down at The Store, Mr. Charlie Owens, manager of the Dabneys' mercantile business, heard the call and the flesh tingled on his turkey-red neck. However, he did not look up from the list of goods he was reciting to the drummer from Mobile.

"A dozen of Hoyt's cologne and four cases of Garrett snuff. Usual amount paregoric and calomel." Mr. Charlie scratched the back of his ear, using his index finger.

The drummer, named Elmo Batson, looked up from his order pad and grinned. "What else, Mr. Charlie?"

The front door rattled open, then banged shut and the heavy tread of Ronnie Sullivan creaked the floorboards of the old store. Mr. Charlie glanced up and he and Ronnie exchanged nods. Ronnie, too, had heard the horn. He was a middle-aged man who bossed the Dabney oxen and wagons that fetched logs from the lumber camp to the little Dabney mill, now insignificant in the shadow of Peninsula's projected huge plant.

Ronnie opened the door of the hot blast-stove and shoved in two pine knots. He turned his back to the heat, warming himself, watching Mr. Charlie.

The merchant droned on while Elmo Batson exuded good will. Dabney credit was good and Mr. Charlie never strained it. "I need some Seltzer Pepsin chewing gum and two Studebaker one-horse wagons." He slipped his spectacles to the bridge of his nose and held his head up proudly. "And one Brighton buggy." There was a flourish in his voice. "Spindle seat and all the trimmings."

The buggy was for Mingo Dabney, younger son of Bruce and Kyd.

Elmo closed his order book. "God a'mighty. I tell you sump'n— that's an order what is an order. Got some calendars for you." He took them from his sample case and said casually, "What's all this talk about Peninsula opening a store in Lebanon?"

Mr. Charlie glanced up and Ronnie stepped from the stove to the counter. "Where'd you hear that?" Ronnie asked.

"Oh, just heard it."

That was the moment Bruce Dabney blew the second call and the echo reverberated down the valley. Ronnie stiffened and Mr. Charlie tapped his fingers on the counter. Elmo Batson listened a second, then said, "Old Bruce?"

Charlie Owens removed his spectacles and wiped them, then put them back on. "Uh huh." He nodded sadly. "He's calling his folks together."

Elmo Batson closed his sample case. "See you next month. If you need me, just holler." He looked up toward the Dabney house. "Ol' Elmo can tell time."

He went to his two-horse buggy and drove away toward the south cut, the road to Mobile. Ronnie dropped another pine knot in the stove and he and the storekeeper peered at each other.

Mingo Dabney was riding up the pike. He was wearing brown Kentucky jeans and a tight-fitting coat. His wool hat, drab and commonplace on other men, looked jaunty on Mingo. His coal-black hair, an inheritance from his mother, showed in masses under the wide brim.

The Dabney mill and The Store were Mingo's responsibilities, but he kept his eyes on the oxen, the forest and the crops. He overlooked nothing; a bargain, a trade, a pretty face. He went one year to college, then assumed management of the mill. It was Kyd's reluctant suggestion, but she, aware of her husband's weariness, was convinced that Mingo was needed at home. He kept his finger on the family ledger while Sans, the other son, felt for the pulse of the people.

Mingo entered The Store and glanced around, nodding to Mr. Charlie. Then, without looking at Ronnie he said to him, "We logging around the stove these days?"

"My crews are working." Ronnie said it without offense. "Did you hear your pa's horn?"

"I heard it. Sans been here?"

Ronnie reached for his chewing tobacco. "Sans is working timber at the south cut. The Peninsula crowd is down there and he reckons he better be nigh."

Mingo said, "If he drops by, tell him I've gone to The House." He walked out, mounted his horse and rode rapidly away.

Ronnie and Mr. Charlie saw him out of sight and the storekeeper said, "Some of the sawmill hands say hard things about Mingo, but he's all right."

"Nothing wrong with Mingo," Ronnie said. "He just don't like to sit around and talk. He's like his mother. Sharp as a meat-ax. Looks sump'n like her, too."

"But he's got Dabney gumption." The old merchant tugged at the lobe of his ear. "Mingo ain't like most of us. Ain't like his brother a-tall. Not a frazzlin' bit like Sans."

The courthouse was New Hebron's only brick building and stood in a grass-splotched square where water oaks shadowed it, softening somewhat the harshness of the red bricks. Across the dusty road was the office of Wyeth Woodward, attorney for the Dabneys. It was a two-room building with a passageway and was filled with heavy furniture, and Woodward himself was a heavy man, stolid behind his thick chestnut-turning-to-gray beard.

The call of the Dabneys that winter afternoon startled him, although he had been expecting it for days. He was in his office talking to Louisa, his daughter.

Wyeth heard the horn and pulled out his heavy gold watch. It was 2:25 o'clock. He toyed with the fob, a piece of broad black ribbon on which were clasped his initials, woven in gold, and his Masonic emblem.

Louisa, standing by the fireplace, watched her father, then glanced out of the window and up the pike toward The House. The sky was cobalt and brooding, a wet chilly wind rustling down from the north cut, down Bogue Homa.

"Mr. Dabney is impatient, isn't he?" Louisa said, and reached for her fascinator. She had her father's full round face and brown hair, and her mother's graceful strength.

Wyeth said, "People usually get impatient when wolves are scratching at the barn."

"You worried, Papa?"

"Scared to death."

She forced a laugh and flipped the fascinator around her head. "Fiddlesticks!" Louisa dismissed the possibility of her father being afraid of anything and said in her sweetest tone, "You'll open a bottle of muscadine wine for Sans when he comes to supper tonight, won't you?"

"Of course."

"And, Papa, will you open another bottle when I ask Mingo for supper?" She pulled her coat collar around her neck.

Wyeth did not answer immediately. He tapped his walking stick against his shoe and said, "Yes. I'll open another bottle for Mingo. But one of these days those two boys are going to compare notes."

"Papa!" she upbraided him. "Gentlemen don't compare notes on ladies."

He looked down at her with his "lawyer look" as Louisa called it and said, "The time is coming when you'll have to make up your mind, young lady. It's contrary to law and custom to marry two men. At the same time."

She tucked the ends of his muffler under his coat collar and handed him his gray hat. "Some day I'll make up my mind, but while it's going on don't fuss at me."

They walked across to the courthouse square where Wyeth's bay gelding was hitched to a runabout buggy. Gar Rivers was waiting at the hitching rack, his throat wrapped in a brown scarf and his bony frame protected by a sack suit of coarse jean.

Gar Rivers was so ugly as a baby that his mother thought he resembled a garfish and so named him. He grew up a slave over in the big river country and loved Wyeth Woodward as deeply as any man ever loved his brother. He educated himself, then opened a little school for Negroes, the undisputed leader of his people in the valley.

"You heard the horn?" Wyeth asked.

"Yes." Gar nodded slowly. "I heard it."

Louisa told them goodbye and walked away. Her father waited until she was beyond hearing and asked, "Wonder if Sans heard it?"

"He's down by the south cut," Gar replied. "I saw Nils Holmquist at the livery stable and told him to tell Sans." Alone with Wyeth, he called white men by their names without titles, a privilege he never used in public.

"What's Holmquist doing in town?"

Nils Holmquist, a Michigan man, was woods boss for the Peninsula Lumber Company and spent most of his time at the company camp southwest of New Hebron.

The Negro unspanned the hitching strap and tossed it to his friend. "He came in to help settle some trouble between one of his men and one of our girls." He held the reins while Wyeth got into the buggy. "Holmquist is an easy man to deal with. He's trying to get along down here."

"I know it," Wyeth said. "But he's having a hard time."

"Any man would have a hard time understanding folks in this valley." Gar said it without bitterness. "The shanty Irish and the shack Negroes. Neighbors, Wyeth. So close they smell the collards cooking in each other's kitchens, and yet miles apart. And then the Cajuns—" Gar held up his hands in a gesture of futility. "Holmquist or no other man can unravel the caste and color lines in this valley."

And Gar was right. First, there were the Irish, and the Irish themselves were divided. Those who had lived all their lives in the valley, drawling Southern Protestants, who loathed the freshly-come Irish imported from the North by the Peninsula people.

Then there were the Negroes, neighbors to the Irish, but regarded by them as inferiors although they lived in the same squalor.

Finally, there were the Cajuns, a mystery people who kept themselves apart from the Irish and the Negroes, although there were traces of Africa in their blood lines. They knew little or nothing of their ancestry and cared less, and if a brown child appeared, an event neither common nor rare, they shrugged; and brown children and blonde children nursed at the same full breasts. They spoke a polyglot of French, Spanish and English, built on a broad African base. Their blood lines went back to Portuguese and Spanish pirates, including Moors, and were crossed and recrossed with Colonial French and Indians and Negroes. They held themselves above the Negroes, yet were unaccepted by most of the whites. These people, proud and sensitive and lusty for life, lived in tidy cabins along Bogue Homa, growing little patches of peppers and herbs and working alongside the Irish and Negroes, but were a part of neither.

The buggy was sagging under Wyeth's weight and the lawyer fingered the reins. "If Holmquist will see that Sans gets the word, we can be going along. Climb in." He looked quickly at Gar. "You're going, aren't you?"

"No." The Negro stroked the horse's ear and the gelding nuzzled him.

"I know I can walk in the front door of the Dabney house and they'll welcome me. Call me Professor Rivers. But they don't want me up there today."

The lawyer stirred uneasily. "Anything that concerns Lebanon concerns the Negroes."

"Maybe. But they'll be talking big land and big money. That's when we Negroes are always on the outside listening in." He slapped the horse's chest and the horse nipped at him playfully. "Tell Bruce Dabney if he needs me, he knows where I am."

He slapped the horse once more and walked away towards the courthouse to warm his big hands before the sheriff's fire. There, too, he was welcome because he was the span between the white man's law and the black man's obedience.

Wyeth touched his horse with the whalebone whip and wheeled around the square, past the bank and the Free Church, past the rickety Jasper Hotel, and up the pike. The raw wind nipped at him and he frowned, not in discomfort, but in worry.

There was much to worry a good man in 1893. Wyeth's talk with Gar reminded him that blacks and whites were farther apart than ever. The unpainted wagons he passed on the road, driven by men who clucked occasionally to their skinny, worked-out mules, told him that the Southern agrarian revolt was starved out and its offshoot of Populism was losing ground to cash and credit, courts and contracts. The blight of Southern Bourbonism was still heavy on the people and although a few men, Northern and Southern, were linking arms to plant the land again, Northern big foxes, a feared breed, and Southern little foxes, a despised breed, were joining hands to glean once more. They intended to own the land; and all the fruits of the land, from ore to timber, would be theirs and whoever got in their way might get hurt.

All this bothered Wyeth and he was troubled, too, by more personal matters; his catarrh and his girth, the ambitions of Laurel his wife, and the behavior of his daughter with eyes for both the Dabney boys, Mingo and Sans, the brothers who really were cousins.

The ridges of Lebanon trooped through the south cut, toward the Gulf of Mexico, seventy-five miles away. In that wilderness were a few scattered hamlets, and millions and millions of virgin yellow pines, a sea of trees, a seething, humming tide of green needles.

Sans Dabney walked these woods with long strides, cruising his timber, judging it. There were hobs in his heavy brogans and rawhide around the legs of his blue jeans.

Although most people forgot it, even those who knew it, Sans

Dabney really was not the son of Bruce and Kyd. He was the post-humous son of Bruce's older brother, Cormac Dabney.

Martha was his mother and planned to name her son for his father, but while the Cajun midwife washed the baby, the old woman muttered, "*Pauvre enfant. Il est sans père.*" In the emptiness after the birth of her son, Martha heard the lament and, fondling her sorrow, decided to make her son a living reminder of the loss of her husband.

So she named him Sans.

Martha died the day he was born and the old Cajun came to lay her out, and, pausing by the cradle, she whispered, "*Sans père. Sans mère.*"

Bruce and Kyd took the child for their own and reared him with Mingo, born less than two years later.

Sans, walking the woods, was thinking of his brother and worrying a bit about him, but not too much. Mingo liked a horse race, but never a hunt. He was tense at the flip of a card and enjoyed a break-down dance in the hills, a waltz in Mobile, a glass of brandy or a dipper of whiskey, a Cajun girl in the moonlight, an Irish girl in the rain. That was Mingo, the younger brother.

The older boy often worried about Mingo, but Mingo never worried about Sans. To the younger brother, the older brother was rock and trees and sky; the steadfast things, the things that never change.

Sans glanced up from the floor of the forest and saw Nils Holmquist ride up over the ridge and sit there, looking about. The Dabney boy cupped his hands and shouted, and Peninsula's woods boss rode his way.

Their ages were different, for Sans was young and Nils Holmquist was in his middle years. Their outlooks and backgrounds were different, too; but they, a Michigan Swede and a Mississippi Dabney, had much in common. Both were woodsmen and too big to see little things.

Nils dismounted and threw the reins over a gallberry bush. "How's it coming?" He was a ruddy man with gnarled hands, broken by trees and chains from the Upper Peninsula to the Gulf, a thousand miles of sawmilling.

"Pretty fair," said Sans. "How 'bout you?"

"All right, I suppose. Saw Gar Rivers in town and he said tell you your father was blowing the horn."

"Then I better be going." Sans was not surprised; he knew that sooner or later the family must gather and decide its course.

Nils offered his horse, for Sans' horse was tethered up the ridge, a quarter of a mile away. Sans mounted and Nils held the bridle a second. "I know that call was something to do with Peninsula." He looked up. "Well, I'm part of Peninsula and we ain't looking for trouble down here."

The Dabney boy gathered the reins in his left hand. "I know it. And we've got no grudge. Least, no grudge against you, Nils." He slapped the horse with the tip of the reins. "Be seeing you."

He rode down the slope to the pike, riding easily and rocking slightly in the saddle. He turned north for the village, pulled his leather cap low over his forehead and put his horse to a gallop.

The wind was in his brown hair and stung his face and he was lighthearted, for the time had come for the Dabneys to turn and fight. He wished he had time to ride by the Woodward place and maybe wave at Louisa, at least pass the house where she lived, the room where she slept.

Chapter two

ALONE IN THE PARLOR, Bruce Dabney sat in his big chair, waiting for his family to gather. There was a fire in the room and the French windows were closed, the green shutters fastened. The glow of the fire was the only light. Bruce wanted a cigar or a pipe, but tobacco was a habit Kyd disapproved of, and he slipped off to the woods or to the sheds whenever he needed to enjoy a smoke. The nicotine stains on his beard were evidence of his transgressions.

Kyd believed tobacco and coffee possibly aggravated the brown lump on his hand. She wasn't a martinet; rather, she was a scolding nest-bird who watched her mate's every move, convinced she herself must protect his happiness and well-being.

She was a Cajun, a Dabney convert, and with the usual zeal of the convert, was endowed with a fierce determination to hold the valley Dabneys together. She sprang from nothing, and now she was somebody and her fire was so bright she wanted the whole family to live in its warmth.

In the beginning, Kyd's matriarchy met no opposition from her lackadaisical husband. He knew the reins of the valley had passed from his tired hands to Kyd's strong hands, and that she was passing them on to Mingo. He didn't really resent the situation, although at times he was irked by Kyd's posing as the high priestess of the temple. He just didn't see any sense in her accentuated reverence for the past, her idolatry of the Dabney forebears. Bruce realized that those hallowed giants buried down there under The Tree were adventurers and rakes, ruthless pioneers who seized what they wanted, sowing a whirlwind they didn't live to harvest.

He rested his elbows on the arm of the big chair and, listening for his wife's footsteps, scratched the brown welt on his hand in sensuous pleasure. Then he got up and was standing before the fire, the glow of the blaze on his white beard, when Kyd swept into the room and glanced around. "Oh, there you are," she said. "They'll all be here in a few minutes. I think you should sit over there by the fire. And, Bruce, stop scratching your hand."

"I'm not scratching it," he said. "Just rubbing it." He said it slowly and Kyd sensed rebellion.

"Wyeth can sit next to you and I'll sit here," she said. "The boys can sit over there on the divan."

Bruce watched his wife a second, watched her bustle around the room, arranging chairs. "We'll need another chair," he said. "There'll be six of us."

"Six?" She stared at him, hiding her sudden agitation. "Certainly you don't expect your mother to attend the meeting?" She nodded towards Shellie's room to punctuate the question.

"That's right." Bruce met the stare. "Mama will be with us."

Tiny icicles of fear stabbed at Kyd's heart. Here was a maneuver she didn't understand. Why helpless old Shellie? Her judgment was of no value. She was an old, old child. Why Shellie? Kyd's mind was separating each fact swiftly, weighing and storing it. If Bruce wanted his mother at the meeting, then Bruce expected dissension, an issue. If an issue arose, a matter of Dabney principle, Shellie would support her son.

Kyd's riposte was adroit as always. "Now, now! You're teasing, Bruce. Your mother is sick. We mustn't subject her to a family meeting."

"We've got some problems to settle this afternoon. Mama will be with us. Now, let's hear no more about it."

Kyd knew when to retreat and said, "Very well. Just the same, it's a little unfortunate a man and his wife can't thrash things out. Don't you think so?"

Bruce might have answered her, but he saw Mingo ride up and watched him toss the reins to the stable boy.

In the hall, Mingo sailed his hat toward the hat rack and walked into the parlor, glancing around and missing nothing: the fire, the position of the chairs, his father's steady gaze, his mother's smile. "Hello, Papa," he said cheerfully, and stooped to kiss his mother's cheek. "So I'm the first one here."

"Yes. The others will be along pretty soon," Kyd said.

"Oh, sure. Sans will come balling-the-jack up the pike in a few minutes." Mingo grinned. "Course, it might take a yoke of oxen to move Mr. Woodward—"

They all laughed and Mingo sat down near the fire. The tension was broken and he held his hands toward the blaze. They were silent for a minute, Bruce dreading the ordeal ahead and Kyd mulling over his maneuver, sulking because he had presumed to plan without her.

Wyeth Woodward's buggy, sagging to the left under the lawyer's weight, came up the pike and wheeled into the lane toward The House. Bruce went to the kitchen to mix toddies.

Mingo stepped in front of the fire and stretched. "Looks like Papa means business."

"I just don't know what's come over your father," Kyd said. "There was no need to call us together like this." She looked up at her son, at his black hair so much like hers, at his smoky brown eyes. "I suppose you know that Sans is going to the Woodward house for supper tonight." She adjusted her cuff. "Has Louisa asked you over?"

Mingo turned toward the fire and pushed the logs with his foot.

He didn't want to talk about Louisa and Sans. "She said something about me coming over in a few days."

"Sans goes tonight—"

"I know it, Mama." He was smiling when he turned to her. "If Sans had his way, he'd be over there every night."

Kyd walked toward the hallway to greet Wyeth, and Mingo walked beside her. "You boys mustn't let Louisa lack for beaux. You and Sans are the only ones around here who're eligible. Nobody else meets her mother's approval."

"You talk to Sans," Mingo said. "He's already in love with her, head over heels."

They were in the long hallway and Kyd said, "But you know Sans. Always in the clouds. Louisa isn't like that at all."

He put his hand on his mother's shoulder. "Now, Mama, I'll pick my girl for myself."

Kyd wanted to continue the discussion, but Wyeth's heavy footsteps were on the porch. She opened the door and welcomed him, and they all walked back into the parlor where the lawyer warmed his hands; then accepted a toddy from Bruce.

They talked about the weather and politics, about many things. "How're your mules?" Wyeth asked Bruce.

"All right. I'm sending up to Maury County, Tennessee, for a jack. Believe I can breed mules to take the place of our oxen."

Mingo crossed his legs and dangled his foot. "By the time you get your breed, we'll have a railroad in here. We'll be shipping lumber in flatcars. Those Peninsula people aim to do business in a big way."

He was not conscious of saying anything unusual. He was only making comment, repeating what was common talk in the village, but Bruce and Wyeth exchanged glances and were silent. Kyd saw the exchange and more than ever was piqued.

A long "Cre-e-e-o-o-o" sounded down by The Tree. It was the catamount cry of the Dabneys, the old family cry of warning and no quarter. Bruce sat erect and his face drained of color.

Kyd was startled. "Good heavens," she whispered.

Mingo went to the window and watched Sans gallop up the lane. He shook his head and laughed. "That crazy scutter. Told you he'd be balling-the-jack." He turned and faced the others. "He don't ride a horse. He just grows to one." Then he noticed how tense his father and mother were.

"Bruce!" Kyd said hoarsely. "Tell Sans never again to yell that cry. I can't stand it." It brought back frightening memories of her childhood, of war in the valley and a Confederate regiment swarming through the north cut to scourge Mississippi's nest of Unionism. "Speak to Sans."

"I will." Bruce touched her hand, comforting her. "I'll speak to him. I'll tell him not to yell that cry. Never again. Unless it's needed."

The fire sputtered and hissed as it ate into the rich pine, and the north wind rattled the shutters.

Sans Dabney was the tallest of his family, as tall as his father who was killed at the north cut when the Confederates invaded the valley, passing to his unborn son the humiliation of defeat and the resolve that never again must an enemy force the gate to Lebanon.

The red of the wind was in his cheeks and he ran his fingers through his tousled brown hair as he strode into the room, bringing a quiet confidence to all of them, even Kyd who loved him so much and understood him so little. There was gentleness in his manner as he spoke to each of them, but there was tenderness when he spoke to his brother. "How you doing, Lebuba?" He had called him that since, at the age of three, he tried to say Little Brother.

"First rate, kiddo."

Bruce waited until everyone was still, then said, "You boys go get your grandma. Bring her in here."

The brothers turned to obey. In the hallway, Mingo whispered, "Good Lord! Grandma going to be there!"

"We'll have to tote her," Sans said.

Shellie was before the fire, rocking and watching the blaze. Her face and her eyes were hollow and her mind was almost so, wavering back ninety years to the Indian wars, to the massacre at Fort Mims. The Civil War and Lebanon's stand for Abolition were but yesterday to old Shellie. "It had to happen." She was mumbling. "Our family was divided and hatred brewed upon our hearth."

Her grandsons had heard her mumble so often that they gave no heed to the drone of her words. "Good day, Grandma," Sans said.

She looked up at the two boys, then away. Sans nodded to Mingo and they lifted her chair and carried her into the parlor, and set her down before the fireplace.

Again Shellie looked around, first at Bruce, then at Kyd. A flick of recognition passed across her face. Then the blank look returned and she began rocking slowly. Wyeth touched her shoulder. "Good day, Mrs. Dabney. I'm Wyeth Woodward. How are you?"

Shellie fingered her black shawl. "Nobody was to blame," she whispered, mumbling again. "It had to happen. Aven was young and beautiful. She took Clay MacIvor from Morna. Morna was sick—"

She was opening the door of the Dabney crypt, mouthing the tragedy of her daughters, Aven and Morna, both long since gone from the valley. It was their fate to love the same man, Claiborne MacIvor, who forsook the valley and joined the Confederacy, taking Aven with him and deserting Morna, his betrothed. MacIvor led the Confederates in their attack against the valley, and paid with his life.

"—Aven robbed Morna of her first love and robbed me of my peace." Her voice trailed off.

The Dabneys looked at one another and Kyd said to Bruce, "I knew you shouldn't bring her in here."

Shellie turned at the sound of the voice. "It's Kyd," she said.

"Yes, Mama," Kyd leaned over her mother-in-law, adjusting her dress. "Anything you want?"

The old one took Kyd's hand and stroked it. "I remember it all. I was the only person to get away from the Indians at Fort Mims. I swam the Alabama River." She pulled the shawl tightly around her shoulders and leaned forward, rocking.

Bruce avoided Kyd's stare and stepped in front of the fireplace. "I called you together because we must make some decisions. It's about the Peninsula people. Wyeth, you take over."

The heavy-set lawyer got up, tugged at his vest and propped his shoulders against the mantel. He cleared his throat and said, "Like Bruce says, it's Peninsula. We might as well get down to brass tacks. They already own considerable land below the south cut and they're going to build a mill down there. They want more land. They want some Dabney land because it joins them, and they need logging roads across it."

Nobody said anything. Shellie's head sagged to the back of her chair and she was asleep. Bruce reached for the poker and stirred the fire.

It was Mingo who took the lead. "We knew this was coming. I say we ought to sell them all they want."

"They want a heap," Wyeth said. "All the land between their mill site and their camp."

"Better still," said Mingo. "More they want, better bargain we get. I say sell."

Kyd looked at Mingo and beamed. Bruce stared out of the window, saying nothing, giving his family an opportunity to speak.

Sans sat leaning back in his chair, his fingers locked behind his head. Twice Mingo glanced at him and once Kyd looked his way and waited for him to speak, but he sat there with his long legs stretched out, gazing past Wyeth and into the fire. Finally he said, "If we sold 'em that land, Mr. Woodward, reckon they'd agree not to log with skidders?"

"No," said Mingo quickly, before Wyeth could answer. "They won't do that. All the big companies use skidders."

"I must agree with Mingo," Kyd said.

Sans shoved his hands deep in his pockets. "Mama, do you know what a skidder is?"

"Course," said Kyd tersely. "It's a big machine."

"That's right. Just a big machine with a long cable that drags logs through the woods. It tears down or pulls up everything it touches."

Mingo hitched his chair forward. "What difference does it make? What's a few saplings? There're plenty trees. Enough trees to last forever, if we keep down fires."

"Forever!" Sans got quickly to his feet and stepped to the fireplace. Something about his bearing prompted Wyeth to move over; prompted Bruce to step aside. "Mingo, do you know how long it takes to grow a tree? These are virgin pines. There never will be any more like them. Never."

At the sound of Sans' voice, old Shellie opened her eyes and fixed them on him, on his hair and his shoulders; then dozed off again.

Mingo stirred uneasily. "Don't start talking like a Populist politician, Sans. It's a fad now to jump on big companies. I like trees as much as the next man, but a pine growing is just a pine. Cut it up and it's a house." He looked around, studying the impression he was making. "It's a choice between a tree rotting in the woods, and a roof over a man. I'm for the man. Besides, trees grow faster than most folks realize."

"Up in Michigan they said trees would last forever. They didn't." Sans said it emphatically. "Peninsula helped wreck that country. Now they're here. They aim to cut our land bare, and that'll wreck us."

Old Shellie looked up at him again, staring at him as he stood tall before the fire, perhaps remembering his father, her eldest son.

"Wait a minute, Sans." Mingo started to get up, but only shifted in his chair. "We been cutting some trees ourselves—"

Sans cut him off. "We log only the big ones, and leave the saplings to come on. Peninsula won't sawmill like that. They'll cut a big tree then skid it through the woods and crush saplings and seedlings. No forest can stand that." Sans was pleading. "And when they're done, they'll get out and leave us in a valley of stumps. They'll take our tress. Then the land will go. Then the people will go. Then we'll go. There'll be nothing in this valley but graves and waste."

Bruce was smiling his pride in the boy. Mingo was awed by his brother. Wyeth was shaken. There were tears in Kyd's eyes. She was annoyed and yet she, too, was proud. She reached out and touched Sans and patted his arm.

"I don't aim to be the burr under the saddle," Sans said. "But I'm against Peninsula. We all knew their proposition was coming and I'm against it." He turned from the mantel and went back to his chair.

Wyeth Woodward cleared his throat. Bruce stared into the fire and Mingo was quiet.

Kyd saw that Sans' plea had touched Mingo and her husband, and decided that delay was the wise maneuver. "Maybe a little coffee will help us all."

"You're right," Wyeth said. "A little brandy in mine, please." He felt in his pocket and found his stogies and pulled out two. "Bruce, have a cigar."

Bruce took the stogy, looked steadily at Kyd, and lighted it. Then he sat down in a chair by Shellie while Kyd went for coffee.

Wyeth studied his notes and, mulling his own ideas, puffed his cigar. To him it was all quite simple, and sad. Mingo was the South of a new day, ready to accept big machines, big corporations, big money. Sans was the echo of yesterday, the South of revolution and rebellion, the vanquished but unconquered South, still at bay, still ready to strike one more blow; the defiant South, so terribly right, so magnificently wrong.

The endless Southern conflict still was joined, and in brothers.

The coffee warmed their spirits. Shellie, strengthened by a little brandy, perked up noticeably and looked around, smiling for the first time. Wyeth tossed his cigar in the fire; then stepped back to the mantel, the well of the forum.

Again he cleared his voice. "As attorney for the family," he said, "let me lay Peninsula's whole proposition before you: then you decide your course. They want to buy land west of Bogue Homa. They aim to dam the branch and build a mill pond."

"They already own the east fork," Sans said. "If they get the west, they'll own Bogue Homa. They can dam the whole creek."

"What if they do?" Kyd's tone was sharp. "What good is Bogue Homa down below the south cut?"

Wyeth blinked and turned away. Sans lowered his head and Mingo blushed. Bruce was gentle, however. "People live down there. Cajuns. If Bogue Homa dries up, their land will be dry."

"Oh," said Kyd, "I forgot."

"Go on, Wyeth," said Bruce. "Get to the main point."

The lawyer rustled his notes and fingered his Masonic emblem. "Peninsula wants a right of way into the valley. They aim to build a railroad to tie up with the Mainline at Ellisville. They aim to come through the north cut, down Bogue Homa, through New Hebron and on to their mill." He folded his notes and stuck them in his coat pocket. "That's the main point."

"I say let 'em in." Mingo said it quickly. "There'll be a boom. Our property will skyrocket."

Sans asked, "Will the railroad be for everybody or just for Peninsula? Can I ship logs on that railroad?"

"No," Wyeth said. "Peninsula wants a private line. It's for them and nobody else."

"Then I'm against 'em." Again Sans Dabney declared himself. "I'm against a private line coming in here. A regular railroad will come in some day. I say let's wait."

No one bothered to reply. Kyd and Mingo were thinking of land values. Bruce was troubled by other matters. Shellie was asleep. The little group was silent and Bruce nodded to his lawyer.

Wyeth, weary of standing, pulled a chair to the side of the fireplace and sat down, sighing as he did so. "That's all I've got to say about Peninsula."

Bruce took over. "There're some things we haven't mentioned. Wyeth, did you bring Papa's will?"

Kyd gasped and sat erect, startled. She remembered Hoab Dabney's will. So that was the reason Bruce wanted Shellie there. Mingo was puzzled, and so was Sans.

Wyeth closed his eyes, resting them. "No," he said. "But I know every provision. Most of Hoab Dabney's possessions were willed to his son, Bruce Dabney." The attorney, pompous in the discussion of legalities, reverted to his lawyer talk.

Kyd knew every provision, too. She had made it her business to know them and was looking from Bruce to Shellie.

Wyeth fingered his beard and frowned. "The will provides that no decision concerning Dabney land is valid unless Mrs. Dabney—" He nodded toward Shellie. "Unless Hoab Dabney's widow approves."

"Provided—" Kyd said slowly, prompting him.

"Provided Mrs. Dabney is capable of a decision."

Bruce dropped his head. Mingo was staring at the floor and Sans looked at his grandmother, withered and helpless, and he was stunned that the valley of Lebanon was held in those palsied hands.

"When you are ready to question your mother," Wyeth nodded to Bruce, "I will be ready. But I want one thing clearly understood." He looked at each of them separately. "If I am convinced Mrs. Dabney is competent of a major decision, I'll go into court and so testify. However, I will not hesitate to hold that she is incompetent, if I think she is."

"Ask her, Mr. Dabney," Kyd said. "Ask her now. Let's get this ordeal behind us."

"Not yet," said Bruce. "First, I want Wyeth to explain the positions of certain members of the family."

"Very well." The lawyer then recounted that while Sans actually was the son of Cormac Dabney, he was the legal son of Bruce and Kyd through adoption. "Then there is Morna Dabney—" Again the crypt was opened but, mercifully, Shellie was sleeping.

Morna was the wife of Keith Alexander the freebooter, the duelist branded by bastardy, who helped brew Lebanon's rebellion against the Confederacy because he hated a South that scorned the stigma of his illegitimacy. He married Morna after MacIvor turned from her to her sister, and killed him after MacIvor led his Confederates through the north cut. Alexander fought the South for four years, then went to Chicago, screening the stigma of his birth behind the millions that testified to his triumph.

"—Years ago when Morna married Keith Alexander," the lawyer continued, "they renounced all claims to any property in Lebanon." He lowered his voice, careful lest Shellie hear the words that followed. "Finally, there is Mrs. Aven Dabney MacIvor. The widow of Claiborne MacIvor was disinherited by her father and has no claims to any Dabney rights."

At mention of Aven, they glanced at one another quickly. Bruce and Kyd wanted to forget Aven, although she was Bruce's twin, and Mingo and Sans never had known her. She did not write to the family but they knew, in roundabout ways, that she lived in genteel poverty in Virginia. To the valley Dabneys, Aven MacIvor was dead. She had never existed after she married her sister's lover and approved his Confederate campaign against Lebanon. . . .

Kyd again was impatient. It was getting late and her nerves were frayed. "I can't possibly see any excuse for dragging Morna and Aven into this. They are no longer part of the family. They have their own lives."

Wyeth puckered his lips and cut his eyes toward Bruce. The Dabney sire, deep in thought, rubbed the back of his hand; then stopped abruptly, conscious that Kyd was watching him. He stepped to the center of the fireplace and, half turning, tapped on the mantel. His manner put them all on edge.

"We are tired," he said. "But, at least, we know where we stand. Therefore, I think this is the proper time to tell you that Aven is coming back to the valley."

He said it so simply that a second passed before the news touched them. So Bruce repeated it. "I said that Aven is coming back. Aven MacIvor!"

Kyd stifled her gasp. Bruce hadn't told her. A demand, a biting demand for an explanation, was on her tongue, but she dared not speak it. Wyeth and the boys must not know that Bruce ever kept anything from her. She sat there dazed, her lips pinched and bloodless.

Mingo was the first to find his voice. "Aunt Aven coming back! She wouldn't dare. She's a MacIvor!"

At the name MacIvor, Shellie raised her head slowly and looked around.

Sans gripped the arm of his chair and his big knuckles were white under the tan. His voice was cold. "She's a MacIvor, Papa—"

Bruce said, "By choice she is a MacIvor. But by blood she is a Dabney. My sister. My twin."

"What is she after?" Mingo's words crackled. "Land? She knows she has no claims to any Dabney rights."

Bruce's tone, usually so gentle, now was harsh. "She has no Dabney rights. But by law she is a MacIvor, and the MacIvor holdings once stretched from Bogue Homa away back over the east ridge."

Mingo sprang to his feet. "Good Lord, Papa! That land was taken over thirty years ago when Clay MacIvor betrayed this valley."

Bruce turned to his friend. "Go on, Wyeth, Let's have it all."

The lawyer folded his hands across his chest, hesitated a second, then opened the crypt all the way. "The MacIvor land was taken over under duress." He said it ponderously, as though handing down a judgment.

"My God," Mingo whispered, and the room was so still that Shellie's easy breathing was heard.

Wyeth looked away from them, first at the fire then up at the ceiling. "Colonel Claiborne MacIvor died intestate. He deserted his land but did not surrender the titles, and the land belongs to his widow."

Kyd blinked and her lips parted. She was breathing heavily, tensed by her anger at Bruce and the news that Aven MacIvor had valid claims in Lebanon.

The lawyer tapped his fingers together, still staring at the ceiling. "Now that Peninsula is here, the land is valuable. Mrs. MacIvor is coming back to claim a widow's rights." Wyeth shrugged his massive shoulders. "If you contest her rights, she will go to court and beat you."

Kyd demanded, "When is she coming?"

"I don't know," Bruce replied.

Sans broke his silence. "If it's her land, then it's her land."

They all looked at him and, for a moment, no one spoke. Mingo edged away from his brother. "We better make some plans," he said. "Quick ones." He was directing his remarks to his mother, expecting her to have a suggestion.

Kyd opened her mouth to speak, to ask more questions, but Bruce moved to the center of the fireplace, to the center of the forum. The way he moved quieted them. He looked at the back of his hand. Then he held up his head. "I'll tell you what we're going to do." The room no longer was a place of shadows and doubts. "First," he said, "we will settle once and for all time whether or not my mother's mind is clear enough for the responsibility my father gave her."

Kyd moved toward Shellie, to arouse her maybe, to touch her and soothe her.

"Sit down, Mrs. Dabney," her husband said gently. Kyd gasped at the order; then turned and went back to her chair.

Bruce went to his mother and stooped, his hand on one of her knees, his face close to hers. "Mama! This is Bruce."

The old woman touched his face. "All right, Bruce. I know you. It's cold in here. Poke up the fire."

Mingo moved to the fire, but Sans motioned him back. Their stares were fixed on the wrinkled old woman. They watched her while Bruce fixed the fire; then he went to her and knelt on one knee.

Again she stroked his face. Her eyes were clear. "I heard the horn," she said. "I know why I am here. Aven MacIvor is coming back. I heard you say it, but she is no child of mine." Her eyes closed and her head sank against the pillow at the back of the chair. "Your father forbade me to mention her name in his presence and I pass on his word to you. Never again must any of you say her name before me. And she can never come into this house." The old eyes opened. "You understand, Bruce?"

"I understand, Mama."

"Do all of you understand?" She looked around and they nodded and were awed. Shellie put her hands over her eyes, pressing her eyes; she was almost exhausted. "That's all I have to say. Take me back to my room."

Bruce whispered, "Yes, Mama. But first I must ask you a question." The old eyes were closed.

"Some people want to buy part of our land, Mama. Maybe we should sell some of the valley. Mama— Mama—"

Bruce touched her, touching her shoulder, then her face.

She opened her eyes slowly, and they were vacant, "I was the only one who got away from Fort Mims—"

Bruce put his head in his hands and sobbed. Kyd wept, and Wyeth's heavy shoulders sagged. The Dabney brothers stared into the fire, staring at the ashes, at the flickering embers.

Wyeth tiptoed across to Bruce and put his hand on his friend's shoulder. "That's all. That's all, Bruce."

Bruce got up. "I have followed my father's wishes." He turned to his sons. "Boys, take your grandmother back to her room."

They lifted the chair and took her away, then came back to their places.

"Now," said Wyeth, "if you want to decide the Peninsula question, I'm ready."

Kyd wished at that second it could be avoided. She must vote to sell because she believed that way. Mingo would vote with her because he, too, believed that way. She was certain of that. She also knew Bruce wouldn't defy her, wouldn't dare go directly against her. That left Sans alone, and she was sorry.

Bruce was standing in front of the fire, again master of the council. "There won't be any voting." He said it softly, so easily.

Wyeth was caught by surprise, and for a moment Kyd was stifled. She started to speak, but Bruce silenced her. He looked down at his feet and traced patterns in the rug with his shoe.

"Boys—" His voice quivered and he went on tracing the pattern of the rug, until he looked at Mingo and Sans. "The time has come for a decision. I will not leave to your mother the responsibility my father left to my mother. The scene you just witnessed will never be repeated in this family."

He studied his sons, their faces, their hands. "You two boys do not always see things alike, and I will not bind you with the tie of common property. Therefore, I am dividing the valley—"

"No, Papa." Mingo started to rise, then sat back and looked at Sans. The older brother's face was in his hands and his shoulders shook.

"I am dividing the valley," Bruce repeated. He reached out and put his hand on Kyd's shoulder and she looked up at him through her tears. "Mingo will manage The Store. When your mother and I are gone, The House will belong to Sans and The Store to Mingo. But from this minute on, all other Dabney property belongs to you, share and share alike. Mr. Woodward will see to a fair division."

The silence brooded over them and they flinched when the fire sputtered, when it found one last morsel of rich pine.

"Is there anything more?" Bruce asked his sons.

"Yes, Papa," Mingo replied. "Who gets the north cut?" That was the gate to the valley, the key to the Dabney holdings.

There was a trace of disappointment in Bruce's voice as he asked, "Who do you think should have it?"

Mingo was aware that Sans was looking away, that Wyeth was watching him. Then the younger brother remembered: it was at the north cut that Sans' father was killed, defending the valley. "I forgot, Papa," he murmured. "Of course the north cut goes to Sans."

"Of course," said Bruce.

"Of course," said Kyd.

The fire was almost out and the room was chilly and growing dark. Kyd wondered if she should fetch a lamp. Nobody moved. They all sat there, staring at the fire; each thinking his own thoughts. Yet all were thinking the same:

The valley of Lebanon was divided.

Aven MacIvor was coming back.

Bruce pulled out his watch and frowned, but didn't mention the time. Wyeth rose and stretched. "I'm hungry," he said. "We'll have a good supper tonight, Sans. And Louisa is expecting you."

"Yes, sir," Sans said, and continued to stare at the fire.

Mingo leaned over and pinched his mother's cheek. "Hope you got a good supper. I'm hungry, too." He laughed and they were grateful to him; gay, carefree Mingo. He stepped to Sans' chair and nudged his brother. "Come out of it, kiddo. We'll live through it."

"Sure. We'll make it." Sans touched his brother's hand.

Wyeth moved toward the door. "I'll be going now."

"Thank you, Mr. Woodward." Mingo offered his hand. "You can tell Peninsula I'm ready to do business."

Sans walked to the lawyer and tried to smile as Mingo did. "You can tell them for me, I have nothing to sell. But I'll let them through the north cut if they'll make it a railroad for everybody."

They walked together out of the parlor and Bruce closed the door. They all stood on the front porch and watched Wyeth drive away.

Bruce slipped his arm around Kyd. The brothers went to her and kissed her. They kissed their father, too; the first time in years.

There was a moment's stillness; then Mingo slapped Sans across the shoulder. "Reckon you want to bathe first. Get yourself all prettified for Louisa. Come on, I'll help you get the water."

"Never mind. You stay here with Mama and Papa."

He lugged his hot water to the bathroom and poured it into the tub. It was a lead tub held in shape by pine boards, rubbed smooth.

He sat in the warm bath and soaked. Then he put on his broadcloth suit and a white shirt with a stiff collar.

It was pitch dark when he went to the stable and saw the horse he'd borrowed that afternoon from Nils Holmquist. He decided to ride one of the Dabney horses and lead Nils' horse back to him.

The Tree was silhouetted, a sentinel over the dead, but he, a young man, gave no thought to the Dabney past. He was thinking only of Louisa Woodward, and, thinking of her, he began singing softly.

His horse flipped back his ears to listen.

Chapter three

Sans Dabney was singing because he was going to Louisa. Down the pike and off in Bogue Homa bottoms, lamps glowed in the cabins of the Cajuns and Irish, the shacks of the Negroes. 'Tite Pierre, the little Cajun with the leg that dragged, lived there. Shane Figgis lived there, and the hair on his chest was like the matted beard of the red thistle. Gar Rivers lived there, and Smoke Jackson whose skin was blacker than tar smoke.

Sans rode into New Hebron, past the blacksmith shop where

Gabriel d'Artois, whose mother was a Choctaw, had shod the horses of the valley for twenty years. He rode past The Store and on to the office of the Peninsula Lumber Company looking for Nils Holmquist, to return the borrowed horse. There was no light in Peninsula's office, but there was one in the bank and Sans went inside. Nils Holmquist was in the rear of the bank, talking to Mr. Stanley, the cashier.

"I brought your horse," Sans said. "Much obliged." He turned to Leslie Beck, the teller. "Working late, aren't you, Les?"

Leslie glanced up from the money he was counting. "Peninsula is paying off tomorrow. Nils came for the payroll." He had an easy little voice like a child.

The door was opened and Ronnie Sullivan came in and went to Sans. "Been wanting to see you. There's an all-day sing at Ellisville next week. Some of the men want to go."

"Then let them go."

"Mingo says they can't."

Sans moved back to the counter and leaned against it. "Why?"

"He says he can't spare 'em."

"I'll speak to him about it." Sans' tone was calm, but there was a sudden firmness in it.

Nils Holmquist raised his voice from the rear of the bank. "Did you catch that fox, Sans?"

"What fox?"

"Wasn't your pa blowing a fox horn?"

Sans understood Nils' rough way and liked him. "Nope. Didn't catch him. We ran him under a stump and left him."

Nils' laughter filled the little building. "Hell, I know about that horn. I know why Mr. Dabney blew it. He wanted to talk to his family about Peninsula. Ain't that right, Sans?"

Sans looked at Ronnie and winked and called back to Nils. "I told you we were running a fox. A red one."

Nils came out of the back office. "That's what you told me before. But you weren't running a fox. You were running from Peninsula. What are you scared of?"

Sans leaned against the counter, his hands in his pockets. "Everything, bud. I scare easy."

Ronnie was picking his teeth with the nail of his little finger, spitting out fragments of tobacco. Leslie Beck still was counting money, wetting his fingertips on a sponge in a small glass bowl beside him. Mr. Stanley left his desk and walked a few steps out of his office but didn't come all the way; he stood there, listening.

Nils said, "What's there about Peninsula that scares you?"

"Your horse is out front." Sans started for the door.

"Wait a minute. Don't go off mad. You people down here are too damned touchy. So touchy most people can't do business with you." Nils' face was flushed.

No one answered him. Ronnie kept picking his teeth. Nils waited, then turned to the teller. "Give me my money."

"If you don't like it down here—" Ronnie loosened a flake of tobacco and spat it out. "Why don't you go back where you come from?"

Nils ignored him. "Listen, Sans. Get that chip off your shoulder. I ask you a civil question and right off you get mad."

"I'm not mad," Sans said.

"The hell you ain't! We want to get along down here." Nils raised his voice. "But you people won't let us. And I tell you something else." He pounded the counter. "I'm tired of hearing about grandpas and great-grandpas. You Southern people are always digging up your dead ancestors. Why don't you let 'em rest in peace?"

Sans straightened out of his slouch. He, too, was weary of the constant talk about the past, but he didn't want any outsider butting in. So he said, "*You* let them rest in peace, Nils."

"No offense intended," the Peninsula woods boss said. "But I'm tired of hearing you Southerners brag about what you used to have, and bellyache about what you ain't got now."

Ronnie Sullivan moved his jaws slowly, then spat at Nils' feet, making a splatter on his shoes. "If there's so God damn much wrong with us, why don't you get the hell-and-gone back where you belong?"

Nils looked down at his feet; then his gaze wandered from Sans to the Irishman and he realized they were two to one. "I'm not talking to you, Ronnie." He turned to Sans once more.

Ronnie put his hand on Nils' arm and pulled him around. "It ain't polite not to answer my question."

"Take your hand off my arm," Nils said, looking at Ronnie's hand, but not moving his own arm. "Keep out of this. Get back to your barn. You'll always make a two-bit living driving your stinking oxen—"

Then Ronnie struck. Nils went down as if he'd been hit with a hickory pole. He rolled over and Ronnie kicked him in the back, and kicked him again. The toe of his brogan hit Nils' spine and the arms of the Peninsula woods boss jerked out stiff, his hands wide on the floor and flapping.

Mr. Stanley came all the way to the front of the bank. "You aim to stop it, Sans?"

"No."

"I don't like 'em fighting here in the bank." Mr. Stanley went halfway back to his office, turned around and watched.

Nils crawled away, his face writhing. Ronnie kept chewing and spitting. Nils braced his right hand on a sand box near the stove, shoved himself to his feet and reached for a poker and swung it.

Ronnie put up his arms, but the poker knocked his arms down and glanced against his head, which began bleeding from the cut. The ox driver felt in his pocket for his knife. "I'm going to cut your heart out." He opened the blade.

"I ain't got a knife." Nils backed away.

"I aim to cut your God damn black heart out." Ronnie moved towards Nils, his knife in front of him ready to jab.

The big Swede caught his arm and jerked him forward and he fell on the floor and Nils jumped on his wrist. Sans heard the bones crack.

Leslie Beck leaned over the counter and touched Sans and opened a drawer, pointing to a pistol. "Take it and shoot him."

Sans shook his head.

Ronnie tried to get off the floor and Nils kicked him in the temple. He rolled over and he kicked him in the throat. He put his heel on Ronnie's mouth and twisted, stomping his mouth and crushing his nose.

Leslie touched Sans again. "Holmquist is stomping hard. Why don't you kill him?"

Again Sans shook his head. "Ronnie started it."

Nils drew back his foot and kicked the Irishman in the jaw and his head swung limp from side to side. He was gurgling his breath.

"I reckon that settles it," Sans said.

Nils kicked Ronnie again and his head snapped far over and stayed there, red slobber trickling down his jaw. The woods boss wiped his feet on Ronnie's coat and turned to Leslie Beck. "Let's have my money." The teller shoved the payroll across the counter, and Nils walked out of the bank.

Ronnie squirmed on the floor, then twisted over and tried to push himself up. Sans wanted to help him but knew his friend would resent help. Ronnie caught hold of a chair, pulling himself to his feet.

"Want a horse?" Sans asked.

"I'm going home." The Irishman went to the door and tried to open it with his right hand, but couldn't. He opened it with his left hand and went out.

Sans followed him. "I've got two horses. Take one of 'em."

"I'm going home." Ronnie stumbled across the pike toward his shack down beside Bogue Homa.

The Dabney boy watched him out of sight and stood there a minute. Ronnie was the valley and Nils was Peninsula, and they had clashed brutally and without reason. The valley had been beaten; badly beaten. The fight was neither fair nor honorable and nothing was settled.

Sans, on his way to the Woodward place, stopped by the livery stable and spoke to the loiterers there, telling them casually, "Ronnie and Nils had a fight at the bank a minute ago. Nils beat hell out of him." He wanted to be the first to tell the news. The people must not think that the brawl was the beginning of violence between the valley and Peninsula.

"How come they fought?" one of the group asked.

Sans said, "It was just a fight between two men who can't get along. You know how it is."

He turned his horse and rode around the courthouse square to the little side street where the Woodwards lived.

Sans was coming to supper with Louisa, but her mother was arranging things. She was particularly interested in her daughter's costume because even in Lebanon, which Laurel often reminded Mr. Woodward was so far from the centers of real culture, she considered the most fashionable toilette *de rigueur* for her daughter.

She bustled into Louisa's room. "You'll be late if you don't hurry."

"There's no hurry, Mama. No telling when Sans will be here. Papa hasn't even come yet."

"Let's see now, which dress to wear?" The mother opened the massive wardrobe with a mirrored front. "I think this is the one. It looks so refined."

She laid out the dress, then chose a corset cover of flowered muslin, edged with deep insertion. Next she selected a Bonton petticoat. sateen in the latest striped pattern and lined with flannelette. She laid out a pair of drawers, Style U, banjo seat with tight fitting legs and elastic cuffs, fastening below the knees. Then she picked up Louisa's B. V. D. Spiral Bustle and stretched it, testing the spring of the wires. It was one of the lightest, coolest and most durable bustles made and was manufactured exclusively by the Bradley, Voorhees and Day Company of New York.

"There now," Laurel said. "I'll send your bath water right up. Do hurry, dear."

Laurel went out of the room as quickly as she came in and Louisa began undressing. Flora Belle, the cook, came in with a copper kettle of hot water and put it on the hearth.

The girl peeled her chestnut-brown hair tight up from her neck, swirling it into a quick ball on top of her head, and thrust in a few bone hairpins.

She lifted the bowl and pitcher set, with the Moss Rose design, and carried them from the washstand to the hearth. The room was warm and she washed slowly, giving no thought to her ablutions; thinking only of Sans Dabney.

Louisa had known Sans all her life and yet, at times, she wondered if she knew him at all. He had kissed her only once, at a birthday party when she was fifteen. Mingo kissed her that day, too, in the parlor during a game and the other children laughed and Laurel smiled. Sans kissed her in the hall, in the shadows of a corner. A serious boy even then, Sans seemed to honor the kiss as a troth, a covenant between them.

Those were her thoughts as she bathed, rubbing the soapy rag across her shoulders and neck. The fire was warm on her flesh and her flesh was pink and tingly. She glanced up and saw herself in the wardrobe mirror and moved her right leg a little behind her, posing. She smiled, tipping her head from side to side and preening. She thought of Sans again and the bottoms of her feet were warm and tingled, and she wiggled her toes.

The voice of her mother, calling from downstairs, startled her. "Do you need any help?" Laurel called.

"No, Mama."

"Well, hurry along."

Louisa tiptoed to her wardrobe, and pulled open the bottom drawer, careful to make no sound.

She reached far back and lifted out a pair of Robbie pants. A saleslady in Mobile showed the pants to Louisa and, in quick excitement, she bought them and her mother never knew. They were thin cotton cloth, adorned with flying cupids in pale blue. She held them up and the light of the fire played through them, and the wavering light made the cupids fly and dart. She drew on the pants quickly and looked at herself again. Never had she seen anything so dashing and adorable as the little cupids sailing mischievously in front of her.

Louisa drew her corset tight, wasping her waist and lifting her breasts. Then she put on her corset cover, her petticoat and bustle. She remembered to hide the banjo drawers her mother selected, and turned to her dresser.

She removed the hairpins and her hair tumbled down over her shoulders. She combed and brushed it, and the color of her hair sometimes was bright, almost auburn, and then it darkened to a deep chestnut in the wavering light.

She heard her father's horse stepping fast up the road and the buggy turning in the gateway to the lane, coming quickly toward the house.

"Louisa."

"Yes, Mama."

"Your father is home."

"Yes, Mama."

Sans Dabney, approaching the Woodward house, heard the low, mournful bay of a hound running a coon down in the bottom lands along Bogue Homa. He knew that hound. It was old Sooner and he won his name because he always got there sooner than the others.

Sans had run many a possum, many a coon behind Sooner and the baying told him the hound was getting close and things were smelling mighty good to him.

That afternoon, at the family meeting, the past of the Dabneys was brought into sharp focus and their future projected. That night, Sans saw a valley man stomped by a newcomer. Yet, down in the bottoms the old, lop-eared hound was running a coon just like always, and Sans was glad to hear him. The baying brought back good memories and eased his worry about the future.

Throughout his life, Sans had heard the valley talk endlessly of an age that was dead, and was aware that Lebanon could not always live in its easy, casual way, drawing its strength from the past. He realized times were changing and the valley must change with them.

But Sans Dabney, being a Southerner, was a phenomenon and a paradox, an agrarian with the prejudices of a ravished land where defeat still was gall, but where the vanquished nourished an embittered pride. He was the South of red hills, of black bottom land, of yellow rivers rolling slow forever; the rope to hang and the same rope for a plow line, the fagot to burn in fury, the same fagot to warm a friend. He was the sensitive South, angry in defense of her own sins, aware of her sins and ashamed, but haughty in the face of critics. . . .

The Dabney boy rode up to the gateway of the Woodward house and turned in, going to the stables. A Negro met him and took his horse. "Too cold to leave him out," Sans said. "So put him in a stall, please." He walked toward the house.

Laurel met him at the door, took his hat and led him into the parlor where Wyeth Woodward was seated in front of the fire, reading the *Mobile Register*.

"I'll call Louisa," Laurel said.

"Come on in, son." Wyeth motioned toward a deep-seated chair, upholstered in blue velvet, tufted and fringed with fat tassels swinging from the arms. "Getting a little raw out there, isn't it?"

"Sort of," Sans said. "Blowing up a little."

"Oh, Louisa," Laurel called. "Sans is here."

"Thank you, Mama. I'll be right down."

Mrs. Woodward turned to their guest. "How's your mother?"

"She's fine." Sans stood by the chair. "How are you?"

Laurel removed her apron and held it properly in her hands. "My risings are troubling me. But I never like to complain." She glanced at her husband as she said it; then turned to Sans. "Have your folks heard anything about when the Thrumbulls are coming down to stay?" She was referring to Peninsula's superintendent and his daughter, Ruth.

Sans was sitting on the edge of his chair, stiffly and uncomfortably. "No'm. I don't know much about 'em. I suppose they'll be down for good when their house is ready." He had never seen Ruth Thrumbull, and didn't care if he never did. He had been on a fishing trip with Bruce when she had visited the valley.

Wyeth looked over the top of his paper. "Supper about ready, Mrs. Woodward?"

Laurel glanced sharply at her husband. "In a few minutes." She turned again to Sans. "Now excuse me. I'll go help Louisa." She hurried up the stairs.

Wyeth laid his paper on his lap, took off his spectacles and looked across at Sans. "Glad we got things settled this afternoon."

Sans, thinking of the fight and remembering Ronnie's bloody face, knew that nothing was settled. He dreaded to tell Mr. Woodward about the fight. "Yes, sir," he said, "I'm glad we had the meeting. Maybe I'm wrong not to want Peninsula in here, but I'm afraid of what they'll do."

Wyeth picked up his silver-framed spectacles by the hooks and swung them, pendulum-like, in front of him. He cleared his throat. "Maybe you're a little hard on the Peninsula folks. It's a good company and I don't think they aim to rob us." He leaned over and tapped his glasses on Sans' knee. "They're just businessmen who put their money to work like your uncle Keith Alexander. The company is made up of investors from all over the country. From every walk of life."

"Yes, sir," the Dabney boy said respectfully, "I reckon it's a good company. I know it's a big one."

Wyeth cleared his throat again. "They're expanding fast. They've opened a mill in Oregon and they've got mahogany concessions in Honduras and Cuba. It's a powerful concern."

Sans shook his head. "I'm scared of 'em, Mr. Woodward. They come in here grabbing things and stomping folks." He knew he must tell about the fight. "Ronnie Sullivan and Nils Holmquist tangled tonight."

Wyeth leaned forward. "Which one whipped?"

"Nils did. He gave Ronnie a good whipping."

The lawyer crossed his legs and swung his glasses again. "So Peninsula's woods boss whipped the Dabney woods boss." He cut his eyes at Sans and grinned. "You superstitious, son?"

Sans grinned back. "You mighty right I am." He got up as he heard Louisa's door open and pulled back his chair, and stood there waiting.

Louisa's dress was dark green and she came toward Sans with her hand outstretched. He offered his chair, but she preferred a lady's chair of walnut, upholstered with horsehair, slick and shiny black. Sans moved it near the fire and she sat down, smoothing her dress primly. Her father put on his glasses and went back to reading the *Mobile Register*.

She glanced at Sans and smiled, and he said, "I sure like your dress. It's mighty pretty."

The girl looked down at the velvet bow on the bosom. "Mama had to buy it in Mobile. It would be convenient if Mr. Charlie kept nice things like this at The Store."

Sans was conscious of her scented rice powder and heliotrope perfume. "You better speak to Mingo about that. He's the real boss at The Store."

Laurel came back to the room and announced supper. Louisa and Sans got up, but Wyeth continued to read his paper.

"Mr. Woodward," Laurel said. "Supper is on the table."

"Be John Brown!" Wyeth ignored her announcement and held his paper close to the lamp. "Pierpont Morgan and August Belmont have gouged us again. They're grabbing a seven million profit—"

"That's fine, Mr. Woodward." Laurel was fidgety. "But supper is waiting."

"Fine! I'll be billy blue blazes if I see anything fine about it!" He got up and they all went into the dining room. Wyeth still was grumbling. He picked up his napkin, tucked one end in his vest and reached for the chicken. "Those rascals took a seven million dollar profit on sixty million dollars worth of government securities—"

"Mr. Woodward!"

Wyeth bowed his head. "Lord make us thankful for these and all thy blessings amen." He reached again for the chicken. "That's robbery. Taking that much money from the people is robbery—here, Sans, have some of this chicken." He passed the platter to the guest and helped himself to sweet potato pudding. "That kind of thievery will put the Populist party in power."

Laurel frowned at him. "Mr. Woodward!"

"The Republicans and their golden calf will drive us into a panic, sure as shooting. Then they'll blame everybody but themselves—"

"Mr. Woodward!"

"By God!" He banged the table and the table shook. "Bourbons are still Bourbons. North and South. They never learn and they never forget—"

Laurel dropped her knife upon her plate. "Wyeth Lowdermild Woodward!"

"All right. All right." Wyeth jabbed his fork into his potato pudding.

Sans wanted to hear more, for Peninsula Lumber Company was his Bourbon; then he felt Louisa's gaze upon him and everything went out of his thoughts except that here he was, and there was she.

The ham was fresh killed and topped by a layer of fat, dotted with cloves, crusted with sugar. Wyeth served Sans the ham, then passed him the rice and gravy, the potato balls, macaroni and cheese, rutabagas, greens, biscuits, butter and fig preserves. He was careful to perform his duties as host, but he was miffed at his wife and didn't talk much.

Flora Belle brought the hot mincemeat pie and egg custard. They ate their dessert and Wyeth pushed back his chair. "Now, Mrs. Woodward, we'll have a little of that muscadine wine. We'll have it in the parlor—"

"Wine is fattening," Laurel said.

"A whole bottle please, my dear. In by the fire." He got to his feet and led the way back to the parlor. There he packed his pipe and raised the lid of the wood box, taking out a splinter of fat pine. He stooped and lighted it at the fire, then lighted his pipe.

The wine was brought in and Wyeth poured. He unbuttoned his vest and sat in his big chair, sighing as he settled in full comfort. "Now I'm ready for some pretty singing."

"Oh, Papa!" Louisa ran her fingers through his gray hair, tousling it. "Not so soon after supper."

Wyeth folded his hands on his stomach and settled himself deeper in his chair. "I'm a little drowsy. If I don't hear it now, I might not hear it at all."

Laurel returned to the kitchen to supervise Flora Belle and the dishwashing. Sans stood by the organ, and Louisa sat down and pumped the pedals, adjusting the stops. The organ was made of rosewood, polished a deep red; ornamented with hand carvings of doves flying with ribbons in their bills.

"What do you want me to play?" Louisa pressed a chord.

"You know," Wyeth said. "And play it soft. And sing it." He reached for his glass of wine.

Louisa looked up at Sans and began singing *Flow Gently, Sweet Afton.* Wyeth leaned over and whispered, "Sing with her, son."

Sans' voice was a mellow one, a baritone, full and deep. He enjoyed singing. Laurel came from the kitchen into the parlor and was looking at Sans and Louisa, thinking how handsome they were. There was something gentle about his face. Perhaps it was his gray eyes. He certainly had a lovely voice. Too bad he wasn't a good businessman like Mingo.

They finished the song and Wyeth said, "Sing that song Gar Rivers taught you, son. I like a male solo."

Louisa pressed a chord and Sans looked away, out of the window, then sang softly:

> "Shall I, wasting in despair,
> Die because a woman's fair?
> If she thinks not well of me,
> What care I how fair she be?"

His voice trailed off and the organ moaned to a stop.

"How charming." Laurel turned to Wyeth and saw that his eyes were closed. "Mr. Woodward! Don't you think it was charming?"

Wyeth grunted and opened his eyes, peering at his wife. He got up from his chair. "Glad you came to supper, Sans. Come back whenever you can."

"Yes. Come back soon." Laurel started for the door, expecting her husband to stand aside and allow her to precede him, but the old lawyer was sleepy and was on his way to bed. His wife laughed lightly at his little gaucherie and said to her daughter, "I'll see you later, dear." Then she followed her husband up the stairs.

Sans put a log on the fire and drew up the sofa. It was small and they were near each other. The fire shadows danced and Louisa wished she were bold enough to turn down the lamp wick. She knew Sans wouldn't do it.

He was staring into the fire, watching the shadows, and began talking, slowly at first. He told her what happened that day, the division of the valley, the fight at the bank. He told her, too, that his Aunt Aven was coming back; and Louisa gasped and said nothing. Then, his emotions soothed by her nearness, he told her all his hopes and dreams, pouring out his heart, emptying it.

Louisa did not question him about Aven MacIvor's return: she was aware the MacIvor tragedy was locked in the Dabney crypt, and only a Dabney opened that door. Besides, she was more interested in the division of the valley.

The lamplight was on Sans' face and she watched him, even as she seemed to look into the fire. She noticed his soft brown hair, the deep tan of his face. He talked on, confiding in her, and she realized more than ever what a dreamer he was.

She wished he would turn and face her, and she slid her hand along the sofa. He put his hand on top of hers. "You are mighty pretty, Louisa."

She waited. He didn't say more and she encouraged him. "Am I?" she whispered.

"You are the prettiest girl I ever saw. And the sweetest."

She turned her hand and their palms met. "You're sweet, too," she said.

He put his arm around her. "I love you, Louisa. You know I do."

Again she waited; then whispered, "Yes, Sans?"

He kissed her, and she closed her eyes, wishing her lips could seal him to her forever. She longed to run her hand through his hair, feeling his hair, and slide her hand across his shoulders and pull him closer to her, press his face against hers.

It was Sans who first drew away and she opened her eyes, and his face was flushed. He held her hand and they looked into the fire, whispering together.

The grandfather clock bonged ten times and Louisa got his hat and walked with him to the door, holding his arm. She told him good-night, but didn't close the door, standing there until he rode out of the lane.

Sans turned and waved to her and she blew him a kiss, a daring thing to do. Then she closed the door gently.

Chapter four

A METTLESOME SPRING, swishing in on the lull of a fat south wind, brought rain and high water to Bogue Homa in 1894 and when the freshet receded, Mingo's fancy Brighton buggy was delivered to The Store by Elmo Batson, in person. The drummer and Mr. Charlie hauled the crates behind the building and unpacked them while a crowd gathered, including Sans and Ronnie Sullivan.

The big Irishman was sullen since the fight, and Nils Holmquist avoided him. Sans was grateful for Nils' tact, and the valley, by and large, had forgot the trouble between the two woods bosses.

Sans and Ronnie assembled the buggy while the laughing crowd offered suggestions and no help. Finally, even the skeptics approved the rig and Sans sent one of the spectators to The House to fetch Chinquapin, the family's best buggy horse. "What about harness?" The older brother turned to the drummer. "Didn't you bring new harness for Mingo?"

Elmo was chagrined and attempted to dismiss the oversight. "Didn't nobody order any." He hooked his thumbs under his suspenders and popped them. "And I tell you sump'n. Ol' Elmo don't peddle nobody nothing he don't want."

The crowd guffawed and Ronnie yelled, "That's right, Elmo. You'd just sell a claw hammer coat to a tumblebug. If'n you could get it on him." Two of Ronnie's teeth were missing and there was a lump on his wrist where the bones had knotted in mending.

Sans laughed. "Mr. Charlie, get your best set of harness and put it down to me."

Chinquapin was hitched to the shining buggy and the crowd stepped back and approved its work. Suddenly Mr. Charlie thought about a whip and hurried into The Store. He came out with a gleaming new one and tucked it in the holder at the right of the dash. Everything was ready, and they sent for Mingo. The younger brother was so pleased that he invited the crowd into The Store for a treat. Elmo Batson was proud and passed out free samples.

"Come on, Sans," Mingo said. "Let's try her out."

They got into the Brighton and the mare shied a bit; then pranced, her head high and her tail waving. The crowd cheered as the buggy skimmed away.

"She's a beaut," said Sans. "Let me drive a little bit."

Mingo handed over the reins and they headed down toward the south cut. Wyeth stood at the window of his office and smiled. The office force of the Peninsula Lumber Company left their desks and crowded around the door, waving salutes. Gar Rivers, resting on a bench by the livery stable, raised his stick and shook it in friendly salutation. The brothers bowed and waved, acknowledging the greetings, and drove on past the new road leading to the mansion Mr. G. T. Thrumbull was building for himself and his daughter. Mingo had contracted to build the house, and the sides and columns already were up.

"Been wanting to talk to you, kiddo." The younger brother said, accepting the reins. "I need more logs than I'm getting."

"I can't cut you any more," Sans replied. "My men are working ten hours. That's all they can stand in this weather. It's getting hot."

Mingo wanted to sell more lumber because he needed money to carry out his plans. Expand The Store. Clean land for home sites. Build houses for Peninsula people already crowding the hotel. "Get your crews in the woods at sunup," he said, flipping the difficulty aside. "Hold 'em till dark."

The older brother's jaw set and he looked straight ahead.

"Course," said Mingo quickly. "I'm not trying to run your business."

"Let's keep it that way." Sans' lip was thin and his tone heated. "My men were born here and expect to die here, and I'm not breaking them down for you or anybody else. We got troubles enough already, and I'm meeting the men tonight to try to figure things out."

Mingo was quick-tempered, too, but he clamped his teeth and didn't reply to his brother's anger. He touched Chinquapin with the whip and the mare high-stepped to the south cut. Peninsula's pond was filling slowly behind the dam across Bogue Homa's west fork and the big mill's boilers and kilns already were in. A little locomotive was huffing toward Holmquist's logging camp. The engine handled more logs in a day than Ronnie Sullivan's oxen hauled in a month.

The Dabney boys sat in silence, watching. Mingo spoke first. "Got to hand it to those Yankees. They're building that mill mighty fast." He wheeled Chinquapin and headed back for The Store. "Have you heard Papa say anything lately about Aunt Aven coming?"

"Not a word," said Sans. He watched the mare's easy pace and, without looking at his brother, said, "Sorry I sort of blew up a minute ago."

"Aw, forget it. I reckon with so much going on around here maybe we're both on edge." He let Sans off at The Store and went on to The House where Kyd and Shellie were on the front porch, the old woman enjoying the warm sun. Kyd saw the new buggy enter the lane and hurried out to exclaim her approval.

Her son couldn't hide his pride. "Hop in. I'll take you for a little go-'round."

"Wish I could but I mustn't leave your grandmother." Kyd looked back at Shellie and was thoughtful for a second. "But I tell you what," she said brightly, as if the idea had just occurred to her. "Go take Mrs. Woodward and Louisa for a little ride. That will please them, and Mr. Woodward and your father are such close friends."

Mingo's eyes twinkled as he looked at her in mock seriousness. "What's really on your mind, Mama?"

"I was just thinking about Louisa. That young lady has a mighty good head on her pretty shoulders. And she sets the style in Lebanon."

The boy grinned. "She hasn't much competition. She buys her clothes in Mobile. The Cajuns and the Irish can't." He wiped some dust off the seat of the buggy.

Kyd noticed the cape jasmine buds were swelling and pulled one to take to Shellie. "That's the point, son. There's no sense in Louisa buying her clothes in Mobile—"

"We can't afford to stock The Store with fancy merchandise just for Louisa Woodward—"

"But what about the Peninsula women? Ruth Thrumbull, for one. She'll be down pretty soon. And there'll be others. Lots of ladies wanting expensive things."

Mingo pushed back his hat. "Say, now. I hadn't thought of that." He leaned over and kissed his mother. "Maybe I will go take the Woodwards riding." He wheeled his buggy around and headed away, mulling what his mother said. Louisa could help him select a line of ladies' ready-to-wear. She could get the trade of the Cajun and Irish girls, most of whom dressed beyond their means, and help him get business from the Peninsula big-wigs, once they moved in.

The redbuds and dogwood in the Woodward yard were in full bloom and Laurel and Louisa hurried to the gate as the new buggy came up the lane. "It's beautiful," Louisa said, and Mingo beamed.

He jumped out and looped the reins over a picket. "I came to take you two riding. We'll have time before dark."

Laurel glanced at her daughter. "Oh, I'm sorry, but Flora Belle is off today and I must fix supper for Mr. Woodward."

"Can you spare Louisa?" Mingo asked gallantly.

"Of course. You go right ahead, daughter, and supper will be a little late tonight. Your father is meeting Gar Rivers and won't be home on time."

Mingo helped Louisa into the buggy; then got in and lifted the reins. She waved at her mother and he tipped his hat. They cut over to the pike; thence across Bogue Homa to the east ridge. Louisa relaxed on the springy seat. It was fun to go riding with Mingo. He was good-looking, and her mother predicted that some day he would be the richest man in Lebanon, maybe in Mississippi. She said, "Twilight is the nicest part of the day."

"Sure is," Mingo said. "Makes a fellow want to sing." He broke into *The Elephant and the Flea*, and she joined in:

"Way down South where bananas grow
A flea stepped on an elephant's toe,
The elephant cried with tears in his eyes,
Why don't you pick on a fellow your size."

They both were laughing as Mingo began the chorus:

"Boom! Boom! Ain't it great to be cra-zy—"

Louisa tapped her foot and moved her shoulders in rhythm as she sang. The land was lush and soft. A few bold lightning bugs came out to test the twilight and, finding it warm, flew across the road. The moon was in its first quarter.

"Boom! Boom! Ain't it great to be cra-zy—"

Gar Rivers came up out of the Bogue Homa bottoms, the Negro quarters, to keep his appointment with Wyeth Woodward. Men who didn't know the gaunt Negro said he was hideous, and rightly named, ugly as any long-snouted gar fish that ever sucked in the mud. Wyeth Woodward and the few who really knew Gar didn't think of his looks at all. They remembered the pride in his voice, and honored him as a man enriched by loneliness and suffering; made strong in his spirit by a solemn, reverent determination to replace ignorance with knowledge, hate with understanding.

The streets and the square were almost deserted and Gar walked more slowly than usual, depending more on his cane. He believed it was good to walk strong and upright before all men and refused to allow the years or the burden of his birth to weigh him down; but in the twilight, when there was no one to see him, Gar Rivers admitted by his gait and to his cane that time and the unkindness of man had sapped his body and forced it to bend.

At Wyeth's office, he turned in and saw his old comrade waiting for him. "I got your message," Gar said.

"I'm glad you did. Come on in." Wyeth got up and shut the door.

Gar took the chair beside the desk and accepted a cigar. It was a luxury he didn't often have, and he liked good tobacco.

"I got a letter from a brother Mason in Mobile." Wyeth leaned back in his chair. "He cautioned me to confidence, and I pass it on to you." He took his cigar from his mouth and rolled it between his fingers. "How much do you know about José Marti—" he held up his hand quickly— "beyond the fact that he's a Cuban revolutionist?"

Gar's face lighted and there was a soft fervor in his voice. "Marti!" The old man nodded. "I know he dares preach freedom for Cuba, and a brotherhood for all men—"

"We all know that," Wyeth said almost impatiently.

"I know Spain has hounded him from dungeon to dungeon for thirty years." He rubbed his bony hands together. "He's in this country now, an exile. But they can't shut him up."

"He's coming to Lebanon—"

"Merciful God! What for?" The old Negro gripped the edge of the desk.

Wyeth turned in his swivel chair. "That's what I'm trying to find out." He unlocked a drawer and took out the letter, handing it to his friend.

The words were blurred to Gar's old eyes and he borrowed Wyeth's spectacles: "This is a message in Masonic brotherhood. I fraternally enjoin you for sanctuary for a man who is coming to you. He is José Marti, Master Mason. He will have an associate with him, a lady. Her name is Rafaela Galban y Torres. Spain's price for her life is almost as high as for his."

Wyeth held out his hand for the letter. "Did you ever hear of the lady?"

"No," Gar said solemnly. "That name is strange to me."

The old lawyer accepted his spectacles and returned the letter to the drawer, locking it. "But why should they come here? Why Lebanon?"

"Sanctuary," Gar said. "We're isolated here."

Wyeth deliberated a moment, his fingers tapping the desk. "I have a feeling it's more than sanctuary." He got up and walked to the window. The spring twilight was drifting in and the village was calm, the supper smoke lifting thin and gray from the chimneys. "Three months ago Spain gave Peninsula concessions to cut mahogany in Cuba. Now Peninsula is coming in here, and José Marti is coming here." He wheeled from the window, returning quickly to his chair and it creaked as he sat down. "I tell you it's more than sanctuary."

"Have you told the Dabneys?"

"No." Wyeth spoke emphatically. "It's only a premonition and they're already worried to death. I'll wait until I know more about it."

The two men talked on, questioning each other and finding no answer, pondering why José Marti was coming to the valley of Lebanon so soon after Peninsula paid Spain's price for Cuba's trees; why he was bringing with him a woman named Rafaela Galban y Torres, both Cubans, both in the shadow of the Spanish garrote.

Sans met his logging crew back in the woods at the stables where Ronnie Sullivan bedded his oxen. All the men were serious, together for a serious purpose. Among them was Joe Doyle, the oldest hand.

At first, the group discussed their problems in generalities. Sans, sitting on the end of a wagon, contributed laconic remarks, letting the men do most of the talking. Finally Ronnie got tired of listening. "Aw, for God's sake. We ain't cutting no mustard. Just popping off. And we might as well tree this coon right here. We're losing more men than we can spare, Sans. Peninsula is outplaying you."

Fishbait Gates, a huge Negro, wiped his nose on his sleeve. "Them what's leaving us ain't much 'count." His voice was deep, hollow-toned. "Most of 'em is like Turkey Daly and he ain't no 'count even when he's sober."

Debo Giles, an ox driver, reached for his tobacco and passed it around. "Ain't all of 'em like Turkey. We air losin' some good hands. Take ol' Rockhead Riggs. He air a good hand."

Sans asked, "Why should Rockhead leave us? He's got a family and a little farm. Besides, he's valley born."

The workmen looked at one another; then at the boss. "It's money," Ronnie said.

Paul de Ru, a cypress logger and a Cajun, reached inside his shirt and scratched. *"Mais, oui."* He heaved up his shoulders, spreading his hands, and there were callouses on his hands as thick as a mule's hide. "It's money, my friend. A stupid one like Turkey Daly does not care for tomorrow. He takes the quick money today."

Debo Giles said, "The valley folks are for you, Sans, but that Peninsula money spends mighty big."

The Dabney boy slid off the end of the wagon and stood up, facing his men. "How can I pay more? I work on a shoestring and I haven't got any money."

Ronnie, getting nods from the men, stepped closer to the boss. "We know what you get for logs delivered to Mingo's mill. And we know what you pay us. It's a hell of a spread."

"I get the drift." Sans slipped back his cap and scratched his head. "But if I raise wages now while things are good, what'll I do when hard times come?"

"What ever'body else does," Ronnie said. "Cut wages."

Quickly, Sans was serious. "You fellows got me where the hair is short. I'll raise wages. Got to. But will you take a cut if things get tough?"

"Sure," Joe Doyle said. "We go up or down together."

It wasn't that Sans Dabney was a particularly generous man. Peninsula was forcing him into a corner. Labor was the key to his living, so he hoped to satisfy his men and benefit himself. He'd share his trees with his men. They'd share their labor with him. It seemed as simple and as safe as that.

Ronnie Sullivan was skeptical. "You aiming to take us in as sort of podners?"

"I'm not just aiming; I'm drawing my bead," Sans said. "But if we try it and a man loafs, he's digging into your pocket, same as mine."

"We'll handle that end," said Joe Doyle, a quiet man.

"We'll go to the bridge with you," said Fishbait Gates. "We'll cross hell on a horsehair for you."

Sans, naive as he was, knew that enthusiasm and loyalty never met a payroll, but he believed men could share and he was determined to try it. They all shook hands with him and went home, all except Ronnie. The big ox boss waited until the others were out of hearing. "Maybe if I looked around, I might find something."

"Then start looking," said Sans.

They went to the far end of the stables and Ronnie lit a lantern. He dug into a pile of straw and came up with a demijohn. "Right out of Ol' Man Pinckney's cornfield!" He was grinning as he pulled the cork. "A bushel of his best!"

Sans lifted the jug and drank, gurgling down the whiskey. He blew out a deep breath. "Jeemeny criminy!" He blew out his breath again. "Don't strike a match, Ronnie, we'll blow up."

Ronnie slung the demijohn over his shoulder, turned his head until his mouth was at the opening; then lifted his shoulder and let the whiskey pour, drinking in the mode of experienced demijohn men. Once he paused to get his breath; then lifted his shoulder again and continued pouring. Eventually, he took down the jug and wiped his mouth on the back of his hand. "Right pert drinking likker."

Sans started to drink again, but lowered the jug and asked, "Think it'll work?"

"A boss splitting with his hands! I ain't never heard of such a thing. But you always were sort of crazy."

The Dabney boy held the jug to his mouth with both hands as a novice will, and drank until he coughed. "Maybe it ain't good business, but my tail's in a crack." He picked up the lantern. "Let's get out in the cool."

They walked out of the barn and over to the brink of the west ridge and selected two trees, close together, with needles thick and soft upon the ground. The two friends sat down, leaning back, the jug between them. There was a light in The Store, far down the slope in New Hebron. The Peninsula office showed several lights and beyond the south cut lanterns and pine torches glowed as the company pushed construction of its mill. The lanterns burned steadily but the flame of the torches bent a little west, away from the light east breeze.

"Ronnie," said Sans, looking around carefully to make sure no one was listening. "I've figured out a way."

The Irishman slowly studied the circle of darkness outside the little yellow tent of their lantern. "A way to do what?"

"To run those Peninsula sons of bitches ragged." He pointed out how much time they lost hauling logs down the slope to Mingo's mill. "We'll lay a double track from here down to the bottom. A loaded car going down will pull an empty up."

The idea almost sobered Ronnie. He stood up and peered down the ridge. "It'll save us half our time." He sat down again, lifted the jug, and leaned against his tree, settling himself in careful comfort. "We'll run 'em ragged," Ronnie boasted. "Give it to 'em nip and tuck. Pull Dick, pull Devil." He handed the jug to Sans. "Let's likker."

Sans steadied himself and steadied the demijohn, fitting his lips to the mouth of the jug. "We'll whip 'em to death."

Ronnie lifted the jug straight up and took a quick swig, then balanced the demijohn on a little knoll. He watched the jug, blinking at it, and turned away, staring toward the south cut, toward Peninsula. He sat there, somber, morose, glaring at the lights. "No good sons of bitches," he muttered. "Steal acorns from a blind hog. And I'm gonna stomp hell out'n Nils Holmquist. I ain't forgetting what he done to me—"

"You stay shed of Holmquist," Sans said. "If you two tangle again it'll lead to a free-for-all."

"Look at this knot on my wrist." Ronnie held out his arm. "He done that."

"You stay shed of Holmquist—"

"You know I can whip him, don't you?" Ronnie demanded. "You know I can whip any son of a bitch in this valley except you—"

"Uh huh. But you leave Holmquist alone."

"All right, Sans. Anything you say. Do anything for you."

The east breeze was freshening, humming through the pine tops, strumming the needles. A hoot-owl, back in the woods, sent its forlorn call looping across the ridge. The lantern was smoking and the big Irishman rolled over to his all-fours and crawled toward it. He felt for the wick and turned it down and crawled back to his tree, stretching on the ground, his hands under his head. "Want you to sing that song for me."

"What song?" Sans mumbled.

"The one Gar Rivers plays on his gee-tar."

The night was still, even the little things in the woods were still and Sans sang:

> "Shall I, wasting in despair,
> Die because a woman's fair—"

The plaintive melody carried down the ridge, but there was no one to hear, no one but Ronnie, and Ronnie was crying. Sans stopped singing and stared. "What you bawling about?" The ox driver was sobbing so hard he couldn't answer, sitting there with his face lifted toward the stars, tears splashing down his cheeks. Sans crawled over to his friend to comfort him. "What you bawling about?"

The Irishman sobbed even louder, wailing his sorrow into the night. Sans watched his friend; then tears came to his own eyes and slid down his cheeks. He put his arm around Ronnie, and Ronnie put his arm around Sans, and they held on to each other, sharing their misery. Still sobbing, Ronnie turned his wet face to his friend: "Let's likker."

Sans nodded and searched for the jug. He picked it up and passed it to his comrade who tilted and drank until the end came, as the end must, and the well was dry. He shook it close to his ear and held it upside down and shook it. "All gone."

They sat there looking at each other, blinking slowly, until they were able to focus; then pushed up from the ground and Sans located the lantern. He took it back to the stables and hung it on a limb. With care and patience he helped Ronnie mount; then put out the lantern and got on his own horse.

They rode down the ridge together and up the pike until Ronnie turned off to go home. Sans went on alone. The moon was dimming, ready to wane. He had no knowledge of time, but he knew it was late and he was sorry he had taken so much to drink. Otherwise, he might ride by and see Louisa and tell her how he and his men were going to run Peninsula ragged.

He felt good; weary and sad and joyful. He forgot there were any other persons in Lebanon, in the world, besides Louisa and himself, and he lifted his voice to his beloved:

> "Shall I, wasting in despair,
>   Die because a woman's fair—"

The more he sang, the louder he sang, and along the pike lamps were lit and people peered out, the young people laughing and the old people shaking their heads. It never failed, come spring. The dogwood in bud, the honeysuckle in bloom, the sap rising in the hickories; and Sans Dabney, the serious brother, on his seasonal jubilee, his wonted salute to spring. The old folks remembered that his father, too, took one spree a year; greeting the dogwood in bud, the honeysuckle in bloom, always in the spring. And his father died at the north cut.

Down in his two-room cabin, Gar Rivers, worried by the news

Wyeth Woodward gave him, was sleepless, tormented by a fore-boding. He heard the song and smiled to himself, calmed by the song and by the man who sang it, and ceased wondering why the valley of Lebanon should be the meeting place for two Cubans who spoke for the right of revolution, and a mammoth lumber company which denied it.

Chapter five

THE LETTER from Aven MacIvor, anticipated and dreaded, came in June. It was addressed to Bruce Dabney, Esq. & Family and told the news simply, pathetically simply, that Bruce's twin sister would arrive at Ellisville the following Monday on train No. 3. The terseness of the message, written in Aven's tight handwriting, was sad; evidence of her apprehension at returning after thirty years to the home she deserted.

Bruce handed the letter to his wife and Kyd bridled as she read it. "She's defiant, isn't she? No need to tell Mama she's coming."

"No. We won't tell her." Bruce took the letter and put it on the mantel. Then, on second thought, he tossed it into the fire.

Kyd watched the letter burn and, without looking up, she said, "I suppose I've forgotten a lot, but I can't hate her as I guess I should."

Her husband stood by her chair and she leaned her face against his arm. "Neither can I," he said. "Thirty years is a long time to hate anybody, especially a sister. She's had a hard time."

He leaned back against the mantel and, his mind far away, he rubbed his hand. "I'm going to meet her."

"Of course you're going. She expects it."

The boys came home for dinner in the middle of the day and

Bruce repeated the news. They were silent, looking down at their plates; then up at their parents. Mingo spoke first. "Do you know what she's up to?"

"No," said Bruce. "Maybe she's just coming down to see about her land."

Sans asked, "Want one of us to go with you to meet her?"

"No. I'll go by myself." He sliced a piece of cornbread and buttered it slowly. "The part I hate most is to drive her right by this house, right by her mother, and take her to the hotel." He looked up at his family. "But that's the way it will be, and I'll ask you to say no more about that part of it." He nodded toward his cup and Kyd rang a little bell by her plate and handed the empty cup to the cook. . . .

The depot at Ellisville, new and ugly, was not so old as the railroad, the New Orleans and Northeastern that, thirteen years before in 1881, was pushed from New Orleans obliquely across the yellow pine wilderness of South Mississippi.

The station was opposite the hotel where Clay MacIvor had his headquarters during the Confederacy's campaign against Lebanon. Adjoining the hotel was the law office of Cephus Hill, a wheedling man whose invalid wife was given to frequent fits of hysteria, then long spells of melancholia. The Dabneys loathed Cephus Hill and pitied his wife. The lawyer was called Windy Hill in Lebanon, but he was a power in Ellisville, a town larger than New Hebron.

Down near the station, in the shade of a red oak, Bruce hitched his horses and pulled a pile of hay from under the buggy seat and scattered it before the team. He was sweltering in his black suit, so he reached to the buggy seat and picked up a palmetto fan, then walked slowly to the depot and sat on a hard bench and fanned himself.

The railroad tracks, simmering and wavering in the heat, slunk into the forests that circled the village, and disappeared. On both sides of the rails, the land was charred from fires set by the locomotives' sparks. Along the right of way a few trees, once a fire threat to the forest, had been girdled and left to wither. They had long since starved to death and, standing starkly, they were waiting to crumble into waste while their trunks shed slabs of bark, and their branches sloughed off hunks of rotten wood.

A freight train, heading northeast, crawled into view, its cars stuffed with lumber, kiln dried and lean streaked, from the mills along the way: Lumberton and Richbourg where, five years before, John L. Sullivan beat Jake Kilrain in 75 knock-down rounds—the last bare knuckle prize fight in the nation. All along the railroad, lumber towns were budding in the woods, and mills were gnawing at the forests they believed would last forever. Picayune, which meant a small coin. Hattiesburg, honoring Mrs. Hattie Hardy. Laurel, built on a gallberry flat and named for the rampant laurel shrubs which were hacked down because they were poisonous to livestock.

Bruce Dabney, fanning himself slowly, wasn't thinking about the dead trees or the living trees, or the towns that lived and died with the trees. He was thinking of what to say when his sister arrived. Should he say, "I'm glad to see you, Aven"? Or should he say what he felt, "My God, Aven! Why did you come back after all these years?"

The freight agent came out of the depot. "No. 3's coming. She's slowing down for the grade."

Bruce walked over to the baggage wagon and leaned against it until the locomotive came swaying out of the woods, smoke puffing in gusts from its tall stack. The old man stood very erect and walked to the spot where he calculated the cars would stop. There was a tight, sharp hurt in his chest. The locomotive slid past him, throwing off a blast of heat.

Several Negroes, laughing about the excitement of the trip, got off their car. Then the white passengers stepped down from their coach, aided by the conductor and porter.

Aven was the seventh, maybe eighth, passenger to leave the train. Bruce saw her step from the platform and, without realizing what he did, held up his fan and waved at her. He almost called out to her, for, at that minute, she might have been Aven Dabney returning from school, and he might have been her brother come up to meet her, as often he had done. For a minute, it seemed she never had been away. This was Aven, the twin he pushed into Bogue Homa that day, forty years ago, the twin who climbed out of the creek and chased him. This was Aven, who scorned a side saddle and rode double with him when they were children.

In the old family, Cormac and Morna were a pair. He and Aven.

And there she stood, her lower lip trembling, home for the first time in thirty years. To old Bruce Dabney, there was no feeling of time, of the page turned. Aven was home and memories made her young again. He folded the years and smoothed them and put them away.

She hadn't changed much. She was tall and her hair, golden red when she went away with Clay MacIvor, still was golden red. She was young for her years. Bruce, her twin, was old for his. She was wearing a gray tailored skirt, and her linen shirtwaist was handmade. Her black sailor straw hat was held in place by a pearl hat pin, and her parasol was closed neatly.

The station agent recognized her and Bruce heard him exclaim, "Good God A'mighty! Aven MacIvor!" One of the depot loiterers sucked in his breath and hurried away to report the news at the livery stable.

Bruce took off his hat and held it in one hand with his fan, and moved toward his sister. She came to meet him in long, graceful strides, trying to speak, but sobbing. Only then did Bruce notice a few hard lines at the corners of her mouth, the tiny vines of bitterness that had seeded in her heart.

The spectators stared at them, but the Dabney twins ignored the oglers. Bruce put out his arms and she met him and pressed her hands against his sides, then to his back. She put her face against his and he felt her tears.

"You all right?" he whispered.

"I'm all right. And you?"

"I'm all right," he said.

She felt his wet eyelashes against her cheek and she patted him. "I'm glad you came to meet me," she said.

He stepped back and looked at her and whispered, "You look fine." Then he raised his voice, "I'll see about your trunk. That's my buggy down yonder." He nodded toward his team and Aven looked around at the station and the people for the first time.

She smoothed her gloves with slender fingers and adjusted her hat pin, then walked slowly toward the buggy while Bruce stepped into the depot. The station agent came up to her and took off his hat.

"I'm Frank Edwards, Mrs. MacIvor. You won't remember me because I was just a little shaver when you left. But my pa was with

Colonel MacIvor. He followed your husband into Lebanon and he never came back, either."

"I'm sorry," she said. "I'm sorry he didn't come back."

She was conscious of the stares of the loiterers as she walked away to the buggy. There she opened her parasol and wondered what was delaying Bruce. Then she knew. He wanted her to be alone with the memories that the first sight of Ellisville must nourish. So she turned her head and looked once and for the last time at the hotel. There her husband slept the night before he invaded the valley. There, the next day, they brought his body. And yonder, beyond the hotel, was the road to Lebanon, the road down which he went, and over which they brought him back.

Ellisville looked so dingy and primitive, only a few comfortable houses and beyond them the shacks and log barns and limitless stretches of pines. This place was dusty and dirty and the skins of the people were brown and hard, and their hands were hard. It was all so poor, so terribly poor, and she drew away from it.

Two Negro men brought her turtle-back trunk out of the station and Bruce helped them slide it under the buggy seat. He climbed in beside her, touched up his team and headed out of town.

"Is Kyd all right?" She closed her parasol.

"She's all right."

Then, since it had to be asked, Aven asked it! "What about Mama?"

"Mama's mind is about gone. All the others are fine."

The dusty road ran parallel to the main railroad line until, a quarter of a mile out of town, they came to the junction where Peninsula's railroad, under construction, led away from the Mainline and headed south for Lebanon. A crew was working at the junction, installing a switch. Several freight cars were waiting, loaded with rails, ready to roll on south toward the valley as the rails were needed.

"How are things in Virginia?" It was meaningless, anything to make conversation.

"I've been very well. Everything's all right. How are your boys?"

"Fine." There was surety and pride in his voice.

"Are they in love yet?"

"Oh, I don't know. Sans has a girl." Bruce chuckled and Aven glanced at him. It was the first time either of them was merry. "And

Mingo—well, Mingo is the sort of fellow who's in love with all the girls."

"Does he look like you?"

Bruce watched his team pull in the deep sand, watched their straining haunches. The horses came to a hard road and snorted and shook their heads, rattling the harness, and Bruce eased the reins and let them go. "He looks more like Kyd than me. He's a brunet, like Kyd."

Aven felt sweat where her back touched the seat and moved away from it. "Who does Sans look like? Cormac?"

"A little, but he's taller than Cormac was."

Aven settled back in her seat. "Now let's see—" She couldn't think of any more specific questions, so she said, "Well, suppose you just tell me everything."

"I think," he said slowly, "that you should do the talking. I think you should tell me why you're here, Aven." The road was gravelly and rutty. But off to the side, Peninsula's railroad was new and smooth and straight.

"I came back," she said, and looked directly at him, "because I want my rights. I am a MacIvor and I want my land."

The road wandered through a bog where hollies and mayhaws were thick. Ferns were green on the banks. "Well, Aven," he said with deliberation, "you are entitled to your rights." Bruce heard his sister gasp and glanced at her.

"There will be no squabble?" she demanded.

"Not over the MacIvor land. But there is no Dabney land for you." It hurt him to say that, but it must be said.

"I don't want any Dabney land." She said it quickly, sharply. "And I'm glad there'll be no trouble over my MacIvor property. I'd hate to drag our family differences into court."

Bruce looked at her and again noticed the tight lines around her mouth. Her eyes, brimming a few minutes before, were hard, too; frosty hard. There was a catch in his heart, and he said, "Yes, that would be unpleasant."

The road meandered out of the swampy land and on to higher ground. Dust spurted from under the horses' hoofs and drifted back, and bushes along the road were dust-white and drooping in the heat.

Suddenly Aven sat erect and almost hissed her words, "What about Morna? Does she own any Dabney land?"

Her brother did not look at her. He leaned far over the dash and watched the left horse, trotting as though a shoe were loose. "Morna gave up all rights to any land in the valley." He straightened up. "So did her husband." Out of deference to Aven he didn't mention Keith Alexander by name.

"She has plenty anyway," Aven said. "Morna has everything."

"Yes, I suppose so. Her husband is mighty well off—"

"I heard she sent her children to school in Europe. I suppose our schools aren't good enough for them."

The remark deserved no reply and got none. Already, Bruce was wishing his sister hadn't come home. She was bitter and unforgiving, milking her bitterness from her memories. "What are your plans?" he asked. "Now that you know there'll be no squabble over MacIvor land, what do you want in the valley?"

His tone impressed her. He, too, was firm. She had forgot how firm her twin could be. So her voice was gentle again. "I have no plans." She put her hand on his arm. "Honestly, Bruce, I have no plans. None beyond getting title to my land. All of it."

"You won't stay in Lebanon?"

"Heavens, no!" She almost laughed. "Stay here? My home is Virginia. I have nothing here." She tapped her gloves against her lap. "Nothing except memories." She looked down at her lap, at her feet. "You and I, Bruce, were the victims of a terrible thing. It just goes to show how the innocent must suffer—"

Bruce Dabney clinched his jaw and choked back a torrent of words. He tilted his chin and a slight breeze rustled his beard. Innocent? Aven innocent? She who had robbed her sister of her betrothed? He wanted to move away from her, to the end of the seat, to be as far away from her as possible. This woman was evil. His sister was pitying herself. She had hurt others, but now she pitied herself. However, instead of saying something to regret, he merely said, "The road is mighty dusty today. It's always bad. We haul lumber over it and I don't see how the oxen make it."

Aven laughed, and it was a merry laugh. "Still using oxen?"

"Uh huh. I'm breeding mules for the work, though."

She turned her head slightly and nodded toward the Peninsula tracks, so new and unused that rust still was on the rails. "That will stop the oxen. The mules, too, won't it?"

"Maybe."

"Maybe!" Aven was puzzled. "They're going into New Hebron, aren't they? Peninsula is building a big mill and laying a railroad right through the north cut, aren't they?"

Bruce checked his team and got out and examined the shoe. It was secure, so he patted the horse and climbed back into the buggy. Only then did he answer her. "They're building a mill, all right. And a railroad. But they're not going through the north cut. Maybe they'll go around the ridges and get to their mill that way, but they're not building a railroad through the north cut."

"Nonsense," said Aven. "That's preposterous." She shrugged her shoulders and gesticulated with her right hand. "Why should they go the long way around? They'll go straight through."

Bruce felt in his pocket for a cigar and, finding none, knew Kyd removed them before he left home. That tickled him, but he didn't smile. Instead, he cocked his head over at his sister and smoothed his beard. "We've divided the Dabney part of the valley. Mingo runs The Store and the mill. Sans owns most of the timber; and the north cut. He says Peninsula won't be coming through there."

Aven felt a shiver along her spine. This was Dabney talk, the Dabney way of declaring they intended to fight. That left her nothing to say.

The road got worse as they neared Lebanon, and Aven, shaken by the buggy and the excitement of her return, felt ill. There was a spring back in the trees and Bruce got out, leading his horses through the woods and across the Peninsula tracks. The spring was dry, sealed by the company so it could not wash the roadbed, and Bruce muttered his grievance.

"That's all right," Aven said. "I don't need any water—"

"You haven't been pulling a buggy," Bruce said impatiently. "My horses need water." He got back in the seat and drove on, and Aven scowled in petulance.

They came to the temporary end of the rails—the end for only a few minutes. For as they watched, Peninsula workmen moved the terminal forward, rail by rail, moving toward the north cut—toward the gate of Lebanon. Bruce had never seen men work as these did, hauling rails to the end of the line, laying them, and stepping aside for the next gang to lengthen the line with more rails, leap by leap to the valley. Aven was fascinated and Bruce was appalled. The tracks were within a mile of the north cut and were heading directly for the pass, down the right of way the company owned, toward the cut they didn't own. All of it was terrifying to the old man, this modernity, this progress of steel and steam; a monstrous djinn creeping toward his hearthstone.

A donkey engine whistled and backed toward Ellisville for another load of rails. Bruce's horses shied as the locomotive passed. Bruce shied, too. But he held his team firmly, and drove on. Home was only a mile away.

Suddenly, there was nothing for him and Aven to talk about. Their worlds were worlds apart. After thirty years, there was nothing to say that hadn't been said.

The north cut came into sight and Aven sat erect, peering at it. How small it was. It wasn't a valley at all. Only two sloping ridges and a gentle pass to the hollow where Bogue Homa flowed. She remembered then. Some called it Dabney's Hollow. At that minute, Aven was sorry she was there. It was so small, not big and lush as she had remembered it. Just Dabney's Hollow, called the valley of Lebanon.

They were nearing the cut and she reached over and touched her brother's hand, and he stopped his horses. "Where did it happen?" she whispered. "Was it here? I must know."

Bruce took off his hat and fanned himself a second, sad that she had asked, but not surprised. "Yes, it was right about here. Clay was coming down this road at the head of the Confederates."

"Yes," she said. "That's the way I heard it. Go on."

He lowered his voice. "It was raining. Keith Alexander walked out of the north cut and stood right about yonder—"

"Go on, Bruce."

He took a deep breath. "Keith called out to Clay."

"He *called* to him!" Aven was stunned.

"That's right. He shouted 'MacIvor!' Keith's pistols were cocked. He was waiting. Clay spurred his horse to ride him down. Keith fired first."

Aven's lips were bloodless and her cheeks white. "How many times did Keith Alexander shoot?" She almost spat the words at him. "How many times did he fire? I've heard several stories—"

Bruce's lips were as bloodless as hers and just as tight. "Keith fired after Clay drew his bead. The first shot hit him in the stomach. Then Keith fired his second pistol." Bruce's voice broke. "His second shot hit Clay full in the face. You wanted to know. And that's how it happened."

Aven slumped in the seat and sobbed. "I'm bitter. Of course I am. But I'm not bitter at you."

He didn't reply.

"Just one thing more," she said. "Is Keith Alexander helping you now? Is he helping you against Peninsula?"

Bruce lifted the reins. "So far as I know, Keith knows nothing about it." He paused suddenly and faced her. "Aven! You're afraid of Keith. After thirty years, you are still afraid of Keith Alexander."

It was her time not to reply, and her brother did not press the point.

They passed through the cut and again Bruce halted his team, giving her time to see the valley, The House over to the right, The Tree and Bogue Homa, the village down the pike. A moment, a minute he waited, dreading what he must say; then he said it gently. "Want me to take you to the hotel?" He heard her quick breath, almost a gasp, and he did not look her way.

"Naturally," she said coldly. "Take me to the hotel." She sat very straight and held her chin high.

Her brother could stand it no longer. He put his arm around her and she put her head on his shoulder and there by the north cut, they both wept.

"Good Lord, Bruce! Don't the Dabneys ever forgive?"

"Have you forgiven?"

She took her head from his shoulder and they looked at each other. "No," she said. "I can't. I hate Keith Alexander. I'll hate him to my dying breath. Take me to the hotel. I'm tired."

The horses, nearing home, took up their trot again and the buggy moved down the pike, past The Tree, past The House. Bruce looked the other way. Aven looked straight ahead.

"Tell me," she asked when they were beyond The House. "Who wanted it like this? Mama or Kyd?"

"Mama," said Bruce.

"Then I want it this way, too. Tell her that for me."

Dust swirled from the pike and settled on the sycamores and

cypresses; but the pines shed the dust, shaking it off. There was the pounding of Peninsula hammers toward the north cut, the whining of Peninsula saws toward the south cut. But in Lebanon the locusts sang, rasping their forecast of dry weather.

Chapter six

THE SUMMER OF 1894 brought the worst drought in a quarter of a century, searing the valley from the north cut where Peninsula's railroad was gouging for an opening, to the south cut where Peninsula's mill was ready for its roof. Stifled and still, Lebanon lay gasping day after day while green things browned and burned.

It was a summer of national bickering and sectional tempers, and gradually the republic floundered into economic and political confusion. Profits fell and bankers called their loans, lamenting that the American way was passing. They found a scapegoat in the Populist Party, branding it revolutionary for advocating such innovations as rural free delivery and parcel post, for daring to preach that gold was not a god. The people, frightened, tried to sell and refused to buy, and the great panic was booming; the whole nation sipping the cup of travail which had been held to the South's lips for three decades.

Peninsula stretched its chain of power, thin but binding, from Lebanon to the North; from Lebanon where the trees grew, to Chicago where the fate of the valley was decided by men who never saw the trees. Orders came down from on high to finish the mill and get into production. Company officials were arriving daily and Mr. G. T. Thrumbull's house was almost ready for him and Ruth.

The drought, the railroad and the mill were the only subjects of talk, and for the first time in the memory of Lebanon, there was no interest in that year's election, due in November. Mr. Charlie was running again for the Board of Supervisors and didn't bother to campaign. However, Sheriff Vernon Boyd did a little politicking.

An occasional brush fire broke out in Peninsula's tinder-dry forests and the company posted its land to keep off careless trespassers. Posted land meant an end to free range for the Cajuns' scrub cattle and razorback hogs. It meant fences and they didn't understand the need for fences. In their puzzlement and anger, they threw lighted pineknots into Peninsula's woods and more fires broke out.

The people had Peninsula's hard money in their pockets, but they were sullen, blaming the company's dam for the parched, cracked banks of Bogue Homa, the dead fish among the reeds; and they cursed the company. Most of Peninsula's executives were baffled. They were paying money to poor people, yet the people didn't respect them, wouldn't come to work when the whistle blew. The people loafed when they needed cash and the company needed labor. Peninsula's executives, wrangling around a table in Chicago, couldn't comprehend that Lebanon's lanky, red-necked poor were men of dignity, sentimental about a vague heritage, and stubbornly suspicious of any effort to change them.

Nils Holmquist understood it all, however, and was worried as he watched the railroad jabbing at the north cut and heard the people grumbling. Mr. G. T. Thrumbull and Ruth Thrumbull, preparing to move to the valley, understood and hoped to do something about it.

Keith Alexander, aloof in his Chicago mansion, understood and didn't care. Long ago he put the South behind him. He hadn't been in Lebanon to see the Dabneys, his only people, in eight years. Keith Alexander was content to live in his citadel with Morna Dabney, and his millions, and his memories.

Lebanon was so hot and dry, the people so listless, that the coming of Aven MacIvor brought only a few stares and nods from the community. Once she established her residence at the hotel, the people forgot her or ignored her. It was far too hot to fret over an old Dabney feud.

Kyd avoided her sister-in-law and Mingo followed his mother's lead. Nor did Bruce call on his sister. They met, as they must, and he talked to her pleasantly and about casual things; but he never mentioned Shellie or the family, and never invited her to The House. Aven felt she was treated as a pariah by her people and scorned them. Her head always was high and several men in the village, mostly Peninsula men, eyed her, but dared not accost the stately widow of Claiborne MacIvor.

She found that titles to the MacIvor land were snarled because of inadequate records and she employed a lawyer in Mobile, visiting there to confer with him. It was cooler in Mobile than in Lebanon and she took a suite at the Battle House.

Peninsula made an offer for her holdings, but she declared their price unsatisfactory and the company quickly ended negotiations with her. Peninsula already had enough land and needed only one more asset in the valley—a right of way through the north cut. Aven did not press a sale, for she was toying with the idea of opening her own mill if she could get backing. She was in no hurry, and spent her days between Mobile and Lebanon, waiting and watching.

It was Sans Dabney who broke family precedent and called on his aunt at her hotel room, a large corner room. He did it because he thought it was the right thing to do. A gasp, then a rush of tears greeted him when he presented himself at her door that sultry afternoon.

He said to her, "Aunt Aven, I'm Sans."

She didn't know whether to kiss him or offer her hand, but she followed the dictate of her heart and put her hands on his big shoulders and looked at him. Then she kissed him on the cheek and motioned to a chair.

"I'm glad you came," she said.

Sans sat stiffly for a few minutes and their talk was awkward. But she was gracious and gradually he relaxed and then they talked freely, and laughed.

"I'd forgot how hot it gets in the valley," she said.

Sans crossed his long legs and grinned. "Mr. Charlie says it gets so hot in Lebanon that hell shuts down for repairs."

She smiled and he was aware how beautiful she was, how creamy was her skin, how soft her hair that defied the parching heat. Only her eyes and the thin little lines about her mouth were hard.

Aven sent downstairs for coffee and they talked of many things, but did not mention Shellie or Kyd or Mingo. She told him stories about his father and as she talked, Sans knew his father for the first time. Even Bruce, as close as Sans was to him, never brought Cormac to life as Aunt Aven did.

"You're a lot like your father." Then her eyes twinkled. "Do you greet the spring with song and—" She hesitated. "Too much whiskey?"

Sans squirmed and blushed.

"Then you're exactly like your father." She was laughing.

"That's what Aunt Morna told me." He said it casually and instantly wished he could take it back.

Her mood flashed to bitterness and, because she was a woman who nurtured her hate, she turned the knife in the old wound. "When was the last time you saw your Uncle Keith?" The cords in her neck tightened and her face reddened.

Sans looked away. He didn't want to talk to her about Keith or Morna or Clay. He didn't want to talk about the past at all. "I saw Uncle Keith about eight years ago," he said, after a moment. "The last time he was here, Aunt Morna was with him. She's been back since, but he hasn't."

"Is she still beautiful?" Aven asked quickly.

"Yes'm. She is very beautiful."

She looked out of the window and once more turned the knife. "You've probably heard only one side of the story," she said. "I'd like for you to know my side."

He was embarrassed and looked down at his shoes. "Yes'm. But it all happened so long ago. Must we bring it up?"

"Yes. I must warn you against Keith Alexander. He's a sardonic, iniquitous scoundrel." Her voice rose and Sans was startled, almost frightened. "I'm glad you have not been around him much. He would warp you in the mold of his own vicious personality."

"Aunt Aven!" Sans got to his feet. "I didn't come here to listen to criticism of my folks."

She bowed her head. "I'm sorry. You must forgive a lonely woman for her unhappy memories."

They exchanged meaningless pleasantries and then Sans picked up his hat and told her goodbye.

From the window of her room, she watched him walk out of the hotel, out into the blinding sun, swinging along, his shirt collar open.

She waited long enough for him to pass out of sight, then changed her clothes and went to the livery stable for a team and driver to take her to Mobile. She wanted wine and laughter.

There was an odor of dust over the valley, the dry, parched smell of the desiccated earth. The white dust lay on everything like a film of chalk, and nothing stirred. The trees drooped in exhaustion, too weary to lift their arms in a plea for succor. Even Bogue Homa, usually red, was a sickly yellow. The slime stank and gave up its dead minnows and crawfish, and its worms turned to parchment.

Despite the heat, Kyd didn't break tradition, and served the family its customary hot supper. She waited until they were drinking their second cups of coffee before she announced she had received a letter from Keith Alexander. Sans glanced up quickly, thinking it strange that his Uncle Keith's name should come up twice that day, once with Aunt Aven and now with Kyd.

"Everything all right?" Bruce asked.

"Uh huh. Morna's in Europe with the children and he wrote mostly about that."

The boys were busy eating but Bruce sat back in his chair. He was smiling. "All right, Kyd. What did Keith really have to say?"

She laid her fork across her plate and looked at her husband. "I wrote Keith not long ago that Aven is here, but he didn't mention her in his letter." Kyd passed the tea cakes. "I also told him about the Peninsula developments."

Mingo glanced up quickly and Bruce frowned. Sans finished eating his cake, then asked, "What did he say about Peninsula?"

They all watched her and she tittered to hide a trace of guilt. She didn't answer Sans directly, but spoke again to her husband. "He says if Sans is smart, he'll sell."

The older brother drank the last of his coffee and got up, pushing his chair back into place at the table. "Next time you write him, tell him I'm not smart." He started to turn away from the table, but didn't. "And I might as well tell you now. I called on Aunt Aven this afternoon."

Kyd gasped and her face flushed. Mingo threw his napkin down next to his place, but Bruce silenced him with a look. He silenced Kyd, too, and Sans stood there waiting for them to rebuke him.

Finally the flush left Kyd's face and she asked, "What did Aven have to say?"

"She said I was a lot like my father," Sans replied. Then he smiled. "She told me Louisa is a pretty girl, and I'm on my way to tell Louisa the same thing." That was all he told them, and saying it, he bowed slightly and asked to be excused.

He stepped down the hall to see his grandmother and finding Shellie asleep, went to his room and got out his white linen suit and broad-brimmed Panama. He was shaving when Mingo came in and sat on the bed. "Came to talk to you about Louisa." The younger brother said it quickly, anxious to break the ice and tell Sans the whole story.

"What about Louisa?" Sans slipped his arm into his shirt.

"She's a smart girl, kiddo." He pulled at his wilted collar. "I'm going to add a ladies' ready-to-wear department to The Store, and she agreed to help me start it."

Sans buttoned his shirt. "That's fine. You were smart to ask her." And he meant it.

"She will be my silent partner, in a way. Do some buying for me in Mobile and New Orleans." He was earnestly laying his plan before his brother. "The whole thing is a gamble. I haven't got much cash and she knows it, but she thinks it's such a good idea she's willing to take stock instead of a salary."

Sans instinctively was cautious, the caution of a woodsman in a strange forest. "Is that a fact?"

The younger brother moved a chair and sat down by the window. "I can dip into my mill money and pay her a salary until the department is paying for itself. But it would be a whole lot easier on me to give her stock, and she's willing to help me and do it that way. What's your idea?"

"I'm not much of a businessman." Sans peered in a mirror, rubbing his chin. "Have you talked to Papa and Mama about this?" He turned from the mirror and watched his brother.

"I figured I'd settle it with you."

The older boy reached for his tie and slipped it under his collar. "If any stock is in the deal, then Papa and Mama would have to have a say. You know that." He frowned slightly. "Papa would be against it. He wouldn't want any Dabney business in anybody else's hands, even the hands of his future daughter-in-law." He looped his collar around his neck, fastening it to the brass button at his throat.

Mingo stared out of the window. "How do you feel about it?"

"I'm against it, Lebuba." Sans said it slowly, shaking his head. "I'm against any stock in any Dabney business going to any outsider. Even to Louisa."

"What are you afraid of?" Mingo demanded, leaning forward in his chair.

Sans touched the younger brother's shoulder. "I'm afraid something might come up to cause hard feelings between you and me. We don't want that to happen."

Mingo put his hand on his brother's hand and for a second they looked at each other. Then Mingo said, "You have no objection to Louisa working with me?"

"Not a bit." Sans smiled an emphasis to his sincerity. "And if Louisa prefers a salary, I'd be grateful if you gave it to her instead of stock."

"If that's how you want it, then that's the ticket." Mingo got up from the chair and stretched. "I just wanted to be the first to tell you. Now you tell me something. What's Aunt Aven like?"

There was no immediate reply. Then Sans said, "Come on out to the stable with me."

They walked together down the hall and Sans stuck his head in the doorway to the parlor and told Kyd and Bruce goodbye. The brothers went out on the porch and a blast of hot air hit them. Mingo grunted, "You able to get any work done in this weather?"

"Not much. And you?" Sans asked.

"Damn little! Why don't you use my buggy tonight? If you get in a saddle, you'll be wringing wet before you get to the pike."

"Thanks. It'll save my suit."

They reached the barn and Mingo said, "I'll hitch up for you. Now tell me about Aunt Aven."

Sans rubbed the back of his neck, feeling sweat there. "Did you ever get a good look at a copperhead?" He stuck his fingers inside his shirt, flipping it back and forth, fanning himself. "Well, I want to tell you that's just how Aunt Aven looked when she mentioned Uncle Keith."

"You can't blame her much." Mingo reached under Chinquapin

for the belly strap and buckled it. "He killed her husband, didn't he?"

"It's eating on her. It's eating her up inside." Sans stepped into the buggy and picked up the reins. "Least, that's the way it seemed to me, but maybe I'm being hard on her."

The younger brother rested his hand on the dashboard. "She's a MacIvor. She deserted the valley." He slapped Chinquapin and the mare pranced, skittish and eager to go. "So long, kiddo. Give Louisa my best."

Chinquapin high-stepped out of the barn and the buggy rounded The Tree and into the pike, the wheels swishing through the sand, the dust churning up. The night was filled with sound, the baying of dogs, and old Sooner was leading the pack. The stars, speckling the sky, seemed to crackle and crinkle.

Sans turned and looked back toward the north cut, at the reflection of the workers' lights. Peninsula was driving its crews, almost at the gates of Lebanon. Far to the south was the glow of other lanterns. They were roofing the mill down there, testing the big saws.

Hammers at the north cut. Saws at the south cut. In between lay Lebanon, hot and panting.

Wyeth Woodward and Gar Rivers were sitting on the front steps of the Woodward house when Sans drove up and tied his horse to a picket near the gate. They moved their palmetto fans slowly, stirring a little breeze.

Sans assumed they were discussing the weather like everybody else. Actually, they were talking again about José Marti and Cuba, still wondering why Marti and Rafaela Galban y Torres were coming to the valley; still puzzling about any possible connection between the revolutionists and Peninsula Lumber Company.

"Don't get up," Sans said as he approached them. "I can step around you. It's too hot to move."

They laughed and Sans rapped on the door, and was standing in the hall when Louisa came down. He took her hand and led her to the parlor.

"Don't mention the weather," she said. "I'm sick of hearing about it."

They sat on the sofa and Sans looked at her. There were tiny drops of sweat just under her hair line and on her neck, and the sweat showed through her dress. Her face was shiny and Sans thought it beautiful. He told all he had done since he saw her last, and he told about his visit to Aunt Aven.

Louisa was taken aback. Her displeasure showed in her eyes and on her cheeks, which flushed suddenly. "You shouldn't have done that. Your mama didn't approve, I bet."

"It was the right thing to do," he said.

The girl dropped the subject. She knew it was wise to drop it. She knew something about Sans that he didn't know about himself; a few prods were acceptable, but one too many was dangerous.

After a minute, as though hesitant to tell him, Louisa began talking of her plans at The Store. She was surprised that he knew already, that Mingo had told him.

"Then you don't mind?" she asked quickly.

"Why should I?"

That, too, surprised Louisa. She would be at The Store all day with the younger brother, yet the older brother apparently gave it no thought. This man was not capable of suspecting those he loved. This man trusted her. Suddenly, Louisa Woodward felt inadequate in his presence. The mood passed quickly, however, and she leaned closer to him. "I think I'll take stock in the department instead of a salary," she said. "What do you think?"

"Salary." He said it bluntly.

She was amazed. "Are you loony, Sans Dabney? That department will be a success. I'll see to it. The stock will be worth a fortune some day and you and I will own it."

The Dabney boy clasped his hands over his knee and rocked a second, staring toward a window. "I am not, and I never will be in competition with my brother, Louisa. Besides, when we get married you will be my wife, not a merchant. Now we'll talk no more about it—"

"Sans!" Her eyes were wide in delight. "I love to hear you talk that way." She put her hand on his, rubbing his hand. "I am going to Mobile to buy goods and dresses. Then I'm going to New Orleans."

"Will you be gone long?"

Louisa laughed. It was a happy, well-fed laugh. "Not too long." She took his little finger and bent it playfully; then put his hand back in his lap, her arm resting a second on his knee. "Will you miss me?"

"Course I'll miss you." He patted her shoulder and she looked up at him, innocence in her eyes and woman in her heart. Sans Dabney saw only the innocence. He kissed her and she melted into his arms, flowing into his arms. He kissed her again and, feeling her tremble, he was caught in a frenzy and fumbled for her breasts. Louisa relaxed in his arms, her body quivering, and Sans cupped his hand over one of her breasts, pressing it.

Her head rolled back against his neck and he felt for her corset cover and, pulling it open, touched her hot steaming breasts; then bent and kissed them. Louisa gasped and whimpered and Sans pulled her to his lap.

"Be careful," she whispered, finding her voice. "Papa and Gar are on the porch."

That broke the spell and Sans lifted his head, and shame was on him. He drew away from her and felt gross and wretched, as if he had done an evil thing. "I love you so much, Louisa." He waited a few seconds. "And when I take you, it will be forever."

She saw in his eyes a thing she had never seen there before, a slow spark burning, almost ready to flame. Her emotions were choking her and she was yearning for an answer to the tormenting riddle. "Forever and ever. I'll be yours forever and ever." She felt sweat on her spine and between her breasts and wanted to wash herself, yet never wash herself.

She clung to him, and he was Sans Dabney in her arms; then he was Mingo in her mind, and she was terrified. She wanted them both, and had room in her heart for both, and would keep them both forever.

She heard Sans' words clearly. "—And when you are my wife, I'll kill any man who dares look at you as I will look at you."

Again she was terrified, but the terror eased for she believed that in her own time, and in her own way, she would resolve it. She pulled his face down to her. "Now you must go."

She got his hat and kissed him goodnight and watched him go out of the door; then went slowly upstairs to her bed and to the feverish dreams she so often dreamed.

Wyeth and Gar still were sitting on the front steps, still fanning and talking, and their presence brought Sans back abruptly to the world of men. Their voices trailed off when they saw him. In the quietness, Wyeth stretched and yawned. He stood up and Gar stood, too.

"She ran you off sort of early, didn't she, son?" Wyeth said, and nudged Gar.

The old Negro was watching Sans.

"Yes," the elder brother said. "She was tired. She wants to get rested before her trip to Mobile."

Wyeth put his fan on a chair, and turned to Gar. "I forgot to tell you. Louisa is going on a buying trip for The Store. Mingo is putting in a ladies department."

Gar nodded and continued to watch Sans. He knew all about the ladies department. "If you are riding toward the pike," the old Negro said, "I'll go along."

"Let's go," said Sans. "I need some sleep."

They bade Wyeth goodnight and got in the buggy together, and the night was so still they heard the whir of the buggy's spokes. They were almost to the Negro quarters when Sans reined the mare and cocked his head to one side.

"Listen," he said. "What's that?"

Gar raised his head and they heard the creaking of wagons up on the pike.

"What the blazes?" Sans whispered. "Wagons this time of night. Must be four or five of 'em. Heavy loaded."

"The Thrumbull wagons," Gar said. "Bound to be. They're bringing the Thrumbull household goods for their new home. Let's go see."

They rode up the pike and passed the wagons, five of them, each pulled by four mules. Sans whistled under his breath, "They sure got a lot of stuff."

Down beyond a bend, out of sight of the two men, the Thrumbull carriage paced the caravan. It was driven by a Negro groomsman hired in Ellisville, and in the back seat Mr. G. T. Thrumbull was dozing. Ruth Thrumbull, however, was awake, watching the trees and feeling the hot night as they rode to their new home. It was she who insisted they accompany the wagons. Their possessions included silver and lamps and Meissen china, valuables left to her by her mother, and Ruth didn't trust the drivers alone from the railhead at Ellisville to the valley.

She was tired from her long journey, and seeing the black shapes of the brooding trees, she was awed by them. In the night and the quiet, she did not see or hear the other buggy pass, because Sans was driving along a little detour beside Bogue Homa.

Ruth Thrumbull passed Sans Dabney for the first time and didn't know it.

Down by Bogue Homa, Sans watched the wagons out of sight and Gar, sensing his mood, put his bony hand on the boy's knee and said, "Worried?"

"Sure. I'm scared to death. Peninsula is a big company."

"Goliath was pretty good size, too," the old man said. "Now take me home, and I want you to sing a little for me."

Sans settled back in the seat, lifted his head to the trees, and sang the song the old Negro taught him:

> "Shall I, wasting in despair,
> Die because a woman's fair?"

The melody drifted away into the woods and the two friends were silent, but down the pike Ruth Thrumbull touched her father, rousing him.

"What was that?" she demanded.

"What was what?" Mr. Thrumbull was nigh exhausted.

"That song. It came from the woods."

The groomsman turned his head. "Excuse me, ma'am. But that was Mr. Sans Dabney singing."

"Is he the Dabney boy I saw when we were here before?" Ruth peered into the woods.

"No," her father said sleepily. "That was Mingo Dabney. Sans is the elder brother."

Ruth Thrumbull was wide awake, all the fatigue out of her. Maybe it was the excitement of her new home, or the trees. Maybe it was the song. There was something so plaintive about it that she hummed the melody, then sang to the night and to the woods, singing back the song whence it came to her:

> "For if he be not for me,
> "What care I for whom he be?"

They passed The Store and turned across Bogue Homa and drove up the east ridge to their house. She instructed the drivers to unhitch their teams and to leave their wagons for the night, to return and unload the next morning.

"We'll go to the hotel, Dad," she said. "We can start moving in tomorrow."

"Anything you say," said Mr. Thrumbull, "but for God's sake, let's get to bed. I'm dead for sleep."

"Are you sure I never saw Sans Dabney when I was here?"

"I'm sure," said Mr. Thrumbull impatiently.

"Drive us to the hotel," Ruth told the groomsman, then turned again to her father. "Which of the Dabney brothers is blocking the company's railroad?"

"Sans," said Mr. Thrumbull wearily. "I told you that before."

She heard the song again, first up the pike, then moving through the woods, then along Bogue Homa to the quarters, to the cabins.

Ruth Thrumbull undressed slowly in her hotel room, across the hall from the room of Aven MacIvor. She sent for a bowl of warm water and bathed, slowly stroking the water from her long legs, removing the dust of Lebanon.

All the valley slept fitfully. The heat harassed the people, and the dogs, tormented, prowled and bayed. There were sledges pounding at one end of the valley, saws turning at the other.

Sans Dabney could not sleep, thinking of Louisa, and Louisa could not sleep, thinking of many things.

As weary as she was, Ruth Thrumbull could not sleep. The song was haunting her, and she wondered about the man who sang it.

Chapter seven

THE THRUMBULL HOUSE was the most pretentious in the valley because Peninsula's superintendent had wanted a mansion and Mingo built him one, taking his idea from post-bellum houses erected on old Southern foundations with new Yankee money.

It took the Thrumbulls a week to move in and Mingo, the contractor, called to pay his respects. Ruth, trying to make the mansion into a home, listed several minor changes to which the builder agreed willingly.

At lunch, she told her father about the changes and he was pleased. She said, "I haven't seen the other Dabney boy at all." Ruth sipped the tea they served instead of coffee.

"Neither have I." Mr. Thrumbull frowned. "He stays in the woods most of the time. But I must see him before long. The company is ready to make that young man just one more proposition."

"Why not have him here at the house?" Ruth asked.

"I intend to."

Their cook, valley-born and the despair of Ruth's life, removed the dishes while they were still at table, and Ruth looked at her father and shrugged. She was learning fast.

"I met Mrs. Wyeth Woodward and her daughter at the Dabney store this morning." Ruth watched the cook go tromping back to the kitchen.

"Like them?" Mr. Thrumbull lit a cigar.

"All right, I suppose. Mrs. Woodward seemed giddy, but the daughter is rather pretty. You know the kind—soft and sweet and Southern." Ruth rang for the cook and asked politely for more tea.

Up at The House, the Dabneys sat down to dinner and the food was steaming. To make it hotter, they dashed pepper sauce on their vegetables. Mingo reported his call at the Thrumbulls' and they all were interested; they all asked questions except Sans, and he visibly was worried.

"That girl is the brains of that family," Mingo said. "She's a lulu."

"Skinny, isn't she?" Bruce looked up from his food.

"Willowy," said Mingo.

The family laughed and Sans joined in.

"She can't hold a candle to Louisa Woodward," Kyd broke in. "Why, she's not in Louisa's class."

Sans spoke for the first time. "Louisa is going to Mobile tomorrow."

"Why don't you use my buggy and take her down?" The younger brother put aside his coffee cup and wiped his lips.

"Mrs. Woodward is going along," Sans said, a trace of bitterness in his voice. "I feel cramped around Mrs. Woodward."

They were silent and Kyd was oppressed by the silence. She didn't like a silent dinner table. The dinner table is a Southern forum, a marketplace for gossip, a bazaar for news. Kyd herself broke the quiet. "Laurel and Louisa met Miss Thrumbull in The Store. Louisa said she is stylish."

"She is," Mingo replied. "She'll be one of our best customers when we get our new department going."

Bruce, paying little heed to the conversation, asked for more coffee. Sans' mind also was in other places.

Kyd called the cook and ordered the dessert. "Laurel said she was scrubbed up like all Yankee women, not nice and soft like Southern girls. But Laurel said some nice things about her, too."

"That's news," Bruce pushed his cake plate aside. "Bet those Thrumbulls wish they were back North. I've never seen such a summer." He excused himself to go take a nap.

Mingo left the dining room and went to his room to sponge and change into a fresh white suit. Sans waited for him, sitting in the shade on the steps, his shoulders propped against a pillar and sweat forming on his brown face.

The verbena around the steps was moist, but the big shrubs were dry and droopy. Mingo came to the porch, pinched off a verbena bloom and twisted it between his fingers, watching his brother. "Too hot to work in the woods?"

"Too hot to work all day," Sans said. His lips came together and he bit the right corner of his lower lip, pulling at the skin with his teeth. "I was by the mill this morning. They told me you are shutting down one of your saws."

Mingo dropped the verbena bloom and spread his handkerchief on the step by his brother. He sat down carefully, sparing his white suit. "That's right. We shut down a saw yesterday. I was going to tell you tonight that I'll be needing only half as many logs as I've been buying."

The elder brother put his hands over his face, pressing his eyeballs, relieving them of the strain of the sun. "How come you shut down that saw, Mingo?"

"I was losing money. I can't ship in competition with Peninsula, and the local market is flooded." Mingo crossed his legs, rubbing his hand over his ankle. "There's no profit any more in two saws. From now on, I'm counting on The Store."

Sans got up and he towered above his brother. "I'll have to cut my logging, if you cut your orders."

"I reckon so." There was an edge on Mingo's words and he wanted the talk to be over. He hated to see Sans in a quandary.

"If I cut operations, I'll have to lay off some of my hands." Sans said it slowly. "The men will be in trouble if I'm in trouble."

For two or three seconds Mingo was silent, staring at the steps, seeking the words he wanted. His first inclination was to be vague with Sans, to soothe him. However, on second thought, he decided to settle the problem firmly and finally. His reply was blunt. "That's tough titty, kiddo. But there's nothing I can do about it."

A cluster of sweat popped out between the tip of Sans' chin and his lower lip. "The hell there isn't. You can sell me the mill. I've got to have an outlet to stay in business."

Again it was necessary to disillusion his brother and Mingo dreaded the chore. He reached into his pocket for his knife and pared his nails. "How can you buy the mill?"

"I'll mortgage my timber."

"The mill is not for sale." Mingo snapped his knife shut and met Sans' look.

"Why?" Sans demanded.

"Because if you mortgage your timber to buy the mill, I'll soon own your trees. I don't want them, Sans. They are you." Mingo was not looking at his brother then, but across the ridges to the forests, listless in the heat.

Sans' stature diminished as he floundered for a solution. "Then I'll borrow from a bank and build my own mill." His words were flat and had the bravado of a small boy trying to boast his way out of a dark corner.

Mingo ran the back of his thumb across his chin and frowned. "If you sawmill, Sans, where will you sell your lumber?"

"In Ellisville."

"How'll you get it there?"

"Oxen."

"Oxen against Peninsula's railroad?" Mingo was a bit annoyed at his brother's persistence. "Wake up, Sans. If the valley can't support my two saws, how the hell can it support two mills?"

There was a tiny furrow between Sans' eyes as he puckered his forehead. "All right," he said wearily. "What would you do?"

Mingo got up and leaned against a pillar. "I'd sell Peninsula that right of way."

"But that'd give them a stranglehold on the valley—"

"Are you stopping them?" Mingo snapped. "All you're doing is losing out." His impatience was obvious. "You're trumping your own cards. You asked me, and I'm telling you. Go on and sell. Cut your crew in half. Cut down your overhead—"

"What about my men?"

"*Your* men!" Mingo snorted. "They're not *your* men. You can't protect them forever. Let them worry about their own problems. Then cut only enough trees to stay in business. I'll buy 'em." He leaned over and tapped his brother on the chest. "Can't you realize that sooner or later Peninsula will cut all its trees? You'll be the only fellow around here with any trees, and you'll clean up. But if you're going to do that, you've got to sell that right of way. And you got to lay off some of your men. So jump frog or drown—"

"I'll drown." It was an outburst of foolish defiance; partly exasperation, partly desperation.

Mingo opened his hand in hopelessness, then walked toward his buggy.

Sans followed him. "You going to The Store?"

"Uh huh. Got to meet Louisa. Got a few things to go over before she leaves."

"I'll go along if you don't mind." Sans fell in step. "I'll be in the woods late tonight and she'll be leaving tomorrow."

The elder brother was morose and moody and his spirits did not lighten when he saw Louisa. Laurel was with her, and Laurel hovered as close as a mother hen. Louisa was so excited over her trip that she talked of nothing else and while she and Mingo discussed merchandise, Sans sat near the front of The Store, scowling into the distance.

It was the first time he had been in The Store in more than a week and he noticed that Mingo had increased prices on virtually all items, even snuff. Mr. Charlie was puttering around the place, casting disapproving looks toward Louisa, and Sans called him over and asked about the price increase.

"Business is booming," Mr. Charlie said. "Town is full of folks and this is the only store. Mingo is getting his while the getting is good."

Sans got slowly to his feet and walked to the back of The Store, to Louisa. There he told her goodbye and reached out and put his hands on her shoulders. Laurel gasped and Mingo grinned as Sans pulled her to him and kissed her.

Louisa was delighted and lifted her face for a second kiss. Several customers in The Store giggled and Laurel demurely put her fingers over her mouth, feigning shock. Kissing Louisa, and particularly kissing her in front of her mother, lightened Sans' heart and he and Louisa laughed. "Take care of yourself, honey." Sans patted her cheek. "And hurry back." Then he reached out and squeezed his brother's arm and walked out of The Store and down to the livery stable where he got a horse and rode to the woods.

His crews were cutting behind the west ridge, hauling logs to the top of the hill and moving them down the slope on the cable cars Sans and Ronnie had rigged. Oxen, slobbering and too hot to move, stood around the crest of the ridge, hitched to their wagons.

Ronnie saw Sans riding up and called out, "We can't do any work. The hinges of hell done melted."

Sans sat his horse for a minute and watched them. "All right, men, let's knock off. All of you. Meet me at the barn." He turned and rode away. His men sensed his mood, glancing at one another apprehensively.

The crew assembled and sat on hay bales and wagons, gulping water from an oak bucket. "What's eatin' you?" Debo Giles asked.

Without haste or concealment, Sans told them the news. There was no grumbling. Ronnie Sullivan said simply. "Can't blame Mingo. If he can't sell lumber, he can't buy logs."

Fishbait Gates kicked off his shoes so he could think. He hung a flat heel on the edge of the wagon and rubbed his long toes. "Mister Sans, if you lay us off, what'll we do? Peninsula ain't hiring no loggers."

"Dammit to hell!" said Paul de Ru. "We don't have no trouble in this valley until Peninsula come."

Joe Doyle said, "They'll buy Lebanon logs in Pascagoula."

"Why should they?" Sans demanded. "They've got their own timber—"

"Ain't got pine like Lebanon's," Joe said. "I heard a while back they want heart pine down there."

"How long ago?" Ronnie asked.

"Oh, I ain't sure. I just heard talk." Joe couldn't see what time had to do with it. Lebanon logs were Lebanon logs.

Ronnie shook his head. "Hard times is on now. Things are different."

"Besides that's Pascagoula," Sans said. "That's seventy miles from here and we can't make money on ox hauls like that."

Joe Doyle said, "We can float 'em down Bogue Homa to Leaf River, then to Pascagoula River and the mills."

The men stared at Joe Doyle. Bogue Homa was so low that the idea of log rafts was crazy. Debo Giles mumbled, "Ain't enough water in Bogue Homa to float a chip. Snaking logs from here to Pascagoula is a damn good way to get killed."

"I'd as leave get killed on a log as starve to death," said Fishbait.

Debo Giles said, "None of us put in a crop this year. If we don't log, we don't eat. It's root hog, or die—"

"Let's root," said Paul de Ru.

Rough, profane talk greeted the remark and Sans moved to the center of the men. They'd worked together for a long time and if they wanted to root, then by God, he'd root with 'em. "All right," he said. "It's Pascagoula. Ronnie, you'll stay here. Take half the crew and keep moving logs to Mingo's mill. And stay shed of Nils Holmquist." Most of the men laughed and Ronnie grinned.

The venture was a gamble, but they might win and Sans was enthusiastic. "Joe, Debo and I will handle the Pascagoula crew. We'll stack logs along the creek, then roll 'em in and high-tail it."

Ronnie scratched his unshaved jowls and spat. "Maybe you ought to ask Mingo about this. Or your pa. You might get caught up a creek without a paddle—"

"If we do, we'll pole out."

Ronnie laughed. "Have it your way. I'll hold up my end."

There was no delay. Smoothly and without haste, Sans split his workers into two teams, leaving the old and the very young with Ronnie. He sent word home not to expect him for several days, shouldered an ax and led his crew into the woods by Bogue Homa. There they felled timber. By daydown, the work was well under way.

Nils Holmquist rode out to see Sans and visited with him a few minutes, then said, "Just dropped by to let you know that some of my men got over into your timber by mistake. They cut a few trees."

"Stealing my timber, huh?" Sans was grinning. He propped his ax, double edged and razor sharp, against a stump. "How many did they cut?"

"About two hundred dollars' worth." Nils spat and wiped his mouth on the back of his sleeve. "That bunch down at the office said tell you to send 'em a bill."

"Tell 'em to go to hell." Sans' face flushed. "I'll do business with you."

Nils was grateful to take such a message to the high and mighty office bosses. "That reminds me," he said. "Mr. Thrumbull wants to see you."

"Well, tell him to come to see me."

The Swede grinned and walked away. Sans was with his men, swinging his ax again, before Nils was out of sight. They worked until pitch dark. Debo Giles went home to his family for supper, but Fishbait Gates sent for food and cooked it in the open. Sans and the rest of the men ate Fishbait's grub and they slept in the woods.

The next morning they had four hours' work behind them when Louisa and Laurel drove through the south cut on the road to Mobile.

Louisa heard the axes back behind the ridge and knew Sans was there. However, she didn't see him.

For three days, the Dabney boy stayed in the woods and the logs piled up. His muscles, always wiry, grew as tough and stringy as the vines of the wild muscadine. His skin burned a reddish brown and his beard bristled on his face. He was standing on Bogue Homa's bank canting logs when Bruce and Mingo drove into camp and greeted him.

Mingo broke into laughter. "You look like a wild man, kiddo."

"How are you doing, son?" Bruce asked.

"All right, sir." Sans dropped his cant-hook and followed them to shade. He reached for a pine needle and chewed it. "Everybody all right at home?"

Bruce took off his hat and ran his finger around the band. "Everybody's fine. Louisa got to Mobile all right. We came out to tell you that Mr. Thrumbull was by to see you."

"What does he want?"

Mingo kicked a pine cone, spinning it away. "He wants you to come over to his house this afternoon."

Bruce said, "He asked nice and polite like. Sort of a formal asking." He eyed his son closely. "I believe I'd go if I were you. Manners are manners and the Thrumbulls are trying to be friends."

Sans nibbled at his lower lip and ran his hand over his face, feeling his beard. "Hey, Debo. I won't be back till dark. Look after things." He walked away with his father and brother toward their buggy.

Kyd met them on the steps of The House and Sans went with her to see Shellie. He'd been in the woods only three days but the family treated him as though he'd been gone for weeks; such was the affection of this family, each for the other. Kyd had an extra good meal for him.

After dinner, Sans bathed and Mingo came to his room, bringing his best blue cravat, dotted with polka dots. "Wear this," the younger brother said. "And you're going to wear a white suit, aren't you?"

"No. I'm going back to the woods as soon as I see Mr. Thrumbull. Why should I get all diked up?"

Mingo went to Sans' closet and picked out the best white suit and laid it across the bed. "You're going to wear this. You might see Ruth.

You're my brother and I got a reputation to protect. Get it on, kiddo."

"All right. All right." Sans combed his thick brown hair. There was a wave in his hair which he was ashamed of and tried to wet and comb away, but couldn't.

"On the side," said Mingo. "Part it on the side and leave that wave in it. The ladies like a wave."

Sans tried to appear displeased, but actually he wasn't. He looked at himself in the mirror, his cheeks smooth, his skin burned brown. It was good to be clean and fresh again.

A gardener, a valley Negro, was setting out shrubs on the lawn of the Thrumbull place as Sans walked up the path to the new house. He grinned when Sans guyed him for planting shrubs in such weather.

"They told me to." The gardener nodded toward the house.

"Did you tell them it's too dry to plant?" Sans picked up a lump of the hard dry clay from around the plants, pressed it with his thumb and it crumbled in his hand.

"I didn't tell 'em nothing. They're paying me to do, not to tell."

"Well, mulct 'em good and soak 'em down." He stooped over and poked the soil, then glanced up. Ruth Thrumbull was on the verandah, watching him and smiling. Sans removed his hat.

"Do you charge for your advice?" she called down.

"Yes'm," Sans said and looked at her, and saw that her eyes were a cool gray.

"What is your fee?" She waited for him on the top step of the porch.

"A smile, ma'am." Sans bowed. "A smile from a beautiful lady."

Ruth was delighted, and there was a ring to her laughter. She stepped down from the porch and offered her hand, a thing Southern ladies never did. "You are Sans Dabney. I'm Ruth Thrumbull. I overheard what you told the gardener."

"Didn't mean to butt in." Instinctively, he was comparing her to Louisa. This woman was tall while Louisa was small. This woman was strong and lithe. Louisa was dainty.

"Do you think I'll ever have grass here?" She walked across the lawn and Sans followed her. Her light brown hair was swept back over her ears, exposing them, and it was tied loosely at the back of her head.

"You won't have the kind of grass you have up North," he said.

"Have you been up North?" She paused by a withered hydrangea and felt its parched leaves.

"No, ma'am," Sans said. "But I have an aunt and uncle up there and they've told me about it. You'll never get that thick green grass you're accustomed to. But if you'll sod and plant Bermuda, you'll have a pretty good yard."

She looked up at him in a frank, friendly way and suddenly he was reminded of the vines of the forest, slender and graceful and strong.

"Any other suggestions?" she said.

"You serious?" He was suspicious again, afraid she might be teasing him. He never had known a Yankee before who asked advice; but, then, he had known only a few Yankees.

"Yes, I'm serious," she said. "I'd appreciate your help."

He glanced around the yard. "Take out that big pine. Haul in some good soil and plant Bermuda. Get some sheep to keep it cropped."

"You talk like a man who knows what he is talking about." She was making mental notes of his suggestions.

"I do," he said simply. "We have two seasons, wet and dry. Rather, hot and hotter."

"And this is—"

"Hotter," he said. "Put in crepe myrtle and azaleas." He pointed as he talked and she was enthusiastic too, envisioning the yard as he planned it for her.

"Are gardenias all right?" She nodded toward a bush near the gate.

"If you like 'em. I happen to hate 'em. Remind me of funerals. We call 'em cape jasmines down here."

They walked toward the house and up the steps. "I want you to meet my father," she said. "He wants to know you."

Mr. G. T. Thrumbull met them at the door. He was a stout man, but not so heavy as Wyeth Woodward. He was a gracious man, too, and his handshake was friendly and firm. They went into the library and Sans stood until Ruth selected her chair. Then he sat down and looked around at the books and statues. She sent for refreshments, whiskey for the men and chilled wine for herself. They drank and talked about the weather, and politics, then the panic.

Sans felt lost. He knew little about national politics and virtually nothing about the results of the panic throughout the country. Mr. Thrumbull blamed the Democrats, especially President Cleveland, but Ruth disagreed with him and, in a respectful way, argued with him.

"It's the same old fight between the haves and the have-nots," she insisted, while her father shook his head and teased her by calling her a political rebel. "If Big Business were only half as wise as it is greedy, it would give an inch today rather than lose a mile tomorrow. Don't you think so, Mr. Dabney?"

Sans looked into his whiskey glass and took a small drink, a very small drink for him. He never had tasted such good whiskey. "I don't know much about it. I'm a logging man and trees don't have panics. But Mr. Wyeth Woodward says it's a matter of not enough folks eatin' high up on the hog."

Mr. Thrumbull sent for cigars and Sans accepted one, rolling the soft Perfecto between his fingers. Never before had he smoked such a cigar, and he said so.

His host appreciated the compliment. "Good cigars and good whiskey are my only luxuries." He fingered his Perfecto fondly. "I get them direct from Cuba, but with the threat of revolution down there I may not get many more."

Ruth spoke forthrightly and without apology. "It will be awful, Dad, if you can't get your Perfectos because those poor people are trying to get a little freedom."

"It's more than my cigars," he explained quickly to Sans. "The company is opening logging operations in Cuba. A revolution would interrupt our program."

Sans thought nothing about it, caring nothing what Peninsula did outside the valley.

Mr. Thrumbull returned the conversation to politics and the panic. "Sound business practices can end this depression. Businessmen made our country what it is. Men like your uncle Keith Alexander."

"Do you know my uncle?" Sans, trying to smoke casually like Mr. Thrumbull, inhaled deeply and almost coughed. The fine whiskey and the fine tobacco were too much for a valley man accustomed to Mr. Pinckney's corn whiskey, and homemade cigars.

"Never met him."

"I've seen him," Ruth said. "I saw him and his wife at a reception in Chicago. Mrs. Alexander is the most beautiful woman I ever saw."

Sans declined another drink. "Tell me something." He looked across the room at Mr. Thrumbull. "Does my Uncle Keith own any stock in Peninsula?" He crossed his legs and puffed on his cigar and enjoyed himself thoroughly, sitting there and talking big business and himself feeling mighty big.

"No," said Mr. Thrumbull. "Peninsula is pretty well a closed corporation. Your uncle doesn't buy into a company he can't control. He won't own anything he can't boss—"

"I challenge that," Ruth said gaily. "He owns Mrs. Alexander, but I'll bet he can't control her."

Sans was the first to laugh. His stomach was warm and there was a glow inside him.

Mr. Thrumbull also refused a second drink and laid his cigar on a brass ash stand. "You mentioned Mr. Woodward a minute ago, Mr. Dabney. He is your lawyer, isn't he?"

"That's right, sir."

"I assume you know Mr. Cephus Hill, our counsel up at Ellisville?"

Instantly Sans was on his guard. He didn't know Peninsula had employed a local lawyer. "Yes, sir," he said softly. "I know Mr. Hill." He could have added that he despised him. "Folks in the valley call him Windy Hill."

Ruth's merry laugh was spontaneous and Mr. Thrumbull hid his grin behind his hand. "It is, perhaps, an understandable sobriquet. Nevertheless, Mr. Hill—Mr. Windy Hill—hoped to be here this afternoon, but my daughter vetoed the plan."

"Thank you," Sans said almost curtly, then realized that in thinking of the shyster lawyer he spoke abruptly. He changed his tone and said to Ruth, "Thanks a lot. I would not have come if Windy Hill had been here. I came to pay my respects and to welcome you to Lebanon. And," he said to Mr. Thrumbull, "I believe you wanted to see me."

The Peninsula superintendent picked up his cigar again. "Yes, Mr. Dabney. My company asked Mr. Hill to handle this, but I thought you and I might settle it in my home, in a friendly atmosphere. I want to talk to you about the north cut and a right of way."

Sans was silent, staring at the floor. Then he looked up at Mr. Thrumbull. "I suggest you see my counsel if you want to discuss the right of way."

"But lawyers—" Mr. Thrumbull frowned. "They complicate things. Ruth and I thought we could approach you better."

"Excuse me, Dad. You thought so," Ruth said.

Sans got up and put his glass on a table. "Makes no difference," he said slowly, "the right of way is not for sale. But I'll say again that I'll give you a right of way if Peninsula will make the railroad a common carrier and let all of us use it."

Mr. Thrumbull glanced at his daughter, then at the ash of his cigar. "I can't give you such an assurance, Mr. Dabney. I can only offer you money and concessions for the right of way."

The Dabney boy shrugged. "That being the case, sir, we're right back where we started from." He rested his hand on the back of a chair and bowed. "Thank you for asking me down and you-all come to see us. Now, if you'll excuse me."

Ruth went for his hat and Mr. Thrumbull walked with him to the door and offered his hand. Sans shook it and accepted his hat. Ruth asked him to drop by again. The Thrumbulls bade him goodbye and watched him swinging down the path. The father sighed the weariness of an honest man troubled. "The company will break his back."

The daughter did not reply. She stood by the door watching Sans Dabney walk through the gateway.

"I said they'll break his back," Mr. Thrumbull repeated, glancing over at his daughter. "He's the kind of man I like, but he hasn't got a chance against the company."

Still Ruth Thrumbull did not reply, her eyes following Sans as he mounted and wheeled his horse. Then she closed her eyes, fearing, perhaps, the revelation of their yearning. "The company won't break his back," she said. "But that Woodward girl will break his heart. She is not good enough for him." She shut the door, shutting out the scorching rays of the late afternoon sun. It was as though her father was not there at all, that she was talking to herself, expressing the feelings of a woman never afraid of her emotions. "She can't hold him."

Mr. Thrumbull looked at his daughter sharply and she turned from the door and walked up the stairs, slowly at first and then faster. She wanted to be in her room by herself, but never alone. She knew that never again did she want to be alone.

Kyd and Shellie were the only persons at The House when Sans returned home to dress for the woods. His mother plied him with questions about the Thrumbulls and he answered her politely, admitting frankly that he was impressed by Ruth. "I didn't see anything Yankified about her. She didn't seem hard and brittle to me—"

"She wears well," Kyd said quickly, praising Ruth and taking exactly the opposite tack from her talk with Mingo. "The more I hear about her, the better I like her."

Sans hummed a jaunty tune as he walked down the hall to his room and Kyd watched him, watching her son as closely as Mr. Thrumbull had watched his daughter.

It was late afternoon, almost dark, before Sans was ready for work again. He kissed his mother goodbye and said, "Tell Papa Mr. Thrumbull wanted to talk about the right of way. I told him nothing shaking." Before Kyd could press him further, he was out of the door and walking toward the stables and his horse.

He rode rapidly through the village and, beyond the south cut, saw the shadow of Peninsula's mill, stretching long and dark away from the low sun. The mill itself was a huge red building and behind the mill, lining the slope where every tree, every sapling, had been cut down, was the mill town—row after row of red houses, each squatty little house exactly like the next.

Each house had three steps, a little porch, two windows in front. Each house had a tar paper roof, and a chimney—a brick stub sticking up. Each house was painted the same red, all painted from the same bucket, with the same brush. Each man's house was like the house of every other man, and no man's house was his own. The town, and the houses, and the sameness of the houses, all were made from a matrix in Chicago and all belonged to the company.

Some of the houses were occupied and Sans rode down a dusty lane between them, smelling the grease and salt of the kitchens, the heat and sweat and diapers. The houses depressed Sans and he was almost past a big unpainted building when he realized he hadn't seen it before. He reined his horse and looked at it in the shadows. It was roofless and smelled new, of resin and pine sap. A warehouse, he supposed, and rode on.

The moon was out before he reached his camp and his crew was working by firelight. He stopped on the ridge and called down to them and they looked up and waved. Then for sheer joy, in the beauty of the fire and the woods, in the comradeship of his men, Sans Dabney tilted his head to the moon and yelled the old catamount cry of the Dabneys, the warning of hell to come. "Cre-e-e-o-o-o!" The cry shrilled through the south cut, through the mill village, and echoed back from Peninsula's red mill.

His men answered him and he galloped down the ridge, slapping his horse with his hat as he galloped, dodging pines, and whooping and yelling.

"Drunk, by God," said Debo Giles. "And spring done gone."

"Nope," said Joe Doyle. "Just full of Dabney beans."

Sans tied his horse and strode up and down the creek bank, examining the logs. "We've got enough. We'll float 'em now and shove off at daybreak. Roll 'em in. Grab a hook and growl."

They grabbed and worked in unison, Sans setting the pace. He regaled them with stories of the Thrumbulls, of the fine liquor, the big cigar. They worked until the moon waned and none bothered to make a bed, but piled pine needles and bedded down, Fishbait Gates leading the crescendo of snores.

Before the sun blazed red over the ridge, the men were off down Bogue Homa, some riding the logs and some walking along the bank, shoving and pushing the pines through shallow water.

It took three days of misery and might to get the logs a few miles to the junction where Bogue Homa dribbled into Leaf River. There was a nice head of water in the river and the men tied their logs together, rafting them down the current. The sun mirrored itself in the muddy water and threw back its heat, burning them.

Joe Doyle sprained his leg and left the crew and hobbled back to Lebanon. Debo Giles mashed his hand between the logs, but kept going. Sans' face blistered and peeled, but they worked on down the river through a wilderness of pines.

For days they moved without seeing a cabin or the smoke of a cook fire, then they glided into Pascagoula River; they were exhausted and lean and hard. The sight of the Gulf and winging gulls cheered them and they were carefree again, singing and cursing and laughing.

They tied their rafts at the river's mouth and Sans borrowed a skiff and rowed across the bay to Pascagoula town. He was proud, even jaunty, when he told a sawmill owner he had logs across the bay. "Lebanon logs. Top grade."

The mill owner looked at him as though Sans were crazy. "Logs! You floated logs all the way from New Hebron?" He shook his head. "Good God A'mighty, man! Ain't you heard of the panic? We ain't buying logs."

Sans Dabney almost wept. He rested his hand against the side of the office shack, steadying himself, scarcely believing what he heard. He knew the panic was bad but he never thought, never dreamed, that any mill would ever refuse Lebanon logs.

"I'm sorry, son," the mill man said. "But we ain't buying nothing."

At Sans' insistence, however, he went with him across the bay and looked at the logs. "I'm a fool to buy 'em," the man said after an inspection. "But they are beauts. We'll trade."

The price was so low that the trip was a waste of time and muscle. None of his men said a word when Sans accepted the money, and there was mighty little talk when he divided it. Fishbait Gates and Debo Giles took their share and went to Pascagoula and spent it: Fishbait on whiskey and old Debo on a young mulatto whore.

Sans was too miserable to leave camp and he lay on the bank of the river, staring up at the stars, until fatigue relieved him of memory and he slept.

The next day they began the long walk home. . . .

Ronnie and his crew knew the voyage had failed when they saw Sans and Debo plodding up the slope back of Mingo's mill. In the disappointment for all of them, there were no greetings and Sans called his men about him, told them the news, and laid off half of them.

One by one, the men drifted away to their cabins, walking through the company town to their shacks along the creek. Sans dreaded to face Mingo, hated to go home. He wished Louisa was in New Hebron. He needed to see her and find comfort in her presence.

Kyd fixed him a good supper and Bruce poured him a drink of

his best whiskey. They all heard his story of failure and all were as sad as he.

"Has anyone heard from Louisa?" Sans asked.

"Yes," said Kyd. "There's a letter for you."

He took it to his room and read it eagerly, searching the precise, exemplary words for a hint of love. But there was no warmth in the letter and Sans was bitter, aware that Laurel was with Louisa when she wrote it. Louisa wrote about Mobile and the things she had bought. She told him she was going next to New Orleans, then Natchez; she wasn't sure when she would be home.

Sans put the letter in his bureau drawer and sat on the bed, staring at the floor. Her mother was taking her to Natchez. Her mother was afraid for her to be with him. Her mother wanted her to marry somebody with a good business, somebody making sure money. A man who was tired and muddy, who floated logs down a puny creek on a fool's errand, wasn't acceptable to Mrs. Woodward.

He tried to put it all out of his mind and went to the porch and sat with his family. Kyd and Bruce had fans and Mingo was sitting on the steps, watching the moon. Even the moon looked hot.

Kyd said, "Bruce, did you tell Sans that Wyeth wants to see him?"

"I was going to tell him later." Bruce turned to his son. "Mr. Woodward wants to see you at his office."

"What's up?" Sans asked.

"Lawyers," Bruce said. "That's all I know."

The Dabneys were silent, each staring into the darkness. And in the stillness, the pounding of the hammers at the north cut sounded clear. At the south cut, the reflection from Peninsula's mill shone bright, glowing with a strong steady light.

Mingo watched the moon a few minutes, then yawned. "Must be rain up there somewhere. Bound to be."

"Rain's coming," Bruce said. "My corns hurt."

Kyd said, "Quit scratching your hand." She held out her own hand and Bruce put his hand in hers.

"Got to go up to Jasper County tomorrow," he told her. "Man up there got some mules I aim to buy. I'll be gone two or three days."

They talked a few minutes about the mules and Sans contributed only a few words, for the black mood was on him and he was restless. "I think I'll go down and see Gar a few minutes," he said. He needed the company of someone who could absorb his worries and give him peace.

Mingo said, "Care if I go with you? I've got the fidgets myself." He stood and yawned again.

Bruce looked his gratitude at the younger brother and he and Kyd watched them walk around the porch toward the barn. They took Mingo's buggy and were past The Tree and on the pike before either spoke more than monosyllables. Then Mingo said, "What's eatin' you?"

"I don't know." Sans was driving and he watched the mare's muscles ripple. "I'm just down in the mouth and want to see old Gar."

Mingo did not try to lighten his spirit, or attempt cheerfulness at all. Instead he fitted his own mood to the mood of his brother and they both were silent, riding along, watching the trees brood with the night. Mingo Dabney loved trees, too. He loved them but did not understand them. The forest was a mystery to the younger brother, a revelation to the elder.

They reached Gar's cabin and the old Negro was joyous to see them together. He offered them cold buttermilk and the three sat on the steps of his cabin, drinking the milk, and each thinking his own thoughts. Sans' thoughts were for Louisa. Mingo's thoughts were for Sans.

"Let's walk around," Gar said. "Do us good to walk around a little bit."

They walked together along Bogue Homa, careful of the brush and fallen logs. They spoke scarcely at all and only of simple things; the weather, the possibility of snakes along the bank, the stillness of the night. Sans began humming his song.

Mingo listened, his head cocked slightly toward his brother and his eyes on the distant ridge. "I don't like that song. Too damn sad for me. But then—" He parted the curtain of a willow tree. "If I was in love like you, maybe I'd sing it, too."

"Maybe."

Gar watched them both, seeing things even the night couldn't hide. Sans took up his song again and the old Negro joined him. A slight breeze, timid and hopeful, rustled along Bogue Homa and caught the words, drifting them down the valley. Ruth Thrumbull, restless in her canopied bed, heard the melody and there was a catch in her heart. So he was back from Pascagoula.

The only reason Sans Dabney called at the office of the Peninsula Lumber Company was because Wyeth Woodward explained it was courteous to meet the company lawyers for the requested conference. The lawyers, Mr. Lewiston and Mr. Irving of Chicago, and Windy Hill of Ellisville, had been in the village for several days, awaiting the return of Sans.

Vernon Boyd, the sheriff, saw them enter Peninsula's office and hurried to the livery stable with news that at last Sans Dabney was visiting the company. Speculation spread through the village and some men bet that Sans would compromise with the company. Nils Holmquist gave two to one that he wouldn't budge an inch. Mr. Charlie made it three to one. Mingo made it five.

Windy Hill was the first to greet the visitors, hopping up from his chair at the side of the conference table and offering his hand to Wyeth, trying to impress his superiors by his friendships in the valley. He didn't offer to shake Sans' hand, however, knowing his gesture would be ignored.

Wyeth asked about the health of Windy Hill's invalid wife. Folks always did that as a matter of manners. "She's mighty po'ly," Windy said dolefully as though his wife's misery were a cross he must bear without complaint.

Then the Ellisville lawyer introduced the Chicago lawyers, and Sans and Wyeth sat down. Windy began talking in generalities, about the weather and the crops. Mr. Lewiston interrupted him and turned to Sans, demanding brusquely: "What do you want for a right of way through your land, Dabney?"

Sans was taken aback by the bluntness of the question. His eyes narrowed slightly and he looked the lawyer over, then nodded to Wyeth.

"A right of way through my client's land is not for sale under present conditions," Wyeth said.

"Can't you let your client speak for himself?" Mr. Irving asked impatiently.

Wyeth flushed and jerked off his spectacles. "You're damn right, mister. My client will speak for himself just as quickly as your client will speak for itself."

"Gentlemen," Windy said. "Gentlemen, please. No need for short tempers. It's too hot."

Mr. Lewiston cleared his throat. "Mr. Dabney, my company has laid its railroad almost to the entrance of this valley. It requires a right of way to get to its mill. You don't expect my company to run a railroad ten or twelve miles around this valley, do you?"

Sans didn't answer.

"Well, speak up, Dabney," said Mr. Lewiston. "You don't expect my company to run its railroad around the valley, do you?"

Sans might have said what was in his mind, but Mr. Woodward was present and out of respect for the old family friend, the Dabney boy checked himself, then said flatly and without equivocation: "This is the last time I'm telling you. No railroad is coming through that north cut unless it's a common carrier."

Mr. Irving scowled and Windy Hill squirmed. "Apparently we can't do business with this man," Mr. Lewiston said, glancing across the table at his associates.

"Oh, yes, you can," Wyeth said. "All he asks is that your railroad be for public service."

"We are in the sawmill business. Not the railroad business," Mr. Lewiston said, almost shouting the words.

Sans got up. "Let's go, Mr. Woodward."

Mr. Irving got up, too. "Just a minute, Woodward. We are filing for eminent domain, naturally."

"Naturally," said Wyeth. "But there is no record of our courts granting a private company eminent domain for private services." He reached for his hat and he and Sans walked out of the room, leaving the lawyers to stare at one another.

Irving was the first to find his voice. "Thrumbull was right. Dabney will fight."

"So will Woodward," Windy Hill said.

"Can't you arouse the people against them?" Lewiston asked.

"This is Dabney country, gentlemen. The Dabneys are the he-coons in this valley."

Lewiston struck a match and held it poised over the bowl of his pipe while he sat still, listening, his head to one side. "My God! Don't tell me that's thunder." Far away, from almost down to the Gulf, came a rumbling and muttering. "Don't tell me it ever rains in this place." He grunted, and lit his pipe. He smoked a few puffs. "Obviously, eminent domain isn't the answer. Take too much time and money."

Irving looked over at his senior. "Injunction, perhaps. Why not enjoin the Dabneys while we lay the road through? Then a writ restraining them against molesting Peninsula in any way."

Windy Hill puffed his cheeks and blew out his breath. "Woodward would be ready for that. So would the Dabneys. You don't want bloodshed do you?"

Irving glanced at Lewiston and both men shrugged. "All we want," said Lewiston, "is a right of way."

"An injunction will do it," Irving said. "After all, the Dabneys can't defy the courts—"

"They defied the whole God damn Confederacy," Hill said.

A breeze came through the window and rustled papers on the desk. They all went to the window and looked out toward the east where a cloud, lumpy and white like cotton, hung in the sky.

Irving put a weight on the papers. "What about the district judge? Will he grant an injunction?"

Windy Hill snorted. "Hell, no! He's as independent as a hog on ice. We'll get an injunction from him only if we have a good case."

"Then we need a new judge," Lewiston said quietly, "a fair judge. Isn't there an election this fall?"

Windy Hill looked from Irving to Lewiston and nodded.

There was a low muttering of thunder again and they ignored it. "You would make a good judge," said Lewiston, sitting with his back to Windy. "Judge Cephus Hill." He turned to him. "How does that sound?"

"Damn good," said Windy, his face flushing.

Irving leaned forward. "How much campaign money will you need? How much will it cost?"

Windy Hill wet his lips and glanced back at the door. He lowered his voice, lowered his usually booming voice to a whisper. "Two thousand, gentlemen. I can carry two counties. I will lose Lebanon County, but I can carry the district."

Mr. Irving shrugged and smiled across the table at his partner. "The South is still cheap," he said "It'd be fifty thousand back home."

"Don't file for office until the last minute," Lewiston said. "Resign from Peninsula's employ on the day you file. Begin your campaign by denouncing the company. That is the procedure." He made a triangle with the tips of his fingers and pursed his lips, apparently pondering the problem. Then he recited: "Of course use white supremacy. Lower taxes. Yankees. Wall Street. And remember, Hill, ample hospitality at the whiskey barrel."

Windy Hill said, "Yes, sir."

Mr. Irving walked over to the window and watched the cloud spreading toward them from the east. He looked at the earth, the poor sandy soil, at the dusty streets and rickety buildings of New Hebron, at the people sauntering by. "So this," he said, "is the valley of Lebanon. Jesus!"

"But it's a gold mine," said Mr. Lewiston. "There are enough trees here to be minted into a fortune."

Irving still was looking out of the window. "So this is the valley for which Keith Alexander fought—"

"Do you know Keith Alexander?" Windy Hill blurted, leaning forward, his jowls quaking.

"I've met him," Irving said. He came back to the table and sat down. "I had occasion to represent him once. He is very powerful in Chicago."

Windy Hill stuck his hand inside his collar and rimmed his neck, and his hand was wet with sweat. "Don't mention his name. Just don't mention his name—"

"Why, Keith Alexander is an old man," Irving said, and laughed. "Besides, he has no connection with Lebanon any more."

Windy Hill shook his head and paled. "You don't know what you're saying. He married a Dabney. And he's still Keith Alexander." He took out his handkerchief and wiped the sweat that beaded about his mouth. "Just don't talk about him. That son of a bitch will never get old. I've seen him, gentlemen, as he really is. I've seen him with pistols. Pistols and riding a white horse."

Mr. Irving and Mr. Lewiston laughed as they looked at Windy Hill, and at his trembling hands.

Chapter eight

THE DUSTY LEAVES of the water oaks around the courthouse trembled, vibrating at the touch of the slight breeze. Sans and Wyeth, walking from Peninsula's office toward Wyeth's office, watched the trees a second, eagerly, hopefully.

Sheriff Vernon Boyd came out of the courthouse and looked around. 'Tite Pierre, the crippled Cajun, got up from the post office bench and peered at the sky. He saw Sans and Wyeth and spoke to them, saying that the miracle of the rain might come to pass.

The breeze was on Sans' forehead and, removing his hat, he felt it in his hair. Wyeth felt it against his beard, and they smiled at each other.

"The breeze is from the east," Sans said. "It might blow up a wet spell."

"Praise the Lord. I'll take even a heavy dew."

All through the village people stirred, watching the sky, feeling the breeze. Sans and Wyeth reached his office and stood on the porch. The dust was moving, churning a bit, and the breeze waved the heavy magnolia leaves and hummed in the pines. The locusts were hushed and birds darted into the hedges, streaking them with quick color, and only the thrush sang, the rain prophet.

Sans sighed and opened his shirt and let the breeze cool him. "I saw heat flashes to the east last night. That's a good sign."

"Lord knows I'll never cuss high water again." Wyeth cut his eyes over at the younger man. "Worried, huh?"

"In a way. I feel like we're fighting a barrel of molasses—"

"We are. They've got tricks. They'll squirm and twist and quote the law from hell to breakfast. But the law is on our side."

A flock of chickens, their necks outstretched, ran frantically across the square, heading for shelter, and the oak leaves swayed. The promise of rain buoyed Sans' spirit but he still was depressed. "Folks can buy the law, can't they?"

"No." Wyeth stepped into the hallway of his office. "Sometimes they buy men who make the law and who are supposed to enforce it. But the law itself is just."

"What'll we do if they start buying?"

"Thrumbull won't stand for that. Neither will Holmquist." Wyeth put the back of his hand under his beard, lifting it and letting the breeze get at his throat. "We'll just sit tight and wait."

A salvo of thunder over the north cut interrupted his words. The echo rolled down the valley, grumbling and muttering away into the distance. A black cloud loomed over the east ridge.

"Good Lord," said Wyeth. "Am I seeing things?"

"It's real. That's a cloud. You know—one of those things that give rain."

They smiled and chuckled and their spirits were caught up by the wind, and soared. Gabriel d'Artois ran out of his blacksmith shop, waving his thick, muscular arms and laughing. Shane Figgis stood in the road and opened his shirt wide, letting the wind blow against his matted chest. The loiterers around the livery stable whooped and pounded one another's backs. At the north cut, the boss of the Peninsula railroad crew drove his men harder, watching the sky as he shouted orders. Bruce's mules perked and twitched their ears. Ronnie's oxen raised their heads, their sad eyes no longer hooded with heavy lids.

A rain was coming: the gentle gift of heaven.

There was another crash of thunder and the wind was sharp and gusty. A tall funnel of leaves suddenly twisted up off the ground and went skimming and spinning over the square and over the pike until, for an instant it hung still, teetering on its point; then spilled back loose and empty to the ground again. Scraps of paper shot into the air only to lose their flight and sag until the wind caught them once more and flung them higher and higher.

Ruth Thrumbull pulled down windows at her house, dashing from room to room. At the Dabney house old Shellie raised her head and mumbled her thanks, and dozed again. Mingo told his sawmill crew to take the day off if it rained.

"Celebrate," he told them. "Get drunk for all I care. But don't get drowned."

Smoke Jackson's little girl, named Mattie Pearl, and black as Smoke himself, came out of The Store, totin' a bottle of coal oil with a corn cob stopper. She looked up at the clouds, then hopped off the porch and scooted for home, skipping along, her bare feet plopping up the dust of the road. Her hair was twisted into little tufts, stiff on her head, each wrapped tight with white cotton string.

Mattie Pearl, blacker than the cloud, gayer than the wind, went running and skipping and swinging her bottle until suddenly the very miracle of life was too beautiful for her—the wind, the sweet smells, the impending storm. She stopped and put her bottle down and held out her arms stiff, then whirled round and round, holding out her hands to the wind and the world, weaving and spinning and chanting:

> "Chick-a-ma, chick-a-ma, craney crow
> Went to the well to wash my toe,
> When I went by
> The well was dry—
> What time it gonna rain, old witch?"

Sans watched her and lifted his eyes from her to the pines on the ridges and the darkening sky. He looked down again and saw the squalid shacks along the creek bank, and the child still dancing. There was a tremble of awe and anger and trepidation in Sans' heart, and tears in his eyes as he watched the little girl, spinning and chanting, "Chick-a-ma, chick-a-ma, craney crow."

"I'm going to The Store," he told Wyeth. "See you later."

He was hardly away from the lawyer's office when the first big drop of rain hit the road and knocked up a spurt of dust. "Here she comes!" The cry sounded over near the courthouse and men shouted and whooped. Mattie Pearl snatched up her bottle of coal oil and darted for home.

Another drop fell at Sans' feet and then little spouts of dust were hopping all over the road, and he lowered his head and ran for The Store. Before he got there, the rain was sluicing down, the squall blustering through the valley and the wind slanting and billowing the curtains of rain. He ran hard for The Store and didn't bother with the steps, jumping from the pike to the porch.

Mr. Charlie was standing at the door and slid his spectacles lower on his nose and peered over them. "Think it'll rain?"

Sans was slinging water from his hat. "Might. If it clouds up." He laid aside his hat and slapped the water from his shirt.

Mr. Charlie jerked up his chin and spat across the porch. "She's a gully washer and a trash mover. Praise be!"

The Dabney boy grinned and slid his hands down his pants legs, slicking off the water. He went to the lee side of the porch and sat on a bench, stretching his long legs out in front of him. He sat there watching the rain pounding, washing the leaves, beating the trees while they swayed with the wind and shivered with delight. New Hebron was deserted and The Store was deserted except for the young man and the old man. Sans said, "Mr. Charlie, let's you and me have a bottle of beer."

They went inside and Sans noticed how orderly The Store was, and how high the prices. Joining the old building at the left, was Mingo's annex for Louisa's department, a fresh pine annex, the yellow boards sweating an occasional fleck of brown, gummy resin.

Mr. Charlie said, "They'll finish it before long." He spat again, not so much to be rid of excess tobacco juice as in professional indignation. "Women in a store! Good God A'mighty! Dabneys selling perfume and hairpins." He took a long drink from his bottle of beer.

Sans grunted and walked back to the porch, to the bench. The top of the bench was a single slab of heart pine, deep rich red and polished through the years by the seats of the long sitters, the long talkers, the slow whittlers. Its front edge was notched and slotted. Initials were carved on it, and a hound running a rabbit; but mostly the lazy, unimaginative knives had dug trenches—just sort of meditated along the top of the bench.

The elder brother crossed his legs and watched the rain, steadying down to its appointed task of wetting the earth. He thought of Louisa. The rain made him think of her. The rain made him melancholy and the black mood was on him.

Mr. Charlie came out and pulled up a chair. He was ready to sit, then noticed a hole in the half-rotten porch. "I aimed to fix that hole many a time," the old man said. "Now I'm gonna do it."

That brought Sans out of his reverie. "How's politics, Mr. Charlie?"

"Slow." The storekeeper went inside for his hammer and walked back and forth across the porch, looking at the signs nailed there, dozens of them. "Don't want to use one of Elmo Batson's signs to patch a hole," he mumbled. "That'd hurt ol' Elmo's feelings."

He selected a tin sign and pried it off, fitting it over the hole, patching his porch with the yellow-and-black sign that proclaimed the Wonder Working Wizardry of "Black Draught" and the endless benefits of "Wine of Cardui."

"Doing any 'lectioneering?" Sans asked.

"Don't have to. Ain't nobody running against me."

"How 'bout Peninsula folks? Can any of them vote?"

"Some of 'em been around here long enough to vote."

Sans reached for his pocket knife and gouged at the bench. "They for you?"

"Got to be. Nobody else for 'em to vote for. It's me or nobody." Mr. Charlie ran his hand along one of the posts, feeling where the whittlers had cut too deep. He ripped a tin sign, tall and narrow, from the wall and nailed it on the post. It was a shield against the whittlers and it proclaimed:

A-yer's Sarsaparilla
Y-our best remedy for
E-rysipelas, Catarrh
R-heumatism, and
S-crofuls.

S-alt-Rheum, Sore eyes
A-bscesses, Tumors
R-unning sores
S-curvy, Humors, Itch
A-nemia, Indigestion *
P-imples, Blotches
A-nd Carbuncles
R-ingworm, Rashes
I-mpure blood
L-anguidness, Dropsy

L-iver Complaint
A-ll cured by
AYER'S
SARSAPARILLA

Sans slid to the end of the bench, leaned over and read the sign.
"Cures about everything, don't it?"

"It won't cure what's ailing you." Mr. Charlie ripped down dodgers
from the notice board by the door.

"What's ailing me?" asked Sans. The rain was making him drowsy.

The old storekeeper took off his glasses, pulled out enough of his
shirt tail to wipe them, then put them back on. "Can't nothing cure
what's ailing you except Wyeth Woodward's little girl. You got it
bad." The wind lessened and the rain fell in a soft even drone on the
shingled roof. Mr. Charlie leaned his hammer against the door jamb
and went over and sat down near Sans. "No use roosting there with
your tail feathers dragging."

"Ain't dragging, Mr. Charlie. Just drooping." He stretched and
leaned his head back and yawned.

Primed by the rain and their mood, Charles Pryor Owens, the ven-
erable bard of Lebanon, took up his saga of the valley, reciting the
annals of things long gone; the good years before Peninsula came,
before a woman threatened his kingdom of coal oil and snuff.

He came at last to an interlude; then saw that Sans wasn't interested, wasn't listening, but was looking past him down the pike.

The storekeeper turned and he, too, stared down the pike, toward
the south cut and Mobile. A two-horse buggy was coming up the
road, the horses pulling low-headed, tired. They plopped their heavy
feet in the mud and it splattered.

"That's Elmo Batson," Sans said. "And he's got his curtains down."

"Elmo's buggy all right. He ain't due till tomorrow."

It was good to see ol' Elmo coming. They could sit on the porch
and listen to his stories, get the latest news. Elmo was a high stepper.
He'd been places. Been to New York, seen Lillian Russell and the
Cardiff Giant.

Mr. Charlie was spitting and fidgeting, his Adam's apple bobbing
in anticipation of an afternoon with his crony and no customers to
pester them. However, instead of coming to The Store as always,

Elmo stopped his team in front of Wyeth Woodward's office. Sans and Mr. Charlie craned their necks. Then they looked at each other. "Elmo Batson ain't never before been in this valley without coming to see me first." The old man was hurt.

The rain was coming down steadily, purring on the roof and spilling over the eaves. Elmo got out of his buggy and unfastened the curtains at the back of the vehicle. A man stepped out and turned and held up his hand. A woman took his hand and he helped her to the ground. The man and the woman hurried into Wyeth Woodward's office, Elmo opening the door.

"Who are they?" Sans kept his gaze on the buggy.

"Never saw 'em before," Mr. Charlie said. "Little bitty fellow, wasn't he?"

"Maybe more Peninsula folks."

"No, sir-e-e. Elmo Batson wouldn't be hauling Peninsula folks."

"The woman had on a veil." Sans tapped his foot against the floor, his curiosity sharpening his impatience.

Elmo came out of the lawyer's office and Mr. Charlie scowled, getting set to rebuke him.

Then, to Mr. Charlie's consternation, Elmo turned his buggy around, heading directly away from The Store, driving toward Bogue Homa, toward the Negro quarters. The old man almost exploded, swelling up like a turkey cock, his neck as red as wattles. He sat glowering and pouting, mumbling his indignation at being ignored.

Sam stared at the buggy until it was out of sight, and still was staring when it came back and stopped in front of Wyeth's office again.

Gar Rivers stepped out and hurried into the building.

That was too much for Mr. Charlie. "I'm going to mosey down that way," he grumbled, "rain or no rain."

"I'll come along." Sans started to get up.

Elmo appeared again and Sans sat back down. Mr. Charlie snatched up his hammer and tore off Elmo's biggest sign, the one with a great bull, his head high, his tail arched. He slammed it over a spot in the floor that looked a little weak and nailed it face down, contemptuously, not even bothering to turn it up so his customers could read that the Prince of Wales smoked Bull Durham Smoking Tobacco.

"He's coming here this time," Sans said, watching the team plod up the road.

"Don't care. Don't give a slick damn where he goes."

The buggy turned toward the porch and Mr. Charlie laid down his hammer and waited. They heard Elmo, behind the heavy curtains, speaking to the horses. Then he tightened his reins and pushed back the curtain flap and called out, "Sans."

There was no cheery greeting from the jovial drummer, no banter. Elmo's face was solemn and drawn, and Mr. Charlie's rebuke died on his lips.

"Sans," he called again. "They want you and your brother at Mr. Woodward's office. Come on. Let's go get Mingo."

The elder brother jumped off the porch and into the rain and ran to the buggy.

"Who are them people?" Mr. Charlie demanded. "Them two strangers?"

"Couple of furriners." Elmo lifted the curtain for Sans. "They are furriners from Cuba." He let the curtain drop and wheeled his team.

The Dabney boy suddenly was alarmed. He had never before seen Elmo Batson subdued; serious as a messenger bringing ominous tidings. The drummer was sodden with fatigue, and his team was nigh exhaustion. The buggy, curtained tight against the rain, smelled of sweat—Elmo's sweat. But there was a lingering odor of perfume, of flowers.

"What's going on?" Sans demanded. "You been driving back and forth like a crazy man."

"I'll tell you when we get Mingo." Elmo's voice was strained. "No need of telling twice. So just keep your shirt on."

They arrived at the mill and Sans shouted for his brother. Mingo ran out in the rain and jumped into the buggy. "What the hell? Anything wrong?"

Elmo headed his buggy back down the pike while Sans explained all he knew, then turned to the drummer. "All right. What's the mystery?"

"Yeah," Mingo said. "Who are these folks and what do they want?"

"Ain't no mystery." Elmo's voice was low, still strained. "Like I said before, they're Cubans. A friend of mine in Mobile asked me to bring 'em up here to see Mr. Woodward. Then Mr. Woodward told me to fetch that old nigger. And you Dabney boys."

The buggy neared Wyeth's office. "But who in the name of goodness are they?" Sans insisted emphatically.

"The man's name is Marti," Elmo said wearily. "The woman's got a name as long as your arm."

"His wife?" Mingo asked.

"No." Elmo reined his team near Wyeth's steps. "They just work together."

Mingo stepped out of the buggy first, and Sans turned to the drummer. "For Lord's sake, Elmo, hurry up and see Mr. Charlie. He's busting a trace."

Puzzled by Elmo's behavior, the Dabney brothers hurried into the shelter of the hallway, jumping lightly to the porch. The door to Wyeth Woodward's office was partly open. They heard a man talking, and hesitant to interrupt, paused by the door. Mr. Woodward was motionless behind his desk, his head slightly to one side. Gar Rivers was near the desk and the face of the old Negro shone with a singular radiance.

The voice in the room was so calm, so firm. "Liberty and brotherhood—that is our covenant." The Dabney boys stepped full into the doorway, seeing José Marti for the first time. He was a small man, slight and pallid. To the right, at the far end of Wyeth's desk, was the woman.

She was wearing a mantilla, a shawl of black lace that covered her head like a cowl. A few strands of white hair showed beneath it. That was all Sans noticed before his gaze was drawn back to the man. But Mingo Dabney held his eyes on the woman and she, feeling his eyes, turned her head and looked away.

Wyeth glanced up at the brothers, then addressed his visitor. "Señor Marti, I present Sans Dabney and Mingo Dabney."

The little man's eyes were wide set in deep sockets under heavy black brows. He shook hands with the Dabneys and bowed to the woman. "Gentlemen, I present you to my associate and confidante, Señorita Rafaela Galban y Torres."

She stood and her mantilla slipped back from her forehead to the crest of her hair, and in quick consternation she drew the covering low again, concealing her hair. She was tall and slender and young, and her hair was silver white; not the cold, dead white of alabaster, but the living silver of hair turned white before its time. Her forehead was high, and her face tapered, thinning down her pale cheeks to a tiny chin. Her lips were full and red, and she was smiling.

Mingo said, "Good evening, ma'am," and took her hand. It was friendly and firm, but her fingers were cold. Señorita Galban sat down again and Mingo took a chair near his brother, staring at her until Sans nudged him and both the boys turned to Wyeth.

"Señor Marti and Miss Galban have come to talk to us," the lawyer explained. "They regret that your father is not here." He folded his hands and leaned back in his chair, then remembered a lady was present and flushed and sat erect, mumbling an apology.

Rafaela Galban smiled in acknowledgment, and Mingo, stealing a glance at her, saw there was no warmth in her smile. Her eyes were unlighted and cold, like the seamless black of a winter night. He looked at her face, at the glow of her hair under the mantilla, and he thought of snow, of all the world cold and under white.

Marti plucked at the full black mustache that hid his lips completely, accentuating his thin face. He crossed his right leg, the crippled one, the ankle still festering from Spanish shackles. His black broadcloth suit was rumpled and his Masonic emblem dangled on a chain across his vest.

Wyeth spoke directly to the Dabneys. "Our guests are exiles in our country because they advocate overthrow of the Spanish regime in Cuba. They are revolutionists."

Rafaela Galban's eyes, cold the moment before, sparked and fired at mention of Cuba and revolution.

"I know you boys are anxious to know why I sent for you, but I ask you to be patient." He settled his bulk comfortably in his swivel chair. "I sent for you as attorney for the Dabney interests." He folded his hands across his bulging middle, revolving his thumbs. "Our guests have come for information about Peninsula Lumber Company—"

Sans eased forward, glancing at Rafaela Galban, staring at José Marti.

"Peninsula Lumber Company is opening logging operations in

Cuba," the attorney continued. "They have purchased concessions from the Spanish crown, thereby aligning themselves against Señor Marti, Miss Galban and their fellow revolutionists."

"Wait a second." Sans could restrain himself no longer. "What's that got to do with Lebanon?"

Marti spoke as quickly as Sans. "A hydra has a head wherever there is something to devour."

Rafaela nodded emphatic agreement, and Mingo saw the color creeping into her cheeks.

The lawyer held up his hand. "I commend patience to all of you. Señor Marti, will you explain to us why a revolutionist is interested in Peninsula's activities here in Lebanon?"

The Cuban girl, disconcerted by Mingo's captivated gaze, turned upon him and coldly stared him down, but the color was higher on her cheeks. Then, in a studied effort to ignore the boldness of the valley man, she gave her attention to Marti, smiling encouragement to her compatriot as he limped to the desk and leaned against it.

"I am here," the exile said, "because Peninsula Lumber Company is opening operations in this valley almost simultaneously with its operations in my country." He paused, selecting his words with utmost care. "The South, whether you gentlemen agree or not, is a colony of the United States, and my country is a colony of Spain. We've had four hundred years of exploitation; you've had only thirty. But now we have a common invader."

Sans interrupted once more. "You're over my head. What are you getting at?" Gar Rivers touched his knee, stilling him. Rafaela flinched, evidence of her annoyance at the interruption. Mingo Dabney heard and saw none of this; he saw only the girl.

Marti was infinitely patient with Sans. "Mr. Dabney." He held out his hands, opening them in the unvarying gesture of his people. "Have you ever considered the similarity between your South and my Cuba? We each are an agrarian society blighted by absentee proprietorship; cursed with one crop, burdened by race antagonisms, poverty, and ignorance."

Wyeth Woodward bridled in the way of all Southerners. "We get along all right down here." He jerked down the flap of his vest. "Now, sir, will you favor us with the reason for your gracious visit?"

Again Marti shrugged, again with infinite patience. "Very well.

What is the connection between Peninsula Lumber Company and the government of Lebanon?"

Mingo looked up then and he and his brother grinned. Wyeth's middle shook as he chuckled at the foreigner's misconception of hegemony in the valley. The government of Lebanon was the Board of Supervisors, the constable, the J. P., the pineboard ballot box, the calaboose with rusty bars. There was an embarrassing silence and Gar Rivers, sensitive to Marti's fallacy, went to his aid. "We do not have a government here as you understand government," the old Negro said.

Wyeth's chuckle rumbled its course and he said considerately, "Some of Peninsula's folks vote here, just like everybody else. But Peninsula's headquarters is in Chicago, and the company itself plays no part in local politics."

The Cuban revolutionists, experienced in the ways of intrigue, gaped at Wyeth in incredulity. He glanced quickly at Rafaela and her astonishment confirmed that he had heard correctly. Then he looked at all of them—the lawyer, the brothers, and the old Negro, slowly apprehending the bewildering naïveté of these provincial people. At that moment he was convinced, beyond a shadow of a doubt, that the Dabneys and their neighbors knew nothing of Peninsula's schemes and machinations. It was in his heart to warn them, but he understood American assurance, had endured it, and knew they would resent the intrusion of a foreigner. Therefore, he must go to Chicago for the screened information his cause needed.

"I pray God you are right," he said, abandoning hope of any enlightenment from Lebanon that might help him fight Peninsula in Cuba. He was weary, resigned to the long and intricate course his revolution must follow. He waited there by the desk a second, watching the rain strike the windowpanes and slide down. Then the little man limped dejectedly back to his chair, bowing the cue to his associate.

Rafaela Galban touched his sleeve. "Do not be depressed, Don José." She raised her head, her eyes misty, and uttered the words she had spoken a thousand times. "It is our custom, wherever we go, to seek aid for our cause. We continuously seek men and money for Cuba's fight against tyranny." Her mantilla slipped back slightly, and again she drew it forward, still concealing her hair.

At the mention of fighting and tyranny, the Dabney boys leaned forward. This was talk they understood. "What kind of fighting?" Sans demanded.

"Yes, ma'am," said Mingo. "Go on."

"The fight of the meek for their inheritance!" The girl, the schooled revolutionist, the incendiary, rose gracefully. She was almost as tall as Mingo, as straight as Sans. "While we sit here, my people are being garroted because they dare hope for privileges you gentlemen accept as your rights." The sound of the rain was heavy on the roof, but in the room there was no sound except the voice of Rafaela Galban. "So we come for men and money. We come in the name of liberty, the seal of the brotherhood of man." Then the evangel, her black eyes burning with a fanatic fire, pointed a trembling finger at each of them. "I challenge you, the blessed free, to share a pittance of your wealth! I cast the gauntlet at the feet of the valiant and, whosoever dares, let him accept the sword and follow me!"

Mingo Dabney stared at this girl transfigured, this apostle, this burning torch. His breath filled his throat and he felt the shock of a hot surge into his stomach, and then it was cold, and he was weak.

Wyeth's eyes narrowed and Gar sat immobile, his bony hands folded in his lap. Sans was breathing shallow, scarcely seeming to breathe at all, astounded by the revelation on his brother's face; himself oblivious to the flamboyant words of the girl, concerned only with their effect on Mingo.

Rafaela walked over close to Marti and he reached up and took her hand, exuding strength. "Spain knows we will strike soon," she said. "And Spain has sworn that my country will be a mountain of bones before we are free."

Here, too, was talk the Dabney brothers understood, and Mingo's fervor dimmed into realities. "There are men around here who'll fight for anything. Work is scarce in the valley." He was thinking of Shane Figgis and other men; Mingo Dabney never thought of himself.

"And we can raise a little money, too," Sans said. "Can't we, Mr. Woodward?"

"Of course," said Wyeth.

Gar Rivers, the living embodiment of dignity attained through suffering, went over to José Marti. "I know men who will pick up Señorita Galban's gauntlet. Will Cuba accept Negro soldiers?"

Marti evinced surprise. "We ask for men, sir."

"But there is peonage in Cuba," the Negro replied.

"Not in *our* Cuba!" Rafaela Galban picked up her own gauntlet.

José Marti gripped her hand again, gaining strength. He was more mature in revolution than his compatriot, much calmer, much wiser and, without her fervor, he declared their faith. "We offer every man a machete. If he be willing to fight for his freedom, then freedom is his. It is the promise of Liberated Cuba to slaves of Spain."

Gar Rivers held out his long, thin hand and Marti grasped it. The talk of freedom and of justice sounded so sweet to the old Negro that tears rolled down his cheeks. He took Marti's hand in both of his and, overcome by his own yearnings and the bright promise for younger men, he lifted Marti's hand and kissed it.

For a moment Marti stood motionless. Then impulsively raising the old man's head he murmured, "*Mi querido viejo*—my dear old one." He held Gar's face in both his hands and drew him close, and kissed him on the cheek. José Marti took his hands away and the anointed one sat down and leaned his head upon the desk and sobbed.

Wyeth wiped his hands with a handkerchief. Sans' face was flushed, a burning red. Mingo, however, was pale. The rain beat against the building, swishing under the building, a rumbling, eerie swishing. The room was very still for a moment; then a shuffling of feet and the moment was ended. The lawyer put his handkerchief away and said simply, "Lebanon will serve the cause of freedom any way it can. There will be men and money."

Gar lifted his head from the desk and affirmed his agreement, and the Dabney brothers reaffirmed it.

"Thank you," said José Marti.

Rafaela Galban murmured her gratitude and, conscious again of Mingo's gaze, she glanced first at the floor and then toward the window; anything to avoid his look.

Marti stood by Rafaela, his shoulders sagging in the weariness of the long journey, the endless struggle. He addressed Wyeth Woodward. "There is one thing more. I come to you in the bonds of Masonic brotherhood. I must go on my way, but this journey is not for my associate. And so, my brother, I seek sanctuary for her in this valley."

Mingo's strength flowed out of him and he was humbled and exalted. He had glimpsed the morning star and was content, and now the sun was rising. The illusion took form; the girl was to remain in the valley.

Without thought of his wife and daughter, the Masonic brother replied immediately. "I gladly offer Miss Galban the hospitality of my home."

The muscles of the older brother tightened, for he had seen the revelation on his brother's face. It was Sans' obligation to speak and he weighed the problem and its possibilities; then spoke the verdict of his family. "No stranger has ever been denied the right of sanctuary in this valley. Miss Galban is welcome."

The younger brother too must speak and, looking at Marti, he spoke to Rafaela Galban. "She has found sanctuary." It was a truth to be expressed simply and it was expressed that way.

Sanctuary.

The girl, hounded by Spain in a dozen lands, breathed deeply, turning in her mind the beauty of the word, the pledge and the covenant. She put her hand on Marti's shoulder, smiling at him, her eyes suddenly flooding tears. "They told us we would find sanctuary in Lebanon."

Mingo grinned. At such a serious minute he grinned like a boy, and his whole face lighted. "There's plenty of room at our house. We'll be tickled to death to have Miss Galban stay with us. Won't we, Sans?"

"Of course," the elder brother said. "Papa would be honored and Mama would be pleased."

Wyeth glanced at Gar, then pursed his lips as though mulling over a question he already had decided. Mingo was impetuous. Kyd Dabney might not be happy to have a strange woman in her house, particularly a foreigner whose face already had lighted a fire in the eyes of her son.

"Just a minute, Mingo. You Dabneys must share this honor with the rest of us." He smiled as he said it and the others smiled. Rafaela tilted her head and laughed freely for the first time, a merry, tinkling laugh of relief and joy. It was good to be wanted again.

Gar understood Wyeth's tact and said, "Half the families in the valley will want Señorita Galban as their guest. It is a detail to be worked out."

"No problem at all." Wyeth lumbered to his feet and bowed gallantly to the lady, and once more she laughed. Marti's pride and gratitude were evident.

Rafaela Galban twisted the ring on her finger, and twisted it again; a ruby given her by José Marti when she was a child. "You are all very kind."

"We're all mighty glad to have you." Mingo's grin broadened. "And you'll like it here in the valley. Just wait until you taste some of my mother's syllabub. Eh, Sans?"

"That's right," Sans answered solemnly.

"I have work to do," Gar said, thinking of boys from Meridian to Mobile, boys he had taught; men who now could fight for the things he taught them.

Then Sans grinned, too, his grin as wide as his brother's. "We better go see Mr. Charlie. He'll be having a conniption fit until we tell him what's happened."

Wyeth picked up his umbrella and accompanied the brothers into the hallway. He lowered his voice. "You boys got to help me look after these people. With my womenfolks away, I'll need some help."

"We'll be over to your place in a few minutes," Sans said.

Mingo did not reply. He was staring out into the rain.

"Stop by The Store and tell Mr. Charlie to let me have something good to eat," Wyeth requested. "And tell Elmo to come back here in a few minutes and drive them over to my place." He handed his umbrella to Sans and stepped back into the office.

Mingo moved away without a word and Sans fell in step with him. They walked through the mud and rain toward The Store. "Hey!" Sans poked his brother, moving the umbrella over him. "Come back down to earth."

They skirted a puddle and went on, Mingo straggling from under the shelter, out into the rain again. "I never saw a woman like her. How old you reckon she is, Sans?"

"Oh, maybe twenty, or twenty-one."

"Did you see that white hair?"

"Uh huh." The older brother felt a twitch in his heart.

"And did you notice her eyes? Did you ever hear anybody talk like that?" Mingo Dabney's face was in the rain, and he was not aware that he was walking in the rain. "She reminded me of a soft green hill, Sans; snow on the top; maybe frost on the horizon, and gone when you get there." Never before had the younger boy spoken such words, speaking them softly, only for himself and his brother. He felt the rain and stepped back under the umbrella.

Sans drew his brother closer, gripping his arm as they walked. A fine mist sprayed through the umbrella, wetting his eyelashes, already wet. "When a man sees all that in a woman, Lebuba, he will go through hell for her."

Mingo repeated her name to himself, stumbling the pronunciation. Rafaela Galban y Torres. He said it again, and this time it was easier to say. And he knew why, for he had seen her in a myriad places. On the green hills, on the horizon, in the fox-glow. All the things he had looked at all of his life, the forest and daydown, now were revealed to him; frost shimmering afar and a woman appearing in the rain, black eyes burning and white hair hidden. He had seen her in a myriad places.

Chapter nine

THE RAIN SHIFTED to the west before the Dabney boys reached The Store, sweeping in over the ridge and drenching the valley. Lebanon was in for high water.

Ronnie Sullivan was sitting on a counter, dangling his feet, a full bottle of beer in his hand and an empty bottle beside him. Mr. Charlie and Elmo were nowhere in sight.

"Where's Mr. Charlie?" Sans asked.

"I ain't rightly sure," Ronnie said casually. "Him and Elmo went down to the south cut a few minutes ago. He told me to keep an eye on things—"

Mingo glanced at the beer and grinned. "Now that's a hell of a come-off." His voice was light and friendly, and Ronnie peered over at him. It wasn't like Mingo to grin while a man was helping himself to The Store's beer.

Sans shook the water from his clothes. "What did he go down there for?"

"I don't know. They got in Elmo's buggy and lit out."

Mingo got a basket and walked along in front of the shelves. "I'll pick out a few fancy things for Mr. Woodward." He reached for a can of sardines and two cans of salmon. "You cut off a hunk of that cheese, kiddo."

Sans lifted the cleaver, turned the cheese hoop and sliced it. "Hey, Ronnie," he called. "Do me a favor."

"Name it."

"Step down to the post office and tell one of the fellows that Mr. Woodward wants Elmo at his office. And you come back here and look after things."

Ronnie finished his beer and walked toward the door. "I'll be back in a second." He stepped outside, braced himself against the rain and walked rapidly toward the post office.

Sans helped Mingo select groceries. "It's not like Mr. Charlie to leave The Store."

"Don't let it bother you," said Mingo cheerily. "Maybe Elmo just wanted to see how Peninsula's mill is coming on, and Mr. Charlie went along to keep him company." His eyes roamed over the shelves and he selected two jars of chili.

They filled the basket and Sans said, "Let's have a bottle of beer before we go over there."

"I reckon not," Mingo said. "I don't want to get there smelling like a brewery."

"Maybe you're right."

They left the umbrella in The Store, threw canvas capes around their shoulders, and dashed out to their horses. They reached the Woodward place as Elmo's buggy drove up. Wyeth Woodward, in his light buggy, was close behind.

Elmo and Marti assisted Rafaela from the carriage. Sans and Mingo helped with the baggage and they all hastened to the Woodward porch where they clustered near the door, scraping their feet and brushing off the rain.

"Anything else?" Elmo asked Marti.

The Cuban shook his head, and Wyeth said, "Won't you have a cup of coffee with us, Elmo?"

"No, thanks," the drummer said. "I got to get some business done with Mr. Charlie. Then I got to go to Ellisville." He addressed José Marti. "Tell you sump'n, my friend. I ain't hard to find. If you need anything, just ask for ol' Elmo Batson." His voice suddenly was tense. "I can tell time, señor. In Spanish, too."

"Thank you," Marti said. "You'll take me back to Mobile?"

"Day after tomorrow. Soon as I get back from Ellisville." He turned to the Dabney brothers. "You two fellows coming by The Store after you leave here?"

"Maybe," Sans said. "Anything important?"

"Nope. Just like to see you before I light out again." He hunched, and ran out to his buggy as Wyeth opened the door, showing his guests into his home. The host led the way to the parlor and apologized for the absence of his womenfolks. Then he asked the brothers to entertain them while he spoke to Flora Belle, the cook. He knew she had roasted coffee that day. In the valley, coffee was roasted fresh every day, but Wyeth wanted to remind Flora Belle exactly how to drip it, black and strong. Blacker and stronger than Mrs. Woodward tolerated.

In the absence of Laurel and Louisa, the Woodward parlor had not been aired properly and the room was damp. Sans opened a window just enough to admit air and assumed the role of host. Mingo stood leaning against the doorway, watching Rafaela while he pretended to watch his brother. Then, realizing he should do something, he began arranging chairs, moving them needlessly. He was moving the same chair a second time when Flora Belle waddled in and told Rafaela to come on upstairs. "I'll show you to Miss Louisa's room," she said.

Wyeth was wearing his prized smoking jacket when he rejoined the men. He believed it looked impressive and, although it was wool and not a summer garment, he was willing to suffer some discomfort to gain a more distinguished appearance. He offered José Marti a cigar. Then he offered one to Sans and Mingo. He had never seen either of them smoke a cigar and was slyly amused at the way they behaved. Sans put his cigar in his mouth and puffed away like a woodsman enjoying a rare luxury. Mingo rolled his between his fingers as Marti did. Wyeth opened a decanter and the men had whiskey.

They sat in the parlor and talked of many things—the panic and politics and the rain. The elder brother did most of the talking for the Dabneys. Mingo was content to sit there without speaking, glancing occasionally at the stairs. Marti was moody, almost distraught. He poured a second drink of whiskey and pulled nervously at his mustache. "Gentlemen, I regret returning to the subject, but I ask your leave to query you once more about Peninsula Lumber Company."

Wyeth waved his arm in an expansive gesture. "What's on your mind, my friend?"

"Can Peninsula's Lebanon mill handle the mahogany logs they are cutting in Cuba?"

The lawyer deferred to Sans, and the woodsman said, "They can convert to mahogany without too much trouble. But they won't do it. They'll never ship Cuban logs to this mill. They'll build mills down there."

"That's what I feared." Marti lifted his glass and drank again.

Coffee was ready when Rafaela came downstairs. She had changed to a black dress, tight at her hips and flowing full around her ankles. The men stood as she entered, and Sans glanced at his brother. Mingo did not see the glance. He saw only Rafaela Galban and he thought again of frost, cool and far away on the rim of the world. Her mantilla was loose, but hid her hair. She smoothed her dress as she sat down on the sofa and accepted coffee, drinking it black. Mingo sat down beside her.

"Does it rain like this in Cuba?" It was the younger brother's opening gambit, the first move in the inevitable contest.

"This!" She blinked at him, then laughed freely. "To us, this is a drought." There was warmth in her eyes, gaiety in her heart; that is what sanctuary meant to Rafaela Galban. The pretense of ignoring him was ended and she looked at his smoky brown eyes, his mouth, his hands. In quick merriment, she spoke rapidly to Marti in Spanish.

Mingo frowned and Rafaela apologized instantly. "Your pardon, sir. It is bad manners to speak a language that any member of the group does not understand. I was telling Don José what a big man you are. *Hombre grande*. Big man."

The younger Dabney blushed and tried to hide his blush behind laughter. *Hombre grande* meant more than a big man; it meant a big heart and a strong spirit. Wyeth Woodward knew what it meant, and so did Sans. Wyeth turned toward a window. Marti stared at the ceiling. Sans watched his brother.

There was an embarrassing pause and Rafaela, aware that she was responsible, sought to bridge the silence. She tilted her shoulders in the way of all Latins, then fingered her ruby ring. "It really means nothing, señor. It is only a saying." A flush of color was in her face as she leaned slightly toward him. "Cubans are great ones for brave names. Don José, for instance, is called 'The Prophet'."

Then Mingo asked the natural question. "What do they call you in Cuba?" He said it merely to make conversation.

Marti's cup rattled against its saucer and he sat bolt upright, rigid in his chair, staring at the valley boy. Rafaela's face suddenly was red; and her eyes, warm the second before, were cold again, black and unlighted. "Why do you ask that?"

Wyeth was abashed by her vehemence. Sans clamped his jaw and felt his temper boiling within him. Guest or not, she might at least be civil. Mingo, however, was flustered. "I wasn't trying to pry," he said. "I was just wondering what they call you—"

"You may call me Miss Galban," she said slowly, and relaxed.

So did Marti.

The atmosphere was strained and Rafaela, feeling guilty, attempted sociable conversation and once it was under way again, she visibly was relieved. Flora Belle came into the dining room and set the table for supper. Rafaela glanced at the tall clock in the corner and her black brows arched in surprise at the lateness of the hour. She excused herself to rest before the meal.

Mingo walked with her to the foot of the stairs and there, impulsively, offered his hand instead of bowing. She took his hand and smiled at him. "I am sorry I was rude a minute ago."

"You weren't rude," he said, as she slid her hand from his. "I had no business asking such a question."

She rested her hand on the newel post and defended him. "Under the circumstances, it was a natural question."

Mingo glanced down at the carpet, at her feet, then up at her face. "No, it was an intrusive question. You are a revolutionist and may have a lot of names. I should have thought of that."

For a long second she did not speak, looking at him; then, in instinctive trust for this man, she confided, "In Cuba some call me *La Entorcha Blanca.* 'The White Torch'." She closed her eyes as if to blot out the significance of the name, then she opened them and leaned against the banister, gazing over his head toward the front door and the rain outside. "I do not like the name. It makes me a symbol, and I had rather be a woman." Her voice was low, so low that he leaned forward to hear her. "They call me *La Entorcha Blanca* because my hair is white." Her hand went to her mantilla and she drew it tight about her forehead.

"Your hair is silver," Mingo said.

"My hair is white, Mr. Dabney."

Mingo touched her hand and she moved it away, smiling as she did so. He stepped back from the foot of the stairs and bowed. "Goodnight, Rafaela Galban." He said it softly.

Her lips parted in the surprise of the second and a warm light was in her eyes. She gathered the front of her skirt in her hand, her hand white as snow against the blackness of her dress. "Goodnight, Mingo Dabney." It was a whisper, and she turned and walked up the stairs, slowly at first and then almost running. Perfume and the rustle of her skirts drifted back to him.

He waited until he heard her door close, then returned to the parlor. Sans was on the sofa and Mingo crossed the room and sat beside him. Wyeth was pouring Marti another cup of coffee and Sans cast his eyes at his brother, then got up. "You gentlemen have much to talk about," he said, bowing to José Marti and Mr. Woodward. "So, if you'll excuse me, please."

Mingo rose, too. "Yes. We better be going." His voice was so low, so unreal that Sans looked at him again, quickly.

"Be glad to have you eat with us," Wyeth said.

Mingo wanted to accept, but felt his presence would be an intrusion. Sans was anxious to go on to The Store and see Elmo Batson. "Thank you," he said. "But Mama will be expecting us home for supper."

The Dabney brothers walked into the rain, now that the rain

was easing a bit. They swung into wet saddles and turned toward Bogue Homa. Mingo felt the rain on his face and pulled his hat lower over his forehead. He was still under the spell of her good-night. Again, to himself, he said her name. Rafaela Galban y Torres. The music of it stirred his imagination into a fantasy of green seas and blue skies, the call of faraway lands. There was a strange urge within him and Lebanon seemed so small, seemed to tighten about him, compressing his restless yearning.

Sans was talking, and, for the first time since they left Mr. Wood-ward's, Mingo became aware of what his brother was saying. "Sure, kiddo." He came quickly back to the minute at hand. "We'll go by The Store. I want to pick up some spices and get Mama to make some syllabub."

The horses picked their way into Bogue Homa's swamp. Mingo's heart was gay and yet he was sad. He was bewildered and yet he was comforted. The trees along Bogue Homa drooped their arms, spilling the rain. All the land on the slope, descending slowly toward the swamp, and the swamp itself was green, except for the glistening limbs of dead trees, writhing black out of the slime of the water.

Then Mingo Dabney saw fox-glow in the swamp. Fox-glow in the rain. And no man could see fox-glow in the rain. He halted his horse and looked again, and there was no fox-glow. It was gone.

"Good Lord!" He stared into the swamp, seeking it again, seeking the glowing will-of-the-wisp.

"What is it?" Sans demanded, checking his horse sharply.

"I saw fox-glow—"

"You're crazy." Sans leaned toward his brother, searching his face. "You can't see fox-glow in the rain. Fox-glow is nothing but a fungus that glows sometimes, but never in the rain—"

"I know all that." Mingo reached out and touched his elder brother, making sure he was there. "But I saw it."

Fox-glow in the rain! An instant of white, of glowing silver. A quick, soft gleam like silver hair lighting for an instant, then hidden by the dark shawl of the swamp. He must tell Bruce what he had seen; what no other man had ever seen. He must tell Mr. Charlie. And then he knew he could tell no man except his brother.

Sans still was watching him and Mingo drew back his hand from his brother's arm. "I saw it, I tell you."

"Then you saw it," Sans said. A man sees what he wants to see and Sans Dabney was not one to question the heart, or seek explanations. He lifted the reins, heading deeper into the swamp, riding on to cross it and reach the pike and The Store.

Mingo rode beside his brother, and the rain beat on his hat. He was awed but not frightened, and he watched the swamp, hoping to see again the white glow in the awesome black; but the rain came down heavy, shutting him in, and Mingo lowered his head against the drive of the squall.

In the swamp the rain eased under the umbrella of the pines, and Mingo rode closer to his brother. "Sans."

"Yes? What is it?"

"How do those words go? The words to that song."

"You know them." Sans looked straight ahead, his heart welling to his throat. It was his song and now he could share that, too, with his brother. Now they could share a song and a song's meaning, which was the love of a man for a woman.

Mingo rested his hands on the pommel of his saddle, swaying in the saddle to the motion of his plodding horse. "I'm not sure of the tune. Sing it to me."

"Sing it yourself," Sans said, for there was happiness in his heart but there was a lump in his throat.

Mingo hummed the song, seeking the melody. Then he sang, and his voice, so often gay and confident, now was gentle, plaintive; Sans felt the tears brimming in his eyes and running down his face, mingling with the rain.

> "Shall I, wasting in despair,
>   Die because a woman's fair—"

Mingo sang on as he rode through the swamp, glancing occasion-ally about him, peering at the dead trees; but Sans Dabney turned in the saddle and looked back toward the Woodward house, toward the room where Rafaela Galban lay sleeping. The room was dark and the twilight hid the room, closing it off from him; and he turned again and looked ahead at his brother, riding on through the swamp and singing as he rode. . . .

Elmo Batson was leaning against a show case in The Store, puffing on the stub of a cigar, a better cigar than any The Store offered to Lebanon. Mr. Charlie was sitting in a chair, tilted back against the wall. Elmo still was serious and there was no suspender popping or spicy stories. Mr. Charlie was serious, too, his lugubrious face long and dismal, his chin resting almost on his chest.

The storekeeper looked up at the brothers, over his spectacles, and waited until they shook the water from their clothes. He peered at Mingo, seeing something he had never seen before, a new light in the smoky brown eyes of the younger brother. Then he spoke to Sans, commandingly: "What about them Cubans? Elmo didn't know much—"

"Just a minute, Mr. Charlie." Sans turned to Elmo. "You've got something on your mind. Let's have it."

The drummer glanced at Mr. Charlie and they both looked at Mingo as he walked toward the back of The Store where the spices were kept.

"You boys tell me about them Cubans." Mr. Charlie fidgeted with his watch fob. "How come they come here?" Righteous curiosity was tormenting him. "What happened down at Wyeth Woodward's office and over at his house—"

"We'll tell you later," Mingo said. "We're in a hurry now."

Elmo Batson rubbed his chin and Mr. Charlie, puffing like a pouter pigeon, tapped the younger brother on the shoulder. "Well, if you're so damn smart, wait'll Elmo tells you what we know."

"What is it, Elmo?" Sans demanded. "What's eatin' you?"

The drummer spoke to Mingo. "I thought you knew."

The younger boy put his hand on the counter, facing the shelves, seeking some tidbit that might please Rafaela Galban. "Knew what?" He was reading the labels on the goods and only half listening to Elmo.

"That Peninsula is going to open a store of its own."

Sans, leaning against a sugar barrel, jerked erect. For a second, Mingo didn't move, then turned slowly and stared at the salesman. "You're crazy." He looked from Elmo to Mr. Charlie, then at Sans.

"Like hell I'm crazy," Elmo said. "*You're* crazy. And sound asleep, too. They're shipping stuff into Mobile by the carloads."

Mr. Charlie looked from one brother to the other, peering at them over his glasses.

"You're crazy!" Mingo repeated it slowly and his lower lip trembled near the corner.

Sans glued his eyes on the drummer. "You sure, Elmo—?"

"Damn right, I'm sure. *I* can tell time." Elmo Batson was irked. "Don't you fellows live here? Don't you know they've got their building almost ready?"

"That big building down in milltown?" Sans demanded.

"That's it." Mr. Charlie got into the conversation. "Me and Elmo were just down there looking at it. He told me the lowdown, and me and him went down there to see."

Mingo said, "You're crazy as a betsy bug. They promised not to build a store in the valley."

Mr. Charlie put his thumb under his suspenders and rocked on the balls of his feet. "Elmo, tell 'em Peninsula's excuse for opening its own store."

"You tell 'em," the drummer said sharply.

Mr. Charlie didn't like to spread bad news, but he was mighty glad to take the lead in the conversation. "Peninsula is getting word around that our store is robbing folks. So they aim to open one to protect their own people."

"I don't believe a God damn word of it," Mingo snarled. Fox-glow was far away at that minute and perhaps never had been at all. This was another matter. Peninsula was crowding Mingo Dabney, and he didn't like to be crowded. "You're guying me. I don't think it's a damn bit funny. Peninsula agreed not to buck me in New Hebron."

"They're not in New Hebron," Sans said. "They're just outside town. They didn't lie to you. They just didn't tell you the truth."

The younger boy tugged at the brim of his hat. His face was livid and the spell of Rafaela Galban was gone for the moment. "I'm going to see Thrumbull."

"I doubt if Thrumbull knows much about it," Elmo said. "He's their mill man. They're sending in a store man."

Mingo ignored the drummer and started for the door. Sans was in step with him, and went with him to the porch. "Want me to come with you?"

"Never mind, I'll handle it myself." He was on the steps and the rain drenched him. "If Elmo is right, they're stomping on my toes."

Sans said, "Hurts, don't it?"

"You mighty come a'right!" Mingo said. "If they don't get off, there will be trouble." He jumped from the steps to the pike and ran for his horse.

Sans returned inside and Mr. Charlie was in his rocking chair, rocking and spitting, his Adam's apple bobbing fast. "Mingo's mad," he said.

"It was happening right under your noses." Elmo shook his head at them. "I thought you fellows could tell time. But if you need any help, just holler."

Sans said, "We can handle it ourselves."

Elmo pulled his belt away from his stomach and smoothed his shirt inside his trousers, then reached for his hat. "Reckon I better be getting on toward Ellisville."

Mr. Charlie stopped rocking. "You ain't got no business starting for Ellisville on a night like this."

The drummer leaned over, patting the old storekeeper on the shoulder. "I can make it. Me and my horses know every inch of that road." He pulled his coat collar tight around his throat. "Be seeing you, Sans. So long, Mr. Charlie. Don't take any wooden nickels." Then Elmo was gone.

Mr. Charlie resumed his rocking and his spitting. Sans looked out at the rain, and down toward the Thrumbull house. He wished he was with Mingo. The younger brother was impetuous and might do something to be regretted; might say something he didn't mean. Besides, Ruth Thrumbull was at home and Sans wanted Mingo to like her because, in a way, he liked her.

The old storekeeper stopped rocking. "Now you tell me about them Cubans."

Sans reported, and the old man was happy at last. The elder brother waited about thirty minutes and when Mingo did not return, he grew restless. He left Mr. Charlie and went to his horse, thence to the south cut, staring through the rain at the Thrumbull house on the east ridge and seeing a light in the library.

Mingo still was there and Sans rode on, the rain beating down on him. He wanted to see Peninsula's store building and he rode past the big mill, silent and dark in the rain. He came to the new building. It looked like a barn and Sans dismounted and stepped to the door.

A watchman was there and, in a Yankee twang, he told Sans that trespassers were not allowed on the property. Sans Dabney just looked at him. A Dabney trespassing in Lebanon! He turned from the watchman and walked back to his horse. He was afraid to stay there, afraid of what he might say, surely of what he might do. He felt sorry for the watchman and yet he had an urge to take the man in his hands and shake him.

He rode slowly back to the south cut, heading for the pike. Up on the east slope, lights still burned in the library of the Thrumbull house and Sans watched them. Then above the swish of the rain and the low moaning of the trees, he heard a horse splashing down the slope, coming from the Thrumbull house. He slapped his own horse and galloped toward the pike. There he waited.

Mingo, hunched against the rain, was riding hard toward him, and Sans saw that his face was set. The younger brother jerked his horse to a stop.

"It's true!" he said. "I saw Thrumbull. It's true—"

"The hell it is!"

"They double-crossed me." Mingo's words were low. "They aim to open a store beyond the south cut."

"And they aim to run a railroad through the north cut. They aim to stab us both." Sans turned his horse toward The House and alongside Mingo, close alongside his brother.

The boys looked at each other. They were the only ones on the road. Mingo hesitated, then leaned out of his saddle and grabbed Sans' arm. The elder brother put his hand over the younger boy's hand, and for an instant held it firmly.

"Let's go home to supper," Sans said.

Together they rode up the pike, toward The Tree, toward The House, their horses galloping in the rain and the twilight.

Chapter ten

THE FURY OF MINGO DABNEY alarmed his mother and taught his brother another lesson in human frailty. It was a tantrum that awed Kyd and she, fearful that he might carry out his threat to burn Peninsula's store building, sent a Negro through the rain to Jasper County to summon her husband. Then she cautioned Sans to stay close to the younger boy and keep him from reckless behavior.

Mingo was in no mood for supper. He went to his room and began figuring, convinced his best weapon for retaliation was money. He put Rafaela out of his mind, or rather, he tried to put her out of his mind—there was work to be done. He had been double-crossed by Peninsula Lumber Company. Well, he'd see about that. Nobody was going to step on his toes and get away with it. He figured rapidly.

"You stay with him," Kyd told Sans. "Your father will be back tomorrow." She tasted her coffee; she had forgotten to put in sugar.

"Mingo will cool off," Sans said calmly, thinking how foolish an angry man can be. "Besides, I'm not sure Papa can get through. This rain is flooding everything."

"He'll get through." Kyd was positive.

Sans tried to divert her by talking of José Marti and Rafaela Galban. "Yes, yes," his mother said impatiently. "Mingo told me about them. The woman sounds like a freak. Young as she is, and with all that white hair."

Sans said, "He wanted to ask them to be our guests."

"Fiddlesticks! He was just being polite."

Sans toyed with his napkin. "Did he say anything about making some syllabub for Miss Galban?"

Kyd poured a fresh cup of coffee, tasted it and pushed the cup aside. The brew didn't taste right. "He said something about it." She looked sharply at the elder boy. "It appears to me you're taking a lot of interest in those people. Mingo said that woman is pretty. Well, you listen to me, Sans Dabney. Don't you get messed up with those people. We've got troubles enough of our own, without fooling around with foreigners. You've got to help Mingo."

Sans drained his coffee cup. The brew tasted all right to him, for he was calm. "Mingo will cool off," he repeated.

"Those dirty Peninsula Yankees!" She flung her napkin on the table. "They lied to us. They're trying to put Mingo out of business. Trash! Yankee trash—the whole kit and caboodle!"

Sans did not look up. "I thought you liked Ruth Thrumbull. She's one of the Peninsula folks."

"Oh, she's different," Kyd said quickly, watching his face. She must not disparage Ruth Thrumbull, the foil she hoped would attract Sans from Louisa. "She is a fine girl. But the rest of that Peninsula crowd are rascals."

The elder boy stared at his hands, then excused himself and went to Mingo's room. The rain was drifting through a window and he pulled it down. The night and the rain made the earth gloomy.

"Go ahead," said Mingo. "Say you told me so."

"No need of rubbing it in. We both got the same bear by the tail."

Mingo bent again over his table and Sans stretched on the bed, staring at the ceiling, waiting for time and the murmur of the rain to quiet his brother's anger. His own thoughts went out to Louisa and it was pleasant to think of her. A locomotive whistle sounded beyond the north cut, a continuous reminder that Peninsula still was there.

Suddenly Mingo shoved his papers aside and returned his pen to the well. "I'll fight the sons of bitches," he muttered. "I'll run both my saws. I'll cut all the timber you can haul me."

Sans said quietly, "If you do that, you'll go broke. Then we'll both be broke. Besides, I can't cut many logs. My men are all scattered." His position was uncomfortable; he moved the pillow. "No, Mingo, my logging business is ruined. Let's not ruin your lumber business."

"Peninsula is grabbing everything. Buying and scheming and grabbing everything we've got."

"No," said Sans. "We've still got the north cut."

"We'll hold it." Mingo hitched his chair forward and stuck his feet on the bed. "You've been right all along about the north cut. Now you talk. I'll listen."

"Cut prices at The Store—"

"Good God!" Mingo's jaw dropped. "I can't do that."

The older brother was patient, remembering when this shoe was on his foot. "Peninsula say you're robbing their workers."

Mingo's anger surged again. "They aimed all along to open a store."

Sans said, "I doubt that. But if their men buy from you, they got to have more money. That'll mean higher wages. So to keep wages down, the company opens its own store." He pulled slowly at his ear. "Now you go on to bed."

The younger brother slipped off his trousers and tossed them across the back of a chair. He sat on the edge of the bed and unbuttoned his shirt. "Listen to that rain; I hate rain at night. It makes me moody." He thought of Rafaela Galban, of the swish of her skirt; of all the things she had said, the things she had done. However, he pried his mind from the pleasant recollections. There was a time for everything, and this was no time for romantic dreaming. He was pulling his shirt off lazily, then suddenly he looked over at his brother in the yellow lamplight. "Wait a minute, kiddo. Didn't Peninsula cut some of your timber by mistake?"

"Uh huh. They cut a few trees."

"Have they paid you?" Mingo's mind was sharp again.

"No. They owe me about two hundred dollars." He swung his long legs off the bed and sat up.

"Sue 'em, Sans. Sue hell out of 'em."

"Aw, humbug. I'm not going into court for two hundred dollars." His eyes were heavy and he yawned.

Mingo was excited. "You can get a big judgment."

Sans stretched, twisting his body and reaching high. He went over to the chair at Mingo's table and sat down. "You said you'd listen to me. This is a good time to start. You go to sleep."

"Maybe I better get some sleep." Mingo pulled back the covers. "But you stay in here with me awhile. I'm in the dumps."

The rain rumbled through the valley. The lamp smoked and Sans lowered the wick. "I'll stay with you."

The younger brother got into bed and turned on his side, facing the window. The black mood of the Dabneys was on him; the usually gay one was somber and melancholy.

It was raining harder, the wind whimpering down Bogue Homa and into the swamp. Sans, too, was melancholy, thinking of Louisa. "I wish I could see fox-glow in the rain."

Mingo turned quickly to him. "I saw it. I did see it, Sans."

"I know you did. I was just saying I wish I could see it."

They looked at each other in the yellow light and Mingo smiled and faced the window once more, watching the world outside, the rain falling. Maybe he could see it again. It calmed him, thinking of the will-o'-the-wisp that some men see while others, stumbling along forever, seek it blindly.

Sans reached for the lamp and put it on the table. He was not sure whether Louisa was in New Orleans or Natchez, but he knew a letter to either place would reach her. So he began writing, telling her all the news of the valley. At times he was almost lyrical and never before had he been lyrical with Louisa.

He told first about the rain because the rain was so important, then about Peninsula's lawyers and Windy Hill, because to him, they too were important, if not so important as the rain. Then he reported the coming of José Marti and Rafaela Galban.

Mingo moved and Sans glanced over his shoulder toward the bed. The younger brother was watching him.

"I thought you were asleep." Sans put the pen away. "I'm writing Louisa."

"Did you tell her about Peninsula's store?"

"I haven't got to that."

"Well, tell her about it," Mingo said. "And tell her I'll write the details later." He turned on his side and looked out of the window again. "I wish Louisa was here. She could help me out." He closed his eyes and went to sleep.

By morning the rain had settled into a siege and Sans was eating his breakfast when Kyd joined him. "I want you to stay with Mingo today," she directed. "Stay with him until his father gets back."

Mingo, freshly shaved and wearing a clean linen suit, joined them at the table. "I'm going down to The Store and check my books. Mama, will you get that syllabub started?"

"I'll go along with you," Sans said and felt the gratitude in his mother's look.

Kyd went to the kitchen to prepare the syllabub and Mingo waited until she was out of the room. "I'm going to see Rafaela Galban today if I have to break a trace. And you see Mr. Woodward about bringing that suit."

"Wait a minute. Who the hell are you bossing now?" Sans was grinning as he said it.

Mingo grinned, too. The black mood had passed. "I'm bossing you this time. See Mr. Woodward about that suit. We're in this thing together."

"I'll think about it." Sans rolled his napkin and pushed it through his napkin ring. He waited until Mingo finished his breakfast, then the two boys dashed through the rain to the barn and hitched a team to a heavy buggy with a top.

Sans waited at The Store until Mingo was absorbed in his books, then hurried down to Mr. Woodward's office. He must talk to him about plans for Rafaela Galban's stay in the valley. There were details to be arranged and, in his father's absence, he was obligated to speak for the Dabneys. She could not remain at the Woodward home after Marti left and before Mrs. Woodward returned. Sans doubted if his mother would welcome her at The House, and surely not if she knew the truth. So Rafaela Galban and the sanctuary she sought meant more problems for the elder brother.

The lawyer was not in his office and Sans was glad. It gave him an excuse to call at the Woodward house—an opportunity to take Mingo with him to visit again with the Cubans. He returned to The Store, but Mingo still was busy with his books and Sans did not disturb him. Instead, he went to the porch and was sitting there talking to Mr. Charlie when Bruce rode in from Jasper County.

Sans never had seen the old man so erect, so dignified. Even the mud, caked on his boots and splattered on his suit, did not lessen the dignity of Bruce Dabney. He swung from his horse with the grace of a young man and Sans knew he had ridden all night, but there was no fatigue in his eyes; only the calm assurance of a man contemptuous of fear and despair.

"I stopped by The House." Bruce stepped to the porch and greeted Sans and Mr. Charlie. "Where's Mingo?"

Mr. Charlie went inside to fetch the younger brother and Bruce sat on the bench and waited. Mingo came hurrying out. "They're going to build a store," he told his father, over and over.

"We heard about it yesterday," Sans said. "A heap has happened while you were away." Then without haste or malice, he told his father about Peninsula's lawyers and about José Marti and Rafaela Galban.

"She shall have sanctuary," Bruce Dabney said simply.

"She's a revolutionist," Mingo said. "She might be in danger. Anyway, Señor Marti wants her to stay here until he sends for her."

"Then she must stay," Bruce said. "I will speak to your mother about her staying with us."

Mingo said, "I knew you would think that way. She needs protection, Papa." He began talking about the exiles and their impending revolution; and the more he talked, the more he picked up the words of Rafaela. There was a fire in the eyes of old Charlie Owens, a glow in the eyes of old Bruce Dabney. Sans eventually got the subject back to Peninsula's store and Bruce looked from one son to the other. His long ride had been unnecessary. His sons could take care of things. "I'm a little bit tired. Think I'll go take a nap."

"Shouldn't you call on Señor Marti and pay your respects?" Mingo suggested. "He's leaving tomorrow."

"You boys convey my respects to the gentleman and to the lady," the old man said. "Now let's go home to dinner."

"What do you think about Peninsula's store, Papa?" Sans asked. "And about Windy Hill lawing for Peninsula?"

Bruce said, "I divided this valley between you boys, and I'm going to let you manage things." He was scratching his hand again and Mr. Charlie looked at the brown skin and the welt.

Kyd plied her menfolks with questions during the midday meal and Bruce told her the news of Jasper County and asked about Aven. Kyd reported that Aven had not been in the valley in several days.

The rain was slacking off. After dinner, the boys rode in the Brighton buggy around to the Woodward place. Mingo's shoes got muddy as he ran to the porch and he stopped and scraped them. Sans gave no heed to the mud. He was impatient to see the Cubans and have the problem of Rafaela's abode settled. He should be in the woods with his men, or at the north cut to check progress of the railroad. There were many places he should be. These visitors were taking his time from the valley.

Mingo rapped on the door and Flora Belle answered, reporting that Mr. Woodward was not at home, but that she had received the syllabub Kyd sent down that morning.

"Where is Mr. Woodward?" Sans asked, giving her an opportunity to invite them in. "He wasn't at his office this morning."

"He's with Gar Rivers," the cook said. "Come on in." She accepted their hats and lowered her voice. "That Cuban gentleman is in the parlor. He's jumpy as a cat."

The Dabney boys stepped to the door of the living room. José Marti was near a window, speaking rapidly in Spanish. The brothers turned toward the divan, expecting to see Rafaela Galban. Instead, Ruth Thrumbull was there, alone with José Marti.

Mingo visibly was annoyed and Sans was surprised, then provoked. She was Peninsula and she had no business there. Ruth smiled at Sans, but nodded only slightly at Mingo, a token of aloof politeness and evidence of reproach. The younger brother had visited her home the night before and now the animosity between them was obvious.

"Ah, the Dabney brothers," José Marti said, waving his hand toward the divan. "Sit there by Miss Thrumbull. I'm happy to see you."

There were footsteps upstairs in Louisa's room and Mingo listened, knowing they were Rafaela's. He crossed the room and sat in a chair, his ears tuned to the footsteps. Ruth picked up a book on the divan so that Sans could sit beside her. "Don't look so surprised that I am here," she said. "I heard this morning that Señor Marti and Señorita Galban were in New Hebron and I came by to pay my respects."

Mingo glared at her, then turned his head, deliberately ignoring her. That was bad manners and Sans glanced at his brother, a trace of disapproval on his face. Mingo had a right to be angry at the Thrumbulls because of Peninsula's store, but he had no right to bring his anger into another man's home. Something must be said to compensate for Mingo's rudeness, and Sans accepted the responsibility. "I didn't know you were acquainted with Marti." He forced himself to be pleasant.

"I didn't know him personally," Ruth said. She gave all of her attention to the elder brother. "Naturally I had heard of him."

Marti beamed. "Miss Thrumbull is well informed on Cuba. And her Spanish is excellent." He fingered his watch chain, twirling the Masonic emblem.

Mingo was sullen, staring out of the window, and Sans began talking about the weather and the effect of the rain on the crops. His words were meaningless even to him, for his mind was on Ruth Thrumbull. She belonged to the enemy's camp and the Cubans belonged to the valley, hence to the Dabneys. She was an interloper and all her charm and grace could not alter that fact; besides, he resented Marti's praise of her, for it made him realize his own provincialism. He turned from her and spoke to Marti. "My father asked me to pay his respects and to welcome you to Lebanon. He needed rest or he himself would be here."

The other boy stood abruptly. "I've got a little headache. I'm going out on the porch for some fresh air." He stepped outside and waited, listening for Rafaela's footsteps.

Ruth touched her lips with her handkerchief and Marti addressed Sans. "If this rain continues, I will be in Lebanon for days and can meet your father." He went to a chair and sighed as he sat down. His fatigue still showed on his face. "I'll send the servant for Señorita Galban—"

"She is resting," Ruth said quickly.

"Then please don't disturb her." Sans was disappointed because he knew Mingo would be disappointed.

"But she will want to see you." Marti turned his head to one side and looked from Sans to Ruth. "My associate was quite impressed by Mr. Dabney. She called him 'Hombre grande'." He merely was making a pleasantry. Cuba was the love of José Marti, and he knew that Cuba was the love and the only interest of Rafaela Galban.

There was formal and accentuated courtesy in Ruth's tone. "I am sure she was impressed by Mr. Dabney."

"That was my brother, Señor Marti. Mingo is the one Señorita Galban called 'Hombre grande'."

"Ah-h-h-h!" Marti flung up his hands, then struck himself on the forehead. "It *was* your brother." He laughed and reproved himself. "I must be more careful not to confuse you gentlemen."

Ruth Thrumbull smiled and her manner changed. She returned her handkerchief to her purse and leaned back comfortably on the divan. Mingo came into the room, glancing up the stairs as he passed them. Ruth spoke directly to him for the first time. "Señorita Galban will join us in a few minutes." The face of the younger brother lighted and he sat down. Sans asked, "Your headache better?"

"It's clearing up."

A gust of rain swept against the house and Marti went to the window, impatiently muttering to himself. Ruth touched Sans' hand to attract his attention. "It's too bad Señor Marti can't remain in the valley for a little while. He needs rest."

Her genuine concern for his welfare pleased the Cuban and he smiled his appreciation. He was impressed by Ruth Thrumbull, perceiving her as an enlightened woman in a valley of provincials. That she was the daughter of Peninsula's superintendent did not disturb him, for she was a free thinker, untrammeled by the traditions of her relationships. He had not questioned her about her father's company, for he chose to make her a friend of Cuba rather than attempt to make her an informer on Peninsula. Besides, she might have rebuffed him.

Ruth acknowledged Marti's smile and again gave her attention to Sans. "Señor Marti is going first to Chicago, then must hasten to the *Junta* in New York."

"*Junta?*" Sans asked.

"Yes." Marti limped across the room and stood in front of them. "A committee of revolutionists. We have them in many cities."

"Is that fair?" It merely was evidence of Sans' curiosity and ignorance. "Is it fair for revolutionists to live in this country and stir up trouble against Spain?"

The pallor left Marti's face and deep wrinkles showed in his high, wide forehead. The internationalist was appalled and had endured his limit of American insularity. Men had a right to live in valleys but they had no right never to look over the ridges. "Fair! You said *fair!*" The little man grew taller. "My God, sir, the time has come for the meek to rise up and claim their inheritance." He glanced toward the stairs and spoke almost in a whisper. "Is it fair that Rafaela Galban is under sentence of death? There are those who would cut out her tongue to silence her. And yet you speak as if revolution were a gentleman's tournament to be played according to rules, with observation of the amenities!" He raised his hands in a gesture of exasperation. *"Santa Maria!"*

Mingo leaned forward to catch every word, his blood quickly pounding and his mind conjuring visions of strength and valor, of gunfire in Cuban mountains; of the meek rising against their masters, clawing for the right of their inheritance.

Sans sat on the edge of the divan, more tense even than Mingo. To the elder brother the meek were the Cajuns and the Negroes along Bogue Homa; the revolution to him was the railroad jabbing at the north cut. He was oblivious that Ruth Thrumbull was watching him, detecting in him a yearning, a call of which he himself was not aware.

Marti limped back to the window and stood there enervated, exhausted by the burden of his destiny, disgusted at the incredible blindness of men who endured the seeding of tares their children must reap.

Again Ruth reached out and touched Sans' hand, shattering the magic. "I'm glad you came. I wanted to talk to you." She looked from him to Mingo. "And to you, too." She crossed her ankles and adjusted her position on the divan. "I need to talk to both of you about Señorita Galban."

Mingo turned on her then. "What about Miss Galban?" he demanded.

The Thrumbull girl glanced his way, then addressed Sans. "I have asked her to stay at our house—"

"She is welcome at our house." Mingo was almost haughty.

The elder boy immediately appreciated the wisdom of Ruth's suggestion. Nevertheless, he resented her presumption. She was butting in again, as Yankees always do. "All the old families of this valley, Miss Thrumbull, will welcome Señorita Galban."

"Of course." Ruth refused to be offended. "I offer our home because Señorita Galban is about my age and I understand her language." Her chin came up and her gray eyes were calm—as calm as her voice. "I discussed this with our visitors and they agreed with me—"

"I thoroughly agree." Marti spoke over his shoulder. "It was very gracious of Miss Thrumbull, and is the simplest solution." He must caution Rafaela never to misuse the hospitality of the daughter by prying into the affairs of the father.

Even Mingo realized Ruth's plan was proper, and told her so. They discussed the entertainment of the Cuban girl and, the details settled, Ruth got up from the divan, smoothing her dress. "I will go up and see if Señorita Galban can come down." She spoke the words to Mingo and walked out of the room, Sans' eyes following her.

The three men were alone and Marti offered whiskey. Sans took a drink but Mingo declined. Ruth returned to the living room and reported that Rafaela would be down in a few minutes. She sat on the divan beside Sans, and Mingo walked to the mantel, restless until he heard footsteps on the stairs.

Rafaela Galban was walking down the steps, her white hand on the banister and her eyes searching the group, searching until she saw him. Her dress was black silk and a tiny cameo was at her throat, held there by a black ribbon. Her mantilla covered her hair completely. It was high on her forehead, but her hair was swept back, concealed beneath the black lace.

Sans stood and Mingo hurried to her, bowing her into the living room. Her eyes were dancing and she exchanged pleasantries, laughing merrily all the while. Marti studied her and his gaze wandered from her to Mingo, thence out to the rain.

They all talked trivia for a few minutes, until Sans, reading the plea on Mingo's face, arose to go. Marti said, "You were kind to call." Then he turned to Rafaela. "I have some letters to write. If you and Miss Thrumbull will excuse me—"

"I must be going, too," Ruth said. She put her hand on Rafaela's arm. "I will be back for you tonight. Your room is ready." Then she spoke to Sans. "My buggy is not here, so I want you to drive me home." She offered her hand to Marti. "I will send my check to the *Junta* in Tampa, and I will raise funds in the valley."

Marti bowed. "I will send you our newspapers." He walked with them toward the door, and told Sans, "Miss Thrumbull has agreed to act for us in Lebanon and help us raise money."

"That's fine." However, Sans didn't like it. One of the valley folks should be treasurer and fund-raiser, but there she went butting in again. Yankee! That's what she was.

They ducked their heads against the rain and ran to the buggy.

He scarcely glanced at her, even when she commented on the beauty of the horse, but slapped the lines and they jogged away. "Yes, nice horse."

"Your brother was pretty upset when he came to our house about the company's store—"

"Upset! He's boiling mad."

The rain splashed against the dashboard and the horse's hoofs sank into the mire. Ruth looked straight ahead and her mouth, usually so generous, was in a tight line. "He insulted my father."

"That's too bad." Sans said it curtly, touching up the horse to get Ruth home and out of his presence as quickly as possible.

"It was a mistake to blame Dad," she said. "He had nothing to do with the store. My father is the best friend your crowd has among the Peninsula people."

Sans hesitated only a moment. The conflict was sharply drawn between the valley and Peninsula, and he might as well make it plain that the Dabneys accepted the challenge. "We have no friends among the Peninsula people." He said it deliberately so she could not mistake his words or his meaning. "And we want no friends among the Peninsula people. If Mingo made a mistake, the mistake is mine, too."

"Then you and your brother see things alike?" Her words were as cold as his.

"We see things exactly alike."

They both were silent, she staring at the rain and Sans watching the road. He was conscious of her nearness, of the smell of good clean soap and light perfume, not the heavy alluring perfume of Louisa. This woman disturbed him, quickening emotions Louisa had never released in him. He said gruffly, "I suppose we should send our money for Cuba to you."

"I suggest so. Maybe you and I can at least agree on Cuba."

"Mr. Charlie Owens would like that collecting job," Sans said, not quite so gruff. "Mr. Charlie is the money raiser in the valley." They reached the courthouse and the square was deserted; the live oaks bending under their burden of rain and the birds huddling for protection. He turned his horse past the livery stable and they started up the east ridge. "Señor Marti is sure a fine talker." He was surprised at the tone of his own voice, now so quiet; not at all as if speaking to a person who annoyed him.

Ruth glanced back toward the Peninsula office where her father was working, then up the ridge toward her house. "José Marti is a poet and mystic. I saw you and your brother under his spell."

"Maybe you're right." He spoke earnestly, as if he were troubled. "I couldn't take much of that man. He got under my skin. He'd make me pull up stakes and follow him to Cuba—"

"No!" The blood rushed to her cheeks. "Don't you dare leave this valley." She held his arm tight, searching his face. "There are folks in this valley who need help as much as any in Cuba. Don't you dare run away from this valley fight, just to get into that fight in Cuba."

Sans peered at her, amazed. The color was bright in her cheeks, and the rain glistened in her hair. He was conscious of her hand on his arm and he touched her hand, and she did not draw her hand away. "All right, I'll tell you." They reached the gate to her yard and Sans halted his horse. "I'll tell you how it is, Miss Thrumbull. I aim to stay here in this valley. I aim to stay—come hell, high water, or Peninsula Lumber Company."

She took her hand from his arm. "I am glad." Then she jumped from the buggy and ran into the house.

Sans watched her running, the wind whipping her skirt. He watched her open, then close the door, and saw her stand by a window a second, looking back at him. He waited until she moved, then drove away toward the village, his mind in a turmoil. Sans Dabney needed Louisa at that minute. She was his comfort and the valley was his anchor, and he must cling to both of them. . . .

Windy Hill and Sheriff Vernon Boyd, ignoring the rain, were in front of Peninsula's office when Sans drove back that way. Lamps were burning in the office, for the day was dark. Sans arrived at The Store and Mr. Charlie met him at the door. They sat on the porch and the old man plied him with questions. Mingo still was at the Woodward house and New Hebron, rain-drenched and forlorn, was brooding in its own dreariness and monotony.

The storekeeper raised his head and looked up the pike, and out of the rain and gloom came Elmo Batson's buggy, covered with mud. "Good Lord," Mr. Charlie said. "Ol' Elmo got through. I figured he was water-bound up the road." The horses came plodding on. "I reckon he'll be heading out, and that little Cuban fellow will go with him."

Sans did not reply, scarcely hearing. So José Marti was departing, and Rafaela Galban y Torres was remaining in Lebanon. The elder brother turned it in his mind, and his mind was troubled. The rain brought the exiles into the valley, and rain was taking Marti away. He was only an interlude, a spell cast by the storm; but Rafaela Galban was a woman with burning eyes and snow-white hair. And Mingo Dabney was a restless man.

Elmo's buggy appeared down by the livery stable, on the road from the Woodward place. A fresh team was pulling hard. The rain was in their faces and they were tossing their heads to shake off the drops. The drummer opened the curtains as he passed and called out. "Mingo said to tell you he'd be along in a little bit." He waved a parting, first to Sans and then to Mr. Charlie. "So long, Mr. Charlie. Don't take any wooden nickels."

José Marti was asleep. The little man sat close to Elmo, his head resting on the back of the seat. He must go to Chicago, thence to New York; maybe then to Cuba. José Marti slept the sleep of the exhausted, the sleep of the almost dead.

Chapter eleven

THE RAIN lasted nine days; it kept Sans from his timber, although it did not slow Peninsula's crew at the north cut where rails were stacked, waiting to be laid into the valley. He fidgeted in his impatience to be in the woods and hung around The Store, keeping Mr. Charlie company.

Ruth Thrumbull shopped every day for her household—made a point of doing it—and when Sans was in The Store she always dallied for a few words with him and Mr. Charlie.

Rafaela Galban was comfortably settled in the Thrumbull house, but only once during the rainy spell did she venture out with Ruth, and that was for a quick visit to The Store. The post office loiterers gawked at her as she and Ruth rode up the pike, and Rafaela was nervous. Her mantilla attracted notice, and the fact that she was a foreigner set tongues to wagging.

Mingo greeted her when she came to The Store that day. She wanted olive oil, an item not in stock, and Mingo immediately instructed Mr. Charlie to order some. Sans grinned as his brother bowed and scraped, showing Rafaela the stock. Ruth also was amused, watching Mingo show off and listening to Rafaela's exclamations of delight over such simple things as colored thread and bottles of gaudy medicines. Mr. Charlie endured it as long as he could—Mingo showing off like that—and then he stepped in and took over, escorting her around The Store, pointing out his prides, the horse collars and the hardware, old cheeses and salt mackerel.

The younger brother drove them home; angry when the people stared at him and at Rafaela. However, he was back at the Thrumbull house that night, and the next night; and soon the valley had its best talk-morsel since the fight between Ronnie Sullivan and Nils Holmquist, since the return of Aven MacIvor. Kyd Dabney was shocked almost to silence that her boy was devoting so much time to that foreigner.

However, she didn't speak to him about it. He might rebuke her and she never wanted to give Mingo a chance to part from her on anything. So she took it up with Bruce and when the old man looked at her gently and smiled and shook his head, she went to Sans.

"You are his brother," she admonished. "I want you to put a stop to this foolishness."

Sans had been expecting such a maneuver. "It's not my place to say anything. Mingo is a grown man."

"But you can't have your brother calling on a freak like that. White hair and hiding it all the time!"

The older son was adroit. "Wait a minute, Mama. The best way to start a match is to butt in and try to prevent it."

"I've never been so humiliated in all my life." Kyd went around the room, picking up things and putting them down. "A Dabney, my own flesh and blood, seen in public with that woman. She's not our kind of folks. We don't even know who she is—"

"Now, Mama!" His tone was sterner. "Don't fly off the handle." He put his arm around her shoulder and patted her, quieting her. "I was fixing to suggest that you ask her up here for dinner. Ruth Thrumbull, too—"

"Are you crazy?"

Sans looked her squarely in the eye. "Think it over and see if I'm crazy. If I were you, I'd ask her here before Papa does. Or before Mingo gets peeved about it."

The mother quickly saw the validity of Sans' suggestion. Better to let this thing run its course—give Mingo ample chance to see her and tire of her.

Bruce was pleased when Kyd announced her intention of entertaining Ruth Thrumbull and her house guest. Mingo was delighted and hugged his mother, then he asked the privilege of extending the invitation personally.

Ruth accepted with alacrity and before the wet spell passed, she and Rafaela broke bread at the Dabney house. Quickly the gossip of Lebanon subsided. If Rafaela Galban was good enough to sit down at the Dabney dinner table, then she was good enough for the valley. Dabney approval was valley approval—even if she *was* a foreigner.

Then Kyd, at Ruth's invitation, went to the Thrumbull house for afternoon coffee. She had a good time—Ruth saw that she did, and Kyd reported her pleasure to her own family. "She made me feel right at home," she told her husband and sons. "Treated me like I was her own age instead of old enough to be her mother." She talked on and on about Ruth Thrumbull, scarcely mentioning Rafaela.

Wyeth Woodward, at Ruth's request, called a rally at the courthouse to raise money for the Cuban revolution. Rafaela did not attend the meeting, not wishing to be conspicuous; but Ruth spoke in public, a thing no woman ever had done in Lebanon.

The people contributed generously, and aid to Cuba became a cause in the valley, a new thing to talk about. A box supper was given at the Free Church and a raffle at the Odd Fellows Hall.

Aven MacIvor reached the valley in spite of high water to see if the storm had damaged her holdings. Ruth called on her for a check and got it. She even wrote to Keith Alexander for money.

Gar Rivers left the valley and went west toward Natchez, talking the cause and recruiting Negroes for the Cuban army.

The first man in the valley to leave for Cuba was Shane Figgis, he of the red beard and the hairy chest. He got crying drunk and cursed the rain and the Peninsula people. He wept on Mr. Charlie's shoulder and cried out for all the woes of man, sobbing his pity for the meek. Then he cursed tyranny and threw a hairy arm around Sans and the other around Mingo and said, "Dammit to hell! I'm gonna fight. I'm gonna fight for them po' little Cubans. I been hearing about 'em. Miss Thrumbull told me about 'em. So did Gar Rivers. If that old nigger can help 'em, so can Shane Figgis. Besides, there ain't no work for me in the valley."

In a flame of glory and whiskey and boasts, Shane Figgis left the valley of Lebanon, heading for the *Junta* in Mobile to offer himself for Cuban freedom.

Three Negroes from Marion County, aroused by Gar's visit there, came through the valley on their way to the *Junta* in Tampa.

Then Debo Giles went, and at last Fishbait Gates pulled out.

"Huh," said Mr. Charlie. "More folks going to Cuba than to Texas."

Sans watched each man leave. The valley was sending her men away, and Peninsula was bringing its people in.

The rain passed and Lebanon steamed; soon the rain was just another thing to talk about, and the people's interest in Cuba waned as they gave their attention to other matters: the crops, Peninsula Lumber Company and a clandestine love affair between one of Peninsula's office workers and a Cajun girl. After all, Cuba was far away and Rafaela Galban was no longer a woman to stare at, but a woman who laughed often, who was seen frequently on the streets of the village, always in the company of Ruth Thrumbull or Mingo Dabney.

There wasn't enough work to keep Sans in the woods every day and he loafed around The Store, doing odd jobs and waiting on customers when two or three came in at the same time. Mingo, awaiting the return of Louisa Woodward before making improvements in The Store, passed on to Sans the chores he once insisted upon doing himself. It would be weeks, maybe months, before Peninsula opened its store and, meanwhile, Mingo spent his time with Rafaela Galban.

The chills and fever of late summer, the plague of dog days, seeped up from the miasmal swamp and Mr. Charlie's stock of tonics was depleted. Where was Elmo? The weeks were passing and Elmo was long overdue, and Mr. Charlie began to wonder about his crony, then to worry about him. Finally, bursting with curiosity and aching with worry, the old man wrote to Mobile, and the letter was returned.

So Elmo did not come back, and his company sent another drummer to the valley. The new man told Mr. Charlie, "I don't know what happened to Batson. He ain't with the company any more. Now, what do you need?"

No more Shane Figgis to get drunk and roar. No Fishbait Gates and no Debo Giles. And now Elmo Batson. Mr. Charlie's face was long. Sans, too, was lonely. Mingo was drawing away from him, and the elder brother was miserable. Ruth Thrumbull did her best to cheer him. They saw each other often in public places and his problems seemed lighter when he was with her, but when he was alone he was miserable.

His spirits were at their lowest—the black mood was on him—when the letter came from Louisa, driving away his despondency. She was in New Orleans, and was coming home without her mother.

"Mama insisted that I stay with her," the letter said. "But I am coming home. I will ride the train from New Orleans to Ellisville. I am dying to see you. Tell Mingo I have many plans for The Store, and some goods that will set a new style in the valley, and turn a fancy profit."

The rest of the letter was about The Store. In fact, most of the letter was about The Store.

Sans was overjoyed. "She's coming home," he told himself. "Now everything will be all right."

He folded the letter and put it in his back pocket and walked down to Mr. Woodward's office. The lawyer was standing on his porch, staring toward the courthouse. His coat was unbuttoned and his collar was wilted. He greeted Sans, then eased his bulk down on the steps and sighed the relief of a heavy man relaxed. "Sit down, son. I'm tired and hot as blazes. I heard from Louisa this morning."

Sans leaned against a pillar and opened his collar a bit more to catch all the breeze that was stirring. "So did I. And I'm mighty glad she's coming home, Mr. Woodward."

Wyeth glanced up at him, then over toward the courthouse square where Sheriff Vernon Boyd was resting on a bench. Mr. Thrumbull came out of the Peninsula office and walked across the square, going to the Post Office Cafe for a cup of coffee. Mr. Irving of Peninsula's Chicago legal staff was with him. So was Windy Hill. Irving and Hill stopped to talk with Sheriff Boyd. Thrumbull kept on walking.

The lawyer watched them a few seconds, then said, "Mingo has been dingdonging me about your suing Peninsula."

Sans flushed. "Mingo has suing on the brain. Nils Holmquist's men cut about two hundred dollars worth of trees by mistake. Nils said the company will pay me."

"Have they paid you?" Wyeth reached for his handkerchief and mopped his face.

"No, sir. But they'll get around to it, I reckon."

The lawyer lumbered to his feet, grunting in the effort. "Have you seen the damage?"

"It's at the far end of my timber. I haven't been there in months."

"I was out there this morning." Wyeth felt for a cigar, and changed his mind. It was too hot to smoke. "I heard that after Nils made his report, the office told him to forget it. They said they'd take care of everything."

Sans jerked his head around and studied Wyeth's face. "Did they? Did they clean it up?"

"No, son. They didn't clean it up until borers got in. Then Peninsula sent in a skidder. They cleaned it up, all right. Cleaned up everything."

The color drained slowly from Sans' face and, without further talk, he went for his horse, riding fast into the woods. He found Ronnie Sullivan and together they rode to the far end of Sans' holdings.

Ronnie began cursing before they got there. They checked their horses and heard the cut-worms boring into good green timber. The worms made a rasping sound, like tiny saws cutting into the wood, and the forest was alive with them, eating sap under the bark, draining the trees and killing them.

"The bastards!" Sans said. "The stupid bastards."

Nils' men had felled the trees while the sap was up. That was all right, had the trees been moved, but they were left on the ground through the carelessness of Peninsula's office force. The sawyers, thick in the fallen timber, were moving into live timber. They would eat through the forest until stopped by axes or cold weather.

The two men rode on until they came to the clearing where Peninsula first had trespassed. All around, for acres, the land was chewed up, the saplings uprooted and the earth scarred. The skidder had ripped and crushed the young trees, and the land was a sandy waste of gravel and dead gray earth. The heavy rains already had begun erosion, gouging gullies in the earth, streaking the earth with destruction, beginning the death march of the land to the sea.

Sans' face was white as he galloped for Peninsula's camp and Nils Holmquist. Ronnie was beside him. The big Swede saw them coming and, sensing trouble, walked to meet them, keeping his eyes on Ronnie. "Hello, Sans. How you doing, Ronnie?"

The valley men dismounted and Ronnie said, "Howdy, Nils."

"Have you been up there where you cut my timber?" Sans asked, his voice low and tense.

"No," said Nils. "The office took me off that job. How come you ask?"

Sans reported the destruction and as he talked, Nils' face, usually pink, got red and sweat stood on his forehead. "The fat fools," he said. "Letterhead lumbermen. Sitting there and letting good timber be ruined—"

"Is it your responsibility?" Sans demanded.

"No. They said they'd take care of it."

"Well, if it ain't your responsibility, I aim to crack my whip."

Nils held the bridle of Sans' horse while he mounted. "Crack it, mister. Crack it God damn hard. I was a timber man before I was a Peninsula man."

Ronnie Sullivan looked down at Nils' feet, then up at his face. "So long, Nils."

"I'll be seeing you, Ronnie."

Neither Sans nor his woods boss spoke a word all the way from the Peninsula camp to New Hebron. At Wyeth Woodward's office, Sans said, "I'll be stopping here." Ronnie rode on to The Store.

The lawyer was waiting. Sans stood in the doorway and said, "Sue 'em, Mr. Woodward."

"How much, son?"

"Two thousand," Sans said.

"That won't cover it. We've got to figure erosion and waste. It's hard to figure wasted land. The Lord forgives a lot of our laziness, but He won't give us back wasted land. And I don't think two thousand is enough."

"Then make it five thousand. Anything!"

Wyeth shifted in his swivel chair. "That's more like it. I'll draw the papers right away."

"What'll they do?" Sans' tall frame filled the doorway and he was so angry he was weak. Ignorant and careless men had wasted his trees. He still heard the rasp of millions of tiny saws, cutting into his trees, killing them. The anger rolled in a fiery ball from his spine to his stomach and burned him.

"They'll try to compromise," Wyeth said.

"We won't compromise."

"Then they'll fight us. They can't afford to lose their first damage suit in this county. If they did, they'd have a hundred suits on their hands in a hurry." The lawyer reached for his pencil and paper. "This is the biggest suit I ever filed. It'll take me three or four days."

"What about Louisa?" Sans asked. "She'll be in Ellisville day after tomorrow."

Wyeth didn't even glance up. "You meet her, son. Do me a big favor and meet her."

The anger passed from Sans Dabney. Louisa was coming home, and he was going to meet her. There was jauntiness in his bearing as he walked back to The Store to see Mingo.

The younger brother and Mr. Charlie pestered Sans with questions about the suit, but Sans was thinking of Louisa. He'd put on his Sunday best. And borrow Mingo's buggy. He'd bring her all the way from Ellisville to Lebanon; alone all that way with Louisa. He felt in his back pocket for her letter, anticipating the pleasure of reading it again. But the paper was wet with his own sweat, and the sweat of his horse. He took it out and looked at it. The ink had run. He held it in his hand for a moment, then squeezed it into a ball and tossed it away.

The sky was without a cloud and Sans Dabney was without a care the day he drove to Ellisville to meet Louisa. He hitched in the shade near the depot, and pretty soon word got around about his new rig. The livery stable owner, wanting to show off, offered a nice price for the get-up. Sans laughed at him and pushed his hat to the back of his head and rocked on the balls of his feet. He felt big and important while the men bragged on Chinquapin and the Brighton.

If they thought Chinquapin was beautiful, just wait until they saw Louisa beside him in the buggy. Just wait until they saw him and Louisa wheel away to Lebanon. The train, northbound to Meridian from New Orleans, was late, as usual, but Sans didn't mind. He walked back and forth in front of the depot, strutting a little, talking to the loafers.

"How near is Peninsula ready to cut timber?" one of them asked.

"Don't know," Sans said. "The mill is about ready. They ought to be able to cut next month."

"They still aim to go through the north cut to their mill? Or they aim to go around?"

"They aim to go through," Sans said slowly. "But down in Lebanon, we figure their aim is bad."

The men guffawed, nodding among themselves. They liked Sans Dabney. The train whistle brought his heart to his throat, and it pounded wildly when Louisa stepped from the coach.

She was slimmer than when she went away. Her clothes were so fashionable the villagers forgot how stylish Aven MacIvor was when she returned. The women in the crowd gaped at Louisa in envy and the men ogled her, her trim ankles, her tightly corseted body. Sans was so proud he grinned like a little boy, then stepped up to greet her.

She called out to him in big-city affectation, "Oh, Sans! Sans!" Before them all, he bent and kissed her cheek and she laughed and held her wide-brimmed hat and said, "Be careful. You will knock off my hat. I'll bet it looks a sight already."

"So do you," he said, "a sight for these lonesome eyes."

"You look tired." She took his arm and the crowd parted and let them through. "Is Papa all right? And Mingo? And your folks? And tell me about The Store." She laughed at her own impetuosity.

"Everybody is fine. I'll answer your questions one at a time." He helped her into the buggy and stood back and looked at her.

This was not the Louisa who went away from the valley to buy goods for The Store. This was not the chubby daughter of a country lawyer. This woman was poised and graceful. She was tiny, trim as a robin. Yet there was strength in her face, and determination. Sans saw it all and was proud.

He went for her trunk and put it under the seat and climbed in beside her, then touched up his horses and felt for her hand, squeezing it. They both laughed and Chinquapin tossed her head and trotted out of Ellisville while the people watched them go, the women nodding and commenting on what a handsome couple they were, the men discussing the beauty of the horse and buggy.

"Now tell me about The Store," she said.

Sans didn't want to talk about The Store or about Peninsula. He wanted to talk about themselves, but, dutifully, he reported all the events, stressing the money Peninsula was spending on its store. The light went out of Louisa's eyes and there was a hardness in them that Sans saw and did not understand.

They came to Peninsula's railroad, where it cut off from the Mainline and ran south to Lebanon. They followed the road beside the tracks and Sans put his arm around her while they talked. He told her about José Marti and Rafaela Galban, scarcely mentioning Rafaela, and never connecting her with Mingo. That was a situation for Louisa to see for herself.

"You wrote me about them," she said tersely. The hardness came back to her eyes. "And Mingo wrote me about that Cuban woman. Said she was pretty, a lot of sense in her head. But you know how Mingo is about a new face." Sans nodded his agreement.

"I suppose she'll be leaving soon," Louisa continued. "I heard that a revolution is going to break out in Cuba any day. I suppose she'll want to be there when it happens." Louisa took off her big hat and held it in her lap. "If Ruth Thrumbull can stand to have her in her house, then I suppose she must be a nice girl. For a foreigner, of course." She looked sharply at Sans. "What is Ruth Thrumbull doing? Have you seen her often?"

"I see her every now and then." Sans cherished the curve of Louisa's shoulders, her tiny nose and rounded chin. "She's Yankee, all right. You know how they are. Busy and bustling all the time."

"That may be so." Louisa said it with authority. "But we mustn't make her mad. I want her trade when I get my department going. Now tell me about Mingo." She dabbed her moist forehead with her 'kerchief. "Hope he hasn't popped off too much about our plans—certainly not to Mr. Charlie. Charlie Owen's the biggest gossip in the valley."

Sans stiffened and a wisp of a frown passed over his face. "If Mingo told anybody any plans, he didn't tell me. I don't know your plans myself, Louisa."

Her merry little laugh drove away his fears. He pulled her to him and she let her head rest on his shoulder. They drove in silence for a while, she looking up at him and he watching Peninsula's railroad as it stretched on and on, through the pines and down toward Lebanon.

"My plans are just the same," she said sweetly, "only more so. I am going to give Lebanon an up-to-date store. I'll teach Peninsula a trick or two."

"Does Mingo know about it?" Sans wondered. "Or Mr. Charlie?"

"Why should Mr. Charlie know? And I'll explain everything to Mingo as soon as I see him." She touched Sans lightly. "I wish you were in The Store instead of cutting timber. And I wish you had some money. We could use some money."

Sans grinned in spite of his forebodings. "I wish I had some money, too. I'm just about broke."

"It's your own fault. There's no need for a man to be broke. Stop the horse. I want to show you something."

Sans reined Chinquapin to the side of the road and, following Louisa's instructions, opened her trunk and handed her a box from the top tray. She opened it and held up four or five packages of cigarettes. They were Dukes and Cameos, Turkish Cross Cuts and Preferred Stock, the popular brands of the day. Sans made a wry face. Only sissies smoked cigarettes. "Coffin tacks!" he snorted. "Mr. Charlie says that when a man smokes a cigarette, there's a fire at one end and a fool at the other."

Louisa picked up several packs. They were small pasteboard boxes, opening at one end. She ripped off the covering and removed the card, a picture of a French bathing beauty, then took out one of the cigarettes. "Don't you make fun of these. Some men in New Orleans already are smoking them. And it's quite the thing to collect the cards and keep them in an album." She opened another package. "They have all sorts of cards to make people buy. Look at this one. It's the American bird series. It's a crane."

Sans examined the picture. "I never saw a crane that looked like that—"

"Don't go laughing at them," Louisa interrupted. "It's the best merchandising plan in years. They give away the cards as premiums. Just look at them." One brand featured a cross-section of arts and sports, including John L. Sullivan in long drawers and Lillian Russell in short drawers. Another brand displayed fancy costumes and flags, and one gave away a 20-page booklet, a story by Horatio Alger.

Sans still was grinning. He felt Louisa's temper rising and he explained hastily, "I'm not laughing at you, honey. I'm just sort of tickled because Elmo Batson tried to get Mr. Charlie to stock some cigarettes, and Mr. Charlie almost blew up."

Louisa said, "Huh! What Charlie Owens doesn't know about merchandising would fill a book. I'm going to get Mingo to stock cigarettes. Try one of them."

"Are you fooling?" Sans drew back, his dignity offended, his manliness outraged.

Louisa held the cigarette toward him, pressing it on him. "Go ahead. Try it. Nobody can see you."

Mostly to please her, but partly because it was a daring thing to do, Sans lit a Turkish Cross Cut. He took a few puffs, then hurled it away and lifted the reins again. "Just a fad," he said. "They'll never sell. Mr. Charlie is right. Just a fad for sissies."

"You'll see," Louisa insisted, bracing her feet against the dashboard. "That's where the money is. Cigarettes and silks and fancy things. Let Peninsula sell salt. We'll sell satin."

A sudden shock came to Sans. This was not the Louisa who went away. This was her mother, Laurel Woodward. This was Aven Dabney MacIvor. Maybe Morna Dabney Alexander. He was disturbed, and although the sky was clear, his heart was overcast. The cities had changed her. Well, Lebanon would change her back. She would be Louisa again. It was strange to him, sadly strange, that Ruth Thrumbull could grow into a valley, while Louisa grew out of it.

To change the subject, he told her about his suit against Peninsula and she sat upright, pulling away from him and staring at him. "Five thousand dollars! And you'll win. They can't beat a Dabney in court. Put that money into The Store."

There was The Store again. She worked every word back to The Store. He said, "I haven't thought about it."

"Well, let's think about it. You can buy into The Store. Forget those trees, darling. Let Peninsula cut the trees. We'll get rich selling luxuries to the Peninsula women."

Sans was wretched and didn't even reply. He reached for the buggy whip and struck his horse, hitting Chinquapin harder than he ever hit a horse before. He wanted to be back in Lebanon; wanted to be with his brother.

Louisa kept talking and the miles rolled by. They passed Peninsula workmen and Sans set his jaw, and Louisa kept talking. Eventually, however, it came to her that he was displeased and she switched the subject from The Store to themselves. She slid down in the seat, relaxing at his side. A breeze rustled her dress, and she sighed at the pleasure of the cool breeze against her face.

"You should be thankful you're a man," she said, "and don't have to wear all these old clothes." She put her hand on his arm and he remembered Ruth Thrumbull had done the same thing.

"Why don't you undo your collar?" he suggested. "That'll cool you off."

"Sans Dabney!" She laughed and glanced behind them. "But why not? Nobody can see me but you. That won't be immodest."

Sans looked at her in amazement, a frown on his face, almost a scowl. Just what her collar and comfort had to do with modesty was a thing beyond him. Conscious of his attention, she unfastened two buttons at her throat, and pulled open her collar and held her dress away from her flesh, feeling the breeze. She laughed in the sheer pleasure of being a woman, and being young.

It was a tempting laugh, and Sans' blood started throbbing. He bent quickly and kissed her throat and she gasped a cry of delight, trying to disguise it as a rebuke. He dropped the reins and the mare slowed down, meandering to the side of the road and nibbling grass. Louisa's fears and desires struggled, churning within her. Sans pulled her to him, almost into his lap, and buried his face between her breasts. She held her breath and her flesh trembled. Then she kissed the back of his neck, and his ears, and the sweat dropped from her chin onto him.

"No." She panted the word. "Not here. Somebody will see us. Some of those railroad men might come by."

He raised his head and cupped her chin in his big hand. It was a rough gesture and he looked at her fiercely, searching her face, seeking something he hoped to find, and then understand by discovery. But he saw nothing except her trembling chin, her forehead and her damp hair clinging there. He saw nothing but a face, a beautiful face. He felt nothing but a supple body shrinking in his arms. Without a word, he lifted the reins and spoke to his horse.

Louisa was so close that he felt her flesh, warm and sticky, through her dress. She pushed against him, moving slowly, and rested her head on his arm. That interfered with his driving and he told her so. She moved her head to his shoulder and began talking again, saying the words she thought she should; while her body, warm against him, told the truth. "We can wait for that, can't we, lover?" she whispered. "I love you enough, but you'd hate me. You know you'd hate me. Wouldn't you? If I gave in to you, wouldn't you hate me?"

"Let's not talk about it."

"You know I love you, don't you?"

"Yes. I know that."

"You know I love you enough to let you do anything. You know that, don't you?"

"I suppose so." He touched Chinquapin with the whip again. Lebanon was about a mile away.

"I love you so much." Louisa put her fingers around his arm and squeezed it. "I have so many plans for us. You are such a silly man in so many ways. A big silly sentimental man. Maybe that's why I love you. Always fretting and stewing about other people." She pushed back her hair and fitted her head into the hollow of his shoulder. "We must work together for ourselves. You never were a good businessman. But I'll teach you. And you will learn that what a man wants, he must take in this old world."

She felt his arm jerk, and knew her words had trapped her. Again she was afraid, afraid and thrilled. She lifted her head, and he was smiling. She saw in his face something she had never seen before, a flick of granite, a trace of lust. She saw the revelation of a man she had seen all her life, but never had known before.

Sans turned his horse toward the woods.

"What are you going to do?" she whispered in awe and anticipation.

He still was smiling and his head was high, and he laughed. "Sans!"

He pulled her into his lap and fondled her with one arm, holding the reins and guiding the horse with the other. They went deep into the woods until the trees hid them, and there he tossed the reins around a bush and stood beside the buggy holding out his arms. "Come on, Louisa."

"I'm afraid. I'm afraid you'll hurt me. Promise me you won't hurt me."

He lifted her out of the buggy, cradling her in his arms, and she held her lips close to his ear and whispered, "Don't let me have a baby." She whispered it over and over.

He laid her down, and the ribbons on her chemise baffled his eager fingers and she untied them for him, babbling as she did so: "Don't let me have a baby."

She pretended terror, and once she cried out, and the cry drifted away into a babble. Then she no longer pretended or cried out, but, whimpering and murmuring, suddenly dug her fingers into his back.

The sweat rolled from Sans' cheek onto her face and there was the bitter, galling taste of her sweat as he kissed her, quieting her. Then he lay on his side, looking at her, seeking an answer to the mystery she had not solved for him.

Louisa was trembling and her eyes were closed. So this was the secret from which she had been protected all her life. This the dare of the flesh and this the answer. There was no shame in her heart, only remorse that the vase had been broken and could not be mended and saved to be broken again. Also in her heart was fear. Someone might have seen them. And, too, there was fear that she might have a baby; then everybody would know.

Sans looked at her and up at the trees and in that interval, if creation can be an interval, Sans Dabney changed from one creature into another creature, changed from a man who had wanted into a man who had possessed, and found his possession a burden. He felt dirty inside himself, and restless. This was no answer. It was only a reply, a reply to the question that had haunted him since he first noticed the swelling of Louisa's breasts years before, and believed that she was the fulfillment of his yearning.

And now he felt unclean. He knew then that he didn't love

Louisa as he must love the woman of his hopes. He wanted dew from life and she wanted damask. He dreamed of stars for a canopy and she wanted only a roof, a roof better than her neighbors. He was sorry for what he had done, and sorry that he was in her debt, that she had a lien on his honor.

Louisa began tying her ribbons, sitting there on the ground. She ran her fingers through her hair, untangling it. There were pine needles in her hair and she picked them out, then dropped them. "I won't have a baby?" She looked up at him.

"No. You won't have a baby." He sat up, also.

"You were the first. You know that, don't you?"

"Yes."

She moved over close to him and they sat there together, he watching his horse and thinking thoughts that a woman never understands, and she watching him. "Was I the first?"

Sans got to his feet and helped her rise. She knew he was not going to answer her question, and she didn't repeat it, sensing something of his mood and knowing her failure with him.

She glanced down at the ground. It had not been as she had dreamed. This man was no lover. She had expected to be transformed, to wander almost endlessly through beauty and joy. But there was no beauty, and the joy was sudden and blind and fierce. Except for a fear knotting in her heart, she felt as she had before she was taken into that valley of mystery about which her mother had whispered. And she was hot and sweaty. She certainly hoped he never expected her to do such a thing again. Never again.

Louisa Woodward knew her girlhood love for Sans Dabney was ended there on the ground, torn and destroyed among the leaves and the pine needles. Her vanity was hurt and her pride provoked, yet she was relieved that the curtain was coming down on the romantic comedy which she had played for so long with this country boy. She had met fashionable gentlemen in New Orleans, danced in Natchez; she had learned how to unfold a fan, to parry a quip, and had attended concerts at the French Opera House. The only music he knew was his own song, the sound of an ax striking, and the bay of old Sooner. There were, however, a few more lines to be spoken, and she spoke them. "I told you you'd hate me."

"I don't hate you." He didn't. She was simply a girl he had

dreamed about so long, wanted so much, and suddenly had lost. He was sorry, and he was terribly lonely.

"Oh, yes, you do. Men always hate women who give in to them before they are married. Mama explained all that to me. Well, Sans." She lifted her chin a little. "I want you to know I am not angry with you. I should have been stronger."

He stood there looking at her.

"And I will never hold it against you." This was a martyr's role, and she played it with the air of a woman who suffered because she was a woman and, therefore, in bondage to man. "I will not hold this as a pledge against you. I want you to know that. You owe me nothing, Sans Dabney. And I owe you nothing." She brushed all traces of the earth from her dress and turned her back to him and said, "Is there any trash on my back?"

"A few leaves."

"Brush them off, please. This is a brand new dress."

Sans picked off the leaves and the wind caught and twisted them as they fell. Leaves from the trees of Lebanon. He picked them off rapidly, for they did not belong where they were; they were not a part of Louisa. Some of the leaves were brown and some were green and he brushed the brown ones off, and lifted off the green ones and they came off easily, never clinging to her brand new dress. He dropped them back onto the floor of the forest. He was anxious to be home, back with his brother, with his trees, with Mr. Charlie and Ronnie, and maybe hear old Sooner leading the hounds.

He helped Louisa into the buggy and Chinquapin picked a way back to the road and broke into a fast, eager trot. There was nothing to be said, although each tried to talk of casual things. Then their conversation mired in its own futility and they were silent, listening to the swish of the wheels. They rounded the last bend before the north cut, and Lebanon lay before them, and they drove on through the cut, still listening to the swish of the wheels, hearing the beat of Chinquapin's hoofs.

There still was no cloud in the sky as Sans Dabney drove back into Lebanon, down the pike to Louisa's home and left her there, hurrying away and out to his woods.

Her father was at the courthouse, and her home was empty. The girl sat alone in her room for a few minutes, staring at the floor; then she bathed and dressed and went out to find Mingo Dabney.

Chapter twelve

SANS DABNEY'S five thousand dollar suit against Peninsula Lumber Co., Inc. caused a hue and cry in the valley and a convulsion of speculation in the company.

Keith Alexander, sitting in his Chicago office and reading reports from his agents, heard the news and was irked by the obstinacy of his wife's family. Lebanon could not beat Peninsula. The odds were too big. So thought Keith Alexander, pulling strings on the destiny of men from his ornate tower. So thought the man who, thirty years before, had stood with Lebanon against the odds of all the Confederacy.

The valley was quickened by the suit and the people talked of little else, all except Rafaela Galban who was interested in the valley only as it concerned Mingo. Besides, there were rumors of gunfire in the Cuban mountains, rumors which accentuated her fears and whipped her emotions into anxiety. Mingo tried to comfort her and keep her mind from the reports that seeped out of Cuba and into Lebanon. He gave so much of his time to her that The Store became a duty and never a pleasure; even his personal fight with Peninsula Lumber Company drifted into secondary importance. To Sans Dabney, however, the conflict with Peninsula still was paramount.

At first, Louisa Woodward was bitterly furious at Mingo's attention to the foreigner. Sans had slipped out of her life, and that did not bother her at all; but her plans included Mingo, and now he was following a strange woman like a schoolboy in the springtime. However, Louisa was too wise to show her hand, and cunningly accepted Rafaela as an object of sympathy, even pity. She was kind to the exile, knowing the Cuban girl would not be long in Lebanon. Let the infatuation run its course and when she was gone, Mingo would remember that Louisa had been kind to her; that Louisa was a sympathetic woman. She spent as much time as possible with Mingo discussing The Store, planning an annex to the old Dabney building, talking of corsets and coats, silks and cigarettes.

Mr. Charlie sat in on the conferences for a while. Mingo asked him to. Then Louisa called Mingo to her house at night for more talk, and they forgot Mr. Charlie.

There was no hardware in the new plan, no coffee beans and coal oil. It was a world passing Mr. Charlie by, leaving him desolate and forlorn, to sit on The Store's porch and talk about the lawsuit with all who came that way, those who had time to sit for a spell and swap talk. Day after day he kept glancing down the road, hoping, even praying, that Elmo Batson would ride out of the dust and heat and come into the valley again with things Mr. Charlie loved—gossip and snuff, chewing tobacco and spicy stories, beer and politics.

Peninsula's lawyers, Mr. Lewiston and Mr. Irving, inclined to scoff at Sans' suit. "Damn nonsense," Lewiston told Irving. "I'd hoped to be back in Chicago before now. All that young whippersnapper's holdings aren't worth $5,000. You prepare a reply."

"I don't like it," Irving said. "These people are tricky. We'd better send for Hill. He is supposed to represent us here."

"Keep that windbag out of this."

Mr. Irving had scarcely started preparing the company's reply before a deluge of damage suits descended on Peninsula. Sans had broken a hole in the dike and shyster lawyers from Mobile and Jackson eased into New Hebron, persuading people they had claims. One man had lost an arm and was entitled to damages. Another's rickety old shack was destroyed by fire started by sparks from Peninsula's locomotive. He wanted three thousand dollars. Another asked five hundred for a finger bruised by his own carelessness. There were scores of similar suits. One farmer contended the company's locomotive frightened his cow and made her go dry.

"Send for Hill," Lewiston instructed Irving. "Get old Tubby-guts here quick. They're swamping us."

Windy Hill was in Jackson talking to officials about eminent domain, greasing his way with whiskey and money, mouthing about

the Bill of Rights, the glories of the Confederate States, and the
public benefits of Peninsula Lumber Company's railroad going
through the north cut. The message from Irving sent him scurrying
back to Lebanon.

"You handle these little suits, Hill," Lewiston said.

Windy emptied a lump of tobacco, chewed and soggy, from his
mouth into the palm of his hand and threw it away. He sucked the
tobacco flakes from his teeth and spat them out. "Want me to settle
any of 'em?"

"Good God, no!" Irving stormed. "The company will never agree
to give these swindlers an inch. One judgment will blow up the home
office." He squinted his eyes at Windy's fat, impassive face. "If we
lose one suit, Hill, your job won't be worth a plugged nickel. We've
got to win them all."

Windy sat in his swivel chair, his belly overflowing into his lap,
his beady little eyes fixed on the blotter on his desk. His hands were
fat, with short, stubby fingers. "How you aim to win 'em all?"

"In court," Lewiston snapped. "No jury in the world will agree to
this robbery."

Windy sucked off another flake of tobacco and tried to spit it out.
It stuck, and he picked it off the end of his tongue. "You don't know
Wyeth Woodward. And you don't know how much folks in these
parts think of the Dabneys." His face grinned, but there was no
interruption of the slow blinking of his eyelids, no merriment in
his voice.

Lewiston glanced at Irving, and they both looked at the fat man.
"Are you serious?" Lewiston snarled. "Do you think we can actually
lose these suits?"

Windy Hill raised his eyelids and looked up. His little gray eyes
were cold and bright as silver dimes. "Hell, gentlemen, it ain't a
question of can we lose 'em. I don't think we can win 'em. Not the
way the cards are stacked."

"Then unstack them!" Lewiston exploded.

"You unstack 'em, Mr. Lewiston." Windy was looking down at
his folded hands and at his thumbs, slowly tapping together. "Or you
tell Chicago to do it. Some day, maybe, you'll learn that cards down
here don't unstack so easy. Folks down here don't like to have their
cards messed with." Windy wiped his mouth, then looked at the palm

of his hand and wiped it on the seat of his britches. "About your only chance, I reckon, is to get a new deck."

Lewiston sprang from his chair and began pacing the floor. Irving leaned back and stared at the ceiling. Windy Hill watched his thumbs.

"Who draws juries around here?" Lewiston stopped his pacing and sat down.

"They are drawn from a jury list," Windy said. Mr. Irving put some cigars beside his papers. Windy reached over and helped himself. "And there's no need in us going all around the world to get to the point. You can't do it just with juries. We won't have a chance unless every official from constable to judge sees things our way."

"You're going to be elected judge," Lewiston pronounced. "That settles the bench. You think we need the sheriff and the clerk?"

"And the Board of Supervisors," Windy assured him. He lighted his cigar, turning the tip slowly in the flame, and puffing. "We'll have to have 'em all. Got to be specially careful about the sheriff because he's the tax assessor, too. Got to be mighty sure the tax assessor is friendly."

"How much will they cost?" Irving asked calmly.

"Yes," said Lewiston. "What will it cost to run a whole slate with you? Men we can trust."

Windy's beady little eyes darted from one to the other. "I can't rightly say. Vernon Boyd is the courthouse, and Vernon runs the county. He never has bucked the Dabneys, but he might could. Yep. If I handled it, he might could."

"Go on," said Lewiston. "Get down to figures."

"Vernon can't run again for sheriff because he can't succeed himself. That's law. But if we got the right fellow to run for sheriff, he could make Vernon his chief deputy. Four years from now, we all could swing behind Vernon for sheriff again." He looked up and grinned and this time there was merriment in it. "It's a sort of flying jenny, gentlemen. You know, a merry-go-round, with the chief deputy and the sheriff getting on and off." The grin was gone and his fat face was blank and impassive again. "That is," he added, "they get on just so long as they see things our way."

Irving laughed. It was a nervous, embarrassed laugh, and there was shame in it. "Jesus Christ! We, the people. Sometimes, Lewiston, I wonder if it wouldn't be more honorable to whore for ourselves than to pimp for the company."

Lewiston cut him off with a quick gesture and a frown. "Don't moralize." He turned to Windy. "Have you a man to run for sheriff?"

"Maybe I have." He held the cigar before him, feeling it and looking at it; then he stuck it back in his jaw and spoke out of one side of his mouth. "Maybe Oscar Hardee is the very man. He lives down in the other end of the county. He's always been a Dabney man, but I can handle him." He took out his cigar, tilted his head, and funneled the smoke slowly toward the ceiling. "Course I could handle Vernon Boyd a little easier, if Mrs. Boyd got a little attention. She likes it. She'd be proud of a brass bed from Chicago."

"Make a note of that, Irving," Lewiston said.

"And she'd be mighty proud if the Thrumbulls called on her, then asked her to their house. For supper or something. Nobody ever paid Shirley Boyd much attention."

"That's out," Lewiston barked. "Thrumbull must be kept out of this."

Irving started to put his feet on the desk, then glanced at Windy, and didn't. "I was wondering about Thrumbull," Irving said. "How are you going to handle him?"

"We'll have the office call him to Chicago," Lewiston explained. "Call him in for consultation."

Windy Hill scratched his head, then scratched his stomach. "You're forgetting Nils Holmquist."

"We'll fire Holmquist," Lewiston declared. "Make a note of that, Irving. Get in touch with Chicago and tell them to fire Holmquist. Disloyalty. Inefficiency. Anything—"

"My God!" Irving grimaced. "He's been with the company twenty years."

"No sentiment." Lewiston glared at his associate. "Holmquist is in the way. Besides, he started the first suit by cutting Dabney timber."

Windy Hill's flabby jaw twisted. There was cunning in his eyes, the look of a weasel stalking a hawk. "Now, if it was me," he purred, "I wouldn't do it exactly that way. Folks are fond of Holmquist. If you up and fire him, he might hang around and make trouble. I'd transfer him back up North. And I'd wait until his mill got running." Windy was looking down at his blotter again and talking quietly, defying Lewiston's edict about no sentiment, and daring the lawyer to do anything about it. "I wouldn't be such a son of a bitch as not give Holmquist the fun of seeing his mill open. He's worked mighty hard to get it going."

Irving and Lewiston exchanged glances and the truth slowly emerged, shaking their Yankee assurance and threatening to strangle it. They were dealing with a new, a raw South without grace, slyly licking its lips in secret, but seeking sympathy by openly licking old wounds and ostentatiously vaunting its legendary pride. This was the new and cunning South, patiently waiting for the North to blunder, as the North always did. Irving and Lewiston suddenly hated Hill and feared him; but they had to have him, and they knew he was right about Holmquist.

Lewiston said, "Very well, Mr. Hill." He said it with respect and loathing, but for the first time he addressed him as Mr. Hill. Windy didn't look up, pretending not to notice that he was being accorded a new deference. The Chicago lawyer continued. "We'll have Holmquist sent back North after the mill opens. Now I suggest we map your campaign. How much will it cost?"

Windy frowned and puckered his lips. "As I told you, I can't rightly say. But you just relax. Just leave the timing to me."

"I wasn't talking about timing, Mr. Hill," said Lewiston. "I was talking about expenses."

"You leave the timing to me. We'll bypass the primary."

"Is that smart?" Irving was impatient. "I thought that down here if you aren't nominated in the Democratic primary, you don't get elected."

"We'll bypass the primary." Windy nodded approval of his plan. "We'll let Charlie Owens and the old regulars win the primary. Then I'll load up and shoot my gun in the regular election. We'll stand as Independent Democrats pledged to clean house. Anti-Peninsula Democrats. It won't be too hard—" He flicked his eyes at each of them. "Provided you don't get in my way."

Irving stared at Windy as if he were a toad. Lewiston filled his pipe and wished his Chicago associates, who considered themselves proficient in manipulating the will of the people, could see the Mississippi lawyer in action.

"Have it your way, Mr. Hill." Lewiston lighted his pipe, then added, "I suppose we can get all these suits postponed? That is, until after the election?"

"Sure." Windy waved the matter aside. "The court always gives ample time for replies. Down here the law is just a little bit personal."

"Now," Irving insisted, "what will it cost?"

"I ain't saying." Windy's words were as final as a door slamming. "I told you I didn't rightly know. And I ain't saying."

It was evident they couldn't pin him down and Lewiston shrugged. "Draw what you need. List it as legislative expenses and good will. And it's company policy, Mr. Hill, that our local representative doesn't add more than ten per cent for himself."

Mr. Hill chuckled and got up from his chair. "Reckon we gentlemen worked out our plans just fine." The coldness and the calculation were gone. Cephus Hill was a smiling, genial hand-shaker again. "Make yourself at home. I'm going over and buy Vernon Boyd a bottle of beer and some cigars. Better take some cigars to Oscar Hardee, too." He reached the door. "Effective right now I'm not lawing for Peninsula any more. But don't forget I'm still on the payroll."

"Naturally, Mr. Hill," Lewiston said.

"And don't be surprised if you hear me low-rating the company in public. Don't get hurt if I call you all a bunch of yellow-bellied Yankees and tail-wetting polecats. I won't mean it." Again he chuckled. "Or maybe I will." He opened the door and went out.

Lewiston peered at the door, moistening his lips. Irving was grinning. "Is there a parable somewhere about the wolves lying down with a snake?"

"There is now." Lewiston pushed back his chair. "Come on, we'll see Thrumbull."

They crossed the hall into the superintendent's office at the rear of the building. Mr. Thrumbull was at his desk. Lewiston went straight to the point. "How quickly can you get the mill in operation?"

"What's the use of sawing lumber when there's no railroad to haul it out?" Thrumbull did not trust the lawyers.

"You leave the railroad to us. We'll have it through the north cut by the first of the year."

The superintendent was dubious. "I thought the Dabneys said you weren't coming through the north cut."

"We say we are." Lewiston snapped. "How soon can you open your mill?"

"By September 1st."

"Then do it. Make it a holiday. That'll get friends for the company." Lewiston glanced at the walls, bare except for maps of Peninsula's holdings. "Once we're meeting a fat payroll, we can handle these pesky people with less trouble."

Mr. Thrumbull picked up a letter from his desk. It was from Aven MacIvor's attorney, contesting a boundary between Peninsula's property and the MacIvor holdings. "What about this claim?" the superintendent asked. "Shouldn't we buy some of her timber and fix our boundaries once and for all?" He passed the letter to Lewiston.

"Refer it to Chicago," the lawyer said. "It's a home office decision. As for me, I think we own all the timber we need in this God-forsaken country. That woman hasn't got a damn thing I want."

"She's got something I want," Irving said, and they all laughed.

An undercurrent of suspicion spread through the valley, threatening any day to break out in a dozen places. The Cajuns and the Negroes whispered in their cabins, and the Irish wailed premonitions of disaster. Gar Rivers fathomed the undercurrent, knowing it was fear and greed, and prayed it would run its course before it roared into the open, into violence.

In all the valley, the man apparently least concerned by the hidden rumblings was Sans Dabney. He went his way, logging on a part time schedule, helping at The Store when Mr. Charlie needed him, and singing and laughing as though he had no worries.

Kyd Dabney saw the change in Sans and wondered. Was he finding a contentment with Ruth Thrumbull that he had never found with Louisa? And when was that Cuban girl leaving the valley? She'd been in Lebanon too long already; she was abusing valley hospitality. When would Mingo be shed of her?

Sans himself occasionally was puzzled because he sang when he should be serious, cocked his hat on the side of his head and whistled a merry tune when he should be worrying about lack of work and lack of money. He never attributed his gaiety to Ruth Thrumbull, or realized how often they laughed when they were together.

He seldom called on Louisa and, although he saw her every day at

The Store, she was just a woman he had loved as a girl. That, and nothing more. She had taught him that the mysteries of life, fierce and compelling, were but an incidental part of contentment. Ruth Thrumbull was teaching him, though he was unaware of the lesson, that the nearness of an unselfish woman is a source of peace. So he laughed and lived with a freedom he had never known before, and still did not understand.

In the surety of youth and the vanity of all men, he believed his gaiety grew from something he himself had done. He had stymied Peninsula. Whipped 'em to a frazzle! The cross-ties were gathering moss and the stacked rails were gathering rust at the north cut, proof that he had blocked them. It was their move next.

Sans was the serious one turned gay, and now it was Mingo's brow that furrowed. The younger brother worked all day at his mill, cutting the few logs that Sans hauled, or pored over The Store plans with Louisa. Under his swift direction and her constant prodding, the builders were finishing the annex ahead of schedule.

However, not even the completion of the annex or the feud with Peninsula held Mingo's interest as the summer waned. Sometimes while working with Louisa he forgot that she was there, and stared down toward the Thrumbull house where Rafaela awaited the summons that would take her out of the valley.

Mr. Charlie sat on The Store's porch and watched it all. His own shelves were almost empty and Mingo would not restock them. That was Louisa's advice and the younger brother followed it. So Mr. Charlie sat and waited and watched. Occasionally he strolled down to the south cut and to Peninsula's store, envying their stock of staples and hardware. He just stood around, his hands in his pockets rattling his keys, as they unpacked and displayed their goods on shelves and counters, getting ready for their opening.

Ruth Thrumbull, buying from Mr. Charlie because she loved the old man, often dropped by and sat on the porch with him, listening to his wisdom and his woes, and learning from him the story of Lebanon. He helped her contact prominent Mississippians in her campaign for Cuba, a campaign in which Rafaela did not participate because she was a foreigner and long since had learned that Americans resented suggestions from an outsider, even while liberally supporting the outsider's cause.

The old man never ceased to wonder about Elmo and because the drummer drove away with José Marti, Mr. Charlie associated his friend with Cuba. His loneliness for his crony was one reason he helped Ruth, and, too, he liked her. She went fishing with him, bringing sandwiches and cookies for their lunch, and she baited her own hook and strung her own fish. He understood why Ruth Thrumbull sought his company; why she was content to sit with him, watching the drama of the valley unfold. She, too, was lonesome. Sans was her companion, but never her comrade. He sang with her, but never to her.

The elder brother visited Louisa often enough to keep the village gossips quiet, careful to hide the truth that the childhood romance had fallen apart. Laurel Woodward came home and instinctively realized that the old ardor had cooled, that Louisa intended to make a new life, and to make Mingo Dabney an important part of it. Then Kyd suspected the truth, that Sans had drawn away from Louisa, and she was as pleased as Laurel. Only Mr. Charlie, with the wisdom that enables some men to see into the hearts of other men, knew that Sans' path and Louisa's path had divided somewhere along the road from Ellisville. He kept his council and he, too, was pleased.

Sometimes when the old man and Ruth were at The Store, he sent for Sans to ask advice about men they should write concerning Cuba's cause. Sans often stayed at The Store and helped them, and Mr. Charlie always opened two bottles of cold beer and served Ruth a celery tonic. Occasionally Sans drove Ruth around the county, to church rallies and picnics where she told the Cuban story. No one thought anything about it, and neither did Sans.

The Democratic primary came and went without excitement and the county renominated all the regulars, including Mr. Charlie for the Board of Supervisors. At the next meeting of the board, Mr. Charlie got to talking about Cuba, and kept on talking until it was too late to vote on Peninsula's petition that the road be improved to their mill, thence to its village and its store.

The valley, trembling in an undertow of an inevitable showdown between the Dabneys and Peninsula, was surprised when Mingo made no effort to open his new department before the company could open its store. He seemed content to wait and was not disturbed when Peninsula's store opened, giving away soda pop and candy. The

people flocked there, delighted to learn that the new store was under-
selling Mingo. There was a whole cent-a-pound difference in coffee
beans. The Company distributed handbills announcing its cut-rate
prices, and these prices made friends. Mr. Charlie's chin hung low in
despair and even Mingo was worried, but not Louisa.

On the Saturday following the opening of the store, Mr. Charlie's
old customers crowded into Peninsula's new place and Mr. Charlie
was alone. The annex for Louisa's department was painted and ready
for showcases. Louisa was at home writing to merchants in New
Orleans. Mingo was at his mill.

Sans, hot and dusty, rode up to The Store for a cool drink. His
crew didn't work on Saturday afternoons and he and Ronnie had been
tramping the woods, looking for signs of turkey and quail to be
hunted that fall.

"Hi, there, Mr. Charlie." Sans threw his reins over a hitching post.
"What'd you rather do or go afishing?" He stepped to the porch and
flung the sweat from his face.

"I'd rather do." Mr. Charlie didn't look up, swinging his foot, loose
at the end of his crossed legs. Two Cuban newspapers lay in his lap.
Ruth read them to him, and Mr. Charlie, when anybody was watching, pretended to read them for himself, although he didn't know a
word of Spanish.

"What's the news from Cuba?" Sans nodded toward the papers.
He went into The Store and came out with a bottle of beer for
Mr. Charlie and one for himself.

The old storekeeper took off his spectacles and blew on them,
wiping them. It was a deliberate gesture. "All hell's fixing to bust
loose in Cuba." He ran his hand around the nape of his neck, scratching the red skin. "Tell you sump'n else—" Mr. Charlie tilted his
bottle and drank, then smacked his lips. "José Martí's in New York
but he'll be heading for Cuba before long. And when he does, Miss
Rafaela will be leaving us."

Sans did not reply.

Mr. Charlie folded the papers and laid them on the floor by his
chair. "What you reckon Mingo will do?"

"I don't know."

A few customers straggled in and the old merchant went inside to
serve them. He came back to the porch with two more bottles of beer

and a handful of gingersnaps. Sans guyed him about eating up his profits.

Mr. Charlie didn't seem to hear the teasing. He set his bottle of beer on the floor beside him and munched his gingersnaps. "You got a heap of sand in your craw these days. Don't seem to be giving much thought to Peninsula. Maybe they aiming to take a tuck in your innards."

"Let 'em tuck. They're bogged down at the north cut and our lawsuit has 'em worried. I feel powerful good."

"But you ain't doing good, son. You ain't cutting much timber. I bet you ain't breaking even."

"Just about even. That's all a man can expect in hard times." Sans nibbled one of the cakes. "I'm eating regular and I sleep like a baby. The fish are biting and the woodbines atwining—"

"And the whangdoodle is making music all the day." Mr. Charlie laughed as he finished the old quotation. "How's your lawsuit coming? I see Windy Hill puffing around, but them Chicago lawyers are just setting. A lawyer setting is like a hen setting. Something is fixing to hatch."

Ruth Thrumbull drove by, saw the two men and waved at them. They watched her until her buggy disappeared down by the court-house square. Sans was thoughtful, his mind returning to Mr. Charlie's words. "The lawyers got to be setting. It'll be months before we go to trial."

"Uh huh," the old man mused. He held up his bottle, squinted through it, then tilted it again and finished his beer. "What you aim to do with all that money if you win?"

"Invest it here in The Store with Mingo."

Charlie Owens crossed his thin legs and propped one elbow on his knee. He was looking at the pike, at the dust, and watching the heat waves shimmer. "Going to be any strings on your investment?"

Sans flexed his muscles, then released them and yawned. The heat made him drowsy. "Won't be just strings, Mr. Charlie. There'll be ropes. I'm a salt-meat and plow-trace man. I got more faith in salt than satin. My money'll go into your part of The Store. Not in the annex."

The old man scratched behind his ear and looked away. "Well, now, I do declare."

"I know you're pretty upset about things," the boy said. "Mingo knows it, too. But he's right, Mr. Charlie. A ladies' department will make money quick. That's what Mingo needs—quick cash. It'll be a cushion against Peninsula's store." He reached out and put his hand on the old man's knee. "You just wait. Everything will be all right."

"A man my age can't wait too long. I'm just about shed of my waiting days."

Sans said, "The Store has always handled general merchandise. Mingo won't change that. As soon as Louisa's department gets to humming, he'll put a lot of his profit in your department. You'll build your business up again. You wait and see."

Mr. Charlie didn't hear him and Sans, expecting a reply, glanced over at the old man, then followed his gaze down the pike, down toward the village. A two-horse buggy, wheeling fast up from the south cut, was passing the courthouse, the Jasper House, Wyeth Woodward's office.

"Elmo Batson!" Mr. Charlie ejected the words as though he himself did not believe them. His face suddenly was tense and his tired old eyes lighted in the beauty of a wish fulfilled. He got up quickly from his chair, craning his long neck down the road, waiting and watching, maybe praying.

Sans blinked his eyes rapidly, resting them from the glare of the sun, then strained his gaze toward the oncoming buggy. It was Elmo Batson all right. Sure as shooting.

The team pounded up almost to The Store, close enough for Mr. Charlie to be certain, and he gasped his joy and jumped from the porch, running for the buggy and calling to Elmo.

"Where you been?" He shouted the demand, kicking up dust as he ran down the road. "Where the hell you been so long and how come you didn't write me?" He reached the buggy and grabbed a bridle, checking the team and repeating his plea. "Where you been?"

Elmo wrapped the reins around his buggy whip and leaped out, embracing Mr. Charlie and whacking his back. They stood there in the middle of the street, in the dust of the hot summer afternoon, hugging each other and laughing.

Sans sauntered over and leaned against a post. The older brother knew why the drummer was back, or thought he knew.

Mr. Charlie held the bridle, walking in the road and leading the team toward The Store, jabbering all the while, upbraiding Elmo for having deserted him. "And that upstart who comes in here calling himself a drummer!" Mr. Charlie spat. "Don't know a shirt from Shinola." He turned around and glared. "Where the hell you been, Elmo?"

The drummer grinned when he saw Sans. It was not the happy-go-lucky grin of other days, not the old jaunty greeting; it was almost a serious grin, a signal of friendship. The Dabney boy raised his hand. "Howdy, Mister." He swung down from the porch. "Been taking any wooden nickels?"

"Hello, Sans." Elmo's grip was hard, a new kind of handshake from the drummer who so long had used a hand clasp to sell goods rather than to seal friendships.

Mr. Charlie, as excited as a boy with a secret, kept nudging Elmo, prompting him, but not giving him time to get in a word edgeways. "Elmo's throwing in with them Cubans," Mr. Charlie said. "He ain't foolin' me. Know him like a book. Ain't that so, Elmo? Ain't you been working with them Cubans? I had a hunch all along—"

Again Elmo grinned at Sans, then put his arm around his crony and together they walked up the steps to the porch. "I ain't got long to stay." He sat on the bench, crossing his legs and looking down the pike toward the east ridge and the Thrumbull house. "Just about long enough for a bottle of beer."

Mr. Charlie sat beside him. "It's them Cubans, ain't it? You're working with José Marti, ain't you?"

Sans said, "Yes, Elmo. What time is it?"

The drummer eyed the elder brother, then looked away again. "It's getting late."

"How late?" Sans propped his foot on the bench, leaning close to Elmo. "How late is it getting?" It was valley talk, the valley's way of asking if a time of decision was at hand.

"Pretty late. Mr. Charlie's right. I'm working with José Marti. I had to do it." Elmo touched one of the old signs on the wall, straightening it, a sign advertising Rosadora soap. "You can't know that man without trying to help him. Things are fixing to bust wide open in Cuba."

Sans dreaded to ask the question that was in his mind, but it must be asked. "If things are fixing to blow up in Cuba, then how come you here?"

Mr. Charlie lowered his head and peered over his spectacles and Sans leaned forward, watching Elmo, seeing the lines around his mouth, the tight lines around his eyes. The drummer felt in his coat for a cigar, bit off the end and spat it out. "I came back to get Rafaela Galban—"

"I knew it," Mr. Charlie said. "Sure as hell, I knew it."

Sans said quickly, "When are you leaving?"

"In a few minutes."

"Where you going? Where you taking her?"

"Sorry, Sans. That's none of your business." He said it gently, but firmly.

The elder brother straightened, then reached over and put his hand on Elmo's arm. "I'm making it some of my business. It's getting late in this valley, too. I'm liable to need my brother. So where are you taking her?"

Elmo's face whitened, the white creeping up his red jowls and across the harsh brown skin of his face. "God A'mighty! It's like that with her and Mingo, huh?"

"It's like that," Sans said.

Mr. Charlie jerked his head to one side, cocking it low over his left shoulder like a wise old rooster. "That's the way it is. So where you taking her? Sans has got a right to know. Mingo is his brother."

Elmo Batson did not hesitate. This was another matter; this now was Dabney business. "I'm taking her to Florida. José Marti will meet us there. After that, I don't know."

"Thanks." Sans stepped quickly to the edge of the porch. "Mr. Charlie will get your beer. You two got a lot to talk about. I'll see you later." He jumped from the porch and walked quickly toward the mill. He must find Mingo. He must tell his brother.

The younger one was not at the mill and Sans hurried back to The Store where his horse was tied, mounted and rode first to The House. Kyd had not seen Mingo since dinner, and Sans galloped back down the pike. Elmo's buggy was gone from The Store, but Mr. Charlie was sitting on the porch, staring forlornly toward the Thrumbull house.

"He's gone to get her," the old man said.

"Have you seen Mingo?"

"Try the Woodward place. Louisa sent for him a while back and he may be over there."

Mingo was on the porch of the Woodward house, studying plans with Louisa. Sans called him to the gate and she followed him. There was neither time nor place for privacy, no chance to speak to his brother alone, so Sans said, "Elmo Batson is back."

The color drained from Mingo's face and the tan of his face was like a mask. "What for?"

Louisa said, "It's high time he got back. If Elmo expects us to do business with him, it's about time he showed up."

Sans ignored her and so did Mingo. The two brothers looked at each other and the elder one nodded, then said, "He's down at the Thrumbull place. You want my horse?"

He handed the reins to Mingo and the younger brother, his lips tight, rode away, leaving Louisa there by the gate, and Sans with her.

"What is it?" she asked. "What's all this excitement about Elmo Batson?" Her mind turned rapidly, fitting everything into place; then she looked up at Sans, the hardness back in her eyes. "It's that Cuban girl. Elmo came back for her."

"That's it." Sans turned away. "It's Rafaela Galban." He'd go back to The Store and relieve Mr. Charlie; he'd give the old man a chance to go to the Thrumbull place and be with Elmo. Besides, if Mr. Charlie occupied Elmo's time, then Mingo might have a few minutes alone with Rafaela.

"So Miss Galban is going away." Louisa called it after him. "I must go down and tell her goodbye. Maybe I can help her pack."

Sans glanced over his shoulder, cringing within himself as he looked back at the woman he once had loved, seeing her as she was, standing there smiling at him, taunting him. "Ruth is at home. She can help her pack."

Louisa drew herself erect in exaggerated surprise. "Oh, but it's only proper for me to bid our guest goodbye. So if you'll excuse me, I'll drive down there and offer my services."

Sans hurried away from her, and on across Bogue Homa and to The Store. Mr. Charlie thanked him, but didn't care to go to the Thrumbull house. "Just don't want to go." His legs were crossed and he was swinging his foot. "I got a feeling, son." The old man got up and wiped the dust off one of the signs that Elmo had tacked there years before. "I got a feeling that when he goes away this time, he won't be coming to see us no more." He reached for a rocking chair, pulled it near to Sans and sat down, slowly rocking.

The two men were silent, each thinking the thing that troubled him; the old storekeeper thinking of his crony; Sans wondering about his brother. The porch was shady and twilight swept down the ridges, the shadows stretching long from the trees.

Elmo's buggy came around the corner of the courthouse and Mr. Charlie stiffened. "Yonder he comes. He aims to go to Ellisville and catch a train for Savannah, Georgia, and then to Florida."

Mingo Dabney was riding beside the buggy, and Sans' heart swelled until it choked him; then seemed to go out of him and down to his brother. Elmo reined his team in front of The Store and Mingo swung off his horse and stepped to the porch. Sans moved over on the bench and Mingo sat by him, watching the buggy, watching Rafaela there by Elmo. She was wearing black and her mantilla was deep over her forehead. She looked straight ahead, up the pike toward the north cut, until finally she turned her eyes toward the porch and her tears brimmed over, wetting her long lashes. "Goodbye, Sans Dabney," she called.

"Goodbye, Rafaela."

She put her handkerchief to her eyes quickly and looked at Mr. Charlie. "Goodbye, Mr. Charlie."

"Goodbye, Miss Rafaela." The old man filled up, but swallowed the lump that clung in his throat. "God bless you."

Mingo stared down at his hands, squeezing his hands, the joints in his fingers cracking as he pressed them. He did not tell her farewell. He did not even look at her, but stared down at his hands, squeezing them.

Elmo reached for his buggy whip and Rafaela turned toward the porch again, looking at Sans and Mr. Charlie; glancing at Mingo. "Thank you all," she said. "You have been kind to me."

The drummer tapped his horses with his whip. He waved his hand at Mr. Charlie. "So long, you fellows. So long, Mr. Charlie. Don't take any wooden nickels." The team pulled away, moving into a quick trot and dust swirled behind the buggy. Then, they were gone.

Mingo looked up, his eyes following the buggy up the pike, past The Tree, up to the north cut. "I didn't get to see her by herself," he whispered to Sans. "Louisa was there. I didn't get to tell her goodbye. Not like I wanted to."

The locusts were out again, rasping their twilight song in the water oaks and the swallows darted low over The Store. Twilight was moving west through the valley and Mr. Charlie went inside and lit a lamp. "You boys want a bottle of beer?" He slapped at a moth that fluttered near.

Sans said, "Not for me. How about you, Lebuba?"

The younger brother did not hear him. He was staring toward the north cut, the dust settling where the buggy had passed. Then he looked up at the sky, a thin red streak low in the west; and dark to the south—dark over the Gulf and south to Cuba.

"Let's go home to supper," Sans said.

"All right." Mingo shook himself and rubbed his hand across his mouth. "Yes. That's all right."

They arose and bade Mr. Charlie goodnight. The old man came to the door and leaned against the jamb and watched the brothers walk together up the pike. The swallows streaked swift to their nesting place. The fireflies came out, dotting the night with yellow.

"Sans?" The word was a whisper.

"What is it?"

"How far is it to Cuba?" Mingo's words were low but to the elder brother they were as loud as hammers striking at the north cut.

The brothers walked the pike, the night wrapping itself about them, until Sans found the words he must say. "Cuba is a long way."

"She said it's about six hundred miles." He looked over at Bogue Homa's swamp where he had seen fox-glow; seen it in the rain. Then he turned to his brother again. "I don't think that's far, do you?"

"It depends on the man who's going," Sans' words came slowly. "And what he's going for. And how bad he wants to get there."

Chapter thirteen

THE FIRST ANNOUNCEMENT that Peninsula's mill would begin operations on Saturday, September 15, 1894, appeared on the bulletin board at the post office. Wyeth Woodward and Gar Rivers wondered why the company was opening its mill before it finished its railroad. Sans, however, showed no concern. He had confidence in the law and in his cause.

It was Louisa who went into a frenzy of activity at the news. Mingo was amazed by her vitality and concentration of purpose, and annoyed by her insistence on talking with him throughout the day, then sending for him at night to discuss the annex and the new stock. Since Rafaela's departure he could not bring his mind back to The Store; he cared not whether Louisa stocked silks or satins, camisoles or carpets, so long as he himself was left free to remember, and dream, and hope.

The elder brother watched the north cut, the way in, where Peninsula bided its time, ready to thrust into the valley. The younger one watched the south cut, the way out, the road to Mobile, to the Gulf and Cuba.

"The company will have a big celebration the day the mill opens." Louisa was bustling about and talking to Mingo. "We can cash in on it. We'll open my department that day."

The showcases were polished and Louisa spent hours training the Cajun girl and the Irish girl as salesladies, teaching them to display the goods, particularly the expensive items. "Flatter them," she instructed. "Tell the fat ones they're thin, and the bony ones they're trim. A woman will go without bread for a bottle of perfume. The profit on bread is two per cent. It's two hundred per cent on perfume." She hung a sign, "Ladies' Department," over the entrance to the annex. It looked strange next to the faded front of the old store.

A band of Irish horse traders arrived in New Hebron more than a week before "Opening Day," as the people began calling September 15. A patent medicine show came to town and Gar Rivers resented the buffoonery of the blackface comedians, although other Negroes in the valley enjoyed it and took up many of the jokes and songs.

Mr. Charlie, as head of the Board of Supervisors, asked everybody to clean up and paint up. He himself dusted the windows of The Store, a few of them.

Aven MacIvor came from Mobile and resumed residence at the hotel. She wanted to be on hand when the bigwigs of the company came down from Chicago.

Mr. G. T. Thrumbull was everywhere, often going at night to his mill to check the boilers and the kiln, fretting that something might go wrong. Nils Holmquist was doing the same thing at his lumber camp.

The Dabneys were in the background. For the first time since the family pioneered into the valley, almost a century before, they were playing second fiddle. Kyd didn't like it and Bruce didn't care.

In Chicago, Keith Alexander read in a trade paper about Opening Day, and, for a moment, considered going to Lebanon and sharing the excitement. He wished Morna were home. They could go together. They hadn't visited Lebanon in years. But Morna was in Europe with the children and Keith dismissed the idea. Besides, he knew that Aven MacIvor was there; and Keith Alexander and Aven MacIvor in Lebanon at the same time might cause tension.

However, three Peninsula executives and their wives journeyed from Chicago to the valley, the women in trepidation, and the men in awe of the vast undeveloped country. The women saw danger and romance behind every tree. The men couldn't see the romance for the trees, and envisioned sawmills and factories in every field. The Yankee women, victims of the Southern myth, saw the Negroes as laughing, shuffling creatures of good will and song. Their husbands saw them as a reservoir of untouched labor, and planned how to tap that reservoir and pipe it north.

Mr. Thrumbull sent two surreys up to Ellisville to meet the

Nabobs, and entertained them in his home. The night before Opening Day, Ruth gave a Peninsula dinner party. She suggested that the Dabneys and the Woodwards, even Mr. Charlie, be invited, but her father wisely vetoed the plan. The railroad might be discussed and cause embarrassment.

All that night Smoke Jackson barbecued beef and pork, cooking whole carcasses over trenches smoldering with red coals. The Ladies Aid of the Free Church made barrels of lemonade. Opening was set for high noon.

By dawn, New Hebron was a mecca for the curious. Wagons rolled in, and in the hickory wagon chairs sat the lanky men and gaunt women, staring, blank-eyed and swag-jawed, as their teams pulled slow to the hitching rails. They came from along Bogue Homa and from across the east ridge.

One little boy in the courthouse square clung to his mother's calico dress and begged his father, "Show me a Yankee, Papa."

Mr. Charlie opened The Store at six o'clock, hoping to catch some of the trade. Louisa, however, set her department's opening for the fashionable hour of eight, and by seven o'clock a crowd was milling around in front of the annex.

Mingo circulated among them, welcoming them. So did Kyd and Laurel. Sans and Wyeth and Bruce sat on the porch of The Store and watched. Mr. Charlie stayed inside, rattling hardware and pretending to be busy.

A few minutes before eight, Louisa rode up in Mingo's buggy. She was wearing a gray dress and a black straw sailor hat. The women in the crowd murmured and stepped back as she walked up the steps, turned and smiled at the crowd, then unlocked the door and invited them in.

The first customer was Ruth Thrumbull. Louisa saw to that and waited on Ruth herself. Then she pinned a flower on her and escorted her to the front of the annex. An itinerant photographer, traveling the country with a Shetland pony, took a picture of Louisa and her first customer. Louisa's sign was in the background. Elmo's sign and the front of the old store were left out.

Windy Hill, smiling and shaking hands, made a purchase for his wife and congratulated Louisa. Vernon Boyd brought his wife and she fingered the silks. Aven MacIvor remained in her hotel room.

She didn't care to stir in the heat, and, besides, it was a Dabney occasion and she was not a Dabney.

Mingo was not needed in the annex and he felt strange, dressed in his best, talking to women and accepting their praise. He glanced frequently at Mr. Charlie's empty shelves, and eventually told Louisa, "I'm in the way. I don't know anything about all these things."

"Very well." She was quick to agree. "You go on about your other business."

"Aren't you going down to the mill opening?"

"Heavens, no. I hate barbecue and I don't want to stand in the hot sun."

The wives of the Chicago bigwigs were impressed by the annex, and more impressed by Louisa. Where was the myth the North cherished about the shy, languid Southern girl? There was the myth, Louisa Woodward! She was smiling and pampering her customers while her memory retained an account of every sale, every dollar coming in.

Sans and Mingo rode to the mill. The plant was new and shiny, its red paint absorbing the sun, its boilers hissing, its saws primed. Nils hailed the brothers. Ruth waved and Mr. Thrumbull tipped his hat. The Chicago women ogled the Dabney boys, particularly Sans, and one of them giggled and whispered to Ruth, and the Thrumbull girl turned away.

At exactly high noon, the whistle of the Peninsula Lumber Company sounded. It was a hoarse, throaty cry, a call for men to come thereafter at dawn, a dismissal at dusk.

Sans Dabney's oxen heard the whistle and were frightened. It was a new sound and the deer heard it and fled.

The people heard the whistle and left off wandering around the streets of New Hebron, or resting on the courthouse square, and they hurried down to the south cut. Aven MacIvor saw them filing past the hotel and only then did she leave her room, going to The Store to see Louisa's goods.

The crowd boarded the company's logging train and chugged out to Nils' camp. There the big Swede was in charge and while the people watched, his double-edged ax bit into a pine. The itinerant photographer took his picture. Someone called out, "Hey, Nils! Watch it! You'll break the camera." Nils grinned at the crowd.

Another shouted, "Let Sans Dabney fell that tree." A cry of
approval went up from the valley folks.

A crew finished the job Nils started, then a skidder gang took
over. The steel cable of the skidder gripped the tree, the big pine
that saw De Soto, remembered Tecumseh, and now was a giant
of heartwood lying helpless on the ground.

"Take her away!" a foreman roared.

"Take her away!" the echo answered.

A winch strained and steam hissed into the sultry air as the skidder tightened, the cable snaking the log through the woods, dragging it from the stump to the logging car.

No oxen. No men.

Steel and steam, and a log ripping through the forest.

Sans Dabney groaned as saplings were snapped and crushed.
"There goes the valley of Lebanon."

"Oh, I don't know," Mingo said. "Pines grow fast. They'll come
back."

The log was hoisted aboard a car. The people climbed on the train
for the trip to the mill, following the first log. Nils rode the locomotive. Officials of the company and their women were in the ca-
boose. Sans and Mingo traveled on the open cars with the people,
in the sun.

Little boys jumped off the train and hopped back on while their
mothers screamed at them. Sans watched and finally could stand it
no longer. He, too, jumped off, ran beside the train, and jumped
back on again. Mingo laughed at him; the dogs running alongside
the train barked at him, and the children called his name.

The first log was dumped into the mill pond and a logger maneu-
vered it to the waiting chains that snared it into the mill. There it
balanced a second. A blast of steam, a whine of steel, and the log,
the Lebanon pine, was shoved into the blade. It trembled and oozed
its sap, bleeding as the steel cut it into a thing of use to mankind,
changing it from beauty and ageless dignity into a roof for a man's
head, a table for his food, a bed for his rest.

Mr. Thrumbull ordered the first piece of lumber sawed into souve-
nirs and gave one to each executive. He kept one for himself. He
overlooked Mr. Lewiston and Mr. Irving, although they were with
the official party; but he went out of his way to give Nils Holmquist
a slab of the wood.

So at last it was done! And the saws kept turning—ripping and whining into more logs. The steam hissed a rhythm. The pumps churned and smoke poured from the stacks, writing a new alphabet: new words and new laws for the valley.

The multitude walked down to the picnic ground and Mr. Thrumbull introduced his guests, and they all made speeches. One said, "That whistle is the cry of progress. That skidder is the chain that will draw the North and the South together forever."

The people had no idea what he was talking about. They were not interested. They were hungry. The children were tired and fretful, and the people wanted meat, not words; they wanted some of that bread stacked in mounds on the picnic tables. They wanted some of the cole slaw, not promises from Chicago. The mill was running. The whistle had sounded. Now, it was time to eat.

They all were mighty glad when Brother Eubanks of the Free Church was called on to say the blessing. The preacher understood, and blessed it short.

Smoke Jackson fixed special plates for the Dabneys and the Woodwards, who, without Louisa, ate together in the shade. Nobody missed Aven. Ruth brought lemonade to Kyd and Laurel, and thanked them for attending the celebration.

All afternoon, the people feasted and talked, the Peninsula crowd keeping to itself and the valley folks to themselves. Gar Rivers ate with the Negroes although the Dabneys asked him to eat with them. Ruth was the only person who went from her people to the valley folks, from Chicago to Bogue Homa.

Kyd and Laurel drove home in mid-afternoon. Wyeth and Bruce stayed until all the lemonade was gone. Mingo returned to The Store, and Sans sought out Ronnie Sullivan; they left the mill and went back into the woods, back to their ox barn.

Ronnie had a jug there and he and Sans drank together. They took only one drink, however. They simply were in no mood for any more. Neither discussed the opening, but sat on a wagon bed staring down toward the south cut where smoke belched into the sky, rising above the pines, rising above everything. Ronnie reached for his tobacco and passed it to Sans. "The fun's over, bub. Now what you aim to do?"

"Cut trees." Sans dared not look at his friend. "We'll start cutting tomorrow back in the east section."

Ronnie scratched under his arm and spat. "How much timber did you sell Mingo last month?"

"Enough to meet my payroll."

"Aw, hell, Sans. You ain't cutting trees. Yonder goes your business in that smoke. You got no more use for a woods boss than for three thumbs."

Sans knew he was right, but he didn't want to face it. "Long as a Dabney tree is standing you have a job."

"Doing what?" Ronnie asked.

Sans didn't reply.

The big Irishman lay back on the wagon bed and stared at the loft of the barn. It was time to feed the oxen. They were restless in their stalls. "Joe Doyle ain't got the heart to tell you," Ronnie said. "But he aims to go up to the Mainline and get a job with Eastman-Gardner."

"It's a good company." Twilight was on them and Sans felt the gathering gloom, the coming of night and the going of his men. He shook off his mood. "Now let's feed the oxen. We'll sell some of 'em pretty quick. No need feeding 'em unless they earn their hay."

He didn't want Ronnie to see his eyes and his trembling lip and he was grateful for the shadows in the barn, shadows easing back into the corners. Fishbait and Debo were gone. Now Joe Doyle. The oxen must go, too. And the wagons. The hardwood spokes would last for years and the iron rims, some of them beaten in place by Bruce Dabney, were on to stay. They would defy rust and time for years and years; but, eventually, they would crumble like all the rest.

"Where you aim to sell 'em?" Ronnie asked, a catch in his voice. "Who'll buy such stuff these days?"

"Take 'em up to Ellisville. Yoke eight oxen to each wagon, and get what you can. We'll keep just enough to get by on." The decision relieved him. He should have sold them weeks before. A man is a fool to let his sentiment dictate to his reason.

The ox boss didn't reply. He closed his eyes and rested his muscles, stretching them. He was a burden to Sans. Or so he thought. He got up and went for another drink out of the jug. Sans declined, and the Irishman returned the jug to the crib without tilting it. It was no fun drinking alone.

Daydown deepened the shadows in the barn, making way for night. The two men lit lanterns and fed the oxen, then drove the beasts into the lot, to water-troughs. The oxen lowed and Sans and Ronnie walked back into the barn and sat on the wagon, waiting for the animals to bed down.

Lights gleamed at the south cut, fires under the boilers of the mill, but there were no lights at the north cut. Work there had ceased.

A horse came pounding up the ridge and Ronnie and Sans strained their ears, wondering who was seeking them at the beginning of night, and why. Then Sans recognized Nils Holmquist and called out to him. The Peninsula man opened the lot gate and entered the barn, eyeing Ronnie in the lantern light.

"What's up?" Sans asked.

Ronnie sat upright, his big hands on the edge of the wagon bed. He never took his eyes from Nils.

"Just riding around," the Swede said. "Thought I'd come see if anybody was here, somebody to talk to." He put one hand on the wagon bed, then the other, extending his fingers, opening and closing his fists. "Got a chew, Ronnie?"

The Irishman handed him his plug. "Take a good bite. You've earned it."

"You sure have," Sans said. "And there's a jug in the crib. You did things up brown today."

"Thanks." The way he said it prompted Sans to look at him closely. He felt tragedy in Nils' words, tragedy and anger and bitterness. One of the oxen nuzzled the Peninsula man and he opened the stall and drove the beast in, slapping his rump as he passed. "Uh huh. They're mighty pleased with the way everything went. So pleased they're giving me a soft job up in Michigan."

"The hell you say!" Ronnie leaned forward. "I didn't know they ever did anything nice for a fellow."

Sans gawked at Nils, at his blue eyes, usually so bright but now sad. Sensing misfortune, he spoke slowly. "Peninsula cut all its timber in Michigan years ago. What kind of job they offering you?"

"Office job. Whittling little sticks, I suppose. They're kicking me upstairs."

"The yellow-bellied bastards!" Ronnie muttered it.

"Then they'll kick me out for good." His distress clouded his blue eyes; his humiliation embittered his words. "The Chicago bosses told me a few minutes ago. Mr. Thrumbull raised a howl, but they shut him up."

Ronnie kept on muttering, "The yellow-bellied bastards—"

"No," Nils said. "I don't feel that way about it. I worked hard and they paid me good." He shrugged his shoulders. "Somewhere along the line, maybe I stepped on the wrong toe. Maybe I'm getting old." He kicked the wagon wheel and spat, knocking up a little spout of dust from the barn's dry floor.

"You going back to Michigan?" Sans asked.

"And let them throw me out in a year or so?" Nils' face was flushed. "Let every woodsman from the Lakes to the Gulf say Nils Holmquist ain't fit for logging any more? Hell, no."

"Then what you aim to do?" Ronnie demanded.

"You can hang around here and starve with us," Sans said.

"Thanks, but you got all the trouble one man needs." He walked to the door of the barn where his horse was tied. He freed the animal and watched him walk over to the water trough. Then he went back to the wagon bed. "Dabney! How far is it to Cuba?"

An ox, patient and strong, crunched hay in the stall nearby. Ronnie stared toward the stall, his face suddenly white and his jaw set firm. Sans looked at the lantern, at the raw, hard light and the night insects beating against the light and dying.

"It ain't far." He said it softly, thinking then of Mingo.

"I never was in a war," Nils said. "I've done a lot of fighting in my time, but I've never been in a war. Looks like those Cubans are about ready to start shooting."

"When you going?" Ronnie's tone was hushed and tense.

"Tomorrow."

"Will you help me drive some oxen to Ellisville for Sans?"

The lump in Sans Dabney's throat was choking him. He wanted to cry out, to hold them both, to cling to them all and bind them all to the valley forever; his brother, most of all.

"Sure." Nils met Ronnie's look and understood it. "You damn right I'll go with you, you red-necked Mick."

"We'll take two wagons. Me and you, bud—"

"We'll take four. I can handle two wagons by myself. Done it many a time—"

"I can handle two with my eyes shut." The valley man jumped off the wagon, swaggering, boasting, and lying. "Me and you, Nils. Then we'll head for Tampa. You got any money? I ain't got a red cent, not a frazzling copper."

Sans waited until Monday to tell Mingo that Ronnie and Nils were on their way to Florida, heading for Cuba. The younger brother said nothing, staring off toward the south cut.

Kyd had a pot roast and rice for dinner, Mingo's favorite, but her son was not hungry and excused himself from the table. That worried his mother and she talked about it. "It's that Cuban woman. He thinks about her all the time."

The elder brother looked quickly at his father, and Bruce changed the subject. The mill whistle blared, and they jumped. It seemed so strange, so out of place, and none of them mentioned it, pretending to ignore it. Kyd clattered the dishes and rattled the silver, making a noise in the Dabney house.

After dinner, Bruce and Sans walked up to the north cut and looked at the rails stacked there, at the cross-ties. The old man kicked one of the ties and slid his foot along the rail, rubbing off the rust.

Sans said, "Has Mingo done any talking to you about Cuba?"

"Not yet. Has he talked to you?"

"Not exactly. It's eating him, though."

Bruce took off his hat and the wind was soft through his white hair and his beard. "It's getting late in Cuba."

"It's getting late in the valley, too," Sans muttered. "Peninsula isn't sleeping. They're just catching their breath. These rails aren't here for nothing."

They walked over to Bogue Homa, searching for signs of bream. Water spiders, perched on their spindly legs, skated swift over the creek, streaking it. Minnows came to the surface, pecking at it, pausing, then darting away. Crawfish wiggled back into their holes, puffing mud into the water. Bruce said, "I'm going home to take a nap."

Sans walked with his father, striding beside the old man until they reached The House. Bruce rested one foot on the bottom step. "Cuba

is a long way. But there are no miles between a man and a woman."
He was looking toward the south cut, slowly rubbing his hand.

The elder son glanced at the purple welt, then stared at it; and
he was much older. His father was an ailing man and he, Sans Dabney, was next in the Dabney line. There was his destiny, the welt
on an old man's hand, and from that hand he must accept the reins.

Bruce walked slowly up the steps and Sans rode down to The
Store. Maybe a talk with Mr. Charlie would brighten things, and
help ease his loneliness. Mr. Charlie, however, was grumpy, stalking
around and shifting goods. The drummer who had taken Elmo's territory was there, and talking fancy about a new style shoe without
pegs and men's short drawers that fastened with a string. The more
the interloper talked, the more Mr. Charlie swelled until finally he
blew up and proclaimed for all to hear, even the women in Louisa's
annex, that Charlie Owens had been buttoning his drawers since he
was a boy and didn't aim to change to newfangled ones. He was
mighty relieved when the salesman left, and he stood in the doorway,
glaring and muttering about a buck with a short horn, and a young
rooster trying to tread an old hen.

Sans hung around, making idle talk with the few customers who
came to Mr. Charlie's department. Louisa's annex was filled with
chattering women and Sans heard the clatter beyond the door, and
went out on the porch and sat down. He took out his knife and
whittled on the bench. Louisa closed her annex at five o'clock, but
Mr. Charlie kept open until six. By dusk The Store was empty and
he came out and joined Sans, taking his place in his rocking chair.
"Where's Mingo?"

"I don't know," said Sans.

The elder brother leaned back and locked his fingers around his
knee, and the old man went on rocking, and they watched the night
gather. Ruth Thrumbull drove by, riding up to The House to see
Kyd. She lifted her hand as she passed, and Mr. Charlie waved to
her.

She was gone only a few minutes, and drove back to The Store
to make a purchase. The storekeeper followed her inside and sold
her a garden hoe. He put the hoe in her buggy and she joined them
on the porch, sitting by Sans. Some of the women who passed cut
their eyes at her and said she was acting mannish, sitting on The

Store gallery. "But," said Velma Downey to Emma Pugh, "they say all them Yankee girls are sort of for'ard."

It was pleasant sitting on the porch, talking a little, but not much. Just sitting quiet in the late afternoon, the three of them watching the people and the wagons go by, the children sauntering along and the dogs trotting behind them.

Ruth said maybe she'd better be going, and Sans began telling about turkey signs he'd seen in the woods, about the crawfish in Bogue Homa. He didn't want her to go away, for somehow she helped ease his black mood.

They didn't mention the mill. It wasn't necessary. The whine and the hiss were a continuous overtone to their talk, shrilling on through the valley until the whistle blew again, spurting its white steam into the air and telling Lebanon it was six o'clock, that day was ended. The people filed out of the mill and filed into their little red houses and the mill was still; the smoke drifting away, the whistle poised and ready for morning.

It was time for Mr. Charlie to close up, but he didn't close. He went inside and got two bottles of beer and a bottle of strawberry soda and they, the old man and the girl and the boy, sat on the porch in the twilight. Sans called it daydown and Mr. Charlie called it the pink of evening. The wagons stopped rolling by. Smoke Jackson's little girl came along, leading their cow from pasture, and sparks streaked yellow and red from Gabriel d'Artois' forge. The shadows were fingering across the valley, feeling their way, and wrapping the land in the first layer of darkness. Ruth sat back on the bench, her head resting against the front of The Store. "It's so quiet," she said. "So quiet and peaceful."

Sans and Mr. Charlie were silent, the old man slowly rocking and thinking of things that used to be. 'Tite Pierre's ancient and decrepit mule moseyed around the corner of the building and pushed his long, gaunt head over the edge of the porch. Sans reached out and scratched his ears and the mule stood motionless. Mr. Charlie went inside and lit the lamp. A customer might come by and anyhow a lamp was company. He returned to the porch and sat down by Ruth. She drew her skirt aside to make room for him.

'Tite Pierre's mule turned and shuffled away, his blunt old hoofs stumbling as he ambled into the dark. The martins were sweeping over Gabriel d'Artois' smithy, wheeling and diving in the sky. Sans was watching the stars come out, watching the birth of night. Then, for a reason none dared ask and a reason he himself didn't know, he began singing:

"Shall I, wasting in despair—"

His words trailed off and he hummed. Ruth waited until the melody was ended. "You were singing that song the night I moved into the valley."

"Was I?" He tilted his bottle of beer, then put the empty bottle by a post, closing his eyes and relaxing, stretching his long legs out in front of him. "I been singing that song all my life. Mingo knows it, too. I heard him sing it one night in the swamp. It was raining."

Ruth said, "He sang it one night at my house. He and Rafaela were on the porch, and I heard him sing it."

Mr. Charlie listened a minute to the tree frogs, scratching their squeaky fiddles, rasping their call for rain. "Elmo Batson liked that song." His words were a whisper of loneliness. "I wonder where ol' Elmo is now. It's a long way to Cuba."

Sans stood up and stretched, poking his arms high. "It's too far for you, Mr. Charlie—"

"Is it too far for you?" Ruth asked quickly.

He looked down at her, looking at her for a long time. "Yes, Ruth. It's too far for me." He heard the quick intake of her breath and he put his hand on her arm. "I told you once before that I'm staying in this valley." He drew his hand away. "Now I got to be going home. It's time for supper." He stepped from the porch and swung into the saddle.

They heard him singing as he rode up the pike, until the song died away and only the echo came back to them. Ruth rose to go, too. She brushed off her dress and leaned down and patted Mr. Charlie on his shoulder. He took off his glasses and peered up at her in the gloom.

"What do you do, Mr. Charlie," she said, "when you love a man so much you hurt inside?"

"You find out if he loves you."

"And if he doesn't?"

Charlie Owens crossed his skinny legs and put his hand on the bench beside him. "Sit down, honey. You may not like what I aim to tell you, but I aim to tell you just the same."

She sat near him, her hands folded in her lap, waiting for him to speak. He mulled his thoughts, feeling for the words and measuring them. "Who do you think is boss in this valley?" He asked it simply.

"Mr. Bruce Dabney. Or Sans."

"That's where you're wrong. Kyd Dabney is the bell-cow of the Dabney clan, and of the whole valley."

Ruth straightened and turned to Mr. Charlie in surprise. "Mrs. Dabney!"

"Yep. Mrs. Dabney. She's the foundation of the Dabney fief, the rock on which the whole shebang is built." Again the old man mulled his thoughts. "She was Kyd Fermat. A Cajun. Born down yonder in the swamp." He pointed his long, lean finger to the marshland across Bogue Homa. "She knew what she wanted, and she went after it. She wanted to marry Bruce Dabney, and she did it."

A mouse squeaked under the porch and Mr. Charlie stomped on the floor and cocked his head, listening. Ruth prompted him. "How did she do it?"

"She's a woman, ain't she?"

Ruth said quickly, "So am I."

"That's right, honey." The old man held up his hand. "But you're a Yankee woman."

The Thrumbull girl was annoyed, for she had been in the South long enough to grow weary of the endless distinction between Northern and Southern. Her manner was tart and her voice sharp. "Don't tell me that you, too, think Southern women are smarter than Northern women?"

"Uh huh. Lots smarter." He cocked his ear again and listened to the mice scampering under the porch, and he stomped on the floor hard and waited until they were still; then he settled back and watched the fireflies speckling the night. "They got to be, 'cause down here they wear the britches. Folks been trying to figure out the South ever since there's been a South. There ain't no secret to it." He glanced at Ruth to see if she was listening. "The South, honey, is a she. From Virginia Dare to Varina Howell—Varina married Jeff

Davis—and on down to Kyd Dabney; the South is a woman, first, last, and always."

Ruth almost smiled; then she was serious. "I can't imagine a man admitting that."

"I wouldn't admit it to any Yankee but you." Mr. Charlie plucked at the loose skin on his neck, pulling it away from his Adam's apple and letting it slide back. "Men down here bow and scrape to their women, and they'll fight you at the drop of a hat about 'em. You know why?"

"Southern tradition and custom—"

"Humbug!" A bullbat swooped so near the porch that Mr. Charlie drew back, and the bird swirled to the road, squatting in the dust, huddling low, then darting away. "When our grandpas first came to the South, they wanted two things. Land, and sons to help them tend the land." Charlie Owens loved to talk and now that Elmo was gone, this girl was his best audience; and he was preaching the Southern gospel that few men dared think and fewer still dared utter. "Land became a God, and sons became safety. Women were mighty scarce in those days and didn't live long, so a man got his sons while the getting was good." He squared around and frowned at the girl. "You following me?"

"Yes." Ruth Thrumbull never had heard talk like this before.

The Southerner got up from the bench and moved over to his rocking chair, the cane bottom crackling as he settled himself. "Pretty soon the women found out they were high up on the pole, sitting on top of everything. So they gave when they wanted to, and they held back when they wanted to. And they gave just enough to get the reins and hold 'em." He paused, granting her time to appreciate what he was saying. "That's the secret that Southern mothers pass on to their daughters, teaching 'em how to get the reins and hold 'em."

"That's no secret. We women know that up North—"

"But you don't practice it," Charlie Owens broke in. "You Yankee women are smart, got a head crammed full of horse sense, but put a Southern girl in the North and she'll be so soft and so he'pless that every man in sight has got to come and hold her up. By the time she gets through thanking 'em, they're all whistling Dixie." He chuckled, sort of proud of the wiles of his womenfolks. "You watch 'em, honey.

A Southern girl can be a kitten one minute and a tiger the next. You watch 'em."

Ruth's laugh was light and airy, concealing the trepidation in her heart. "Are you suggesting that I turn kitten or tiger?"

"Be both!" He was stern, almost scolding her. "You aim to marry Sans Dabney, don't you?"

She hesitated, then said boldly, "Yes. If he loves me."

He got up and, in the fervor of his doctrine, banged the post, rattling one of Elmo's signs. "Out-Southern these Southern girls! That's the ticket." He took her hand and held it. "Don't be so dadblame smart. Let him be the smart one. And poking out a little curve here and there never did no harm, neither."

She almost laughed, but it was no time to laugh. This was what she wanted to hear. Even if it hurt her pride, she wanted to hear it. "Is that all?"

He loosed her hand and peered up the pike, toward the Dabney house. "A little perfume goes mighty good, too. Ain't nothing wrong with clean smelling soap; but that's the trouble, it's too clean smelling. A man's nose is mighty pert. Lot's sharper'n his eyes. Excuse me for saying it, but that's a fact." He nodded slowly, pondering and approving his maxims. Then he said, "When it comes to women, men just naturally ain't interested in brains. At least, not at first. You following me?"

"I'm ahead of you, Mr. Charlie. At least, I plan to be." And now she laughed, for it was the time to laugh. "Just one thing bothers me. If you know so much about women, why didn't you ever marry?"

"Because I know so much about women." The braggart winked at her. He went inside and blew out the lamp, closing the door and putting up the oak beam that fastened it. "I'll see you to your buggy."

"There's one thing more." She put her hands on the old man's shoulders and looked up at him. "A Southern girl would kiss you goodnight." She kissed him quickly and ran down the steps. "Goodnight, Mr. Charlie."

Chapter fourteen

THE LATE SEPTEMBER RAINS bathed the valley and Indian summer dried it and dressed it for winter. Mingo, unable to meet Peninsula's local competition for pine, converted his little mill to hardwood and Sans logged two days a week to keep his brother's saw turning.

Ruth Thrumbull, not so precisely groomed but surely more feminine, devoted less time to raising funds for Cuba and more time to herself and her clothes, shunning the plain and practical garments she had worn and selecting softer materials: lawns, batistes, dimities, some of them embroidered, some ruffled. She took more care in arranging her hair, trying one arrangement and then another, until she found one that suited her. Sans teased her about some tiny curls at the back of her neck and called them drakes' tails. She blushed and pressed them up under the comb, but not all of them. She touched perfume behind each ear.

Mr. Charlie watched it all and smiled to himself and sometimes nodded to Ruth, approving her behavior.

Sans was not conscious of any change, but he just looked at her, studying her and wondering, puzzling over the little things about her; her small ears, the warm depths of her gray eyes, her slender wrists. He saw her only in public places, casually at The Store and at the post office. It never occurred to him to be surprised that, morning after morning, she called for her mail at the same time he called for his. He came to expect her to be there and then one morning, at Mr. Charlie's suggestion, she wasn't there and Sans brooded that day. Something was missing and he didn't know what it was, but he was moody and sullen.

He spent much of his time loafing around The Store, moving inside with Mr. Charlie from the porch to the fat-bellied stove as the season changed and the chill came on. He helped his father breed mules and came to know Bruce Dabney better, and, knowing him better, loved him more; although he was aware that Bruce was the first Dabney to surrender to the matriarchy that Kyd and other women like her were fastening upon the South. Bruce knew it, too, and one day, fishing a branch that fed Bogue Homa, he told his son, "I want only peace." Their woods-going, and their easy ways in general, sharpened Kyd's tongue until Bruce quieted her. "Two things are difficult to live with," the old man said. "A nagging woman and a smoking chimney."

Sans saw his brother mostly at mealtime, for Mingo, prodded by Louisa, was concentrating again on his work. She drove with a new intensity, praising him when he worked with her late at night, coddling him when he tired. Her department turned a bigger profit the first month than The Store turned in three. She trained another clerk and opened a millinery line.

Mr. Lewiston counseled Thrumbull's presence in Chicago, and the superintendent was ordered to report to the home office. He asked his daughter to accompany him. Ruth visited Mr. Charlie and the old man encouraged her to go. "Absence makes the heart grow fonder," he said, "unless the absence is too dadblamed long. Go on up there and let him moon awhile. Do him good. You don't miss the water until the well runs dry."

Sans called to tell her goodbye and she tried to arrange for them to be alone on the porch, but Mr. Thrumbull joined them and spent the evening talking about timber. Ruth and her father left the valley the next day, and Ruth went away without the one thing she wanted most: a goodbye kiss from Sans Dabney.

Aven MacIvor spent more time in Lebanon, now that the weather was cooler. Sans and Bruce saw her frequently on the street, and once or twice a week they dropped by her hotel. Kyd and Mingo, however, shunned her. The valley long since had accepted the situation and it brought no comment.

"Time," said Mr. Charlie, "helps everything but butter."

Louisa's department was patronized at first by only the well-to-do; but as the women of Peninsula's bigwigs began wearing silks, the women of the poor began to yearn. Saturday afternoons in Lebanon became parades of contrast: silks for the well-off, gingham for the poor. The company's ladies rustled their silks against the gingham dresses of the workers' women; at the post office, at the courthouse, at the Free Church on Sundays. Gradually gingham became a badge of servitude, and silk a symbol of superiority. And so, because people are people despite the fat ledgers in Peninsula's home office, the women of the poor began pleading for silks. They turned to their husbands for the things they wanted, nagging at first, then weeping.

Eventually, as so often happens, one of the very poorest broke the line and shattered the caste. A Negro, hoarding his pay and ignoring his children's needs, bought his wife a silk dress from Louisa's department. The white women berated their husbands and their husbands scowled at the Negro. "Gettin' uppity. Damned nigger gittin' out of his place." The Negro wanted only the peace at home that Bruce Dabney wanted; he wanted only to appease the shining, sweaty woman who gave him what little pleasure his barren life enjoyed.

Mr. Charlie shook his head and told Sans, "That silk dress is going to cause more hell than the north cut ever will. We been waiting for a boil to pop out here in Lebanon, but we've overlooked the pimples. That silk dress makes that Negro as big as the best, and better than most, and a lot of low down white folks won't stand it."

Louisa snatched the chance to increase profits. She stocked a line of cheaper silk goods and the poor bought things that helped keep them poor. Soon there was silk in the cabins of Lebanon, even though there wasn't enough corn meal to last from payday to payday.

The workers, having bought luxuries, now lacked necessities; and they demanded credit at the company store. It was refused. Peninsula, unlike the Dabney store, was not geared for credit. Peninsula bought in bulk, played the discounts and sold only for cash. The workers, caught between urge for silks and need for bread, demanded credit to get bread.

Sans saw it and Mr. Charlie saw it. Mingo, however, was not aware of the trend, for the opiate of work no longer quieted him and, restless once more, his eyes were on the south cut, the road out, and his mind was in the mist of his memories. Louisa, grabbing at every straw, suggested to him that Mr. Charlie's department be stocked heavily.

"My department is in good shape. Take some of the money I've made for you and buy enough goods to swamp Charlie Owens. Staples and coffee beans and snuff. Open a little line of furniture. Golden oak. The company store is heading for trouble. We'll tighten our grip and cash in on it." She patted his cheek as she said it. "We'll make a world of money."

The younger brother laid her plan before Sans, seeking his advice for the first time on business matters. Mingo was not so confident of his judgment as he had been, no longer so sure of himself as he had been before he saw fox-glow in the rain.

Sans agreed with Louisa, and Mr. Charlie beamed when Mingo told him to stock up. "Pull out the plug," he said. Mr. Charlie cautioned him that it would take time to restock.

Meanwhile, the workers, forced to pay cash at Peninsula's store and desiring the luxuries in Louisa's annex, were caught between vanity and need; pricked from one side by things they wanted, stabbed from the other by things they had to have. So they grumbled and blamed the company.

Peninsula's executives were astounded. The company was running the Lebanon mill in time of panic, operating at full capacity while most mills were closed down. The company paid every Saturday in hard cash. And yet the people grumbled! They had red houses. They had little garden plots. They had a company store that sold things cheaper than the Dabney store. And yet the people grumbled!

The executives didn't remember that the people always had bought on credit. Throughout their lives they had been in pawn to the future. They wanted credit now, wanted to buy on Thursday and pay on Saturday. Peninsula tried to explain that credit was expensive, that credit meant prices must go up. The company was trying to say, in a vague, digressive way, that credit was faith; and was unwilling to admit that it had no faith in the people. The workers simply didn't understand. They had spent their money. They wanted bread. "Gimme a loaf. Pay you Sad'day."

Peninsula's store manager, worrying about his own job, tried to talk to his customers. "Good Lord, men, if I credit one for a few days, I'll have to credit all. Somebody will run up a bill and walk off. I'll get it in the neck. Or I'll have to pass on the loss to you, and that'll make things cost more."

"The Dabneys always gave us credit," one of the workers said.

"But your women weren't wearing silk petticoats then," the harassed manager argued. "Things are different now."

"They sure as hell are."

In desperation, the manager sent a memorandum to the home office and a conference was called. Mr. Thrumbull, fuming because of delay in Chicago, was invited to attend and dared not refuse, although, as a sawmill man, he knew nothing about merchandise.

In the valley of Lebanon, Mr. Charlie sat by his stove and rubbed his long, bony hands gleefully. "Now the ninnies will issue scrip. They set the trap and baited it. Now they'll blubber when it catches 'em by the bohunkus."

In Chicago, in the sumptuously furnished offices of Peninsula Lumber Company, Inc., a young member of the board, son of a deceased older member, impressed his associates by suggesting that the company store, in far off New Hebron, Mississippi, issue scrip.

"We'll pay our workers in token money, good only at the company store." The young executive never had seen a company store.

Mr. Thrumbull protested. "You don't know those people."

One of the vice-presidents demanded, "You know anything about merchandise, Thrumbull? Know anything about running a store for a bunch of red-necks?"

"No," said Mr. Thrumbull. "But I've been in the South long enough to know the people. I've learned respect for the red-necks, the peckerwoods, the crackers, the swamp rats, the hillbillies, and all the other names we call them." Mr. Thrumbull was indiscreet, implying criticism of his bosses, stepping on the wrong toes. "They have hookworm and lean faces; but, by God, they'll fight. We're sowing a bad harvest down there. Tomorrow we'll reap."

The members of the board plainly showed their surprise at his audacity. They ignored his advice and sent him out of Chicago on a tour of their other mills. Ruth, treasuring two letters from Sans and several from Mr. Charlie, was ready to go back to Lebanon, hungry to go back; but now, with her father possibly in disfavor with the company, she went with him without hesitation, traveling by palace car to Oregon where Peninsula was building mills.

An order for tokens ranging in value from one cent to one dollar was forwarded to a Philadelphia company. The Philadelphia concern

suggested brass instead of pewter. Brass lasted longer and was harder.
Each token bore the name of the company. A U.S. quarter said: "In
God We Trust." The token said: "Peninsula Lumber Company." A
U.S. dime proclaimed: *"E Pluribus Unum."* The company stated:
"Value Ten Cents."

It was all legal. Nobody was trying to rob anybody. The workers
had their little red houses, and their brass money. And the company
money bought more at the company store than silver money bought
at the Dabney store. And yet the people grumbled.

"Funny money," they growled. "They're paying us with funny
money and making us buy at their store. They're robbing us, coming
and going."

Windy Hill, circulating among the people, whispered, "Wall
Street! That's how come I quit the company. Wall Street Yankees,
skinning good Americans like us. Taking our money, and living rich.
Playing up to 'Koons, Kikes, and Katholics'."

The company was trapped in a pit of its own digging. A dusty little
valley in Mississippi, Dabney's Hollow, poor and bare in the fall of
1894, was pressing against one store and Peninsula's pyramid was
threatened. The situation became serious enough to justify a board
meeting.

Keith Alexander, there in Chicago, got reports that Peninsula's
store was in difficulty, that one tiny gear was slipping in the sprawling machine. Alexander mused, then was proud; for he was certain
that the Dabneys—his people and Morna's people—had a hand in it
somewhere, somehow. They'd always fought in Lebanon! Keith Alexander was proud.

Mr. Charlie's new stock began arriving and his customers returned
in droves. The old storekeeper put his cards on the table with Mingo.
"You've let Louisa run her department, and I aim to have the same
right."

Mingo went to Sans for counsel, and the elder brother urged that
Mr. Charlie be given a free hand. Mingo didn't hesitate. He told the
old man to figure it out to suit himself, and that same day Charlie
Owens cut prices.

"I aim to sell more and more for less and less," he announced to
the people.

Then he hired Sans, and the older boy became a clerk in the family
store.

Mingo was embarrassed, and hid it. Kyd started to protest, and Bruce silenced her. Laurel Woodward sneered; Wyeth lowered his paper and looked at her over his spectacles, and she left the room. Louisa was indignant. A Dabney boy working for wages in the Dabney store! How could the valley maintain tradition if a Dabney worked as a common clerk?

"Tradition of what?" Sans asked, and Louisa stamped her foot and stalked away.

The division in The Store was sharp and Louisa strictly stayed out of Mr. Charlie's department, avoiding Sans. She was a manager and he was a hired hand; the cash till was a gulf between them, the ledgers were mountains. Eventually, however, there was a showcase in her department to be moved quickly and dusted. She asked Sans to do it, and he did it. He grinned as he moved the showcase, a menial chore. Charlie Owens fumed, but kept his peace. Mingo didn't know about it.

Another day a box of goods was to be moved. Again Louisa asked Sans to favor her, her tone sharper this time. And still he grinned.

Then she ordered him to empty some trash. Sans looked at her. Suddenly he remembered her under a tree on the road from Ellisville —and he laughed. He stood on the back steps of The Store and tossed the trash on to a pile. Bits of paper fluttered to the ground, reminding him of leaves he picked from Louisa's new dress that day.

Mingo walked over from his mill and stood on the back steps by his brother, looking down at the trash pile, then up at Sans. "Wait a minute, kiddo." There was a strained pallor on his face. He reached over and took the can, and picked out a few bits of paper clinging there and threw them on to the pile. "Dammit to hell, you don't have to empty trash."

They turned from the trash pile and walked into The Store. Sans said, "Don't say anything about it. Just let well enough alone."

"All right." Mingo glanced toward Louisa's department. "But you don't have to empty trash." He stomped out of The Store and back to his mill.

Sans sauntered among the customers in Louisa's annex, swinging the trash can. "I emptied the trash. Anything else?"

Louisa pretended to be busy, but her face flushed. "That's all. Thank you."

Sans winked at the Irish salesgirl, and strolled back to his department. There he unpacked a crate of soap and Charlie Owens watched him work, then turned to the invoices before him. He glanced at his calendar, for he was checking dates and figuring discounts. Neither he nor Sans saw Mr. Lewiston and Mr. Irving leave the valley in a rented buggy: Mr. Lewiston heading for Chicago and Mr. Irving for Ellisville.

It was October 3, 1894. However, it was not the date that caused Mr. Charlie to stare at the calendar and blink. That was one of Elmo Batson's calendars.

Gar Rivers, at the courthouse to check a tax lien against an illiterate Negro, was the first of the Dabney faction to learn that Windy Hill had filed as candidate for judge. He bent over, reading carefully, studying Windy's notice of intent to seek public office, subject to the will of the people.

The old Negro glanced at Sheriff Vernon Boyd, glanced at his eyes, and for the first time in Lebanon saw hatred in the eyes of a white man looking at a Negro. Gar looked again and, without a word, turned away and crossed the street to Wyeth Woodward's office.

The lawyer's jaw, square and massive under his heavy beard, trembled as he heard the news. For a few seconds he slumped in his chair, gaping at Gar. The pimple had spread into a boil and Wyeth Woodward, seeing far ahead, knew better than most men, and far better than Peninsula Lumber Company, that the boil must run pus before it formed a scab, and that the scab would leave a scar. "My God!" He said it over and over. "My God! To cut a few trees and make some money, they have poisoned the well. They have fouled the spring. Don't the fools know that they, too, must drink the water? Lord have mercy on us."

"It was the way Sheriff Boyd looked at me." Gar Rivers shook his head. "He acted like he didn't know me. Like he had never seen me before. I could see 'nigger' on his lips. A fagot in his eyes."

Wyeth reached for his hat and by the time he and Gar got across to the courthouse, Windy Hill's entire slate of candidates, from constable to judge, had filed notice to run in the November elections.

The lawyer tapped the page on which the names were written. "Can you explain this?" he asked Boyd.

"Don't need no explaining," Vernon Boyd said. "Just means we aim to get a little of that gravy the Dabneys been sopping up. And some of the gravy Peninsula is sopping." He was speaking his piece glibly, grinning, red-faced and red-necked and pleased with himself. "You look after the Dabneys, Mr. Woodward. Peninsula looks after herself. Me and Mr. Hill aims to look after the people."

Wyeth rested his hand on a stack of tax books. "I hope you got cash, Vernon. I hope you didn't take promises. When you sell your soul, always get cash."

"I don't aim to take none of your lip." The sheriff was indignant. "I'm supporting Oscar Hardee for my office. Me and Mr. Hill are tired of the people getting squeezed between Peninsula Lumber Company and the Dabneys."

The lawyer scowled around the room, and walked out. Gar followed him. They went to The Store and informed Sans and Mr. Charlie. Charlie Owens was so excited that he closed his department, and they set out for The House, Sans going to the mill to get Mingo.

In the parlor they sat down to coffee, and Bruce tried to quiet Wyeth's fears that Windy Hill was heading for power in Lebanon. He didn't believe money could undermine the people. Wyeth was skeptical and angry. Gar Rivers was afraid, and Mr. Charlie was heartbroken. "I wanted to see this country united before I died," he said. "That's all I wanted. Now we're back to carpetbag days."

Wyeth said, "Peninsula Lumber Company isn't carpetbagging. They'll be with us a long time. They're stalking behind Windy Hill and he'll spawn a breed that'll plague the South for a hundred years."

Bruce Dabney simply did not understand the implications of what the lawyer was saying. "Windy is a mountebank," Bruce declared. "A rascal and a coward. A man like that won't cut any mustard."

Sans understood better than any other member of his family that Cephus Hill's candidacy was a muffled shot in a new kind of war in the South. One of the first of the demagogues was giving notice, and the South was not giving heed. Sans could not read the full meaning of the auguries; but he was troubled, fearing that even the little valley of Lebanon, Dabney's Hollow, might be passing from the hands and the backs of those who were willing to sow, into the grasp of those who wanted only to reap.

The land already had passed from the mansions to the merchants, from cotton to the moneychangers. Now the land was passing further, was dribbling down to the red-necks, the peckerwoods, to those scorned so long. Southern land and Southern power were passing into the hands, the sweaty hands, of those who sawed the timber and combed the earth. And Windy Hill was scheming to control those sweaty hands. He was granting the people power, and scheming to take it away. He was teaching them the might of the ballot box, even as he was arranging to take the ballot box into his grasp.

Kyd Dabney scoffed at the whole thing. "Fiddlesticks! If Peninsula is putting up the money for Mr. Hill, it'll be simple to expose the cheats."

Wyeth was patient with Kyd. "We have no evidence of collusion. There's not a single Peninsula bigwig in the valley. Lewiston and Irving are gone. Thrumbull is somewhere out West. Even Miss Thrumbull and Nils Holmquist aren't here. Windy and the company timed it perfectly."

"Well," said Kyd. "If they fight like that, then why can't we do it? Fight fire with fire."

The family lawyer looked away. Bruce was rubbing his hand. Mr. Charlie mumbled to himself and Sans and Mingo stared at their mother.

Mr. Charlie reckoned he'd better get on back to town. Sans went with him. They went directly to the sheriff's office and Charles Pryor Owens, President of the Board of Supervisors, nine times elected, peered over his spectacles at Vernon Boyd. Sans slouched against the doorway.

"Who's dealing, Vernon?" Mr. Charlie asked. "You, or Windy Hill, or Peninsula?"

"I hope you ain't looking for trouble," Boyd said.

Sans moved from the door to the desk near the sheriff and waited.

"You back Hardee this go-round and be his chief deputy, and he backs you next time. Is that it?" Mr. Charlie sniffed and glanced around. "Windy takes from Peninsula with his right hand, feeds you with his left, and stuffs his own fat face with both hands. Is that the deal, Vernon?"

Vernon Boyd grinned. "You're a right smart man, Mr. Charlie."

"Swapping?" The President of the Board arched his thin eyebrows.

"Maybe. Maybe we might do a little swapping with the right folks.

All you got to do is support Mr. Hill for judge, and we'll re-elect you to the Board."

Charlie Owens reached across the sheriff's desk and took a cigar from a box, and smelled it. The box was a gift from Windy Hill. Mr. Charlie rolled the stogy between his fingers. "Well, I'll be damned," he said. "Cheap. Why, Vernon, I been in political campaigns where we gave better smokes than this to white pimps for hustling yellow whores." He flipped the cigar back into the box. "Maybe the cigars were better because the pimps were better."

Vernon Boyd started to get up, and Sans said, "No need getting up. We'll be leaving. Come on, Mr. Charlie."

A group of valley folks were on the courthouse steps and Mr. Charlie and Sans stopped there and shook hands with them. "Boys, I just learned I've got opposition," the old man announced.

Sans said, "I suppose you fellows heard that Windy Hill and Peninsula are running a whole pack of feist dogs for office."

"Uh huh. We heard it. We was aiming to talk to Mr. Charlie about it." The farmer addressed the storekeeper. "You always been the bell-cow in county politics, Brother Owens. Where you stand now?"

At that minute, the fate of the valley of Lebanon was in the hands of Charlie Owens. All he had to do was raise an eyebrow or smile knowingly. All he need do was trade, and all his life he had been a trader. "I stand right where I've always stood," he said humbly.

Sans felt the sinews swelling in his arm and he was conscious that battles are not always fought at Armageddon. Great battles sometimes are fought in the hearts of men, and the field might be the steps of a county courthouse—a small, backwoods courthouse basking and bathing in the October sun.

"Tell us sump'n, Mr. Charlie," one of the men said. "Is it true that the county spent a heap of money on a nigger school, while I ain't got a road back to my place? That's what Cephus Hill says."

"We gave all we could to our Negro school," Mr. Charlie reported.

"Is it true you're giving them niggers a school, when they don't pay enough taxes to grease a nit's eye?"

"That's true," Mr. Charlie said. No need trying to explain the whys and wherefores.

"Is it true Gar Rivers calls Wyeth Woodward by his first name? And he don't take his hat off when he talks to Bruce Dabney?"

Sans edged forward. "That's none of your business."

"Oh, yes it is, son." Mr. Charlie was emphatic. "Windy Hill has made it their business." He faced the men, the voters, the people. "Now let me ask you sump'n. How come you paying so much mind to Windy Hill? He's sneaked into bed with Peninsula Lumber Company. They're sleeping together when it's dark, and playing like they're mad when it's day." The old man's Adam's apple was bobbing. "And I tell you sump'n else. You put a son of a bitch like Windy Hill in office, and your grandchildren will pay for your sins. You sow it. Your young 'uns will reap it."

The men looked from one to the other. "But Mr. Hill busted up with Peninsula. He quit lawing for 'em when they started meeting their payroll with funny money. Mr. Hill told us so, hisself."

Charlie Owens blinked his eyes and spat. "Well, now. I do declare. And if a polecat told you it was perfume, you'd smear it in your beard."

They guffawed, then returned to the attack, firing the little popguns Windy Hill had loaded and handed them. "Brother Owens, do you think Peninsula is a bunch of weasels?"

Again Charlie Owens faced a decision, a decision to be made on the steps of an old courthouse in an isolated valley. "No," he said slowly. "They are not weasels. A few weasels in the crowd, but not all of 'em."

"Mr. Hill says they all are. You say they ain't. Looks like you're for 'em. And he's agin' 'em. You air a Dabney man. So it looks like the Dabneys and Peninsula have got together to give us po' folks a riggin'. Like Mr. Hill says."

Sans started to speak, but Mr. Charlie put his hand on him, quieting him. "You men will find me at The Store if you need me. I'm running for my same old office. Go back to the forks of the creek and tell your folks that Charlie Owens is still running. Tell 'em I ain't budging an inch. Tell 'em I got to face my God, after I face the voters of Lebanon County."

He walked down the steps and across the square, his head high and his eyes burning. Sans walked with him. He was naïve in politics, but he knew Charlie Owens had signed his political death warrant, and in doing so had signed a warrant for the Dabneys.

Chapter fifteen

CEPHUS HILL had only a month to deliver the valley of Lebanon into the hands of Peninsula Lumber Company: thirty days to sow and thirty years to reap. A week longer might have been too long, for the seed must be planted quickly, lest the people learn. He planned his campaign meticulously, bewildering the people, including the Dabneys, by the sheer ferocity of his attack.

Even Peninsula was appalled, but it was too late for the company to stop what it had started.

Cephus Hill was a red-neck whose barren life had spawned hate in his heart, and he fought with malevolence and guile against any who opposed him. Again in the struggles of men, destiny and the man had met—this time in a little valley, a poor land of trees, isolated in the heart of a poor state.

The first public shot in Lebanon's new kind of war was fired in New Hebron by Windy Hill when he dubbed the Dabneys "overlords." He slurred the word, twisting it. "Them Dabneys are aristocrats," he told his first rally. "An aristocrat is a man who eats his supper with his coat on."

His hearers snickered. The red-necks could see the Dabney house and it was larger than their shacks. That made the Dabneys aristocrats. It wasn't a matter of family or wealth; it was simply that the Dabneys had a heritage and lived in a better house.

Bruce was amused and Kyd secretly was pleased. Mingo chortled at the idea of being a nabob. Only Sans saw the poison and analyzed it. He realized Cephus Hill was trying to set the Dabneys apart from the people, trying to set them up as masters so the people would resent them, then hate them.

The sneers against the family went unanswered. The Dabneys disdained wallowing in the mire. Their failure to answer and attack, to fight back, caused the people to whisper.

The candidate, having nurtured distrust, began the more important job of flattering the red-necks, telling them they were better than other men.

Windy knew something about his own kind that all the South knew, which the North could never see because the truth was hidden in the haze of the Southern myth. The red-neck, the man at the fork of the creek, he of the barren life and quick resentment, was a rebel at heart, a revolutionist. His father never owned a slave, never lived in a white house. The poets and the romanticists had lied. The Southerner always had been poor. He had a stooped back instead of a slave, but it stooped over a heart flaming revolt. He was a rebel against all things, except one: He wanted no change, he would tolerate no change, in the relationship between himself and the Negro. His one claim to superiority was his belief in white supremacy.

Cephus Hill, suckled in the venom, fed it freely to his thirsty listeners. Sure of his doctrine, and bolstered by the ignorance of the mob, he told the voters, "Now, I'm a friend of the darkey so long as he stays in his place. It's none of my business if Gar Rivers goes into the Dabney house by the front door. Gar is a good old darkey. But, my friends, there ain't no nigger coming in my front door. The back door is good enough for any nigger, because this is white man's country."

Oscar Hardee recited the same creed, mouthing different words. "Them Peninsula Yankees are building privies for their nigger workmen. Ruining good old Southern darkeys. Me and you know niggers are just like children, and you can't pamper 'em too much."

That night one of the valley Irish and one of the valley Negroes fought a stabbing brawl at the livery stable.

Sans wanted to strike back. Wyeth and Mr. Charlie restrained him. "Anything you say will make it worse," the lawyer said. "If you Dabneys get in the mud, that's all they want."

Then Cephus Hill called the Dabneys traitors to the South. He lowered his voice and spoke in awed tones. The Dabneys had no right to walk the fair and soft Southern soil wherein lay the bodies of the heroic Confederate dead. The Dabneys had fought the Confederacy. The Yankees had fought the Confederacy. Therefore, the Dabneys were Yankees at heart. Peninsula was a Yankee company.

"Put it all together," Windy said, "and you'll get the truth. Them nigger-loving, aristocratic, Yankified Dabneys are hand in glove with them rich, nigger-loving, Yankees of Peninsula." His voice was vibrant with his indignation. "Sans Dabney's suit is just a trick to fool you hard-working folks. I know it's a trick. Didn't I work for Peninsula until I saw the light?" He raised his face and lifted his hands to the light, and the people roared their approval.

Wyeth Woodward went to the hustings then, up to the forks of the creeks, the springhead of the South, the source of its beauty and its brutality, its wisdom and its ignorance. His daughter volunteered to leave her annex and drive him around the county. Her heritage, for one stirring hour, was stronger than her ambition; and she helped her father in his labors to mend the rents that Windy was ripping in the fabric of Lebanon's life.

Mr. Charlie left The Store in Sans' care and took to the byways, shaking hands and counseling. He and Wyeth and Louisa were effective, and Windy Hill fired another shot.

Keith Alexander married a Dabney. Keith Alexander was rolling in money and he lived in Chicago, up North with them Yankees. "I hear tell," Cephus Hill said, "that his office is in the same building with Peninsula. I hear tell he owns the building."

Then old bones were dug up, and the Dabney crypt was opened in public. The Dabneys were responsible for the death of their son-in-law, Colonel Claiborne MacIvor, that peerless leader of a tattered Confederate host. "Keith Alexander killed him," they whispered. "But the Dabneys were responsible."

Aven heard and tried to answer. "I am the widow of Claiborne MacIvor. I can fight my own fight." She almost was a Dabney then.

Mrs. Oscar Hardee, prompted by Cephus Hill, preached: "Aven Dabney's own mother, old lady Shellie Dabney, won't let her in the house. That's the kind of folks they are. Shut the door on their own flesh and blood."

Oscar repeated the story and Sans reached for a buggy whip. Mingo stopped him.

In the far end of the county, Jeb Slade announced he aimed to stick by the Dabneys. His stand brought a quick rumor that he had sired two Negro children.

Two weeks before election day, Windy Hill drew enough money

from Peninsula to give the people a barbecue and there he told them, "The top rail has been on top long enough. I aim to put the bottom rail on top, and you are the bottom rail."

Leslie Beck, the bank's teller, proclaimed his loyalty to the Dabneys. He was fired that day and next morning Peninsula Lumber Company deposited fifty thousand dollars in Mr. Stanley's bank. Mr. Stanley was promoted from cashier to vice-president.

Paxton Badham, who trapped for his living, cheered at one of Wyeth Woodward's rallies. The next day the mortgage on his traps was called.

G. T. Thrumbull was inspecting Peninsula's far western mills when he and Ruth got reports that Lebanon was in turmoil. Thrumbull wired his company for permission to return to the valley. He was told to continue his tour. The message ended, "It is a policy of the company to remain aloof from local politics."

Ruth, however, left her father and journeyed alone back to the valley. What she saw made her ill, then furious.

She called at the Dabney house and that was a mistake. She went to The Store to see Sans and Mr. Charlie, and that was a blunder. "Stay away," Mr. Charlie said. "The best thing you can do is to cuss all the Dabneys. Cuss 'em in public."

"I'll not do it." Instead, she buttonholed men as they went in and out of the post office, pleading the cause of the Dabneys.

"Huh," Mrs. Vernon Boyd snickered. "She's panting after Sans Dabney like a minx in heat. Brazen Yankee trash!"

Then the pack turned on Mingo for one final snarl at his family. . . . "Thinks he's better than folks around here. Valley girls ain't good enough for him." It was a whisper. . . . "Lost his head over a foreigner." It was a sneer. . . . "Mooning around like a puppy in love, making a dunce of himself over that white-headed Cuban."

"Lots of niggers in Cuba. Folks all mixed up in Cuba, white folks and niggers."

"She's a Cuban, ain't she?" Somebody started it.

"That's how come she wears that shawl all the time. White hair, all right. But kinky." Somebody else took it up.

"A nigger's a nigger, and one drop of nigger blood is all it takes." Mingo Dabney was in love with a nigger woman!

"Them Dabneys asked her to their house, just like she was good as white folks."

God damn Peninsula Yankees! And them God damn nigger-lovin' Dabneys!

Ruth was the first of the Dabney supporters to hear it. Her cook told her, and wept when she told her; frightened by what had been said, terrified of what might happen.

"Keep it to yourself." Ruth reached for her coat. It was late afternoon and she must find Sans Dabney and find him quickly. She did not wait for her buggy, but flung a sidesaddle over her horse and swung up, tucking her dress under her legs and racing toward The Store. He was not there. Mr. Charlie hadn't heard it. She knew by his bearing that he hadn't heard it. He told her Sans was back at his barn with his oxen, and there she hurried.

The Dabney boy came out of the ox stables, dusting cottonseed meal from his hands and picking hay straw from his coat. "What's the matter with you?" He propped himself on the gate and looked at her.

"Sans—" She put her hand on his arm, and then she told him. She felt his muscles tighten and saw all the color slowly drain from his face.

"Go home, Ruth." The words were hollow—cold and stern. He walked toward his horse tied to the fence.

"I'm going with you—"

"You go home." He touched her, patting her arm. His touch was as cold as his words. "I've got to head off a killing. Now you go on home." He left her and picked his way down the ridge, wheeling into the pike at the south cut, then on up the road to the courthouse.

Windy Hill was in Vernon Boyd's office and Sans entered without knocking, scarcely glancing at Boyd, but looking down at the puffy-faced lawyer slouched in his swivel chair. "Windy," he said, and was surprised at the calmness of his voice. "I want to see you alone. Just me and you."

Vernon Boyd accepted Windy's nod as a gesture of dismissal and walked out, closing the door behind him.

The candidate reached for a cigar and tilted back. "Have a seat, Dabney." He pointed at a chair.

Sans said, "I'll stand."

Cephus Hill lifted up his beady little eyes to the elder brother, then quickly looked away, seeing something in the face that alarmed him. "What's on your mind?" He was sorry then that Vernon Boyd was gone.

The Dabney boy wet his lips and rested his hands on the desk, leaning toward the shyster, the politician. "Windy, you're a son of a bitch—"

"Now, wait a minute," Cephus Hill moved to rise.

Sans caught his flabby shoulder, holding him in the chair. "Keep your seat. I won't be here but a minute. It's about six o'clock. Almost supper time."

Windy's eyes darted around the room, then back to Sans. "What are you getting at?"

"Some folks are saying that Miss Rafaela Galban is brushed with the tar."

The candidate feigned surprise, even shock. "Is that a fact? This campaign is getting bitter. I never had the pleasure of meeting Rafaela Galban—"

"Miss Galban, Windy."

Cephus Hill hesitated, then lowered his eyes and mumbled, "Miss Galban."

Sans released Windy's shoulder. "That lie hasn't spread far yet. I just heard it."

The lawyer tilted back once more, locking his fingers behind his head and staring up at the ceiling. "What do you want me to do about it? I didn't start it."

"It's six o'clock—"

"You said that before."

"If that story isn't scotched by six o'clock tomorrow morning, I'll kill you." He was as calm as the twilight that shadowed the room. He gripped the edge of the desk, and his knuckles were white and his face was white, but his voice was as calm as judgment. And he was judgment. He was judgment and death—and Windy Hill knew it.

The demagogue licked his lips nervously and his mouth twitched. He could not bring himself to lower his eyes from the ceiling and face the Dabney boy. "I'll do what I can."

Sans put his hands in his pockets. "You'll do more than that. You'll scotch that story once and for all. I've never killed a man, but I'll kill you. I'll stomp the living hell out of you. I'll do it to keep my brother from doing it." He turned and walked to the door, opening it wide and going out without looking back at Cephus Hill.

Windy got up and went to the window, watching him ride away. Then he began pacing the floor, waddling as he walked, and puffing his cigar. He paced the floor until dark; he had no appetite for his supper. That night he drove with Vernon Boyd to a rally down in the southern end of the county.

The candidate for judge spoke last at the rally, using the occasion to praise the valley of Lebanon as sanctuary for all oppressed people. "When José Marti, that Cuban revolutionist, that peerless leader of a fearless people, needed help he came to Lebanon and was welcome." He said the words slowly and distinctly, pounding their import into the minds of his henchmen, of all who heard him.

He raised himself to his full height and lifted his arms, his little eyes glowing in the fervor of the moment. "When Miss Rafaela Galban—" He let the words sink in, holding his sentence while his eyes turned from one sycophant to the next.

The people stared at him and his cohorts nodded their understanding. Cephus Hill would never call a nigger woman *Miss* Rafaela Galban.

"A flower of Spanish womanhood!" He honeyed his words, dripping them slowly. "A daughter of glorious Castile!"

He lowered his hands and lowered his voice. "I had the pleasure of knowing Miss Galban personally. I donated to the Cuban cause. I am a poor man—" Windy laid his hand upon his chest. "But I gave without stint. She promised that some day she would come back to Lebanon, and did me the honor—me, a poor old Mississippi boy, a peckerwood just like you—the honor of accepting an invitation to my humble home."

It was done. Windy Hill spoke his reprieve, and Rafaela Galban y Torres was a white woman again.

The calumny died that night as quickly as it was born. Windy Hill didn't need it, anyhow. The cheers of the people told him he didn't need it.

Mr. Charlie and Gar Rivers and Wyeth Woodward knew the cause was lost several days before voting time. The Dabneys did not believe it could happen in the valley of Lebanon, in Dabney's Hollow.

A wagon load of whiskey moved into New Hebron the night before election and there was a torchlight parade for Windy Hill. His followers shot anvils and threw their wool hats into the air, shouting for the new order. The bottom rail was on top.

Gar Rivers was the first man at the polls, presenting himself for the right to express his choice, evidence of his consent to be governed. One of the Hill faction demanded the Negro's poll tax receipt and Gar produced it. "This is a general election," he said, calmly. "It is not a primary, but here is my receipt."

A poll watcher scowled at the old man. "Can you read and write?" "Yes." He read and he wrote.

"Do you comprehend the Constitution?"

"I think so. We, the people of the United States, in order to form a more perfect union—"

"The State Constitution?"

They asked Gar Rivers questions about the Constitution of Mississippi, and he answered them. "Aw, let him vote. He's the last nigger who'll vote around here for a long time. Judge Hill aims to reorganize the primary. He'll make it a white primary; then the general election won't be nothing but a way to shut up the folks in Washington."

None challenged Wyeth Woodward or Mr. Charlie, but one of Hill's supporters dared question Bruce Dabney. The old man looked at him and held out his hand for his ballot. It was given to him and the crowd was silent; the white hair, the frosty eyes silenced them.

They did their best to trap Mingo until he suggested they let Oscar Hardee interpret the Constitution. They gave him his ballot quickly and ordered him to maintain the legal distance from the polling place.

Sans voted with Joe Doyle who came all the way down from the Mainline to help the Dabneys. One of Hill's henchmen grinned at Sans. "You ever read the Constitution, my boy?"

"Yes," Sans said quietly. "It gives me the right to defend myself. I'll have my ballot, if you please."

The polls closed at six o'clock, and by six-thirty, as the November night was wrapping the valley in blackness, it was apparent the Dabneys were defeated in their own bailiwick. By seven o'clock it was a rout, and Mr. Charlie went home. He led his ticket; but even he, the old wheel horse, was snowed under by the Hill slate, by the new order.

Wyeth drove home early and drank more than was his custom. He went to bed mumbling his contempt for Yankees too greedy to see, for Southerners too lazy to open their eyes.

Ruth Thrumbull, alone in her big house, sat by her window and watched darkness creep over the valley. Then she shuddered and wished for Sans Dabney.

The Dabneys, at their supper table, stared at their empty coffee cups. There were few words. Eventually, however, Sans broke the sullen, awed silence. "Good Lord! We are in the back seat."

"We aren't even in the buggy," Bruce said.

"Then what's left?" Mingo demanded. "What is there to fight for?"

"People," his father said. "Still people."

In the village, the people celebrated, drinking and dancing on the courthouse lawn. It was cool there, but the whiskey and the flush of triumph kept them warm. Somebody suggested burning a Negro shack just to show who was on top. Windy Hill restrained them. "I'm a friend of the darkey," he said. "No rough stuff, boys. Just keep the darkey in his place."

While his followers celebrated, Judge Cephus Hill slipped into the courthouse, lit a lamp and went to work. There must never again be another general election of any significance in county affairs. Of that Judge Hill was confident. And it was so easy. One party, one primary, a white primary to name all officers; a general election to confirm the result of the primary, to make it legal and keep it sounding like democracy.

It was so simple. No ballot at all for the black men and a ballot for the poor white only at the sufferance and maneuvering of Judge Cephus Hill. The man at the fork of the creek must be called up and used on voting day, then sent back to dwell in darkness until needed again. His reward was his belief that he was playing some part in his government. His solace was the tradition that he was better than a nigger.

Vernon Boyd resigned as sheriff and Oscar Hardee took over. The new sheriff's first chore was to appoint Boyd chief deputy. The power behind both the sheriff and his deputy was Windy Hill. The power behind Hill was the surrender of the people. Now let the people take heed!

In a dozen cities and states, shrewd men like Cephus Hill pricked up their ears and sniffed the breeze. They had his voice and his heart and his cynical disdain of integrity, and they were daring. In Alabama and Illinois, in Georgia and Pennsylvania, in Oklahoma and Ohio, from Jersey City to Kansas City, from New Orleans to New York—the voice of Jacob was the hand of Esau. Tribute from business so business could have its way. Tribute big enough for the manipulators to get all they wanted, and still have enough to toss coppers to the people.

Mr. Irving, now that the bottom rail was on top, came back to the valley and made Peninsula's first demand on Judge Hill. The Peninsula lawyer called for the company's initial dividend on its political investment—the settlement of all lawsuits.

Wyeth Woodward perceived the handwriting long before the words were written. He went to Sans and advised an immediate compromise. Sans was incredulous. "Give in before we have a hearing?"

"That's right. The jury lists are already rigged. If we wait until after the first of the year, when Cephus Hill takes office, we'll not even get our case to trial."

"What about the north cut?" Sans demanded. "Have they got us by the neck there, too?"

"No. That's a question of eminent domain. That's for the state to say, and they don't own our state government. Not yet."

Sans settled for three hundred and twenty-five dollars and turned the money over to Mingo to be invested in The Store, in Mr. Charlie's department. Peninsula settled some of the other suits at ten cents on the dollar. Most of them were thrown out.

Judge Hill told the people that Sans' settlement was more evidence of his collusion with the company. "He got a heap of money," Judge Hill said, "and you folks got nothing."

Mr. Thrumbull was sent back to his job with instructions to remain aloof from politics. He did. "Can't you see what you're doing?" Ruth pleaded. "We're at the mercy of Cephus Hill. He's selling the South down a sewer to make a profit. You're helping, by doing nothing about it."

"I do not appreciate a lecture from my daughter," Mr. Thrumbull said sternly. "Just because you're in love with one of the Dabney boys is no reason to condemn your father."

Ruth's jaw trembled and she ran to her room, flung herself across her bed and wept.

Peninsula's next demand on Cephus Hill was for a way through the north cut. The message of instructions was couched in flattery and, reading the words, there was no incrimination. Between the lines, however, Peninsula stated its case; they were calling on Cephus to pay further dividends on their investment. The judge read the letter twice, then filed it in his safe. It was cunningly written, but he might be able to use it if he and the company ever fell out.

It was time for Cephus Hill to build his poltiical fence into a stone wall. All he needed was to absorb the opposition. He put on his hat and went to The Store to see Mingo Dabney.

Mr. Charlie saw him coming and Sans saw him, and suddenly there was a great fear in the heart of Charlie Owens. Cephus Hill was an ambitious man and Mingo Dabney was a restless man; and Mr. Charlie knew that the new power was seeking an alliance. Sans suspected as much, but there was no fear in his heart.

Judge Hill took off his hat when he entered The Store. He looked around and offered his hand to Sans and to Mr. Charlie. They declined it and Hill said, "I came to see the boss. Where's Mr. Mingo Dabney?"

Sans said, "He's over in the other department. I'll call him." He went for his brother and then he and Mr. Charlie retired to the back of The Store.

Mingo leaned against a counter. "What's on your mind?"

"I just dropped by," the judge said. "I want to bury the hatchet. Me and you are home folks."

The younger Dabney didn't move. "What's on your mind, Windy?"

Sans and Mr. Charlie were waiting and watching.

Judge Hill hooked his thumbs in his vest pockets. "I just dropped by to see you. Maybe your taxes are a little high. Our new tax assessor is a good friend of mine."

Mingo Dabney, once the carefree brother, now the restless one, looked first at Windy's heavy ankles, then at the horseshoe stickpin in his brown tie, then at his red galluses. He scarcely turned his head over his shoulder, calling to his brother. "Kiddo! Open both the front doors. This son of a bitch is a little on the fat side. I need both doors wide so I can throw him through."

Judge Cephus Hill looked from one to the other and walked out. He was not angry. He didn't say a word. There was no need to waste a second shot on a thing already dying.

Louisa Woodward, standing by the door of her annex, watched him walk down past her father's office, thence across the street to the courthouse. A tiny frown, a calculating little frown, wrinkled the bridge of her nose. She stood there a minute, then reached for her coat and hat, adjusting her hat carefully before a mirror and brushing her coat. She bit her lips, reddening them, and walked out of her annex and down the street, the same route Judge Hill had taken.

The daughter passed her father's office and did not look in; then, lifting her skirt properly, she stepped from the sidewalk into the street and across the street to the courthouse lawn. There she hesitated a second under a water oak, staring at the courthouse as though rededicating her mind to her purpose. Her gaze moved from the old courthouse down to the south cut, to the company's store, huge and raw and red.

She would paint it white; have a gallery, wisteria on the gallery. She envisioned the sign across the front of the store, bold letters: Louisa Woodward, Manager. All she wanted was a reasonable salary and considerable stock. Louisa Woodward didn't have to marry a business; she was smart enough to take one. An understanding between her and Judge Cephus Hill—for business purposes, of course, was the right beginning. It was good, sound common sense.

Louisa took a deep breath, summoning her courage. She gathered her skirt in her hand, lifting it carefully, protecting the fine woolen hem from the old gray dirt of the courthouse lawn, the brown leaves and the patchy winter grass. She held her head high and walked into the courthouse, walking down the hallway to the office of Judge Cephus Hill, going to new vineyards, seeking new vines to destroy.

Her strong, straight back and her swaying hips were toward her father's office as she trod the long distance between yesterday and today; and her back was to The Store, for Louisa Woodward was deserting a tradition that she, too, knew was dying.

Chapter sixteen

THE AUTUMN OF 1894, the year of panic and portents, shed its robes of red and brown and surrendered wearily to winter. There was a snow in Lebanon that December, one of the few Sans ever saw. It robed the earth and cowled the trees, and the elder brother thought how good the snow was for the land. Mingo looked at the slender young pines crowned with white and again remembered Rafaela Galban.

The lull of the busk season, of harvest ended, soothed the valley, and Sans hunted the ridges. His mind was at peace while he was in the woods, for the stillness of the woods spoke to him and the earth was sure under his feet, but at night, the long, somber nights of winter, he sat by the family hearth and brooded. The rails were ready at the north cut, and the mill fires were bright at the south cut, and the welt on his father's hand was dark. Each day he saw Ruth Thrumbull at The Store, but at night he brooded.

Quail whistled in the broom sedge and geese flew high, calling as they winged their way south. Some of the Cajuns, the superstitious, said the geese soared because they were afraid of the earth. It was an ill omen. The brothers watched the white wedge piercing the sky, and the far-off calling drifted back to them. The elder brother wondered whither they went, but the younger brother knew they flew on south toward the scattered islands, toward one island the restless, lonely Mingo could not banish from his mind.

There came reports of gunfire in Cuba's hills. Ruth read about it and Mr. Charlie and Sans talked about it. Mingo rode the ridges, looking beyond the valley, his dark eyes smoldering. And the geese were flying high, afraid of the earth.

Then came a whispered word, swelling into a lament. Fishbait Gates was dead, felled by yellow fever in Florida, trying to get to Cuba. He and his two-edged ax had felled a thousand trees for the Dabneys.

Ruth and Sans arranged a memorial service for Fishbait. Wyeth spoke and Gar Rivers spoke. Judge Cephus Hill appeared at the service and, without introduction, rose in the congregation and delivered a eulogy. "Fishbait Gates was a good darkey." The judge exuded fellowship as he called him, "My old friend, Fishbait." Some of the Negroes were notably impressed, and flattered to get a crumb from the table of the mighty.

Shortly thereafter Cephus Hill, apparently without design, met Louisa Woodward in front of the post office and handed her a wordy, ironclad document, an agreement between them. He told her to study it, and there was no need for her father to examine it. Then the judge closed his office in New Hebron and went back to Ellisville, back to his home and his invalid wife, and set about weaving the pattern of things to come, planning a new order, planting a new Southern vineyard.

Vernon Boyd and Oscar Hardee sauntered along the streets of New Hebron. The red-necks perked up as they passed and called them by their first names. The Negroes got out of their way.

Aven MacIvor returned to Mobile to confer with her lawyer about settling her dispute with Peninsula, and to plan for her holdings.

The sun came out again and winter drew away her white cape, leaving the woods too wet to log and too wet to hunt. Sans Dabney worked in The Store, learning merchandise from Mr. Charlie, and the boy's presence at The Store brought trade because people liked him. The bitterness of the political campaign passed and many of the voters were ashamed of some of the things they'd said. Sans Dabney wasn't an aristocrat. He was just a fellow with brown hair, friendly and willing to do a favor, working like ordinary folks for his living, working in his brother's store and shining up to Mr. G. T. Thrumbull's girl.

There was enough business in Lebanon for both the Dabney store and the company store, but gradually, reluctantly, Peninsula was forced to surrender the best trade and handle only the second-class stuff Mr. Charlie scorned. Mingo was secure again, and boasted, "Sans and I have whipped 'em to a frazzle. He's got 'em stopped at the north cut and we're running 'em ragged at The Store."

Mr. Charlie answered him. "A snake never dies until sundown. It's getting late around here, but not that late." The old man nodded, emphasizing the wisdom of his words.

It was mid-December, that day Louisa stepped to the door between her annex and Mr. Charlie's department, and motioned with her finger for Sans to come to her. He was prying the lid off a crate of Christmas raisins and he reached in and pulled out one of the brown bunches and walked toward her, munching the dried grapes. "Want some?" he asked.

"No, thank you. Meet me back in my office. I want to talk to you."

He grinned. "Got some more trash?"

She walked away, her head high, her heels rapping the floor. He followed her into the annex and noticed for the first time that her stock was low. He and Mr. Charlie were stocking heavily for Christmas, but there were gaps in the shelves of the annex and the displays in the showcases were skimpy.

Louisa closed the door to her office and sat down. She allowed only one chair in her office so people would not tarry there. Sans stood by the door and watched her. "What's on your mind?"

He was nibbling the raisins and it infuriated her for him to treat her so casually. She smoothed her skirt and crossed her feet. It was ladylike and businesslike. She picked up a pencil and tapped it nervously against her knee. "I will get right to the point."

"What point?" The room was stuffy and Sans was conscious of her heavy perfume, mingling with the smell of sweetened rice powder. Then it came to him that Ruth Thrumbull used perfume; he had smelled it, but never been conscious of it before. It was not like Louisa's perfume, not like incense; more like a nosegay with a little fragrance that darted away and never lingered.

"You're the one who prevented me from getting stock in The Store." Louisa tossed the pencil back on the desk. "I've worked my hands to the bone for this store. I've made a lot of money for Mingo—"

"Why tell me about it?" Sans' grin vanished and he put his back against the door, leaning there. "It's not my business. Mingo runs The Store."

"But you run Mingo," she said tartly. "Ever since Rafaela Galban was here he's been a different man. He leaves everything to you. All you do is blink your eye and he jumps—"

"What's on your mind, Louisa?" Sans' voice was quiet. "Let's have it."

"Very well." She said it haughtily, tilting her chin in defiance. "I'm warning you, Sans Dabney. I'm giving you fair warning."

He looked down at her, studying her. Was this the girl he'd kissed almost with reverence when he was a boy? Was she the one who left his heart empty when she went away, and tightened his heart when she returned? Was this the girl he'd longed for, ached for, and planned his world for? "You are warning me. How, Louisa?"

"Yes. I'm giving you fair warning." She was nervous then and did not look at him, did not meet his gaze. "Peninsula Lumber Company has asked me to manage their store. Unless I get a fair share of the money I've made for you Dabneys, and some stock in this store, I'm going to take their offer."

The room was quiet and Sans stood there a moment longer, looking down at her; then he turned to open the door. "This is a matter for Mingo. I'll call him."

"No you won't!" Her voice rose and there was a hint of hysteria in her shrill tone. He had never seen her lose her poise before, her surety of herself. "I want you to take it up with Mingo. He'll listen to you."

"If he does, you'll mighty soon be working for Peninsula Lumber Company." Sans still spoke quietly. "You can't be very loyal to Mingo if you're dickering with them."

Her face was taut, her lips tight as she glared at him. "If I leave this department, there will be no department. The trade will follow me."

He said nothing, but turned to the door again, putting out his hand and touching the knob.

"Don't you dare get Mingo!" She caught his arm, and he pulled his arm away from her. She spat her words at him. "I don't want to talk to him. I want you to settle it for me."

Sans ignored her contemptuously and stepped out of the room, drawing the door closed behind him. He walked out into the annex and spoke to one of the clerks, a Cajun girl. "Madeleine, would you mind stepping over to the mill and telling Mingo that Miss Woodward is waiting for him?" He passed through the doorway and was back at his own work when Mingo came from his mill and walked directly to Louisa's office.

"Sump'n going on around here?" Mr. Charlie glanced at Sans, then peered toward the annex.

"It sure as hell is." Sans was opening a sack of coconuts. He picked up one and held it close to his ear, shaking it, listening to the milk inside. "Mingo will tell you about it."

The younger brother came out of the ladies' shop a few minutes later and his face was pale, his jaw set. He called the two men back to Mr. Charlie's office and, without beating around the bush, announced: "Louisa is leaving us."

Mr. Charlie's eyes popped open and his Adam's apple bobbed. "Well, now, I do declare—"

"She's going to work for Peninsula. Going to run their store." He actually seemed relieved, as though happy to be done with an association that had become a burden to him.

Mr. Charlie shook his head. "It'll break her father's heart. His only daughter working for Peninsula."

"She's grown," Sans said. "She has a right to make up her own mind."

Mingo agreed, and Mr. Charlie said, "Reckon you're right. But Wyeth Woodward is going to be mighty put out. Him lawing for the Dabneys and his girl working for Peninsula."

"That'll make no difference in our feeling for Mr. Woodward." Sans glanced at his brother, and the younger one nodded.

Mr. Charlie scratched behind his ear and scowled his suspicion that all the story had not been revealed. He poked his tongue in his cheek and cocked one eye at the ceiling. "Louisa was doing all right with us. Making good money. She was her own boss. Them Yankees must have put up powerfully heavy to get her."

"They offered her stock," Mingo said.

"Is that a fact?" Mr. Charlie still was skeptical. "Ain't like Peninsula to be handing out stock."

The Dabney boys gave no particular heed to his words. Mingo

was concerned with more pressing matters. He had a ladies' ready-to-wear department on his hands and no one to manage it.

Sans asked, "What you aim to do?"

Mingo pushed aside a stack of papers and sat on the desk, dangling his feet. "Louisa ain't the only smart girl around here. I can get somebody as good as her, maybe better."

"Who?" Sans demanded quickly. "Who you got in mind?"

"Ruth Thrumbull. If Peninsula can hire one of our crowd, then I'll hire one of theirs."

Sans picked up an eraser, tossing it into the air and catching it, deliberating. Mr. Charlie was watching him, his old eyes weary and wise. Sans put the eraser back on the desk. "I'd be might grateful if you kept Ruth out of this."

"I was waiting to hear that," said the younger brother, himself suddenly serious.

"Well, you've heard it. This store sort of changed Louisa. I don't want Ruth changed a bit."

Mingo slid off the desk and glanced around, first at his brother and then at Mr. Charlie, then at the calendar placed over the desk by Elmo Batson. "That settles that. Either of you got any ideas?"

"Get rid of the damn stuff," Mr. Charlie suggested vigorously.

Mingo hesitated. "It's valuable merchandise, and I don't feel like taking a loss on it."

"You won't have to," Sans said. "Sell it to Peninsula. They'll grab it. Save them haulage. You know what it costs to haul stuff in here by wagon."

The younger boy tilted his head to one side, studying his brother and pleased by his business acumen. "What'll we do with the annex if we unload the stock?" Mingo asked.

"Make it into a furniture store," Sans urged. "Put in a good line." His brain was turning fast, revolving his long-range plans for the valley, for the Dabneys. "Hire an experienced manager. Plenty of them in Mobile. Sell on installment payments. A lot of stores are doing it."

Mingo whacked him across the shoulder and grinned at Mr. Charlie. "Looks like he's got it figured out. Let's have a bottle of beer."

The report that Louisa was leaving the Dabneys for Peninsula, at first a rumor and then a public announcement by Mingo, caused only a ripple of interest in Lebanon, not nearly the comment that Louisa expected. It was too near Christmas for the folks to chew long on that morsel. Louisa's resignation was to be effective January 1, 1895.

Her decision brought only scorn from Kyd Dabney, and for a while the mother was furious at her best friend's daughter. Louisa was deserting Mingo! She had counted on Louisa to help shape Mingo's life into the mold of a successful businessman, a good provider, a faithful husband, and a dutiful son. And now the little snip was trading her heritage for a mess of Peninsula pottage. If she'd only played her cards right, she might have become a Dabney, like Kyd. The little fool! Kyd stewed inside herself until her pride prevailed and she decided to ignore the whole thing. If Louisa didn't have gumption enough to stick with The Store and try to win Mingo, then the Dabneys were downright lucky to be shed of her.

Bruce shrugged it off and Laurel Woodward tried to explain it away, using the post office forum, church suppers and meetings of the Eastern Star to get her daughter's position over to the people; and Louisa's position simply was that Peninsula was a big concern willing to pay for brains, while the Dabneys were just fairly well-to-do folks, working for their own living.

Wyeth took it mighty hard. He asked his daughter only if she felt sure she was right; then accepted her affirmative verdict and stood ready to defend her. However, he hung his head just a bit and confided in Bruce that his mortification was deep.

Old Bruce Dabney put his foot down then. He didn't aim to see Wyeth Woodward mortified. The Dabneys and the Woodwards were friends long before Peninsula ever came to the valley, and Bruce asked Kyd to invite the family to supper. Kyd protested and Bruce demanded that she heed his wishes.

Louisa and Laurel did not want to accept the invitation, but Wyeth stared them down and instructed his wife to go up to The House and tell Kyd Dabney that the Woodwards were honored by the invitation. That settled that.

It was a good supper. The ham was hot and juicy, and the fire was warm. The candles were gay and bright, and so were the Dabney boys. So was Louisa Woodward. It was their duty to be gay,

and Lebanon understood duty. The Store was not mentioned. Neither
was Peninsula.

And neither was Cuba.

Sans saw Ruth at The Store every day, and sometimes at night
he went to her house and they sat together in the library, she listening to his plans, his hopes, and wondering if she were a part of them.

Mr. Charlie crowded The Store with a gay Christmas stock.
Boxes of candy stood open on the counter—lemon drops, striped red
and white sticks of peppermint, licorice plugs, sticks of banana and
sassafras. Mr. Charlie didn't mind when his customers helped themselves to a nibble, but he snorted when Mr. Stanley, the bank's vice-
president, helped himself to a handful.

Golden-haired dolls sat upright in their boxes, staring out with
big blue eyes and holding out stiff little hands. Red and green and
blue tops were jumbled all together; but the marbles were separated,
the lowly jinks and jugs in one compartment, the gleaming red
agates and stonies in another. Boxes of oranges were opened and
tilted back against the counter. Barrels of apples had their lids broken
in. The sweet aromas mingled and all Lebanon knew that Christmas
was near.

December was turning the last few of its pages, fast to the aging
and slow to the young; and the year was drawing its cloak around
its old frame to go away and join all the other years at the endless
encampment of time.

Christmas day was warm and muggy, and the Peninsula crowd
celebrated the feast. The Dabneys and most of the valley were
Twelfth Night Christians, following the old cult that observed the
ancient rites of Epiphany, the feast twelve days after the Nativity.
Old Christmas, they called it. The valley was divided even on such
a sacred thing as the birth of its Lord.

Mingo closed The Store on December 25 in deference to the day,
and the Dabneys rested. Ruth Thrumbull came to The House late
that afternoon and brought the family some of her fruit cake, juicy
with raisins and nuts, currants and citron, and moist from a long
whiskey soaking. Kyd welcomed her as she had never done before,
serving her pound cake and coffee, and Bruce enjoyed her visit. She
asked permission to take Shellie a piece of her cake, and the old

woman ate it, working at it patiently with her toothless jaws. "Who
are you?" she asked.

"Why, I'm Ruth Thrumbull, Mrs. Dabney." Ruth picked up some
of the crumbs that Shellie spilled on the afghan across her knees.
"I live over on the east ridge."

"Ay—" The old woman nodded. "You're Sans' girl." Then she bent
forward and poked a gaunt finger against Ruth's shoulder. "I've
heard the boys talk about you." She nodded again, tapping her ear.
"They all think I'm deaf, but I know what's going on around here.
And you're Sans' girl."

"That's right, Mrs. Dabney. I'm Sans' girl." She was laughing as
she leaned closer to the old woman. "And I wish you'd tell him so."

Ruth joined the family in singing the old songs. Once she looked
at Sans with a request in her eyes and he interpreted it, knowing
the song she wanted; but he shook his head. Kyd saw the gesture
and Mingo saw it. Ruth ate supper with them and Sans drove her
home.

The week after Christmas was a busy time at The Store. Mr.
Charlie and Sans took inventory, Sans working his way from the
front to the back of the building, calling out the number of lamps
and horse collars, plows and coffins, the number of canned goods
and the size and length of chains. Mr. Charlie wrote it all in his
ledger and figured his needs.

Louisa Woodward came to the annex each morning and super-
vised the checking of her stock by Madeleine, the Cajun girl, and
the Irish girl, Mamie Daly. Louisa hardly bothered to speak to Sans
or Mr. Charlie, and talked to Mingo only about the sale of the stock
to Peninsula.

"It's all very shopworn," she said. "But I'll have a sale. I can dis-
pose of it, I guess."

"You don't have to buy it," Mingo said. "Leave it here and we'll
have a sale."

She tossed her head and walked behind the counter; picking up a
baby's bonnet, she glanced at it, then threw it back into its box.
"No. It costs too much to haul things into the valley. The wagon
charges are outrageous."

The stock of the annex was not all listed by the end of the year;
Louisa gave final instructions to Madeleine and Mamie Daly on

how to complete the inventory; then told them goodbye. At the exit, she stopped and glanced about her; the shelves she had planned, the hats she had trimmed. Then she turned quickly and walked into Mr. Charlie's department. She shook hands with him and with Sans, and stalked out of the old store; her head erect, never looking back.

Mr. Charlie cleared his throat. "Let's me and you have a bottle of beer, son."

They drank their beer, the old man sitting at his desk and Sans on a barrel of flour. Mr. Charlie was silent and Sans' beer was bitter.

The night before Epiphany, as was the custom, Bruce and his two sons went together to feed the mules and the cows, the horses and the sheep. During the year they were stock, but on the eve of Epiphany they were beast-things to be fed well and fondled. A man must be kind to his beast-things for they, too, were creatures of God; and they ate well and the Dabneys fasted, symbolizing their willingness to fast that God's creatures might feast.

There was bread and milk on the table and the Dabneys broke the bread. Bruce took a portion to old Shellie, dozing in her chair, too feeble to come to the table. Then the family ate the bread and drank the milk. The milk was the wine from the beast-things and the bread was the body from the field, and the Dabneys ate and drank and shared in the sacrament.

After supper, they gathered in the parlor and Bruce read the Bible, the story of the visit of the Magi bringing gifts to the Christ child, as it came to pass in Bethlehem.

The last thing Bruce did before bedtime was to go with his sons and scatter grain in the yard, so the birds might find it at the dawn of Epiphany.

Kyd had one of the Negroes stay with Shellie, and she and all the family went to the Free Church the next day and heard Brother Eubanks preach about Joseph and Mary and the child Jesus. The Dabneys sat together on the hard benches and when they knelt, they knelt on the bare floor. The Woodwards were there and all the old valley families, and each family sat together. Only Mr. Charlie was alone.

Back home, the Dabneys feasted and exchanged gifts. The little ceremony was held in Shellie's room so she might share in the thanksgiving and the bringing of gifts. Then Kyd and Bruce took a nap. Sans and Mingo went walking in the woods, this time without guns for God's creatures must not be disturbed on the day the camels brought the Wise Men to Christ and found Him in a stable for beast-things.

The brothers walked over to the north cut, thence down Bogue Homa to the edge of the swamp. Mingo sat on a fallen tree and Sans leaned against a live tree and they watched the creek. In the stillness of the woods, and after the day of worship, the younger one was restless to unload the burden from his heart. "I've been wanting to talk to you."

Sans flaked off a piece of loose bark from a pine and dropped it in the creek. "I reckon I know what it is, Lebuba."

Mingo picked up a leaf and twisted the stem between his fingers, watching it as it turned. "I reckon so. A blind man can see what's happened to me."

A red-tailed hawk screamed high up on the ridge and screamed again, and Sans saw the flash of the sun on its wings. "What you aim to do about it?"

"That's why I want to talk to you." Mingo flipped the leaf aside. "I got to talk to you. I can't put it off any longer."

Sans nodded. "I've seen the geese." He scuffed off a piece of dry bark with his heel and picked it up and thumbed dust from its edges. "They are flying south."

The younger brother didn't look up. "That's the way they're going."

"Do you know where she is?" Sans crushed the bark in his hand and opened his hand and spilled it.

"Florida. She's in Florida. And I got to go."

A wood-bug scurried into the open and Sans watched him run. "There's going to be a showdown in the valley pretty soon."

"How soon?"

Sans shook his head. "I don't know."

Mingo pushed himself up from the log. "That settles that." He caught his brother's arm. "I'll stay as long as you need me. But when it's all right to go, you tell me."

"I'll tell you."

The Dabney boys walked slowly beside the creek, walking on together and a flock of larks rose, whistled their little tune, and settled again. A squirrel barked, then leaped to an oak branch and flattened himself, the red fringe of his tail lifting in the light wind. They came to a sycamore that the lightning had struck and the wind had tugged over, sprawling it on the floor of the forest. Mingo put his foot on the tree. "There's something else." He looked squarely at his brother. "It's about Louisa. You said the other day that The Store had changed her. Do you blame me? Am I to blame for it being off between you two?"

"No. There is no blame." He met his brother's look and went on talking, slowly, choosing his words. "You had nothing to do with it. Louisa just started looking in one direction and I was looking in the other. A man and a woman have got to look together if they aim to make it." He touched a pebble with his toe and it tumbled down and hopped into the creek.

They walked away from Bogue Homa and on toward The House. They did not talk, and the woods were still and all Lebanon was hushed. The silence of a holy day was upon the valley and they went on until they came to the lane, and there Sans stopped. "I think I'll go see Ruth Thrumbull. She came to see us on her Christmas."

"It's fitting you go to see her on ours." Mingo walked on alone toward The House, and Sans turned toward the east ridge and the Thrumbull mansion.

There was humility in the heart of Sans Dabney as he walked through the valley of Lebanon on this day that the Pledge was fulfilled, when man learned the Child was born; on this day when all the water of the earth was pure and cold, and the trees sighed for the burden of the crucifixion. The Dabney boy looked at the dogwood stems and did not see them red, as faith promised them to be; he passed under a cedar tree and the wind was only the wind, and not the angels singing. He looked at the young ferns, and the fronds were not a Christmas star.

At the Thrumbull house, the superintendent of Peninsula's mill met him at the door, and there was friendship in his face. "A joyous Christmas to you, Mr. Dabney."

"And a joyous Christmas to you, sir." The barriers between Peninsula and the Dabneys melted for the moment and the two men shook hands warmly, bound together by the benediction of the day.

"Come in and join me in a glass of wine." Mr. Thrumbull opened the door to his home and led the way into the parlor. He filled two glasses. "Your best health."

The wine was sweet and strong. Sans accepted a chair and refused a cigar.

"Ruth will be sorry she missed you," her father said.

"She's not here?"

"She went for a little stroll." Mr. Thrumbull lighted his cigar and threw the match in the blazing fireplace. The two men drank their wine and talked about the beauty of the day that was no longer warm and muggy, but was cooling slightly; the sun clearing the air and crisping it, a light wind blowing down from the north. Sans stayed as long as politeness dictated, then he put his glass aside and stood.

"Come to see us again." Mr. Thrumbull went to the door with him and saw him out. "I'm not sure, but I think Ruth went down toward the south cut."

Sans found her on the ridge, on the path to his ox barn. She was wearing a green coat and a green tam-o'-shanter; the wind had brightened the color in her cheeks and had loosened wisps of her brown hair from under her tam. He took her arm and she fell in step with him and they walked on through the woods together. "I've been drinking your Christmas wine," he said. "Your father was mighty nice to me."

They turned from the path that led to the barn and walked off under the trees. The tang of the pines was sharp in the air; the smell of the earth was moist.

"I wanted to come to your service this morning," Ruth said. "I wanted to come to the Free Church."

"Why didn't you?"

"Oh, I don't know."

He told her about old Christmas, that all the streams of the world flow backward briefly at the hour of the Star. The cattle kneel and confess with soft lowing, and the fowls bend their heads in an attitude of waiting. Many birds sing during the hour and their voices are divinely beautiful.

"Where did you learn all this?" She looked up at him and there was a mist in her eyes. Her hands were thrust deep in her coat pockets.

"I never learned it. We folks in the valley just know it. It's our kind of faith, I reckon."

He taught her that the wind is still, the whole earth hushed until the Star appears and then everything rejoices. The little things of the woods run and dance and cut capers, ducks and geese march, roosters crow, the singing birds get high in the trees and sing an anthem, and the owl floats about, rising and falling, dipping joyously.

Her hand slid from her pocket, and he took it and held it. "They say, too, that the dogwood stem turns red."

"Have you ever seen it?" she asked.

"No."

They paused at the top of the ridge and gazed down into the valley. The sun was gone from the earth but there was a shawl of gold across the sky and a shower of gold upon Bogue Homa. They walked on to the north cut, and there was a soft lowing from the valley, and the wind was still. They stood motionless in that hushed instant, and then, back in the valley, a cock crowed. Ruth loosed his hand and pointed quickly to the ridge. "Look, Sans. The dogwood stems are red."

He looked at the ridge, then down at her, and put his arms around her, drawing her to him. "The dogwood stems are red." He said it softly, and he kissed her, upon her hair, her forehead, upon her waiting lips.

A wedge of geese, flying high, tilted and circled the valley, hovering over the valley. The boy and the girl looked into each other's eyes, and held each other tightly, and they kissed again.

An owl flapped out of the forest and flew away, rising and falling, wheeling and dipping; and the little birds sang their vespers, puffing their throats and singing loudly, then tucking their heads in sleep.

Sans' face was flushed and he cleared his throat. "I want to ask you to marry me. But I can't rightly do it. At least not now."

"Why? Why do you say that?"

He took both her hands. "Because all I've got is a clerk's job, a few oxen, and my trees."

She moved closer to him. "You've got me."

He kissed her again and they walked back down the valley, and she talked of plans, rattling them off, and Sans was surprised how plainly she saw the problems of the valley and the prospects of making a living, listing a dozen ventures that Mr. Charlie had described to her: Dabney oxen to haul gravel, Dabney crews to build roads, the Dabney mill in the shingle business. She talked on, weaving their lives together.

Darkness was seeping in and her hand was under his arm. "Would you like to come home with me for supper?" she asked.

He slipped her hand into his coat pocket, holding it there. "You must come home with me. We Dabneys always eat together on Twelfth Night."

They turned into the lane and passed The Tree, and walked on.

The day of the Magi, of the Wise Men, was observed by Judge Cephus Hill, up at Ellisville, polishing the final touches of a court order.

It was an injunction in the name of the public weal, a document instructing Sans Dabney not to interfere with Peninsula Lumber Company in the construction of a railroad into the valley of Lebanon.

He dated it for the next day, January 7, 1895, and handed the injunction to Sheriff Oscar Hardee. "Serve it tomorrow."

"Then duck?" Sheriff Hardee asked.

"Then duck. Find a good reason to be out of the valley and see that Vernon Boyd is out, too."

Oscar Hardee was afraid. "Somebody is liable to get hurt."

"Maybe. But it won't be us."

Judge Hill waited until the sheriff was on the road back to Lebanon, then caught a train for Jackson, the state capital. The legislature had authority to commit his wife, and insanity was grounds for divorce. Perhaps Louisa Woodward was as good in bed as she was in business.

Chapter seventeen

ONCE A YEAR, always the day after Twelfth Night, Charlie Owens slept late, and Sans opened The Store that morning. He built a fire in the fat-bellied stove, and the tabby cat, Lydia Pinkham, came out yawning and stretching. She rubbed against his leg and he opened a can of salmon for her. The morning was sunny, but a cold breeze was whipping in from the west.

The wide door between the general store and the annex was closed. The goods Louisa had purchased were being moved to Peninsula's store and it would be weeks, maybe months, before the department was ready for business as a furniture store. The annex was cold and gloomy, the curtains drawn and the goods collecting dust as the closing-out inventory was being completed.

Sans watched Lydia Pinkham finish her food, then lick her paws, stretching them wide and yawning her contentment. He laughed to himself, and walked to the front window and looked out. Workers, hurrying to Peninsula's mill in the streaky dawn, were heavy-eyed and weary, for most of them had celebrated late the night before. A blast of steam hissed into the frosty air and the mill's whistle sounded, echoing up the valley. Some of the workers, already late for their jobs, rapped on the window and waved at Sans as they hurried by.

A few customers, mostly children, came in. They wanted things their mothers needed quickly; soap and starch, coal oil and medicine, and snuff. The children were bundled in coats and scarves, and huddled by the stove, whispering and giggling, while Sans filled their orders.

The Cajun salesgirl, the one named Madeleine, arrived at the annex shortly before eight o'clock to inventory the goods and pack them. She waved to Sans and commented on the sermon Brother Eubanks preached at the Free Church the day before.

"Where is Mingo?" She was bustling around, checking dresses piled on the counter. The valley girls always asked about Mingo.

"He's at his mill." The elder brother was warming himself, watching the sunlight change the cool morning into a pleasant one.

"Sans Dabney!" Madeleine stood in the doorway, her hands on her hips. "Come over here and build me a fire. It's cold in this gloomy old place."

He apologized for the oversight, and was back at his own stove when Oscar Hardee walked in. Sans made no move to wait on him. "What can I do for you, sheriff?"

"You can take this paper." Oscar Hardee handed the notice of injunction to Sans and he accepted it, peering at it.

Hardee turned and walked quickly away.

The import of the document did not impress Sans immediately. The legal phraseology confused him, and then he saw the signature of Judge Cephus Hill. He stuffed the paper in his coat pocket and reached for his hat. "Madeleine, look after things a minute."

Out of the door and down the sidewalk he strode to Wyeth Woodward's office. The lawyer was reading his morning paper and smoking his first cigar.

"What's wrong with you?" Wyeth turned in his swivel chair and faced his client.

Sans didn't reply. His lips were compressed. Anger and fear were churning in his stomach, spilling over into his chest. He tossed the paper on Woodward's desk.

Wyeth took time to adjust his spectacles, and the first word of the injunction brought him to his feet. "My God!" That was all he said and all he could say.

"What kind of shenanigan is this, Mr. Woodward?"

The lawyer stepped quickly, very quickly for a man of his bulk, to the rack and reached for his hat. "It's a court order instructing you not to interfere with Peninsula until a hearing can be held." His beard was trembling, and under his heavy beard his skin was white.

"Is it legal?"

"Hell, no, it's not legal." Wyeth Woodward was so angry his voice cracked. "But there it is, and we've got to act fast."

"They may be coming through right now." Sans was controlling his fury.

The lawyer put his hand on the doorknob. "I've got to find a judge to enjoin Peninsula, and hold them up until the hearing." The Dabney boy said nothing, merely looking at the attorney, and Woodward was ashamed for his calling. He felt responsible for the rebellion and contempt he knew was smoldering within Sans Dabney. "Judge Russell over at Leakesville will support me," Wyeth said. "Judge Phillips Russell is an honest man. He's our nearest hope."

"It'll take you most all day to get there," Sans said slowly. "And most all night to get back."

Wyeth didn't answer directly. "I'll need your horse. A buggy is too slow." He opened the door.

Sans followed him into the hallway and called after him, and Wyeth dreaded to face him. "What about me?" The boy's voice rose for the first time. "While you're hunting an honest judge, what do I do? Hang around and wait, while the law lets Peninsula steal my birthright!"

Wyeth Woodward hesitated for a second only. "Son, if a man came in my house and stole my coat, I'd prosecute him. If he came on my land to steal my heritage, I'd fight him." He turned and lumbered up the sidewalk to Sans' horse, grunting as he pulled his bulk into the saddle. He galloped back past his office, glancing neither to the right toward Sans, nor toward the left at the courthouse.

Sans stood there a minute, his whole body sagging and his mind baffled into indecision. Then he saw Oscar Hardee and Vernon Boyd leave the courthouse and drive away in a buggy. The sight stiffened his body and quickened his mind, shaking it free of all doubt. He walked rapidly, sometimes running, toward Mingo's mill.

The younger brother was at his desk and saw Sans coming, running along the path. Mingo jumped from his chair and hurried out to meet him.

"They're coming through," Sans called out. "They're coming through the north cut." He was breathing heavily by now.

Mingo was hatless; he started for his horse, then realized Sans was afoot and they both glanced around quickly, almost frantically. Smoke Jackson, driving an old mule and an older wagon, was approaching the mill for a load of slabs. The two boys ran to the Negro and climbed into the wagon. "Take us to the north cut," Sans said. "Whip up your mule—"

"They're coming through." Mingo pointed up the valley. "They're coming through the north cut!"

Smoke Jackson doubled his reins and beat his mule with the free end. "Lawd God A'mighty," he prayed, and his wagon jolted away, over to the pike and past The Tree. Sans told Mingo about the injunction and his teeth rattled as he talked. It was an old wagon and an old road.

One of Peninsula's locomotives was outside the cut, waiting there, puffing a friendly rhythm in the morning air. A flatcar was coupled behind the engine and eight or ten men were sitting on the car, their legs dangling over the side. They were smoking and talking, watching a surveyor set up his instruments.

Sans and Mingo jumped out of the wagon and ran into the cut. The surveyor looked quickly at them, then back toward the engine. "Get out of here," Sans ordered.

"Now wait a minute," the surveyor protested. "I was hired to run a line through here."

"Get out!"

Mingo leaned against the bank of the cut, watching the flatcar and the men on it. A tall man, as tall as Sans, swung from the car and stepped toward him. "Hey! Who the hell are you?"

Mingo straightened, and Sans said, "Who the hell are you?"

"You are Dabney," the stranger said. "Well, Mr. Dabney, I'm the new boss on this job. Peninsula sent us in last night and told us to lay tracks through this cut."

Sans tapped his foot against the surveyor's tripod. "I'm saying you ain't."

"I don't want any trouble, Mr. Dabney." The stranger's eyes were friendly but firm, and the twang proclaimed him a Yankee. "I don't know anything about all this ruckus. They pay me to lay rails, and I'm going to lay 'em. I'm coming through this cut."

"You, and who else?"

The boss pointed toward his men. "Me and them."

Sans studied him. There was no personal fight between them. This stranger was only a gear in a machine set in motion in Chicago, and oiled by a thieving judge in Mississippi; but suddenly Sans Dabney hated the intruder. He didn't have to obey orders blindly and do a rotten job, just to make a living. In his quick hatred, the elder brother wanted no more talk. An invader was at the north cut and Sans was a Dabney. He turned his head and Mingo nodded, and Sans' gaze moved back to the stranger.

Smoke Jackson ambled from his wagon into the cut and stood there, near at hand.

Calmly and without haste, the older boy reached out and lifted the brass instrument from the tripod, and handed it to the surveyor. "Here's your doodad. Now get out." He lifted the tripod, broke away one of the legs and tossed it to Mingo. He grasped the second leg and threw the third aside.

At that minute Mingo swung.

The foreman threw up his arms to protect his head, then cried out in surprise and agony as the heavy wood cut into his flesh, drawing blood. Mingo swung again and Sans ran to the far end of the cut, ready if the men on the flatcar started in.

And they started. One lifted a heavy spike and hurled it at Sans and the others grabbed pick handles and slid off the car, coming his way. The surveyor scampered up the side of the cut and ran toward the engine. The foreman, backing away from Mingo and looking for an opening, retreated slowly out of the cut, passing close enough for Sans to hit him. The Dabney boy let him pass.

The foreman walked toward his men and held up his hand. "Don't go in yet. Take the engine back to camp and get some more men."

Sans heard him, and Mingo heard him, and the younger brother grinned. Mingo began laughing at the men climbing on the flatcar to go get more men.

Smoke Jackson heard the order and ran back to his wagon. He must get Gar Rivers, because when Smoke thought of men in the valley to save the valley, he thought only of Gar Rivers.

The engine disappeared around the bend and the foreman and the Peninsula crew waited at a safe distance, watching the brothers. The wind was veering from the west to the north, and was colder.

Mingo ran his hand along his cudgel, the smooth hard wood of the tripod. He stepped to the entrance of the cut and leaned against the bank. Sans moved to the other side.

"Good sermon Brother Eubanks preached yesterday." They were

Mingo's first words since their arrival at the cut, and they were trivial words; but anything to relieve those hard, taut lines in his brother's face.

"Too long," Sans said. He glanced up the railroad tracks.

There was silence for a minute as the Dabneys watched the foreman and his men. Mingo held his club out in front of him, squinting along it, balancing it. The whistle sounded around the bend. The train was at the camp.

Peninsula's foreman stood beside the tracks leading to the cut. He cupped his hands and called, "I've got two hundred men back there."

"That's a hundred apiece," Mingo jeered.

"For God's sake use your heads," the foreman pleaded. "Somebody might get killed."

"Folks been killed here before," Sans said. The engine, chugging in the distance, was coming back. He fastened his eyes on the bend, watching until the engine crept around, billowing smoke. There were ninety or a hundred men on the flatcar. He never knew how many.

There were Negroes from the shacks of Mississippi and Negroes from the slums of Chicago; big, black and brawny. There were Slavs from Illinois and hillbillies from Tennessee. They had no stake in the valley. They wanted only to lay tracks and get their money, then go back to their women and spend it, far away from this grubby land.

They piled off the car and milled around, looking from their foreman to the Dabneys, then back to their foreman. One of them, a Negro with a stick in his hand, started laughing. "Great day in the mawnin', boss!" His laughter echoed in the north cut. "You aimin' to use all of us to handle them two white boys?"

The Dabney brothers recognized the flat, easy drawl, the hallmark of the Mississippi river country. Sans saw his opportunity and reached for it. "That's right, bud," he shouted. "A hundred to handle two. They aim to come in here and ruin the rabbit hunting. You know how Yankees are." It was the same old cry, the same old challenge that a boundary along the Ohio River makes men different.

Several Negroes guffawed and one of the white men, a Georgia Cracker, yelled. "Rabbit hunting pretty good?"

"Used to be," Mingo answered. "Birds, too. The Yankees shot 'em on the ground. You know how Yankees are." The same old battle cry; the same old bloody shirt.

The foreman glanced around at his men. He was baffled and angry. His Northern workers were just baffled. There had been quarrels and fights between the Northern and Southern Negroes, between the Northern and Southern whites, over food and whiskey and women; but now the Northerners were puzzled by the sudden bonds of camaraderie that stretched from their fellow workers to those two strangers there in the cut.

The foreman was on the defensive before his own men. That made him even more angry, and he tried to explain. "I figured those two fellows would hightail it. I don't want nobody hurt. I figured to scare 'em away."

Mingo's laughter rang in the cut and Sans was smiling. He stuck the leg of the tripod under his arm and called to the Negro with the stick. "Looks like you could handle an ax. I could use a good hand like you. Pay off Friday and hunt rabbits Saturday." About half the Negroes broke into raucous laughter and the Southern white men joined the merriment.

The foreman kicked the ground in sheer disgust. His face was livid. It was hard to arouse a hundred men against two strangers. His ruse was not working and the initiative had passed to the Dabneys; two men laughing at his hundred.

Thwarted and angry, the foreman grabbed a pick handle and walked toward the brothers, walking alone for a few steps until some of his men followed him. Sans and Mingo braced themselves.

Smoke Jackson's wagon entered the cut, unseen and unheard by the Dabneys. The first inkling that Gar Rivers was there came when one of Peninsula's Negroes called to another, "Look ayonder. Look at that garfish walking up that bank like a man."

Sans looked back and saw the wagon, then up the side of the cut. Gar was standing alone on the top of the bank, facing the crowd, looking down at Peninsula's mob.

The men began muttering and the foreman stopped. "Where'd that dinge come from?"

"God knows," one of his men whispered. "His name is Gar Rivers. He's a sort of prophet to the colored people."

Gar stood very straight on the brink of the slope, his old shoulders

squared and his eyes roaming over the crowd. He said not a word,
standing alone, a block of gnarled black granite. There stood judgment. The foreman knew it and was awed. His men were awed, too,
for on the bank above them stood one righteous man against the
multitude.

"That damn jiggerboo is the man to watch," the foreman said.
"Keep your eyes on him and I'll handle the Dabneys." Again he
moved forward, moving toward the brothers, but his eyes were on
Gar Rivers.

"Just a minute!" Gar held out his hand, pointing his lean finger at
the foreman, then speaking to the crowd, especially the Negroes from
the big river country. "He called me a dinge." His voice was clear
and firm, without rancor, without fear. "Dinge and jiggerboo in a
Yankee twang—nigger and coon in a Southern drawl. It is all the
same." Gar's voice was rising. "I was once a slave, but I'm an old man
now and I've learned to know my friends. You should know yours.
I am a Southerner and you are Southerners. The South has given you
little but servitude and sweat, and the right to die in the land of
your fathers—"

"That's right!" one of the Northern Negroes yelled. "That's all a
black man gets in the South!"

"The South has given you little, but what has the North given
you?" Again he pointed his finger, his black bony finger, at Peninsula's foreman. "They gave you a promise and didn't keep it. They
made a covenant, a covenant in the name of freedom. And they
broke it. They painted for us a mansion in the sky, and they tore it
down and let it fall about our heads." His voice was trembling; his
whole body was trembling and he flung the words at them.

Sans felt his blood pulsing and he wanted to shout. Here was
justice, black and unafraid. Here was a prophet preaching brotherhood at the north cut. The foreman was motionless, staring up at
Gar. His Southern workers were staring, too.

Gar lowered his voice. "I am a Southerner and I love this old ashy
earth, the tall trees and the yellow rivers. My people are buried in
the black mud of the big river country. The South is my home, and
here is my debt." He walked down the slope toward the foreman.
"All that this man represents, lied to us. His masters sold us back
into bondage because they are as greedy as our masters. A black

kinky head is worth two dollars a day in Chicago and a dollar a day in Mississippi." The indictment was spoken in gall and wormwood. "Go where you will in our nation, the mind of a dinge and the soul of a jiggerboo is measured in money—"

The foreman leaned toward his straw boss and whispered, "Stop that damn nigger. He'll turn our own men against us."

"Shut up, you old fool," the straw boss yelled at Gar. "Shut your mouth or I'll shut it for you."

Gar kept walking toward the foreman.

"Don't tell the man to shut up!" one of the Negroes shouted. "He ain't bothering nobody."

The straw boss balanced a spike in his hand, then hurled it. Sans saw him. He saw his face. He saw the upturned visor of his cap. Mingo saw him, too, and Mingo cried out.

The spike struck Gar above the bridge of his nose and he went down. He fell in the gravel and dirt of the slope, his head toward the foreman. Then he tried to rise.

Sans started running up the side of the slope to reach him. The foreman moved into the cut, swinging his stick, advancing on Mingo. Gar was on his knees, struggling to get up, and the second blow fell. There were men around him, yelling and screaming and cursing and Sans didn't see who struck the blow, but he saw the man with the upturned visor.

The club landed across the base of Gar's spine and he collapsed. His head twisted and his hands quivered as he clawed the gravel. Then he lay still.

Sans screamed his fury and lunged for the man with the upturned visor.

"They killed him!" The cry came from one of the Negroes near the car.

Nobody ever knew exactly what happened or how it happened, but in an instant Southern Negroes and Northern Negroes were fighting among themselves; hurling spikes and swinging pick handles and clubs.

The foreman heard the cries and heard the curses, but saw only Mingo Dabney, who had struck him, and he swung his stick. Mingo ducked the blow and the two men grabbed each other and wrestled. They fell to the ground and rolled over, each trying to choke the other.

Around the flatcar a score of Negroes were fighting. Northern and Southern white men took up their cudgels and waded in. There was no color line. It was the same old brawl, men born in Southern shacks fighting men born in Northern slums.

Two or three men went down. Several ran away and some limped away, nursing cuts and bruises and mouthing promises of death, pledges to be fulfilled another day.

No man knew his enemy and none knew his friend. Rails were pushed off the car and into the roadway. One burly man lifted a sledge to smash the engine's piston and was knocked down by a Negro with a club. Another man was pounding at a coupling when felled by a shower of slag.

Sans was fighting his way along the top of the slope toward Gar. Mingo picked up a rock and beat the foreman in the head, then jerked free and ran to join his brother. A flying spike struck Mingo in the shoulder, ripping it open, and he staggered.

Sans broke his cudgel across the head of the nearest man, and stood for an instant looking down at the bleeding gash. A blow across his back felled him, and he went down, grabbing at another man, clawing at him for support.

The straw boss, the man with the upturned visor, was standing over Gar, staring in bewilderment at the helpless old Negro. Sans Dabney sprang, riding the man to the ground, ripping his face and beating his head in the gravel.

The man kicked Sans in the groin, then staggered to his feet and tried to run away. The Dabney boy caught him and rode him down again and jumped on him, grinding his heel into his back and kicking his head into a bleeding mass. The man whimpered for mercy and tried to crawl away. Sans flung him over and caught his throat, choking him until his face was blue and his tongue stuck stiff from his mouth, swollen and blue and bloody.

He might have killed him. It was his intent to kill him. Death was his urge, but suddenly he glanced up as though hearing an order, unspoken, but still an imperious command.

He saw his father.

Bruce Dabney was walking into the cut, walking alone. The wind was in his white beard, blowing it. He had been there before, many years before, that day the Confederates came through and he fought them with dirks. Without haste he walked into the cut and the men parted and let him pass. Here was a thing that struck terror—an old white-bearded man with frosty blue eyes walking unafraid through a screaming multitude. Mingo started to call out, then was awed and stepped aside. Sans relaxed his grip and got up. All the men saw Bruce Dabney, and a whisper swelled among them.

"Old man Dabney! That's old man Dabney."

Bruce climbed the bank and went to Gar. The men around the fallen Negro moved away, melting away in silence. Bruce knelt and felt Gar, running his hands over the body of his friend. "Paralyzed," he muttered. "He's paralyzed."

The foreman knew the fight was over, and the Dabneys knew the fight was just beginning.

Sans hurried to his father and Bruce stood to meet him. Again the wind was in his beard. All the men saw the white beard, but Sans saw his father's eyes, and he was afraid of his father. "Son," Bruce said, "you and Mingo go home. Tell your mother I'm bringing Gar. He'll need a bed."

"Yes, Papa."

Peninsula's workers muttered and fell back to the car. Even the foreman moved back, moving away from the silent wrath of Bruce Dabney.

"We can take him home in Smoke's wagon," Mingo said.

"I'll tote him." Bruce knelt by his friend. "He's not heavy and a wagon is rough. I'll tote him."

The Dabney boys walked away from the north cut. Mingo's shoulder was bleeding and Sans was limping, dragging one foot.

Bruce lifted Gar, cradling him in his arms. The crowd was hushed, fearful and sullen; afraid of judgment, afraid of an old man with a white beard who was holding in his arms another old man who was helpless. Bruce looked at them, from the foreman to the men; then he turned his back and walked down the slope and into the cut, taking Gar Rivers toward The House.

The crowd shifted nervously and even those with wounds walked back into the cut, watching old man Dabney carry his burden away. The straw boss was stroking his throat and gulping. The foreman wiped blood from his head. "Get the hurt ones back to camp. The rest of us will start laying rails."

The brothers heard the engine whistle, heard the steam, the rattle of the cars and the ringing of steel. They didn't look back, knowing their father was behind them. Neither Sans nor Mingo spoke, but walked on down the pike and were almost to The Tree when Louisa rode up in her buggy.

"What is it?" she demanded, glaring at Sans. "What have you done now?" She saw the blood on Mingo's shoulder and moved to get out of the buggy and go to him.

"We don't need you," Mingo said. "Go on back to your store. Back to Peninsula. This is valley business."

"Yes," said Sans sharply. "Go back. Stay out of this." Then all the bitterness of his defeat welled within him. She was Peninsula, and he hated her. "Just go away and leave us alone. For God's sake leave us alone."

Louisa started to reply, to berate him, but something about his bearing warned her not to tread too far, so she struck her horse and drove away toward milltown.

Sans and Mingo walked on, past The Tree and up the lane to The House. Kyd ran out on the porch, looking first at her sons, thence up the pike at Bruce. Ruth Thrumbull was directly behind her and the two women stood there on the steps, Kyd looking at her sons and Ruth looking only at the elder one.

"Gar is hurt bad," Sans said. "Send somebody for a doctor and we'll fix a bed for him."

"We'll put him in the big room." Kyd's face changed from anger to dread, then back to anger.

Ruth's face was white and tense, her gray eyes wide in fear. Sans scarcely noticed her, taking her presence for granted. She belonged there, at the Dabney house in this hour.

Kyd examined Mingo's injuries and called for servants to bring rags and hot water. "Did they get through?"

"They're coming through," Mingo said. "They're coming through now."

Ruth felt cold inside and turned away, following Sans to the big room. She helped him throw back the counterpane and together they adjusted the pillows. They were standing there when Bruce brought Gar in and stretched him on the bed. The old Negro still was unconscious.

"I sent for a doctor," Kyd said. "Are they coming through, Bruce?"

Her husband didn't reply. He fluffed the pillows around Gar's head, then straightened and started out of the room.

"Where are you going?" Kyd's tone was calm.

"To get my dirks. You boys get ready."

Sans and Mingo looked at their mother, wondering about her reply, and Kyd answered, "Your dirks are in our closet." Her tone was as calm as the hushed hour before a tornado, the dead, motionless minute before a cyclone. The red rush of anger flushed her olive cheeks and her black eyes mirrored the fury of her mind. "Come on, Bruce. I know right where they are. You boys get ready to help your father."

Ruth Thrumbull put her hands to her cheeks, and her hands were cold. My God! Was this to be her life? A family where the mother handed dirks to the father, and the father told his sons to get ready? Was this what she wanted?

This was what she wanted.

The Dabneys, the three men and the two women, walked from the big room into the parlor, thence down the hall past Shellie's room. Mingo got his shotgun and dropped shells into his pocket. Sans got his rifle, and as he lifted it from the pegs behind the door Ruth was standing by him and she touched him, saying nothing. He covered her hand and kissed her cheek, then looked around for Mingo. The brothers came back into the hall and Bruce and Kyd stepped from the door of their room.

Mingo said, "Papa, do you want me to get some of my mill hands?"

"No." Bruce felt the blades stiff against his sides.

Sans said, "Do you want me to get somebody? Mr. Charlie? Paul de Ru? 'Tite Pierre?"

"No, son."

Then the father and his two sons, the mother and a frightened girl, walked down the hall toward the front door. Kyd was the first to hear the command from Shellie's room, the call from behind the closed door.

"Bruce!"

Each looked at the other and Bruce opened the door. Shellie was in her rocking chair, staring at the hearth, at the fire. There was a hallowed hush in the room and he went to his mother and stood by her chair.

"So they're coming through—" Shellie didn't look up. "I heard you talking. There's fighting at the north cut again."

"Yes, Mama. Gar was almost killed. My boys and I are going back."

Old Shellie was the widow of Hoab Dabney who fought the Confederates at the north cut until he bled from a dozen wounds. She was the mother of Cormac Dabney who was killed when the Confederates came through. She was the mother-in-law of Keith Alexander who almost stopped them.

"Put those dirks away," she whispered. "Put 'em back, Bruce. Tell your boys to put their guns away—"

"I can't do that, Mama."

"Put 'em back!" The old woman's eyes, vacant so often, were sharp and blazing. "I still speak for this family. Put 'em back!"

Bruce bowed his head, his body shaking in agony. "You're robbing me of my right to defend my home and the valley."

"There was a man who helped your father. That same man will help you." They all heard her above the spluttering of the fire. "Send for Keith Alexander. Tell Keith I need him."

Chapter eighteen

THE SNOW CLUNG to the hard earth of Keith Alexander's Chicago estate and within the mansion the vain, arrogant master was standing before his gold-framed mirror, brushing his hair. Keith Alexander was the fountainhead of a hundred legends, the flamboyant tragedian of a melodrama of his own making, and he liked the role and played it constantly.

He was jaunty that morning because Morna was on her way back to him. He smiled into the mirror and the mirror returned his smile. It was a gilded mirror and he owned it. Like everything else he owned, it told him only what he wanted to know.

Morna's ship from Europe would dock that night, and she would hurry to him in his private railway car. His car, too, had a gold-framed mirror, and he owned that. Morna Dabney, his wife, was the only thing Keith Alexander possessed and didn't own.

In the anticipation of her return, he hummed to himself, humming in gay memory of his young manhood.

> "Western wind, when wilt thou blow;
> That the small rain down can rain?
> Christ, if my love were in my arms,
> And I in my bed again!"

He stroked his hair, brushing it back loosely past his ears. He wore his hair long and it still was black except for a faint sheen of gray above his temples. His mustaches, trimmed precisely, were blacker than his hair and Keith smoothed them, first on one side and then on the other. He leaned close to the mirror, examining his mustaches. The white did not show. Keith turned his head slightly and nodded approval to Robert, his valet. He owned Robert, too, and Robert was content to spend his years dyeing the mustaches of his master, making sure the mirror told Keith Alexander only what Keith Alexander wanted to know.

He was an old man now, scorning age as he had scorned life, defying time as he had defied man since he, bastard son of a Southern statesman, began writing and acting his melodrama. He was an old man, but no one dared cross him, for Keith Alexander still was feared, though now he used his purse to crush men as ruthlessly as once he had used his pistols.

He submitted to the final ministrations of Robert, and the valet swiftly adjusted the ascot and the broadcloth coat, inserting a silken kerchief in the outer pocket so that only two tips showed.

"Thank you, Robert."

"You look well, sir. Mrs. Alexander will be happy to see you looking so well."

Keith went down to breakfast and a butler brought the newspaper. A horseless carriage had been demonstrated in New York. Keith was not interested in such gimcracks. He was wishing he had gone east to meet Morna.

He finished his breakfast with fig preserves, each fig dripping its own golden syrup. Then he lighted a cigar and walked to the top floor of his mansion, to the hothouse he had built so Morna might have roses all winter.

His wife said, many years before, that dying roses made her sad. So Keith built the hothouse and told her it was for her. Actually, it was Keith Alexander who hated to see things pass, to see things age and wrinkle and fade. He stopped and cut a red bud, drew it through his buttonhole, then walked downstairs and to his carriage.

An hour later he stepped briskly from his private office into the conference room where the directors waited. They broke off their conversation and turned to him. He was in gay humor and chatted lightly. A secretary placed a folder at the head of the table. The directors sat down, silent as they waited for Keith Alexander to speak.

"Gentlemen, thirty railways operate in and out of Chicago." He opened the folder, but did not consult the notes and statistics. "Chicago has become the roundhouse of America." Keith glanced toward the door, frowning as the secretary stepped inside the room. "Yes, Walters, what is it?"

Walters went to him. "I thought this was urgent, sir."

Keith took the telegram and glanced at it. It was from Bruce Dabney and said simply:

"Come at once. Mama needs you."

Morna was on her way home and Morna's mother needed him in Lebanon. He didn't want to go to Lebanon. Never again did he want the ageless pines to mock his years, and the ridges to echo the mockery. But there was trouble in Lebanon; bound to be. In all the years, Shellie Dabney never had asked for help. Now she needed him.

Aven MacIvor was in Lebanon the last time he heard from Kyd. She probably still was there. That disturbed him, then alarmed him. Was the widow of Clay MacIvor the cause of the trouble? His better judgment convinced him the idea was absurd. Shellie and Kyd could handle Aven. There must be another reason.

Rapidly his mind assembled the potential problems and sorted them, seeking a reason for the summons. Bruce? No. Bruce sent the message. A death in the family? Such news would have been revealed. Not Aven. Not money. They never asked for money. He glanced up at his secretary. "What is the latest report on Peninsula's operations in Mississippi?"

"A memorandum went out this morning to stockholders," Walters said. "The railroad is being finished. Peninsula will be shipping from Lebanon within a few weeks."

The directors glanced from one to the other. Keith ignored them. "Any report of trouble?"

"No, sir. Shall I investigate further?"

"No." Keith Alexander had no patience with Peninsula Lumber Company, declining flatly to invest because he distrusted the business judgment of the concern. Too lax and too greedy.

"I hope it is not bad news," Walters said. The directors looked intent and nodded.

"I think not, but I must go to Mississippi." He reached for a pad and wrote a note to Morna, telling her he was called to Lebanon and allaying her fears. "Please come direct from New York to New Orleans. I will meet you at the St. Charles." Suddenly he was pleased. This was Carnival Season and the idea of the carnival and Morna, of good food and wine, pleased him.

He handed the message to Walters. "Have this delivered to Mrs. Alexander when her ship docks. Make my reservations on the earliest possible train. Have Robert pack a bag and meet me at the station." His face hardened and he touched his mustaches, smoothing them. "Have Robert pack my pistols."

The directors glanced from one to the other, and the secretary hesitated. "Is that all, sir?"

"Let me know when my train leaves. Have a carriage waiting."

Alexander turned to his associates. "Sorry for the interruption, gentlemen." He explained that Chicago could no longer operate railways upon surface lines only. "The tracks in the center of the city must be elevated. I have various estimates for the job. One is as low as thirty-five million dollars."

The freight agent and station master at Ellisville, his pencil stuck behind his ear, came out of the depot. "No. 3's coming." A

Negro, limp with sleep, pushed himself off a baggage wagon and pulled the wagon out of the shade and alongside the tracks.

The loiterers straggled around in front of the depot. Since early morning they'd been waiting, some of them whittling, others trimming their fingernails; all of them cussing hard times and taxes, and running the all-fired hell out of red foxes. They were lean, angular men with long red necks, slow thinkers, stubborn as the mules they plowed. Their black wool hats were stained salty with sweat and dust. Their patched blue shirts and denim overalls were bleached pale by innumerable dippings in strong, homemade soap. They were the gaunt backbone of the South, these red-necks, and without them the South could not stand. Some were propped against the depot. Others squatted on their hunkers, their haunches swinging low, almost touching the ground, and waited.

There was distinction in being the first each morning to hear No. 3, and Seth Faulkner, his head cocked as he listened, was quick to announce, "She acomin'!" Old man Hargrove was just about deaf, although every morning for nigh twenty years he was the second man to hear the train. "Yep." He nodded in sure agreement. "That's her, all right. She's comin' in."

They watched to the north, looking along the tracks to the trees rimming the clearing. Then it happened! The miracle happened again, and old No. 3 came puffing out of the forest, her bell ringing, her whistle blowing. "Hot damn!" said Seth, looking at his watch as the locomotive slid past him, spitting steam in shrill spurts. "She's right on time."

Some ladies got off first. Mr. Tom Bigelow, who had been to Meridian, got off. A man with black hair and black mustaches, wearing a gray felt hat and a broadcloth suit, got off. The loiterers looked at him, looking particularly at his lavender cravat, then peered inquiringly at each other.

"Before God—that's Keith Alexander!" whispered old man Hargrove.

A whistle slipped from Ed Fenton's lips. "Jee-sus Key-rist!" he said, and lit a shuck for the livery stable. Here was news that required fast traveling, or somebody else might get there first.

Keith Alexander!

The old men said his name, and some smiled and some frowned, but all remembered. The young men stared. The legend actually lived. He had returned!

They heard the news at the livery stable, and they got up from their chairs quick and came out fast to see for themselves.

They heard the news in the Ellisville Hardware and General M'd'se and they came buzzing out, climbed on their horses and into their buggies, and headed for the depot.

"Keith Alexander!" Al Jenkins was riding alongside Branch Merritt and he reined his horse in close. "Why, I hear'd my pa say that man could take them two pistols of his'n and knock out a gnat's eye at fifty yeards."

Mr. Renfrow, red-faced and fat, his bulk sprawling almost across the buggy seat, was r'ared back, talking big as his ramshackle old horse clopped on toward the depot. His audience was Mort Whittaker who'd asked him for the ride.

"I heard my pa talk about Keith Alexander," Mr. Renfrow said. "My pa told me that Mr. Alexander walked out in the road, and stood there in the open, and shot Clay MacIvor. Ain't no telling how many Confederates he killed there at the north cut thirty ye'r ago. He durned near whipped 'em by himself." Mr. Renfrow bobbed his head in wonderment at the things his pa had told him. "Yes, siree, that Keith Alexander was a stomp-down killing man." He slapped his horse with the cotton reins.

Other buggies came on toward the station, and the tongues of the old men wagged as they remembered Keith Alexander riding his white horse across Mississippi, marking his irascible path with the graves of men foolish enough to mention his illegitimate birth, daring enough to debate his honor.

Keith was amused by the stares of the gawking yokels, but too much an actor to ignore an entrance, even for this rustic audience. He dawdled until the crowd assembled; then, granting them a good look at him, he threw a silver dollar to a gaping colored boy, tossing him a fortune. "Bring my bag to the hotel." The crowd opened before him. He smoothed his mustaches and bowed slightly.

"Thank you, gentlemen." He made a casual exit across the street and into the hotel, smiling as he went inside. These men weren't interested in Keith Alexander, the millionaire. They came to see the most celebrated duelist of his day, the man who walked under the oak seventeen times, and seventeen times walked away. He was pleased that the saga of his pistols still resounded in Mississippi.

"I wish a room," he said to the proprietress. "I will use it only long enough to freshen up a bit."

She did not hear him. "Aren't you Keith Alexander?"

"Yes, ma'am." Again he was flattered to be remembered.

"For a minute I thought I was seeing a ghost."

"No, ma'am. I am very much alive."

"I saw you once before. It was many, many years ago." She handed him a key. "That's our best room. It'll be thirty-five cents."

Keith paid her and went along the hall to his room. The colored boy followed him and put down the bag. "I want you to go to the livery stable," Keith said. "Tell them I want to buy a horse to take me to Lebanon. A white horse."

He took off his coat and hung it on the bedpost and went to the washstand and poured out a basin of water. He started a song but the song died away and, like a man who can play a part no longer, he was tired. He turned from the washstand and sat down in the gooseneck rocking chair. It was a big room. The four-poster walnut bed had a feather mattress. Keith looked about him and saw it all, and suddenly he was old and weary, too tired to pretend.

The hotel hadn't changed much in thirty years. Here Claiborne MacIvor was quartered, this old place was headquarters for him and his Confederates. To this hotel Morna Dabney came to MacIvor on the night before the attack on the valley. In one of these rooms, maybe this one, she slept with him.

Alexander looked at the fireplace, at the iron grate. Perhaps Mac-Ivor had a fire burning that night, and Morna warmed herself before the fire.

She wore a green dress that night. Keith remembered it. He saw it the next morning when she came back home and talked to him, and lied to him. Then he went out past the north cut and killed Claiborne MacIvor.

He remembered it all, and he was an old man sitting alone in a room. He knew that after all these years he still did not fully trust Morna. But he loved her, and that was enough. She was peace for his restless, hindered spirit and he gave her that love which is too wise to examine itself, and which lonely, disconsolate men sometimes give to a woman as solace for their disappointments.

There was a mirror in the room. It was in a walnut frame. Keith went over to the washstand and looked at himself. He didn't own the mirror in the walnut frame and the mirror told him something of the truth: the white was showing in his mustaches, the lines of his face were deeper. Chicago was three days behind him. This was the South and in the South he was Keith Alexander, the bastard who used his pistols to protect a name that was nameless, a heritage only as old as himself.

Keith washed his face and changed his linen. He wondered again why Shellie had sent for him, and was resentful that he had been summoned from his mansion on a mission that wasn't explained.

There was a knock on the door. "I'm Rufus Tolbert," the caller said. "I own the livery stable. And I got you a white horse."

Some of Keith's old buoyancy returned. "That's very handsome of you, Mr. Tolbert. I will send you my check." Then he was cautious. He wanted information, but was not willing for anyone to know that his mission was a mystery to him. "I hope it's a fast horse. I am in a hurry."

"He's fast, all right." Rufus Tolbert shifted from one foot to the other, bolstering himself to familiarity with the legend. "Now that you're back, Mr. Alexander, I reckon Peninsula will tone down. I reckon they'll quit stepping so almighty high and wide."

Keith put his soiled linen in his bag and fastened it. "We'll see." He paused, hoping his guest would go on talking.

"I don't like Peninsula," Tolbert said. "You can't tell me they don't own Judge Windy Hill. And I figure they're aiming to own everything else."

Alexander pushed his bag near the washstand. "I haven't heard any news in the last few hours. Any developments?"

The visitor felt mighty important. Keith Alexander asking him questions! "I ain't hear'd nothing new since old man Dabney—I mean Mr. Bruce Dabney—and his two boys fought 'em at the north cut. But I hear tell Bruce Dabney aims to fight 'em again."

So that was it. Another fight at the north cut. Keith's blood warmed and he glanced at the walnut mirror. He was younger at that minute, and the mirror told him so. In Chicago, they fought at a table. In Lebanon, they still fought at the north cut. "Mr. Tolbert. Please have my horse sent to me immediately."

The livery stable man saw something in Keith's face he hadn't seen before. "Yes, sir." He backed out of the room and went running along the hall.

Alexander opened his bag and took out his pistols. He thrust them into the belt of his trousers and, having worn them there for so many years, it was natural to feel them again, tight against his belly. He drew down the bottom of his vest, covering them, then hurried out.

A Negro was leading a white stallion toward the hotel. Keith waited at the bottom of the steps, smoothing his mustaches and aware that the loafers across the street were staring at him. He tossed a silver dollar to the Negro boy and caught the bridle of the white horse.

Then Keith Alexander held his breath. He must do it just so, and he was afraid he couldn't do it. He put his foot in the stirrup and swung free, then over. He adjusted himself proudly, his head erect. The loafers looked at one another and nodded.

"His name is Shannon, boss," the boy yelled as Keith dug his heels into the horse and galloped down the dusty road. "That stallion's name is Shannon."

Old man Hargrove, leaning back against the depot and watching Alexander disappear, said to the other loafers, "Well, gentlemen, there goes hell on a white horse."

Seth Faulkner peered across the road at an office with the shades pulled down. "Wonder what Cephus is athinkin'? Reckon them fat guts of his'n are jugglin' round right smart, now that them pistols are back."

At the junction where Peninsula's roadbed spurred from the Mainline, heading south for Lebanon, Keith turned his horse and sped beside the company's right of way until he was out of sight of his audience. Then he slowed Shannon to a walk and breathed deeply, letting his head fall forward, resting his neck. His pistols pinched his flesh. The stallion was eager to be on his way, but Keith already was feeling the strain. "It's not fair to my horse," he mumbled, masking his weariness and his years even from himself.

He put Shannon into a fast trot, moving over the hard road, through the sandy stretches and through the bogs. He was a thousand miles from Chicago, a lifetime from his golden mirror. Morna probably already was in New Orleans, or nearing there. And he was an old man on a white horse, riding the road to Lebanon again.

The way was not long because memory lessened the miles, and he was thinking of Morna when he came to the spot where Clay Mac-Ivor died. Remembering MacIvor and his death—a shot to the stomach, a shot to the mouth—Keith Alexander thought of Aven and dreaded seeing her, hoped she was gone from New Hebron.

He rounded the last bend and there lay the north cut, the railroad already through and far into the valley.

Alexander rode down the pike, the reins loose in his hand, and swung into the Dabney lane, a pageant of memories flooding his heart as he passed The Tree. At the porch of The House, he slid stiffly from the saddle, glancing around and thanking God nobody saw him get off. He strode inside without knocking and called, "Bruce! Bruce!"

Kyd hurried out of Shellie's room, running to him and hugging him. She tried to speak and her emotions smothered her words. He felt his own tears surging to his eyes. "None of that. Where's Bruce?"

She took her handkerchief from her apron pocket and dabbed her eyes, then used the same handkerchief to dry his tears. "He and the boys are down in the village. There's been fighting at the north cut—"

"Has Bruce struck back—"

"No. He wanted to, but Mama sent for you. It's Peninsula."

His relief was so evident that Kyd felt his confidence. "I will take care of Peninsula. Is Aven still here?"

"At the hotel. But I never see her."

So he had come a thousand miles to stop Peninsula. That's what they wanted. He could have stopped Peninsula with one word in Chicago. However, he was glad he came. The trees on the road to the valley made him glad.

"Bruce didn't want to send for you, Keith. Mama insisted."

"Take me to her." He was smiling as he leaned over and kissed her cheek. "And get that worried look off your face."

She led him toward the door and he went inside. The sight of old Shellie shocked him. Could anyone be so old? His hand rose to his own face, his fingers sliding along the lines there, touching and lingering upon the mustaches where the white was showing.

Shellie was wearing a gray Mother Hubbard. A counterpane lay across her knees and a blue shawl was draped around her shoulders. Her hair was white and scanty and Kyd had arranged it in a little knot on the top of her head. Only the fire, spluttering red and blue, seemed alive in the room. Even the clock was stopped, for Shellie didn't need a clock. A clock can only tell the present, and Shellie knew only the past.

Alexander stood by the chair and reached out, putting his hand on her shoulder. She opened her eyes and looked up at him. "So you got here. It took you a long time."

"I had to come a long way, Mrs. Dabney." He knelt beside her and her hand trembled over his hair.

Kyd tiptoed out of the room and told a Negro to go for Bruce and the boys.

Keith drew back from the trembling old hand. "Why did you send for me?" he asked gently.

"Because I need you. Now tell me about Morna and the children."

He answered her questions, then said, "Morna's hair is white."

The old woman pulled his face close to her. "And you look young, Keith. Very young for your age. When will you bring Morna to see me?"

Kyd came back into the room, tiptoeing over to the fireplace.

"Real soon, Mrs. Dabney. Now, why did you send for me?"

Shellie let her head rest against the back of her chair and closed her eyes. Kyd moved over and looked at her, then at Keith. "She often drops off like this." Kyd closed the shawl around the thin shoulders. "I'm surprised that she recognized you."

Alexander started to draw away, but Shellie opened her eyes and motioned for him to sit beside her. "I sent for you to put an end to this fighting. Did you bring your pistols?"

"Yes."

"I knew you would." The voice shrilled. "But they're not what we need. You men never learn. You think it's pistols we need. Bruce wanted his dirks. The boys wanted guns." Her eyes were so bright that the fire reflected in them. "There has been enough killing in this valley. Do you hear me? Do you hear me, Keith Alexander?"

"Yes, Mrs. Dabney."

"Put your pistols away!" The mistress of the fief still was commanding. "Don't you dare flaunt them before Bruce! Or the boys! That's all they need. Put them away!"

Keith looked at Kyd, and she nodded. He turned back to the old woman. "There will be no more fighting, Mrs. Dabney. You have my word for it. I will handle Peninsula otherwise."

"You tell Bruce and tell the boys there'll be no more fighting. They'll listen to you. I saw the Indians scalping at Fort Mims. I remember the Battle of New Orleans. And the Alamo. Good Lord, I measure my whole life by battles."

"So do I," Keith Alexander said. "So do I, Mama."

Shellie spoke so softly they scarcely heard her. "I have earned the right to die in peace. That is all I ask. Let me die in peace—"

The room was still again and Keith walked into the hallway, then on into the big bedroom, the guest room. He went to the mantelpiece, slowly pulled the pistols from under his belt, and laid them there. He was not swaggering and there was no melodrama in the gesture. He simply put his pistols on the mantel and felt better because he was rid of them.

Then he returned to the parlor and Kyd brought him a cup of coffee. They drank their coffee together, waiting for Bruce and his sons to come home.

Chapter nineteen

THE NEGRO MESSENGER rode first to The Store seeking Bruce. He was not there, and the boy shouted the words, "Mr. Keith Alexander's back! Him and them big pistols!"

Charlie Owens kept on filling orders, walking from his shelves to his counter, mumbling as he worked. He was glad Sans was at the mill with Mingo. Mr. Charlie had known Keith Alexander a long

time and was aware, calmly aware, that if Keith went with the
Dabneys to the north cut he must go, too. "Let's see," the old man
mumbled to himself. "The Dabneys and Keith and me and Wyeth.
That's six. 'Tite Pierre and Paul de Ru and Smoke Jackson. That's
nine. Wish Ronnie was here. Or Elmo."

As ripples begin in a lake where an acorn drops, so spread the
news that Keith Alexander was back. "Him and them big pistols."
Windy Hill, the sweat cold and dripping from his face, carried the
news to Mr. Irving, and Irving telegraphed Chicago. Oscar Hardee
heard it and was afraid. The sheriff had in his pocket an injunction,
obtained by Wyeth, instructing Peninsula to delay its railroad until a
hearing decided the issue. The sheriff had neglected to serve the
paper, and now he was afraid. He sent for Vernon Boyd. They sent
word to the livery stable to hitch up a team and keep them ready.

Wyeth Woodward heard it and was troubled. Alexander's pistols
were all the Dabneys needed to send them back to the north cut.
Wyeth wanted no more fighting, but he sat in his chair and counted
on his fingers. "Let's see. The three Dabneys and Keith Alexander.
That's four. Me and Mr. Charlie. That's six. 'Tite Pierre. Paul de
Ru—"

Gar Rivers, paralyzed in a bed at Woodward's house because
Wyeth insisted he be there, heard the news of Alexander's return
and closed his eyes.

G. T. Thrumbull heard it. Keith Alexander is back! Louisa Woodward, invoicing new goods in Peninsula's store, heard it. Well, Judge
Hill was stronger than Keith Alexander.

The men in Peninsula's office heard it. Keith Alexander is back!
The men in Peninsula's mill heard it. Him and them big pistols!
Peninsula's saws whined the chant and the loggers took it up. "Alexander is back! Alexander the duelist. Alexander the vain one. The
arrogant, the sardonic rake. Keith Alexander the bastard!"

In her room at the hotel, Aven MacIvor heard, and there was a
quick hard lump in her throat. So he was back! He had dared to come
back! She went to her window and looked out, up the pike toward
the north cut where her husband died; toward The House that was
denied her by her own mother, but where a nameless adventurer
found open arms.

Alexander killed her husband. He prepared for her a widow's

couch. Her eyes were dry and her breathing was slow as she thought of him, wondering if all the world together could hate as much as she hated Keith Alexander.

Bruce was at the post office and sent to the mill for his sons. They rode home together, Mingo in the buggy with his father, and Sans on a horse.

Keith hurried to the porch and watched them ride up. Bruce looked older and his beard was whiter. He raised his hand to Keith, and Alexander waved. The debonair Mingo was haggard, but not haggard enough to hide his resemblance to his mother. Keith's eyes were drawn to the other nephew. This boy was big and lithe; he had brown hair and large hands, something like Cormac, his father.

Bruce and Keith embraced. The boys shook hands with their uncle, then stood back and looked at him in awe and silence. Mingo glanced at Keith's belt and saw no pistols. Sans was watching his eyes. Here was the avenger. Here was the legend riding into the valley on a white horse, coming to help them subdue evil.

They went into the parlor and Sans put wood on the fire and Kyd brought out her best peach brandy. Bruce told Keith all that had happened. The brothers sat on the divan, listening and watching, and did not contribute a word to the account. Kyd, hearing Shellie call, reluctantly left the meeting, and Bruce related every detail while Keith leaned back in a chair and took it all in.

At times there was a trace of a smile on his face, and again his face was dark. He asked only a few questions and one question was directed to Sans. "Why didn't you sell them the cut in the first place?"

"Why should I sell to them?"

The uncle looked quickly at the boy, quickly and closely, and Bruce finished his story. He was rubbing his hand. "And now, Keith," he said, "I'll take one of your cigars. Kyd won't like it, but I feel like I want a cigar."

Alexander gave him one and finished his peach brandy. He went over to the fire and kicked a log into place. "Send for Mr. Woodward. You can't beat Peninsula with clubs. I'll handle Peninsula. Get Woodward."

Mingo rode for the lawyer and Bruce and Keith began recounting the old days, much to the delight of Sans. Yes, Charlie Owens was all right. Ronnie Sullivan? He'd gone to Cuba to fight the Spaniards.

Fishbait Gates was dead. Keith heard it all, then said, "The valley doesn't change very much."

Wyeth Woodward's heavy footsteps sounded on the porch and Keith walked out to shake hands with him. They returned to the parlor and Wyeth accepted a cigar.

"I have the Peninsula situation clear," Alexander said. "I'll bring them into line. Their stock is available to the right buyers and I'll buy enough to be heard—"

"Is it that simple?" Wyeth looked at the ash on the expensive Corona.

"It's just that simple."

Mingo and Sans exchanged glances, and Mingo grinned.

"There will be no more fighting at the north cut." Keith said it sternly. "I made that promise to Mrs. Dabney—"

"There will be more fighting at the north cut unless we get justice otherwise." Bruce said it quietly.

Again the brothers exchanged glances.

Keith softened his tone and shed his peremptory manner. This was no Chicago conference table. This was Lebanon. "It will not be necessary to fight at the cut." He crossed his legs. "Peninsula understands only money. I have enough money to encourage their understanding."

"What about the railroad?" Bruce asked.

Wyeth was watching Keith intently. Sans tilted his head a little more to one side, listening. Alexander rubbed his hand across his forehead. They simply did not comprehend his power. They thought of him only as a man they used to know, the husband of Morna Dabney. "We'll let them finish the railroad." He sighed. "Don't enjoin them. Let them do all the work. I'll see they make the road into a common carrier, and that they pay a top price for the right of way."

"Sounds mighty easy," Mingo said.

"It is a matter of pressure," Keith explained. He did not like to explain. "Start preparing suits, Mr. Woodward. Nuisance suits. Dozens of them. File them the day the line is completed."

The valley lawyer did not reply.

"I want those suits to get to the Supreme Court," Alexander continued. "Before I'm through with Peninsula, they'll beg for a common carrier franchise." He laid his cigar carefully on an ash tray and poured a small drink of brandy.

There was no sound except the crackling of the fire. Wyeth shuffled his feet and changed his position. Bruce stared at the blaze and the brothers were silent, watching their uncle, watching and wondering. Mingo was fascinated.

"And now," Keith said, "we come to the plague of rats. To Judge Cephus Hill. Peninsula is only a temporary pest. His is a permanent problem."

Bruce was surprised. "Good Lord, Keith! Windy Hill is only a tool."

"You're wrong. Peninsula came in to cut lumber, get money, and get out. Windy Hill expects to eat the fat while Peninsula is here, then stay and gnaw the lean forever. We've got to get rid of him." He turned to Wyeth. "How much did Hill cost?"

He had cost Wyeth Woodward his daughter, but the lawyer didn't know that. "I've no idea how much he cost."

Alexander was annoyed. "How much did Peninsula pay to put Hill and his crowd in power? I must have a figure to work on."

"I don't keep books on politicians," Wyeth said.

"Well," Keith snapped. "How much did your side spend?"

"I spent four dollars," the lawyer declared. "Hay for my horse. Gar Rivers told me he spent sixty cents. Postage. Charlie Owens didn't spend a dime. You know Mr. Charlie."

Alexander was dumbfounded. Was he really that far from Chicago? "My God!" He laughed as he turned to Bruce. "You didn't expect to beat Peninsula with pin money, did you? Why didn't you write me for help?"

"Keith," the old man said, "you've been away a long time."

The returned prodigal snorted. "And you folks haven't changed. It's high time you started if you expect to survive." His words were hard and his temper was rising. "Our first task is to learn what Windy Hill paid for votes. We'll have to out-bid him. We'll have to pay more than he did."

Bruce stared at Keith as if he were a man from another world. And he was. Wyeth kept rolling the Corona between his fingers; then suddenly he threw it away, hurling the expensive cigar into the fire, into the logs gathered from the ridges of Lebanon. The blood mounted in Mingo's face, and drained from the face of Sans Dabney.

Alexander did not feel the chill in the room or detect the mood of his audience. He had been away too long and had owned too many audiences. "Don't worry about money," he directed his remarks to Woodward. "Get a slate of officers—men who'll do as they're told. The power today is politics. Get ready for a new kind of fight. Get ready to fight in the tax office, in the bank."

Wyeth Woodward put his hands on the arms of his chair and raised himself to his feet. "And while you're getting, Mr. Alexander, get yourself another lawyer." He looked at Sans and smiled at him sadly, then walked out of the room, an honest fat man walking away from one of the richest clients in the world.

Keith was shocked and anger rose within him. He leaped up and almost shouted at Wyeth, almost commanded him to return. But the words never came. He watched the old lawyer go to the porch, and waddle down the steps toward his buggy.

The prodigal sat down, awaiting an explanation that was not offered. "I'll send for one of my lawyers," he growled. His vanity was bruised and he was a bitter old man. "Woodward always was a nincompoop."

Sans got up, walked to Midas, and stood by his chair, just looking down at him. "I own the north cut, Uncle Keith." He said it slowly. "And I don't want another lawyer."

"You don't understand." Keith waved the boy aside. "If you want me to handle this, I must have my way."

"I don't want you to handle it." Sans spoke softly, almost sadly.

"Son!" Bruce said. "Remember your manners!"

The uncle was peering up at the boy, a searching light in his eyes, the bitter smile of his youth curling his lips. "I suppose," he said sarcastically, "that since you started that fight, you want me to take my pistols and go up there and finish it for you—"

"We have pistols," Bruce said quickly, his words as biting as Keith's. "And I have my dirks. I'd rather fight again at the north cut, alone with my boys, than to foul my own nest."

Keith scowled and whirled in his chair and spoke to Mingo. "What about you? I haven't heard anything out of you."

Mingo came and stood beside his brother. "Sans is speaking for me."

Then old Bruce Dabney spoke for all of them, for all the Dabneys. "You made a pledge to Mama. You are the peacemaker. But you aim to buy peace. Me and my boys ain't buying." The sire clenched his fist, pounding the arm of his chair. "I don't know how much money you've got, but it's not enough to buy this family's honor—"

"Honor!" Keith jumped up. "Words! More damn silly Southern words! What'll you fight them with? Put your honor against their power and see what happens."

Sans' jaw trembled his indignation. "You're telling us two wrongs can make a right. I don't hold with that." He turned his back on Midas and faced his father. "I'm ready to go back to the north cut any time you say. Now I'll be going to The Store. Mr. Charlie might need me." Without a glance at his Uncle Keith, Sans Dabney left the room.

He hoped Ruth was at The Store. He wanted to be in the presence of something he could look up to.

Mingo came to his father. "I better get to my mill. I'm ready any time you say."

Keith watched him follow his brother, then turned to Bruce and there was a question in his eyes, a riddle, and a longing. For one of the few times in his life, Keith Alexander was humble.

Bruce spoke quietly, himself humble, "That's the way it is."

"Merciful God!" Keith murmured. "They turned their backs on me. They threw my purse in my face!"

"They're good boys. Both of them are good boys." There was a burst of pride in the father's voice.

And there was pride in the uncle's voice. "Mingo is you and his mother. That other boy is his daddy. He's Cormac himself." Keith's voice almost broke. "No, Bruce. You don't need my money or my pistols." There were tears in his eyes and he was not ashamed of them. "This day I have seen four honest men. You. Wyeth Woodward. And those two boys."

"Thank you." Bruce stared out of the window toward The Tree, thence down the valley of Lebanon.

The prodigal stepped to the mantel and rested his arm there, gazing down at the fire. "Four honest men! And for one honest man, for Lot alone, the Lord saved a city. I'm glad I came home, Bruce."

And Keith Alexander was home again. Back to the trees, the tall pines and ashy earth. He knew then, in a blinding instant, how much he loved it, and always had loved it. This was his South. The smoky blue haze. The people tormented, the earth torn, the yellow rivers rolling forever.

"We're all glad you came home," Bruce said. He put a log on the fire and walked softly out of the room, leaving Keith Alexander alone.

The tragedian sat there a long time without an audience, and wanting none. Keith Alexander never knew how long he sat watching the fire and listening to the winter wind whip the dry shrubs against the sides of the house the Dabneys built. He thought of Morna and his youth, of men he had killed, of his bitterness and bastardy. The Dabneys had a heritage of honor; and he had naught except his purse and his pistols. And yet, the wind in the pines was his. The right to sit by this fire was his. The blessed right to hope, and to cherish the knowledge of four honest men. He sat alone, tallying all that was his. "What a rich man I am. I am rich beyond all counting."

He bowed his head, resting it, then stood and walked into the hall. It was empty. They were cooking supper and Kyd was in the kitchen talking to the servants. The door to Shellie's room was closed. Keith put on his hat and went to the porch, then down the lane to The Tree, pausing there in an elegy, peering at the ground where his comrades were buried.

The cool wind cleared his head and he walked up to the north cut, along the railroad tracks lengthening down the valley to the mill. Peninsula's workmen were chanting and grunting as they laid rails; Negroes and whites, Northerners and Southerners working together in harmony again. A dollar a day is a good peacemaker.

They ignored Keith. Most of them never heard of him. He stood in the north cut and all the travail of the valley came back to him, fastening itself on his mind and encompassing his spirit.

He strolled to the east ridge, over to MacIvor land, and thought of Aven. In this hour of his own loneliness, he thought of her—how lonely and miserable she must be, and her misery saddened him.

The weeds on the east ridge, thick upon the MacIvor land, were dead and dry and they crackled in the wind, bending and breaking when he trod upon them. There the ghosts gathered too rapidly, and Alexander hurried away, almost fled.

He walked down to Bogue Homa and sat on a log, turning up his collar against the wind. Here, at this spot he first knew the love of Morna Dabney. Here she first came to him, giving her violent, reckless love for the joy of giving, asking no pledge. To an old man the shrine of the first sharing is always a holy place.

Bogue Homa was sparkling clear. The muddy rains of fall had flooded away and the clear cold dress of winter was on the creek and on its banks. He looked at the reeds bordering the water; watching the floating leaves, the slow-drifting leaves of the willows and oaks.

He looked at himself in the water: Bogue Homa was framed in winter reeds, and the mirror of Bogue Homa told him the whole truth. "You are an old man, Keith Alexander, with nothing to show for your age but your purse."

Keith stared into the creek, knowing then that his gold-framed mirror was a mockery, and knowing that the little reed-framed mirror was telling the terrible truth: "You are old. Your comrades are gone. This valley is their monument. But where is your monument, Keith Alexander? You are an old man with no testament to proclaim that you lived; and soon even your enemies will forget your name, your story."

The old man was frightened.

The voice of his vanity whispered to him in the silence of the woods. He wanted to cry out and, in his sudden fear, he looked down into the valley. There lay the land so long promised to the people. There lay Canaan! He, Keith Alexander, would give the land to the people. Canaan would be his monument.

He would make the dream of the Dabneys come true, and turn this valley into a haven for men of good will. The valley of Lebanon would be his monument. All of this Keith Alexander was thinking as he sat by Bogue Homa, a rich old man musing by a country creek.

"I'll buy Peninsula Lumber Company. I'll let Mingo run it. I'll buy the woods and the trees and give them to Sans."

The dream began shaping itself, stilling his fear. He glanced toward the south cut and saw the smoke coiling black toward the sky. He saw the rows of little red houses. He must change them, paint them white and, if Morna approved, put green shutters on them.

It all began to take form, the things he must do. It was all so simple. Buy a paradise! He forgot that he had bought in New Orleans. Bought in Natchez. Bought in Chicago. Bought and never built.

A hospital for the sick of Lebanon. A school for the children. A new front for The Store. Retire Charlie Owens, give him a good pension. A fountain near the courthouse.

Keith Alexander saw Samaria in the village of Lebanon. He was the Good Samaritan and would not pass the city by. He would pour in finest oil and wine.

The old man felt younger and smiled to himself. Morna would be proud. He would build a house for her on the west ridge, and there they could rest and watch their handiwork. On the morrow he would meet with Bruce and Wyeth Woodward and the boys, the four honest men, and tell them his plans.

He got up from the log and walked toward the pike. There was a swagger in his walk. The Good Samaritan was swaggering.

He strolled past the courthouse, past the hotel where Aven lived and he thought again of Aven living under a hired roof almost in the shadow of her own home. She did not belong to the valley. Well, he had enough money to make Aven happy in Virginia.

Keith turned and headed back, not caring to pass the livery stable and the loiterers there. He did not want to talk, to sit and visit and answer questions. He wanted to be back with the Dabneys, to be at home when Sans and Mingo returned.

However, he wanted to see Mr. Charlie and shake his hand. There was confidence in his bearing as he walked rapidly toward The Store. Aven MacIvor stepped out of the post office and came toward him.

Keith Alexander was startled. He wasn't ready to meet Aven, and dreaded the ordeal. She wasn't so beautiful as Morna after thirty years, but she was graceful and dignified, defiant and proud as she moved toward him, her little chin slightly tilted and her eyes straight ahead.

There was only one thing for him to do, and he did it, stepping aside to let her pass. Keith Alexander stepped aside for the widow of a man he killed. He touched his hat, giving her an opportunity to recognize him, offering her a chance to speak and bridge the chasm of thirty years. It was his peace offering, a plea that the past be covered, that the dead be allowed to bury the dead.

Aven swept toward him and he was watching her face, her eyes;

and he saw her eyes waver in his direction. The bridge across the chasm was forming.

He lifted his hat and she stopped and turned, never smiling, never lowering her chin; but she stopped.

"How are you, Aven?" he asked.

"I am fine. How is Morna? The children?"

"They are all right. Morna is in New Orleans. Lebanon has changed, hasn't it?"

"Yes."

A few of Lebanon's people hurried along in the brisk winter afternoon, and they stared at Keith Alexander and Aven MacIvor. Keith felt their stares and knew that Aven, too, was conscious of them. He motioned toward a bench on the courthouse lawn. "Do you care to sit down?"

"It is too cold." She hesitated and looked at him. "But I do want to talk to you. I must talk to you. Maybe you can help me."

The bridge across the chasm was almost strong enough to bear his weight and he tested it cautiously. She was asking him for help. "It will be an honor to serve you." He meant it.

She stepped back from the sidewalk, back to the shelter of a building. "I want to leave here. I hate it here. I want to talk to you about my holdings. Will you call on me?"

"Of course. At your pleasure."

"Tomorrow. At the hotel." She raised her eyes and looked at him. "About ten."

Keith bowed. "At the hotel at ten. I will be there."

She nodded to him and murmured, "Thank you."

Aven moved away. He fell in step with her, walking beside her, escorting her to her hotel.

The few who saw them together whispered, but Keith Alexander didn't mind. She was born a Dabney, and he was going to buy Samaria. This was the beginning of the span across thirty years. He was walking down the road to Samaria, taking her to the inn. He felt noble and he was happy.

He bade her goodbye at the door of the Jasper House, and waited for her to offer her hand. She didn't.

"At ten," she said. "And thank you again."

He turned and left her. Yes, he would buy the MacIvor holdings and let Aven go back to Virginia: seal off that chapter—close it and seal it forever. But first, she must go home again. She must go home and see Shellie. The Good Samaritan would take Aven by the hand and lead her to her mother. Shellie could not refuse him the boon.

The wind was against his cheeks and his cheeks tingled. It was too late now to stop and see Mr. Charlie. Besides, he didn't want to sit and talk about the past with an old man. He was young and he wanted to plan the future.

> "Western wind, when wilt thou blow;
>   That the small rain down can rain—"

Keith Alexander was humming the song of his youth as he hurried toward the Dabney house, striding gaily across the bridge of thirty years.

Chapter twenty

BRUCE SENSED A CHANGE in Keith when he returned to The House, reading it in his bearing, in the calm glow of his eyes. Kyd, too, saw a change, and, lacking Bruce's reticence, asked what had happened.

"I've been out walking." Keith was as pert and mysterious as a little boy with a secret. He heard the brothers riding up and went to the porch with Bruce to meet them. "Come into the parlor. I want to talk to you." He stood before the fire and waited until they were seated. The old actor was setting the stage again, getting ready to play his greatest role. The Good Samaritan. "First, I want you to know I'm proud of you." He was smiling. "I have plans for you and for this whole valley. In a few days I'll see Wyeth—" He called him

Wyeth. "We'll work out the details, then present the plan to you."
Sans and Mingo were flabbergasted.

Bruce said, "That's mighty nice of you. Now let's go to supper."

Kyd gave Keith the chair at her right. Bruce said the blessing. Alexander bowed his head and remembered it was always this way with the Dabneys. A blessing, and then a feast and fellowship. He slipped back easily into the old ways. "Thank you for the muffins. And I'd like another slice of that ham, if there's plenty."

"There is plenty," Bruce said.

Mingo kicked Sans' foot under the table, directing his attention to their uncle. Sans cut his eyes at his brother and grinned, wondering what miracle had come to pass, that Midas now was so carefree and gay. He wished Ruth were there at that happy minute to share the gaiety of the family. He would go down and get her that afternoon and introduce her to his uncle.

They sat around the table and talked. Keith and Bruce told stories of their youth, and Kyd blushed at some of them. Keith turned to the brothers. "Your Aunt Morna was the prettiest girl in the valley but your mother was second, and was first for being spoiled."

Kyd was pleased. "I was only a child when you came into the valley. I thought you were a knight when I saw you on your white horse. Then Morna looked at you, and you were only a man, and melted. You melted just like tallow, Keith Alexander."

Bruce began rubbing his hand, smiling and remembering; the memories were kind and gentle.

Kyd asked, "Have you seen Charlie Owens?"

"Not yet. I'm going to see him tomorrow." Keith began laughing. "Did you boys ever hear the Mr. Charlie story about the pretty girl and the drawers—"

"Keith Alexander!" Kyd laughed, too. Bruce was smiling.

Keith lit a cigar and handed one to Bruce, looking at Kyd as though daring a protest. "Charlie was a young man in those days." He glanced over at Sans. "Your father was alive—"

"So was grandpa," Bruce said. "I was about knee-high to a grass-hopper."

"Good Lord!" Keith said. "Was it that long ago? Anyhow, Charlie fancied himself as quite a hand with the ladies. A pretty girl came in The Store one morning—" He looked over at Kyd. "She was Mary Ellen Ragland. Whatever happened to Mary Ellen?"

"She married and moved to Arkansas," Kyd said.

Keith watched Bruce enjoy his cigar, then said, "Anyway, Mary Ellen walked in The Store to buy a pair of drawers. Mr. Charlie was sort of shy, but he sure enjoyed selling drawers to pretty girls—"

"Get on with your story," Kyd ordered. "If you must tell it, then tell it and be done with it."

Sans and Mingo were grinning and Bruce was chuckling. There was merriment in The House, a lilting merriment. It was like old times before Peninsula came.

"Mr. Charlie asked Mary Ellen what color drawers she wanted. Then what size she wanted. He strung it out as long as he could and Mary Ellen began to get enough of it. Finally, Mr. Charlie said, 'Do you want the kind that open across the back, or open down the side?'" Keith's shoulders shook at the recollection. He took a sip of coffee. "Well, sir, Mary Ellen just looked at him and said, 'Charlie Owens, you get that look out of your eyes. You don't have to be so dang particular about them drawers. I'm buying 'em for a corpse.'"

Sans and Mingo had heard the story a dozen times, but they laughed to be polite and because they enjoyed hearing their Uncle Keith tell it. They laughed, too, because the strain of the day was broken.

The family went to the parlor and sat around the fire, talking and listening to Keith's stories of the old days. The wind was blowing from the north.

"You're tired, Keith," Kyd said at last. "You're bound to be tired. It's bedtime."

"So it is." He stood and stretched and spoke to the brothers. "Boys, would you mind seeing if my horse is all right? His name is Shannon." He asked Kyd for paper and pen. "I must write Morna. She's in New Orleans by now." They all told him goodnight and left him with the fire and the lamp.

He turned up the wick and moved his chair nearer the light, and began writing to Morna. First, he explained why he was in Lebanon, telling her about Peninsula and the fight at the north cut. Then he revealed his plans for the valley—how he would change it into Samaria.

"At last," he wrote, "I can do something with money. I love this country. I love it because it gave you to me. You think, and all men think, that I hate the South because it scorned me. I confess now that I love it so much I weep over its plight. I gain strength merely by walking its ridges." He told it all to her, a young man sharing his dream with the woman he loved.

"Aven is miserable. Some of the responsibility is mine. She does not belong here and I intend to buy her holdings and let her return to Virginia. However, first I will bring her home, take her by the hand and lead her to her mother. It is the right thing to do and I will do it—"

The wind was stronger against the windows and the fire was dying to embers when Keith went to bed, and to sleep.

Sans was pleased to take morning coffee and a kettle of hot water to the big room, and his uncle was awake when he went in. "Good morning, sir. Here's your coffee." He put the cup on the table and the kettle on the washstand. "And here's your shaving water. Breakfast will be ready in a few minutes." He left his uncle to himself.

Keith shaved and stood in front of the mirror, running his fingertips over his face and peering at himself. There was a pair of small scissors on the washstand and he picked them up. He looked at them a moment, shrugged and clipped away the black from his mustaches, leaving only the white.

"Folderol!" he said. "Damned folderol for a man my age to dye his mustaches."

In the dining room the family was waiting. Keith sat down and Bruce asked the blessing. The guest, bragging on Kyd's cooking, ate four biscuits, a piece of sausage and two eggs, besides melting a dab of butter in his grits. His doctor in Chicago would have a fit.

"I'm going to see my mules this morning," Bruce announced. "Be proud to have you come with me."

Keith gave Sans the letter to Morna. "I want it to get out in today's mail."

Bruce was proud of his mules and Keith thought of something else he could do in Samaria. He could buy Bruce the finest jack in Missouri. Oh, there was so much he must do in Samaria!

They were standing by the stables, resting, when Keith said, "I'm going to see Aven at ten o'clock this morning. She wants to sell her holdings."

Bruce watched one of his mules go to the trough and drink, then looked away. "She's had it hard, Keith. And she's bitter. She might not receive you kindly."

"I happened to see her yesterday and she asked me to call." He almost told his plan to bring her home; but decided not to until after he had talked to her, and she agreed to come. A Negro led Shannon from his stall and Keith mounted. "Anything I can do for you in the village?"

"No," Bruce said. "I don't think of anything."

"Tell Kyd I'll be back for dinner." At The Tree he turned and waved to his brother-in-law, still standing by the stable. Bruce raised his hand.

The people of New Hebron stared as Keith Alexander rode into the village on his white stallion, the legend proving himself to the people.

"That's him, all right," they said.

"He looks like an old man to me."

"He may be old, but I wouldn't cross his path."

"Wonder what he aims to do—"

"Take a tuck in Peninsula Lumber Company, that's what he aims to do. He loves them Dabneys, and he's goin' to run Peninsula to hell-and-gone out of here—"

It was exactly ten o'clock when Keith Alexander walked into the Jasper House and told the clerk he was calling on Mrs. MacIvor.

The clerk gawked and swallowed.

"She is expecting me," Keith said. "I'll go up."

The clerk still was staring. "It's the room at the front end of the hall."

"Thank you." He went up the steps, climbing the stairs to the bridge across thirty years. There was a soft singing in his heart because The Good Samaritan was bringing oil and finest wines to pour into old wounds.

She was wearing blue, a blue velvet dress. Her chin was high. She did not hold out her hand.

"Good morning, Keith. Come in." She stepped back for him to enter.

"Thank you." He bowed and went into the room. A fire was burning in the grate.

She closed the door. "Take that chair. Take the rocker."

"No, Aven. You have the rocker." He pointed to a straight-back chair. "I'll sit here." He sat down and laid his hat on the floor beside him.

There was a heavy oak bed with a high headboard, festoons of leaves carved across the top. A cotton coverlet was neatly smoothed on the bed, its knotted fringe hanging at each side and tucked in at the foot. Over the mantel hung a brightly colored lithograph, "Jesus Feeding the Five Thousand." It was flyspecked. On the dresser was Aven's sea shell jewelry box. In front of the box lay her silver comb, brush and hand mirror. At one end of the dresser stood a picture in a heavy silver frame. It was a picture of a young man in a Confederate uniform; a picture of Claiborne MacIvor.

"The weather is cooler today," he said.

"Yes." A door of the washstand was cracked open and she crossed the room and closed it, smoothing the corner of the coverlet as she passed the bed. Then she went to her chair and sat down.

"I want to sell my holdings." She was looking into the fire, not speaking directly to him at all, merely saying words that must be said. "I want to leave here. I must sell my land."

"I think that can be arranged." Keith answered her mood and spoke quietly.

"I hate this dampness. I hate it when it rains. I hate it when it's dry, the heat and dust and gnats." She got up and adjusted a shade. Keith watched patiently, understanding her nervousness, her tension. "I hate these people. Dirty and sweaty." She returned to her chair but didn't sit down, standing behind the chair, her hand resting on the back. Keith saw her wedding band gleaming in the firelight.

"All right, Aven. We'll arrange things ourselves or let our lawyers do it. Any way you want."

"I've had a hard time. I don't want to sell my land. I don't want to sell my MacIvor heritage." She drew her hand from the chair and stood more erect. "But whether I want to sell or not, makes no difference. A widow must live. I've had a hard time, Keith Alexander."

Keith stared at his hands, folded in his lap.

"While Morna is traveling around Europe, and living in a mansion, I've had to work. I've had to slave to keep body and soul together." She walked to the dresser, turned, and faced him again. "I've had a hard time. And I want you to know it."

He didn't look up. "I'm sorry you've had a hard time—"

"You're sorry!" She glared at him. "*You* are sorry. You're to blame for it all."

Then he looked at her. "I am sorry. And I'll give you a top price for your holdings. I'll give you anything you ask for them."

"You—give!" She was standing close beside the dresser. "You never gave anything in your life. All you've done is take away. You took my husband. You made me a widow, Keith Alexander. I've had a hard life. And all because of you."

He sighed and looked down at his hands again. In Chicago he would have ended such a tirade in an instant. But this was Lebanon, and he had brought oil and finest wines to pour into old wounds. He was sorry for Aven MacIvor and sorry for himself. His offerings were being refused and the old wounds would not heal. The dead would not bury the dead. They still lived to haunt and torment.

"Aven," he said, "there's no use in our talking like this. I'll send my lawyers—"

"You'll sit there and listen. I've had to live with it for thirty years. Now you'll hear what I have to say." She walked closer to him. This was the man who killed her husband, calling out before he shot him, "MacIvor!" Her voice was low and she spoke slowly, "May God damn you, Keith Alexander!"

He stooped for his hat, then pushed back his chair. "You may believe me or not, Aven, but I am sorry for your unhappiness." He began walking toward the door.

She opened the dresser drawer.

His hand was on the knob of the door when she called, "Alexander!"

He turned. Keith Alexander never saw the pistol **in her h**and until she fired.

The first bullet struck him in the stomach, knocking him back and he caught the knob of the door, clinging to it. She moved closer to him and he made no outcry.

"You shot him the second time in the mouth." She raised the pistol and fired a second time.

He fell, pitching forward. Aven stood above him a moment, cringing from the horror.

Then she closed the dresser drawer. She threw a coat over her shoulders and walked out of the room, and was going along the hall when the clerk reached the top of the stairs. He saw her coming, the pistol in her hand, and he stepped aside, pushing himself against the wall to let her pass. Two or three men ran into the lobby. They stared at Aven MacIvor as she walked out of the hotel and across the street.

Sheriff Hardee was running toward the front door of the court-house when she walked in. He put his hand against the wall and stared at her, slowly blinking.

Aven handed him the pistol. "I killed Keith Alexander. He came to my room and I killed him."

"Great God A'mighty." Hardee barely whispered the words, and his face went white. He was still standing there when Vernon Boyd came hurrying into the courthouse. "She killed Keith Alexander," Hardee said, staring helplessly at his chief deputy. "Hadn't we better get Judge Hill?"

"We better get set for trouble. Them Dabneys will be coming—"

"But a Dabney killed him! She's Bruce Dabney's twin! They won't do anything—"

"She's a MacIvor!" Boyd shouted the words and reached out and took Aven's arm, leading her into the sheriff's office. "You sit right there, Mrs. MacIvor. Don't you move from that chair. Oscar, you send for Judge Hill. And keep your mouth shut. Alexander went to her room and she shot him. That's all there is to it. Keep your mouth shut."

Aven began weeping. "That's right. He came to my room—"

"He killed your husband," Hardee said. "Maybe that's why you shot him—"

"Keep your God damn mouth shut, I tell you," Boyd bellowed. "And send for Judge Hill. Them Dabneys will be swarming."

Sheriff Hardee ran out and Aven watched him go. "Am I under arrest?"

"Yes'm," Vernon Boyd said. "Sort of protective custody, Mrs. Mac-Ivor. It ain't a regular arrest because this is Mississippi, and I reckon a lady still has some rights in Mississippi."

On that day of all days, Lebanon expected to hear again the horn of the Dabneys and held its breath, awaiting the summons from the big house up the lane from The Tree.

Ruth Thrumbull announced firmly to her father that she was going to The House. She anticipated a protest and was prepared for a showdown. However, Mr. G. T. Thrumbull said softly, almost humbly, "That's all right, Ruth. I'll have one of the Negroes hitch up for you." She began weeping then and he wept too, and they held each other tight. He was without a wife and was to be without a daughter, alone in his mansion; but when she raised her head and dried her eyes, he opened the door for her and she went out.

Windy Hill rode in furiously from Ellisville, verified the report, then sent a messenger galloping back with the news that Keith Alexander was dead. The single telegraph wire from the depot at Ellisville hummed the news. Chicago heard it and Alexander's associates were frightened; their world trembled.

Sheriff Hardee slumped at his desk and Vernon Boyd paced the floor, endlessly rolling an unlighted cigar in his mouth, chewing it. Frequently one of them walked to the window, looking out, listening for the call of the Dabneys, awaiting some sound from the big white house on the west ridge, high above Bogue Homa.

And the horn of the Dabneys was silent.

Throughout the morning and into the afternoon of that somber day, the horn hung untouched on its rawhide thongs in the big room, hanging over the mantel where Alexander's pistols lay. The family gave the horn no thought. They were assembled in Shellie's room, alone with their grief and shame, while the old woman mumbled her rosary of sorrow, telling her beads of evil and distress. "Fort Mims," she moaned. "The north cut. Blood and hate and death. Now one of us has killed one of our own."

Kyd sat on the bed and Bruce sat in a chair by his mother. Ruth rested on a stool, a stool of hickory and oxhide, near Kyd, occasionally glancing at Sans, at his hurt eyes; and her heart cringed for his despair.

The brothers sat on Shellie's trunk near the window, each staring, each stunned into silence. The rain was beginning, coming down softly, and old Shellie talked on and on, mouthing her words until the family scarcely distinguished between her mumble and the mumbling of the rain.

Mingo didn't hear her at all. He was listening to the wind through the tall pines, whispering its summons, and Kyd and Sans, too, were hearing the wind. It was a moan to Kyd, the wail of her failure to hold her son, but it was a wild fierce cry to Sans, the cry of a winged flight divided.

Sans looked at Kyd, at her dry tortured eyes, and he felt a tenderness for her, a sonship. His eyes moved to Ruth and he was stronger because she was there. He looked over at Bruce and loved him, a great gentleness surging up in his heart as he looked at the old man and saw his white beard, saw his hand and his tired eyes and sagging shoulders. The elder brother looked at the family, seeing the years past and the years ahead, and knowing that he was anchored here, to this heritage and to this valley.

Mingo did not look at his family or give thought to the years past. He was looking only at Sans, hoping for the sign that would set him free, loose him from the valley. It was an old valley and Mingo was young. He had seen fox-glow and frost on the rim of the world, and he must touch the frost and find it warm. He was young, but the valley was old because the people were old. Their sinews were weakened and their souls dimmed because they didn't think for themselves, or stand up in meeting and declare their rights. In laziness and selfishness and ignorance, they fumbled on down the endless furrow; today was still yesterday, and it was too much trouble to look up. It was a tired, old valley, and he was young.

In mid-afternoon the body of Keith Alexander was brought to The House in a wagon. Mr. Charlie was in charge. Smoke Jackson and three of Mingo's mill hands carried the body into the big room, then tiptoed out.

Mr. Charlie and Wyeth Woodward stayed by the bier to watch. They sat before the fire, rocking and thinking the troubled thoughts that come to men in the presence of the dead.

"What'll they do?" Mr. Charlie asked.

"Nothing," Wyeth said. "The grand jury won't indict. Keith went to Aven's room, and this is Mississippi. The law hasn't been written in this state to convict a white woman under such circumstances." The old lawyer sighed his worry and his grief. "Anyhow, Bruce will never let his twin sister go to trial."

Mr. Charlie poked up the fire, then walked over and rearranged the gray shroud. "I hope Peninsula lays low. The Dabneys won't take much more. Old Shellie can hold Bruce just so long, and he can hold those boys just so long."

Wyeth moved his heavy hand over his beard. "Maybe a lot of us have taken about all we're going to." He almost choked up. "I carried Gar Rivers back to his cabin yesterday."

Mr. Charlie said, "It was the best thing to do."

"It was the thing I had to do." Wyeth stared down at his hands, clenching them, and his old, massive shoulders sagged under the weight of a burden felt but seldom revealed. "I had to decide between my wife and daughter, and my friend."

Bruce came into the room and Wyeth and Mr. Charlie dropped the subject of Gar Rivers. The Dabney sire glanced over at them and crossed the room and looked at Keith's body. The mustaches were gone and his jaw was gone. Mr. Charlie said, "I did the best I could. There wasn't much left to work with. Have you sent for Morna?"

Bruce nodded. "She'll be here in a day or so. I don't know exactly when, but she's coming."

"What about Keith's children?" Mr. Charlie asked.

"We don't know his children very well. We'll leave that to Morna."

Mr. Charlie was looking up at the horn and the pistols. "You aim to wait until she gets here to bury him?"

"No. We will bury him tomorrow."

The storekeeper peered at Bruce. "Where you aim to do it?"

"Under The Tree with the family. Morna may not want him to stay there, but there's where we'll put him for a while anyhow. Now, what about Aven?"

Wyeth got up and took Bruce's arm and led him to a chair. "Oscar Hardee took Aven to his house. Windy Hill called the grand jury and they'll meet, but it's only a formality. There'll be no true bill. By tomorrow Aven will be free."

"She will never be free." There was no bitterness in Bruce's tone, only a slow, deep sadness. He rose from the chair and walked back to Shellie's room. The rosary was almost told.

A few friends began arriving shortly after noon and Kyd received them and took them into the parlor. Ruth Thrumbull, watching Kyd and learning the customs she expected to obey in the years to come, put on an apron and went to the kitchen. There she helped drip coffee and prepare food. Laurel Woodward came to The House and burst into tears and took Kyd into her arms. Louisa was with her mother and murmured condolences. The Woodward women stayed only a few minutes and did not see Ruth Thrumbull, did not even know she was there.

There came Ruth's father, riding alone from his big mansion. He went straight to Bruce and offered his hand and Bruce said, "Ruth is helping out in the kitchen. Want me to call her?"

"Never mind," Mr. Thrumbull said. He went with Bruce into the big room and looked at the body, and shook hands with the men there.

The mill's whistle sounded, low and ominous, sounding notice to still the saws and bank the fires, to close the mill for the people to troop to the Dabney house and view the body of Keith Alexander, to see the legend dead.

All the people came from afar to see, riding up out of the swamps and down from the scrubby ridges, swarming into the valley, their long red necks swathed against the rain. Even their dogs were gaunt, their heads drooping, and their oxen and mules were slow and plodding. They came in their creaking wagons, the wheels wobbling; came poking into Dabney's Hollow. The South was creeping out of her myth, exposing herself long enough to bury one of her legends.

Past the Jasper House moved the long, solemn file, silent except for the squeak of the wagons, the muddy squish of the hoofs, and the faint clank of the harness chains. It moved on in a single curving line past Oscar Hardee's house where Aven MacIvor walked the floor, and walked the floor, alone in a room, occasionally gazing out of the window at the drizzling rain and the blank, upturned faces staring at her refuge.

The rain passed in the late afternoon, but the clouds came down, settling over the valley, drifting low and gray. The naked oaks dripped and the earth was sodden. Darkness crept in and the folks crept away, squeaking back to their swamps and scrubby ridges.

The Negro grave diggers under The Tree measured with their shovels, and when the grave was deeper than a handle they put their shovels on their shoulders and they, too, went away.

The family was alone again and insisted that Mr. Thrumbull share their supper. Ruth fixed a plate for each of them, and her father looked at her a long time, then his eyes wavered. Her eyes did not waver. Sans stayed close to Mingo, and Bruce was always near Kyd.

It was late, past eleven o'clock, when Brother Eubanks arrived in his buggy. The pastor of the Free Church apologized, "I was in the far end of the county when I heard about it."

He brought news that the grand jury adjourned without indicting. Aven MacIvor was back at the hotel. They gave her another room and she moved in. She was alone. She wanted it that way.

The pastor took a chair in the parlor and sat a while with the men. Then he said, "Brother Dabney, I'd like to talk to you and your boys."

Bruce led the way into the hall. Sans and Mingo followed. Brother Eubanks said, "I've been wrestling with my conscience. I cannot eulogize Keith Alexander at the service tomorrow." The pastor was an honest man, humble and devout. "Keith Alexander rode a white horse and yearned for a white plume." Brother Eubank's voice rose slightly as he was stirred by his imagery. "But in the old days only the dedicated knights rode the white horse, and earned the accolade of the white plume. Keith Alexander was not one of them."

Bruce spoke quietly, "Nothing said at a grave ever increased love or lessened hate. I suggest, Brother Eubanks, that you read Keith's favorite verse, then ask God's mercy."

"What was his favorite verse?"

"In Ecclesiastes. The one about there's a time for things."

"Yes," Brother Eubanks said. "I know. A time to love, and a time to hate."

Sans knew it, too, and he looked at Mingo. A time to go away; a time to remain at home. It wasn't in the Bible, but it might have been.

Shortly before ten o'clock, one day after his death, the body of Keith Alexander was moved from The House to The Tree. Only a few friends were there. The Woodwards; Louisa and her mother standing close together, and Wyeth near them and yet closer, perhaps, to Mr. Charlie. Mr. Thrumbull was with his daughter, and it was Bruce who reached out and took Mr. Thrumbull's arm, easing him and Ruth closer to the Dabneys.

Mr. Charlie nodded to Brother Eubanks and he stepped to the head of the coffin. "This man had many enemies. And this man had many friends. His friends loved him surely as much as his enemies hated him." The pastor opened his Bible, thumbing the pages slowly, wetting the tip of his fingers as he thumbed. Then he read:

> "To everything there is a season,
> And a time to every purpose under the heaven:
> A time to be born, and a time to die—"

His voice droned on and Sans' mind took up the rhythm of the words, their eternal beauty. A time to sow and a time to reap. A time to go away, and a time to remain behind.

Wild geese called over the north cut, winging high above the valley, winging south, hurrying on toward the Gulf, and calling. Sans glanced at his brother, feeling Mingo's gaze and Mingo's question. And Sans Dabney looked south, watching the white wedge piercing the sky, and he cried out for them to turn and come back; but the wild geese flew on, calling.

Brother Eubanks ended the service. "We ask the mercy of God upon the soul of Keith Alexander."

That was all. They lowered the body into the ground and the people began moving away. Ruth went home with her father. There had been a few tears during the service, but now Kyd wept from the sheer strain of the ordeal. Mingo touched his father. "I will be home directly." He put his arm around his mother and held her for an instant. "I want to talk to Mr. Woodward and I want Sans to be with me."

Kyd started to speak. She, too, had seen the flight winging south, had heard the wild geese calling. She, too, knew the cord was severed. She started to speak, but Bruce looked at her and the words never came. She took her husband's arm and they walked to The House.

Sans and Mingo called Mr. Woodward aside and they moved up the lane, beyond hearing of the others. There was no haste in Mingo's words, only a firm resolve. "I've got to talk to you."

"When do you plan to leave, son?" Wyeth used his foot to roll a pine-cone out of the path, tapping it aside. Then he glanced up at the brothers, seeing the surprise on Mingo's face, the loneliness in Sans' eyes.

"Did I make it that plain?" the younger brother asked.

Wyeth turned his head toward the south cut. "I felt it since that day Rafaela Galban left. When do you aim to go?"

"Right away, Mr. Woodward. And I want to talk to you about my business."

Wyeth Woodward knew there was a time for leaving, and the time had come for the younger brother. He was watching Sans, however; watching the one who must stay, as some men must always remain to weave the threads left in the loom, and gather the harvest left in the field. "I reckon you better not hurry, Mingo." Wyeth wet his lips and frowned slightly. "Maybe you better wait until your Aunt Morna comes. Your family might need you."

"I'll stay as long as I'm needed." Mingo's heart was light at last. "Then I'm going."

Wyeth patted the younger brother on the shoulder. "We'll take care of things." He turned toward his buggy, toward his wife and his daughter.

The brothers walked past the grave and on to The House. The sun came out timidly, brushing away the mist and warming the land, warming the raw earth mounded under The Tree where Keith Alexander lay.

Chapter twenty-one

A SPECIAL TRAIN sped Morna Alexander from New Orleans to Ellisville. She brought only one bag and a dossier on Peninsula Lumber Company's venture in Lebanon, compiled swiftly at her command by her husband's agents. The widow of Keith Alexander, the eldest of Shellie's living children, wanted the file to learn of any affiliation, secret or admitted, between Peninsula and Aven MacIvor.

Morna's hair was white and was combed back from her forehead.

Her life with Keith Alexander, his abject devotion, had mellowed the violent temper of her youth, her quick hatreds and sudden fits of anger. But nothing could change her endless hatred for Claiborne MacIvor and for Aven, her sister.

She sat under the swaying lamp of the palace car, studying the report, her nervous fingers turning the pages. She noted an entry concerning Louisa Woodward that disclosed an alliance between Louisa and Judge Cephus Hill, but no details were revealed and the entry obviously was slurred, hiding the facts. She was not concerned at that minute with Louisa Woodward and Judge Cephus Hill; her concern was Peninsula and Aven, for surely the jackals had leagued together to kill the lion.

However, the file contained only one mention of Aven MacIvor; an unimportant notation about a boundary dispute, and it was buried on Page 12 under "Minor difficulties." Finding no evidence of compact between the company and her sister, Morna flung the report aside. She wrapped her scarf about her, drawing it close about her shoulders, and stared out into the darkness, her blue-green eyes blazing anger as the train rattled on. Suddenly she rose and sweeping her scarf about her, strode to the end of the car, summoned the conductor and demanded that the train go faster.

Rufus Tolbert's swiftest team was waiting for her at the Ellisville depot. It was four o'clock in the morning, but Windy Hill knew of Morna Alexander's message ordering the horses and he was up and watching. He saw Morna arrive in Ellisville and saw her leave, her driver lashing the team.

None saw her enter the valley of Lebanon. She came through the north cut before dawn, never pausing to look at the spot where Claiborne MacIvor died and her family bled.

"Whip them up," she ordered as the team pounded through the cut. "We're almost there."

"They can't stand it, ma'am," the driver protested. "We'll kill 'em."

Morna reached for the whip and lashed the horses. Soot was on her green coat, and cinders in her white hair. This was not Morna Alexander of Chicago and the watering places of Europe; this was Morna Dabney of Lebanon.

The Tree was still in the shadows of the first gray of dawn, and The House was a brooding refuge on the ridge. Morna took the

reins and swirled the horses into the lane and past The Tree, seeing
the raw earth and knowing its story. She tossed the reins to the driver,
then swung from the buggy and on to the porch as Bruce came hurrying along the hall, holding his lamp high and calling, "Morna?
Is that you, Morna?"

"Yes."

She reached for the door and flung it wide. Bruce opened his arms
and held his sister, and he sobbed for the first time since he met Aven
that day in Ellisville. Kyd and the boys came from their rooms and
Kyd was crying. But not Morna. She stood in the doorway. "Where's
Aven?"

"At the hotel," Bruce said.

"Hotel!" Morna pulled off her hat and threw it on the table. "My
God! Don't you put people in jail for murder?"

"She's been freed," her brother said. "It's an unwritten law—"

"Then I'll write it." Morna ran from the porch to the buggy,
snatching the reins from the driver. He leaped from the buggy and
she wheeled the horses, lashing them into a gallop. One stumbled
and she lashed him again.

Her family stood silent in the doorway.

The clerk in the Jasper House never had seen Morna Alexander
before. Her hair was falling to her shoulders. Her coat was muddy.
"Mrs. MacIvor will be leaving in a few minutes—"

"She gave no instructions," the clerk said.

"I am giving instructions. Mrs. MacIvor will be leaving in five
minutes. Have a team and buggy here for her."

"I have nobody to send to the stable," the clerk protested. "Besides,
Mrs. MacIvor is a guest at this hotel—"

"Go yourself." Morna stepped close to the desk. "I am Morna
Dabney. Have a buggy here in five minutes. Which is her room?"

"The one halfway down the hall, on the right," the clerk stam-
mered.

Morna went up the stairs and to the door of Aven's room. She
knocked sharply. "Open the door! Open this door, Aven!"

Before she could knock again, Aven opened the door. She was
wearing a blue velvet dress. "I knew you would come."

The elder sister looked first at her eyes and then down her slender
body. Aven drew back.

Morna did not speak to her, but shoved her aside and reached under the bed for a suitcase. She dragged it out and threw it in the middle of the floor. She jerked open the drawers of the dresser and dumped clothes into the suitcase. "Now lock it. You're leaving Lebanon. Pick up your bag and get out."

Aven moved back toward the door, moving away but still facing her sister. "You can't make me get out."

Morna slapped her across the mouth. Then spat on her. "I can present evidence that my husband came here to take you to your mother." She slapped her again and Aven covered her face with her hands, whimpering. Her sister scorned her. "The MacIvors always whimpered. My husband came to your room to buy your property and help you—"

"He killed my husband. He caused all my trouble." Aven began screaming. "He killed my husband—"

"*Your* husband!" Morna caught her hair and jerked up her head, then slapped her across the mouth again. "Claiborne MacIvor made love to me the night before he was killed. He forgot you! He came back to me."

All the blood drained from Aven's face.

"I don't believe it." She gripped her sister's arm. "I don't believe it. You're lying. You're trying to rob me of my last memory—"

"He lay in my arms all night." Morna said it slowly, lingering on each word, burning them into Aven's heart. "He lay in my arms and he forgot you. I was the first who had him. I was the last. And I left him and came back to Keith Alexander. Now get out." Morna put her foot against the suitcase and shoved it toward the door. "Pick it up and get out."

Aven lifted the bag. It was heavy and she struggled down the hall, down the steps and into the lobby where a crowd was gathering. The clerk stepped forward to help her, and Morna looked at him and the clerk stepped back. Oscar Hardee came forward and reached for the bag.

"Leave her alone," Morna commanded.

"I'm Oscar Hardee. I'm the sheriff—"

"I'm Morna Dabney." She strode toward him and he drew back, stepping slowly backward and watching her.

The door of the hotel opened and Bruce and his sons came in.

Bruce reached for Aven's suitcase and carried it outside and put it in the buggy.

"Take this woman to Ellisville," Morna said to the driver.

Bruce said, "Have you any money, Aven?"

Morna gave Aven no chance to answer. She snatched the whip from her own buggy, struck Aven's horses and struck them again. They galloped wildly away, the driver holding hard on the reins.

The crowd mumbled and Sans and Mingo looked to their father for instruction. Bruce turned and faced the people, looking squarely at Sheriff Hardee. "This is a Dabney affair. We need no help in this matter."

They were silent, and Morna got into her buggy and drove away. The Dabney men mounted their horses and rode slowly behind her. Bruce's old eyes were flaming and Mingo was tense, but Sans was wretched. A sister driving a sister out of the sanctuary of the Dabneys!

Morna reined her horses near The Tree and waited. Bruce and the boys drew alongside and together they rode up the lane. Kyd was on the porch, gazing toward the north cut.

There was an echo from the cut, an echo of pounding hoofs, and Aven MacIvor was out of the valley, forever.

The Dabneys went into The House and Morna asked about her mother. "Is she awake yet?"

"Yes. She's asking for you," said Kyd. "She knows you're home."

Morna went to Shellie's room and over to the bed where the old woman lay. "I'm back, Mama." She touched her mother's hair and kissed her cheek.

"What did you do to Aven?" Shellie demanded.

"I drove her away. I drove her out of the valley."

Shellie struggled to sit and Morna helped her, propping a pillow at her back. "You did right," the old woman said. "She is a MacIvor and didn't belong in this valley."

Morna sat on the edge of the bed, fighting sudden exhaustion that almost overcame her. Then she wept, for the first time. She put her head on the pillow of her mother's bed and cried like a child. "You know how much I loved him, Mama."

"I know." She felt for her daughter's hand. "Now go to sleep. You need rest."

Morna Dabney lay on the bed beside her mother and the old woman's hand trembled over her daughter's hair and down her cheeks, soothing her. In the quietness of the room, Morna drifted off to sleep.

The family ate breakfast in silence, glancing occasionally at Mingo as though expecting him to tell them a thing they already knew. However, something restrained him, perhaps the yearning in Kyd's eyes.

Bruce sensed the tension, and broke it. "Your Uncle Keith's stallion needs exercise, Mingo. Maybe you better go ride him."

The boys went out together, and the younger one saddled Shannon, cinching the straps tight. Sans saddled his own horse and he and Mingo rode across Bogue Homa. The creek was swelling from the recent rains and Shannon stopped and drank, then suddenly flung his head high, his white mane showering. The younger brother got off the horse, slowly, deliberately, and handed the reins to Sans. "Here, kiddo. You ride him first."

The elder brother accepted the reins. Never had Sans Dabney ridden such a horse, for the white horse was free and untamed, prancing with high hoofs, shaking the earth as he galloped. His spirit seeped into Sans and there was an urge to cry out to the land, to the trees, to shout that he, too, was free and young and strong. He, too, had heard the wild geese calling and his eyes had followed them.

Over the west ridge he rode, back into his woods, galloping wildly under the pines in a freedom he knew was for a moment only; but in that moment all the shackles were torn away. He was free from the bondage of the valley, free from the loom that other men had set, from the harvest other men had sown. He was free because his fancy was free, running wild in the world beyond the pines, racing beyond the ridges of Lebanon.

Then it passed: the moment of fancy passed into the years of truth, and there was the mill at the south cut, the railroad through the north cut, and this was Lebanon and he was Sans Dabney. However, no matter the shuttle that lay waiting for him, or the hoe that stood ready for his hand; he had ridden the mountains of his dream; he, too, had been in Arcady.

He checked the stallion, knowing that never again must he ride a white horse; for there is a lure in a white horse that leads a man away. And he knew that some men must stay behind, remain forever to weave and plow in the valley of their fathers and their sons.

He wheeled the horse and rode him back to Mingo. "Take him, Lebuba. He's not my kind of horse."

Mingo looked at his brother, seeing everything that Sans wanted to hide; and there was nothing that could be said, so the younger one mounted Shannon and the brothers rode away.

First down to the cabin of Gar Rivers for a glass of buttermilk. An old Negro woman was tending Gar. Mr. Charlie had been to see him that day and so had Wyeth Woodward. He knew all about Aven, all about Morna, yet he did not discuss it with the Dabney boys.

They rode down to the south cut, thence around the west ridge, circling the valley, watching the day bloom and fade; the brothers riding together.

It was late afternoon when they returned to The House. Mingo fed and watered the stallion. Sans did not touch him, turning his back to the white horse and feeding the Dabney horses and his father's mules.

Ruth Thrumbull was in the kitchen talking to Kyd, and Sans kissed her. It was the first time he had kissed her before a witness. Bruce was with Morna in Shellie's room.

Supper was almost ready and the brothers bathed and shaved and joined the family at the table. Ruth was at Sans' side and Mingo's place was set across the table, next to his Aunt Morna.

The younger brother went to Morna's chair, and stooped and kissed her cheek: "I've always heard you were the most beautiful of the Dabneys. That's one family story I believe."

She was pleased and smiled and they all were relieved because she smiled. Her hair shone soft and white and her dress was green, low at the neck. A cameo hung at her throat, held by a black ribbon. "I had a good rest," she said. "And Kyd scrubbed my hair. She took off part of the skin, I think." She looked closely at Mingo. "Bruce tells me you've been riding the white horse."

The old man bowed his head to say the blessing and they waited. "Mingo," Bruce said, "will you return thanks?"

This was the family again. Morna was hungry. "Thank you for the cornbread. Another slice of the chicken, if you please." She drank buttermilk and buttered her biscuits, pausing to pass the plates that moved her way.

"Bogue Homa is rising a bit," Bruce said.

"The foxes are coming in close," Sans said. "It means a hard winter."

Ruth said, "The winters here are so mild compared to Chicago that I never think of them as being really cold." She fitted so naturally into the talk.

Morna looked over at her. She fitted, all right; she belonged. She belonged right over there by Sans until the time came, as it must come, when she moved down to the end of the table and Sans took his place at the head.

Kyd asked the cook for more bread. "Viola Vance is expecting in a few days. I must go down there tomorrow."

Ruth said, "Rhoda Fulton is down with chills and fever. We'd better go to see her, too."

This was the forum, and the talk drifted on, but Aven MacIvor was not mentioned. Sans moved his foot and his foot touched Ruth's, and he left it there, touching hers. Mingo said nothing because he knew that night he must say so much. Morna said nothing because her thoughts were under The Tree.

They finished their meal and Kyd poured coffee and they sat back, looking at Morna, giving her the right to speak first. They all were looking at Morna, but Sans and Bruce were thinking of Mingo, wondering when he would speak.

"I'm glad you put him under The Tree," Morna said. "I'll leave him there. There is where he belongs, under The Tree and in the South." She fingered her cameo, turning it slowly. The time had come for her to talk and she was telling all that was in her heart. "No one really knew Keith Alexander but me. He was not merciless. He was sentimental and romantic. He thought the South hated him and he tried to hate the South, but he failed. It was one of his few failures."

Kyd moved to get up for more coffee, but Ruth motioned for her to remain seated and went herself to the kitchen. Sans sat back and crossed his legs, watching the lamp and Mingo.

Morna went on talking. "He made many plans for the valley—"

"What plans?" Sans asked quickly.

"I'm not sure. His plans died with him." She reached for her napkin, smoothing it. "However, I know one thing. Had he lived, he would have destroyed Windy Hill."

"We'll take care of Windy Hill," Bruce said. "The South will take care of him and his ilk."

Neither of the brothers commented. Sans lacked his father's surety about the future and Mingo's mind was elsewhere.

Morna said, "I hope you do. But, Bruce, if the South accepts the Windy Hills then it must not whine. I am no longer a Southerner and it's not my fight. It's a bed the South is making, and on it the South must lie. I am the widow of Keith Alexander and I am going back to Chicago, to live there with my children." She paused while Kyd poured fresh coffee.

"We don't need the North to help us solve our problems. We never did," Bruce said sternly. "Yankee money put Windy Hill in power, bought him and tied him around our necks. But we'll get rid of him."

Morna remembered then her dossier's disclosure of collusion between Louisa Woodward and Judge Cephus Hill. She started to speak, but checked herself. No need to point out to them that the South herself was betraying herself. They would find out soon enough. She sipped her coffee. "Some of Keith's plans I do know. I know he intended to buy the MacIvor holdings. So I will send my lawyers to Virginia and they will buy every MacIvor tree, every MacIvor bush, every grain of MacIvor sand in this valley. I'll buy it for Sans and Mingo. Keith wanted to do it."

Mingo was staring at his coffee cup, but now he looked up. "No, Aunt Morna. Whatever your plans are, they must not include me—"

"Cuba again!" Kyd said it sharply. "It's Cuba and Rafaela Galban."

"When are you leaving, son?" Bruce asked.

"Tonight." Mingo said it softly. He heard Ruth gasp and saw the startled look in his mother's eyes. His gaze moved from one to the other until it rested on Sans. "There's no need waiting any longer."

"I told you," Kyd said to Morna. "I told you this afternoon not to include him. I told you he was going to leave."

Mingo said, "You have plans to discuss, and I must see Mr. Woodward. You'll excuse me, please. This is no surprise to any of you. If I was abrupt, I'm sorry." He got up from the table and walked toward the door.

Sans rose, too, putting his hand on Ruth's shoulder, patting her. He walked around the table and touched his mother's cheek with his hand, caressing her. Then he walked out of the room with Mingo, out to the barn where they hitched Chinquapin to the Brighton. "I'll be waiting for you," the older brother said.

"I won't be gone long. I want to see Mr. Woodward about my business. You'll stay in The Store?"

"If Mr. Charlie needs me," Sans said. "I'll stay for a while, anyhow. Until Ruth and I get our plans worked out."

Mingo nodded his understanding and drove out of the lot and on to the village. There was a light in The Store, for Mr. Charlie was balancing his accounts. There was a light in Peninsula's office. Mr. Thrumbull and his staff were working late. The courthouse was dark and Mingo turned down the road to the Woodward house.

Louisa was in the parlor, sitting on the divan. He saw her through the window and wished she was not there. But if he must face her, he must; so he knocked and stepped back and heard her walking to the door.

She peered into the darkness and said, "Oh! It's you. Come on in."

Mingo followed her into the parlor and waited, his hat in his hand. "I came to see your father."

She glanced at him and went back to the divan and sat down. "When are you leaving?"

"Tonight."

A sudden coldness passed over her and her stomach knotted. She leaned back, steadying herself. "I thought maybe after all that had happened, your family bowed down with grief, you'd change your mind."

"No." He paused, glancing toward the stairs, hoping to hear Mr. Woodward opening the door of his bedroom. "I'm leaving."

Louisa felt the color burning in her cheeks and she shifted so that the light from the lamp was not full upon her face. He was actually leaving the valley. She had never believed a Dabney man would go away. She glanced at him, at his black hair carelessly combed, his smoky brown eyes.

"Why are you leaving, Mingo? Is it that woman?"

He picked up a little cranberry glass vase, glanced at it and put it down again. "We won't talk about it." Then he looked directly at her. "I came to see your father."

"I'll call him in a minute." She had been unable to hold the elder
brother, unable even to quicken the heart of the younger one; but
all that was past and Mingo was leaving the valley. She was glad
to be through with Sans. He was stubborn and not her kind of man;
but she could have managed Mingo. She didn't want Mingo Dabney
to go away and she smiled up at him, her sweetest smile. "Before I
get Papa, I want to tell you some good news."

Mingo waited, standing by the door, his hat still in his hand. She
moved slightly on the divan, drawing her skirt aside, making room
for him. "What is it, Louisa? What is the news?"

"Peninsula's railroad is going to be a common carrier. I spoke to
Judge Hill about it." Again she smiled. "I certainly wasn't going to
pay those outlandish prices for hauling things by wagon into the valley. So I spoke to Judge Hill, and he's having Peninsula make the
railroad a carrier for everybody."

Mingo didn't believe it. He and his brother had gone to the north
cut and Gar Rivers was lying paralyzed in his cabin. He didn't believe
that this girl could accomplish what the Dabneys had failed to accomplish. He just didn't believe that Louisa Woodward and Windy
Hill, the new order, were sly enough, and shrewd enough, and ruthless enough to achieve all that the open forces of the valley had
failed to achieve. "Peninsula is a big company, Louisa. You can't
make them turn the road into a common carrier."

Again she drew her skirt aside and her hand moved to the divan
beside her, touching the divan, inviting him to sit beside her. His
eyes were brighter than she had ever seen them before. "I've already
done it," she said. "I spoke to Judge Hill, and he told Peninsula
they'd have to haul freight for everybody. For the Dabney store and
everybody."

He felt sick inside. "I don't believe it."

Louisa's temper flared but she caught her words. Now was no time
to make him angry. She was too near losing something she wanted.
Even though she had flipped off to Peninsula's store, she might
wheedle things, and fix things, and have her way, after all. She
never had realized how tall Mingo was, how tall and straight. She
looked up at him. "It's true, Mingo. And I'm happy I can do something for you Dabney boys."

He stared down at her. It was true, and he knew at that moment it was true. The new order was on top. Mingo was disgusted that greed had succeeded where faith had failed; he was miserable at the thought of Sans learning that the common carrier, the blessing to all the people, would be slimed with the schemes of Windy Hill and Louisa Woodward. However, the railroad and even the north cut seemed far away to Mingo Dabney, and he moved to the foot of the stairs. "Mr. Woodward," he called.

The heavy tread of the old lawyer sounded above, and his door opened. "Didn't know you were down there, son." He was wearing his woolen smoking jacket and he glanced from his guest to his daughter, her face flushed, sitting on the divan. "Louisa, I think your mama wants to see you."

"Yes, Papa." She started from the parlor. As she passed Mingo, she hesitated. "I will see you again, won't I?"

"No. I'm leaving tonight."

She hesitated an instant longer, then put her hands to her cheeks, cupping her face, and ran up the stairs.

Wyeth nodded toward a chair near the fire. "Sit down, son."

The younger brother was holding his hat in his hand, fingering the brim. "I won't take much of your time. I want to thank you for all you've done for me and my folks."

The old man lumbered across the room and put his hand on Mingo's shoulder. "Don't thank me, my boy. You and Sans are like sons to me, and I'm proud of both of you."

Mingo held his hands out to the fire. "Thank you, sir. I want you to fix it so Sans will have control of my mill and my timber."

The lawyer nodded. "We'll go over to my office and draw the papers."

"The Store belongs to Mama and Papa. I was just running it for them, and I want Mr. Charlie to have my say-so at The Store."

Wyeth took off his jacket and put on his coat. He took his heavy black hat from its peg on the halltree. "We'll go fix things." He opened the door. "It's chilly." He buttoned his coat.

They walked rapidly to Mingo's Brighton buggy and drove away, Chinquapin stepping high in the frosty night air.

The darkness swallowed them and Louisa, standing at her window, watched them out of sight. It might be the last time she saw Mingo Dabney. Her shirtwaist was untied and her bedcovers were turned down. She could have managed Mingo, and together they could really have been somebody.

She knew then, and admitted that she wanted Mingo Dabney. For a moment longer she stood still, peering out; then she tied her shirtwaist hastily and ran downstairs, and threw her coat over her shoulders.

Chapter twenty-two

THE DABNEYS still were at the supper table, the coffee cold in the cups, the dining room fire almost to ashes. The knock on the door startled them. Maybe it was Mr. Charlie. They hoped so.

Bruce called out, "Come in. Come on in."

Louisa Woodward walked into the hallway, and their surprise showed on their faces. Bruce got up and offered her a chair and Sans stood. Ruth and Kyd stared at her and Morna looked her over. So this was the girl who'd formed an alliance with Cephus Hill.

They all were silent and Louisa stood fingering one of the buttons of her coat. She was embarrassed and suddenly was frightened as she faced the Dabneys. Her eyes lowered before Morna's gaze and she wished she'd not acted so impulsively, that she'd planned more carefully how to say what she'd come to say.

"Good evening, Louisa." Bruce offered his chair. "Won't you sit down?"

"Thank you. But I haven't time to sit down." There was a catch in her voice and her eyes were drawn to Morna, only to shift away again. "I just found out that Mingo is leaving."

Kyd spoke for the family. "He told us he was going to your father's house."

"I had to come, Mrs. Dabney. I just had to." Louisa was speaking

rapidly, her breath coming in little gasps. Maybe she had been un-
wise to come, foolish to confront the Dabneys in their house; but
she saw a chance to upset Mingo Dabney's plans and, maybe, hold
him in the valley. It was a chance, too, to humiliate Sans for the way
he had treated her, and take the rest of the Dabneys down a notch
or two for the way they'd acted about The Store. It was too good a
chance to miss, but now she was frightened as she stood before these
people peering at her so coldly. She swallowed and rested her hand
upon the door. "It was my duty to come," she said.

Old Bruce sat down, taking his place at the head of the table. Sans
put his hand on the back of Ruth's chair, his face set as he watched
Louisa fingering the button of her coat. "What is it, Louisa?" he
asked. "What is your duty?"

She took one step into the room and faced Kyd, partly turning her
back to Morna. "I don't know how to tell you, Mrs. Dabney. Mingo
and I played together when we were children, and our families always have been so close. Just because I don't work at the Dabney
store any more doesn't mean I don't have your interest at heart. If
something like this were about to happen in our family, I know
you'd come tell me—"

"What is it?" Bruce spoke then. He rested his hands on the edge
of the table and spoke with authority.

Louisa took a deep breath. "I was afraid to tell Mingo myself. I
was afraid he wouldn't listen to me." She was facing Kyd and speaking to her, "But maybe he'll listen to you." She squared her shoulders
and lifted her head. "I came to tell you, Mrs. Dabney, that this
woman Mingo is going to, this Rafaela Galban, has nigger blood in
her."

There was agony in Bruce's eyes and quick horror on Kyd's face.
Ruth Thrumbull was the first to recover. She didn't have the heart
to look at Sans. So the calumny had only smoldered, and a woman
was fanning it into fire again.

"It isn't true." Ruth spat the words.

Kyd started to get up, then slumped back in her chair. "It's a lie."

"Come on into the parlor." Ruth arose and walked toward Louisa.
"I want to talk to you."

Louisa glared at her. "I have nothing to say to you. This is none
of your business. This is strictly a Dabney affair."

"That's right, Miss Woodward." Morna spoke for the first time. "This is a Dabney affair. Therefore it concerns Miss Thrumbull. Go into the parlor with her." Morna Alexander got up from the table. "I'll join you there in a minute."

For a moment Louisa made no move to follow Ruth into the parlor, and then, seeing the Dabneys staring at her, she lifted her head high in a courage she did not feel and walked from the room.

Ruth closed the door to the parlor, shutting herself and Louisa off from the family.

"Louisa Woodward!" Ruth struggled with herself, striving to control her anger. "It's a lie, and I know where it came from."

"You stay out of this. Everybody knows you're running after Sans Dabney, but you haven't got him yet. So keep your mouth out of this!"

The door opened and Morna swept in. The dossier on Peninsula Lumber Company was in her hand and she motioned to a chair. "Sit down, Miss Woodward." She studied Louisa a moment, looking at her eyes, then down at her feet and back to her eyes. "I said sit down!"

Louisa put out her hand, feeling for a chair, and slid into it, the mask of courage falling and fright showing in her face. "I won't be treated like this. I came here to tell you something I thought you ought to know—"

"Never mind why you came here." Morna flipped the report until she found the page she wanted. She laid it open on the table before her and nodded toward another chair. "You sit there, Ruth."

There was a moment's stillness, and Louisa started to speak. Morna silenced her with a glance. "An agreement for Miss Woodward to manage Peninsula's store was arranged by Cephus Hill. He worked through one of his company's lawyers." She consulted her file. "A Mr. Irving." She smiled and turned to Ruth. "I know Mr. Irving. A rascal and a scoundrel. A lawyer whose services and integrity are on the auction block."

Louisa slipped further back in her chair, drawing away from Morna, but staring at the dossier. "What's in that file? You Dabneys have been spying on me!"

Morna scarcely noticed her, speaking to Ruth. "This is a report on Peninsula's activities in Lebanon. It will be complete when I hire

Mr. Irving away from Peninsula and have him fill in the details."
She closed the file and held it in her lap, turning to Louisa. Morna
was composed, coldly dignified, but she lashed at the cringing girl
as surely as if she struck her with a whip. "You, the daughter of
Wyeth Woodward!" There was loathing in her voice. "You and
Cephus Hill! The South has spawned strange bedfellows, Miss
Woodward."

Louisa covered her face and Ruth recoiled from the viciousness
of the blow.

Morna Alexander was relentless. No pity was deserved and none
was given. "The valley knows nothing of your contemptible alliance
with Cephus Hill, and God help you when your father finds it
out."

Ruth Thrumbull was wretched and wanted to be out of that room
and back with Sans. Louisa Woodward was terrified. Morna Alexander smiled and rose. "We will now go back into the dining room,
and Miss Woodward will tell my family that she was wrong about
Miss Galban, and that she regrets being a muckworm."

"I won't do it." Louisa sat erect. There was one last spark of defiance left in her. "You can't make me."

"In that case—" Morna toyed with her cameo. "I'll use a weapon
that you and Judge Hill understand." She still was toying with her
cameo, turning it in her fingers. "I'll buy you. I'll use one of my
husband's petty-cash accounts to buy you, and Judge Hill, and your
little store." There was no evidence then of age about Morna Alexander, none except her soft white hair. Some women never really
grow old. "Now we will go back, and you will apologize to my family."

Louisa looked around frantically, and then, because she recognized
power and feared it, she opened the door, holding it open for the
widow of Keith Alexander. They returned to the dining room and
Ruth, her cheeks still white, touched Sans as she passed, reassuring
him. She smiled at Kyd, smiled wanly, but conveying confidence that
all was well. Morna stepped to Bruce's side and announced to the
family, "Miss Woodward has something to say to all of us."

Windy Hill's disciple put her hand against the door to the dining
room, then took it away. Her coat was rumpled and she smoothed it,
gaining time to bring herself under control. Then she looked at all

of them, fear and hate in her eyes, mumbling her penance, "I was in error about Miss Galban. And I ask your pardon."

She looked at Morna and Morna nodded her dismissal. Louisa turned away from them, holding herself erect as she turned her back on the Dabneys. Sans stepped to the front door and opened it for her, and Louisa passed through and out of The House.

Morna glanced at the lamp flickering on the sideboard, at the candles spluttering on the table. "She will not bother you any more." The words were hollow and without comfort.

No one in the family looked at the others; they all looked away, afraid to see one another. Each was thinking the same thing and, after a time, Kyd expressed their fear. "What if she was telling the truth?" Her throat tightened as she said it. "Cubans are all mixed up. Maybe my boy has been tricked. What do you think, Bruce?"

The old man fumbled with his napkin ring, his hands suddenly clumsy. "I doubt that."

"So do I," Ruth said, and Morna and Sans nodded their agreement.

Kyd pulled her chair closer to the table and slid her coffee cup aside, the cup rattling in the saucer. "I've got to know. If Rafaela Galban is part Negro, we'll have to tell Mingo."

Bruce's hands were steady and he rolled his napkin slowly, slipping it through the big silver ring on which his initials were engraved. "You will tell him. I won't."

"I will tell him," the mother said. "If it is true, I will tell him. A Dabney going all the way to Cuba for a woman who is part Negro—" She shuddered, and looked at each in turn, first at Bruce, and then around the table at all of them. "I've got to know before my boy leaves this house. How do you feel about it, Ruth?" She appealed first to Ruth Thrumbull.

"I'd rather not say—"

"You must say."

Ruth hesitated, wondering what Sans wanted her to say. Then her voice was low. "If it were my son, I'd want to know."

"What about you, Morna?" Kyd's eyes darted to her sister-in-law.

Morna looked away, at the darkness outside the window. "I'd not dignify this thing by an investigation." Her words were not convincing, for she spoke from her mind and not her heart.

Kyd turned to the elder brother and he answered quickly, "I'd let sleeping dogs lie. Maybe you better think twice, Mama—"

"All of you together can't stop me." She glared at her husband and old Bruce turned his head. "Gar Rivers will know, and I have a right to know—"

"What if Gar says Louisa was telling the truth?" Sans spoke so softly they barely heard his words. "If it's true, then what?"

Kyd was appalled and her voice rose. "Why, I'll tell Mingo—"

"And if Mingo goes to her anyhow, then what?" Sans looked at his mother, compassion in his look. "If Mingo leaves this house to find a woman he knows is part Negro, then what, Mama?" He hesitated for an instant. "I'd let well enough alone, if I were you. Mingo will learn the truth, sooner or later, and will decide for himself."

Kyd's eyes flashed around the table again. "You're all against me. But I've got to know." She was the Southern matriarch, the proud, frightened priestess of the cult, eyeless in Gaza, ready to pull down the temple rather than surrender one jot or tittle; ready to destroy the South rather than admit the tradition both false and foolish. "Bruce! I insist that you go to Gar Rivers and find out about this."

"I will not go."

"Then I will." Kyd pushed back her chair and got up.

"Keep your seat, Mama." Sans placed his feet squarely upon the floor and rose slowly from his chair. "I'll go. But will Gar tell me the truth?"

"Of course he will." Kyd was triumphant in her house again, speaking to her son and through him to her husband.

"I'm not so sure." Sans rested his hands on the back of Ruth's chair. "Once such poison starts, it saps the truth and finally eats it up."

Ruth rose. "I'll go with you."

"No, honey. I'll drive you home."

They walked into the hallway together and he helped her with her coat, and they left The House together. He lifted her into her buggy, then mounted his horse. The moon was sweeping in over the east ridge and a light burned in The Store. Mr. Charlie still was working at his accounts, getting them ready in case they were called for. There was a light in Wyeth Woodward's office and Mingo and the lawyer were at his desk. Sans kissed Ruth goodnight, and she clung to him, then stood by her door watching him ride away down Bogue Homa toward Gar's cabin.

The old Negro lay helpless on his couch, a lamp glowing on a stand by his head and a book on a homemade rack across his chest. He was propped on pillows. The woman who tended his needs was in the kitchen and Gar pointed to a chair for Sans, using his left hand to point, the one that was not paralyzed. The elder brother pulled the chair close to the couch, a straight-back chair with a cowhide bottom.

"Is it getting cold outside?" Gar closed his book and pushed his rack away.

"Pretty snappy. I'll build up your fire." Sans went over to the hearth and put on some wood and returned to his chair.

Gar did not question him. Only a matter of urgency could have brought the boy away from his family on this night, and Gar had no idea what it might be. It was not Aven. That chapter was closed and Gar knew the Dabneys well enough to know it must never be opened again. Keith Alexander was dead and Peninsula was through the north cut. The face of the old man, so ugly, so strong, was imperturbable; wise and warm.

"Want a glass of buttermilk?" Gar moved his pillows with his one good hand, and Sans stood over him quickly, fluffing the pillows. "We just churned."

"No, thank you." The boy sat down again, folding his hands and slipping them over his knee, drawing up his knee. "Mingo is leaving tonight."

So it was Mingo, the younger one leaving the valley the night of the day that Aven MacIvor was driven out. That explained the visit. "Maybe it's the best time for him to go. How's your mother taking it?"

"All right. She knew it was coming." Sans squirmed in the chair, hitching himself forward. "I've come to ask you something. Something I've got to know."

"What is it, boy?" Gar shifted as best he could, so that he saw Sans better, and the lamplight flickered in the old man's eyes.

Sans wondered how to say it; then, after a moment's deliberation, said it straightforward. "There is talk about Rafaela Galban." The elder brother bit his lip, betraying his nervousness, his embarrassment for his mission. "There is talk that she is part Negro. I must know the truth." It was said, and he leaned back, free of the words and yet never free because he had uttered them.

Gar Rivers' eyes flamed brighter, the flame steady in his eyes. He was helpless in his bed because he went to the north cut for the valley of Lebanon, for Dabney's Hollow. This was his home, his hearth, and here was a Dabney asking a verdict about a woman who might be Gar's own kind. "Who sent you here?" The old Negro's tone was cold, crackling like the wind on the broom sedge. "Did Mingo send you?"

"No." Sans was hurting within himself. The lamp was too bright and he wanted to turn it down, wanting the shadows instead of the pure bright light. "So far as I know, Mingo has never heard the story. I came on my own hook."

A sadness eased over the face of the old man and he closed his eyes, shutting out the glowing light. "Your mother sent you—"

"Mama has a right to know." He went quickly to Kyd's defense. "Mingo is her only son, and this is the South."

Gar opened his eyes, fastening them on his inquisitor, burning his indictment. "Yes, this is the South. Still the South."

Sans Dabney reached out and touched Gar, touching the withered right arm and his touch was sealed to the black arm, welded there by two hundred years, by the fetid ships of the slave traders, the auction block, the long furrow that began in pride and power and ended in spiritual degradation. "Don't blame Mama." He opened his confession, seeking his own absolution. "I had to know, too."

"Of course you did." There was infinite patience in the words, infinite sadness in the meaning.

"I am a Southerner!" The words poured from his lips, bitter, sickening him as they boiled from the cauldron of two hundred years. "I am a Southerner. My mind cries out that there is a brotherhood. But my heart and my heritage hold back. I am not yet ready to face the truth. I can't. I admit to you that I do not want my brother to go to Rafaela Galban if she is part Negro. I can't help it. I'm a Southerner—"

"I am a Southerner, too." Gar reached his left hand across his chest and found the white man's hand. "And I understand what you say. I understand better than you and your people will ever believe." He held Sans' hand firmly, gripping it. "It took courage to tell me this, and there is hope in courage." He searched the white man's face and saw the mortification and understood the shame. "Your generation is not ready. Maybe the next, or the next. The worms still are crawling in the breast of the South, in the loins of the nation. The truth is hidden behind the fears of your people; under the ignorance and fears of mine. A lie is still the master and truth has not been freed."

"Then tell me the truth about Rafaela Galban." Sans took his hand from the withered flesh of the old man, and the touch was broken. "Tell me the truth and let me go."

"She is white." Gar struggled, reaching over and turning down the lamp. The effort brought lines of pain to his face. Yet he did not ask Sans to do it; he did it for himself. "There is no Negro strain in Rafaela Galban. No Negro heritage."

It was the truth and the elder brother had received the verdict he wanted, but there was neither peace nor comfort in his heart, for the purpose of his mission still hurt him. He knew he could never be relieved of the burden of having come this night, to ask this question. He got up slowly, standing by his chair. "I'll be going now. My folks are waiting."

Gar pushed his head back into the pillows, closing his eyes; a trace of bitterness spread over his face. The calm was gone and he opened his eyes, a resolve shining where the light had been. "I hope José Marti never comes to me as you came tonight. And I'm glad Rafaela Galban never came to me as you have done."

"Why do you speak of José Marti?" Sans frowned his bewilderment. "What has he to do with this?"

"He has the welfare of Rafaela Galban at heart. He has a right to know as much about Mingo as you demand about Miss Galban. So I'm glad he never came to me, and I hope he never will. I would have to lie."

"Why should you lie?" Sans stood over the cot, his tone quickly cold. "What are you getting at?"

All men have pride, even the meek. Therefore, there was a thing Gar must do, a lesson he must teach to the white man, a blow that his pride must strike. "Yes." He said it again, very slowly. "Rafaela Galban is white. The noble breed, son." He turned his head, looking compassionately at the elder brother, then out of the window at the night, at the valley of Lebanon. "But I cannot accord the same honor to Mingo Dabney. The same unimpeachable heritage."

It was spoken.

Sans Dabney's face flushed his sudden anger, the color creeping red from his neck to his cheeks. "What the hell are you saying—"

"I am telling you something I might have spared you had you and your people been one bit considerate of me and mine." His words were as cold as Sans'; as fearless. "I am telling you something because it is in my heart to tell it, to strike back and humiliate you as you have humiliated me. It will scar your pride and crush your heart but, I pray God, it will help your soul! Rafaela Galban is a white woman but Mingo Dabney is part Negro." His voice quivered, then was steady again. Perhaps it was a cruel thing to do, to stir the ruins of the fallen temple, smear the hearthstone of the Dabney fief; but long enough had Gar Rivers bowed his head under the stings of the white man's arrogance. Dinge and jiggerboo; nigger and coon. Now he was lashed by one with whom he had eaten salt, and he struck back.

"You're crazy." Sans recoiled from the burning glow that had returned to the old man's eyes. "You're crazy. There is no Negro blood in the Dabneys."

Gar reached out and gripped the book rack, pulling himself high on his pillows. "Kyd Dabney was a Fermat. She is an orphan; a Cajun from Bogue Homa's bottoms. She was taken into the Dabney home when she was but a child. She does not know that the blood she dreads in Rafaela Galban is in her, and in her son."

The elder brother stood motionless for a second, a second that stretched back for two hundred years. "My God!" He whispered it. "Good God in heaven! Mama of all people! Who knows this?" It was a plea.

Gar studied the face of the white man, and slowly into his own face, so deeply marked by multiple scars, the tenderness returned; the longing to ease the agony of another man. "Those under The Tree knew it." His voice was low, like the far off tolling of a bell. "Keith Alexander knew it, but now he, too, is under The Tree. Soon

I will be gone, and you will be the only one who knows the truth."

Sans Dabney bowed as though blows were falling on his head and on his shoulders. "My God!" He said it reverently, piteously. "It would kill Mama if she knew. Maybe Mingo. It wouldn't bother Papa too much. But it would kill Mama—"

"By the law of your people. By the law of your state. By the tradition of your South—" Gar was sparing nothing. "By that law and that tradition, Mingo would have to be segregated down here with us, and his father and mother could be imprisoned. They have committed the crime of marriage."

The Dabney boy lifted his hands to his face, covering his face, and then, without shame and in the deep humility of a strong man chastened, he knelt beside the cot and put his head on Gar's withered arm, sobbing like a child. "God have mercy on us all."

The old man touched him, stroking his hair as Abraham might have stroked Isaac's hair, as Isaac might have touched Jacob, knowing it was Jacob and never Esau. "God have mercy on you, son. Only the strong can bear the truth." He laid his hand on the white boy's head, anointing him with sorrow, blessing him with solace.

Sans Dabney pulled himself from his knees and Gar felt for his arm, holding him. The boy drew away. "I'll be going now. I must go to my brother."

A sob of righteous joy came from the wrinkled lips of Gar Rivers and his eyes shone with a wondrous light. "I was never wrong about you. You are strong, and in strength there is hope. Let men preach a brotherhood. I have seen it!"

"I am going home to Mingo." Sans stood straight and tall. "Between your house and my house I will talk to my God. If He can forgive me, maybe you can."

"All that's behind us now," the old man said. "Tell Mingo goodbye for me."

The elder brother reached for the lamp. "Shall I blow it out before I go? Maybe you want to sleep. Shall I blow out the light?"

"No. Let it burn."

Sans walked across the floor, the boards of the cabin creaking under his weight, and he opened the door and stepped out into the night. The moon was low over the east ridge and the stars were bright, brighter than he had ever seen them before.

The family was in the big room and Mingo had not returned. Sans stood in the doorway, looking at each of them, quickly at Bruce and Morna, a long time at Kyd Dabney, the proud chin, the questioning eyes.

"Everything's all right," he said to them. "She is white. She is fit for a Dabney."

Kyd said, "Thank the Lord I don't have to carry that cross. Thank the Lord."

Morna said nothing, and Bruce nodded toward a pot of fresh coffee. Sans shook his head and went to Mingo's room and packed his brother's saddlebag. Kyd joined him and put in an extra pair of socks. "Gar was sure, was he?" She asked.

"Yes, he was sure. It is closed, Mama."

"All right, son. I just wanted to be sure."

They heard Mingo come in the front door and Kyd ran up the hall and greeted him, putting her arm around her son's waist and walking with him into the big room.

Sans followed them and threw the saddlebag across a chair. Mingo looked over at him and grinned, "Much obliged, kiddo."

The mother lifted the coffee pot and poured two cups. Sans leaned against the mantel, standing under the horn of the Dabneys, near the pistols of Keith Alexander. Mingo sat in a chair by his father. "Did you get everything fixed?" Bruce asked.

"Yes, sir," Mingo said, a light of anticipation in his face, joy and excitement. "I'm all set to go."

Bruce was calm, but suddenly there were tears in Mingo's eyes. Kyd struggled to hold back her tears, and Morna was smiling at him, proudly.

"Do you need any money?" the father asked.

"No, sir. I have enough."

"Where can we reach you?" Kyd asked.

Sans had nothing to say, just looking at his brother.

Mingo put his cup on the mantel. "I'll be in Mobile awhile. I aim to get track of Elmo Batson. Then I'm going on to Florida, or wherever she is." The cup rattled as he put it down and his hand trembled. "I'll be going now. Tell Grandma goodbye. And Mr. Charlie. Did Ruth go home?"

Sans said, "Uh huh. She was worn out, so I took her home. You'll stop by and tell her goodbye?"

"No. I'm ready to go. You tell her goodbye for me." He stepped to his mother and held her, kissing her forehead and her cheek. Then he kissed Bruce.

Morna spoke then. "There's something I want you to do, Mingo. I want you to have his horse. I want you to ride a white horse out of the valley."

Mingo bit his lip, hard. He kissed her quickly and walked out of the room, and out of The House, and his brother went with him.

It was Sans who saddled Shannon, and led the stallion out in the moonlight. He handed the reins to his brother and Mingo threw his saddlebag into place.

"You'll ride to the south cut with me?" Mingo asked.

"Yes. I'll go with you."

They swung into their saddles, the elder brother on a bay horse and the younger brother on a white one. Mingo kicked open the gate to the barn lot and Sans shoved it open wider and they rode through, down past The Tree, and wheeled into the pike. Neither looked back, each knowing the family was at a window in the big room. The village was still and there was no light in The Store. Mr. Charlie had balanced his accounts.

A light burned in an upstairs room of the Woodward place, just one light. The shades were drawn, but the light shone through. It came from Wyeth's room.

There was a light in the Thrumbull library and it shone brightly.

The horses' hoofs were muffled in the deep sand and the brothers looked straight ahead. Past the courthouse. Past the hotel. Sans saw all the familiar sights, but Mingo did not look at them; there was no need to look again, for the landmarks were in his heart forever.

He was leaving his valley, his home and heritage; he was the young South going away, stepping out of the furrow, turning his back on the land—the fruitful and the barren, the scarred and brutal land. From a thousand valleys, a thousand hollows, ten thousand of the young were leaving the land, all on a quest. A quest for anything; anything to be out of the endless furrow, the furrow stretching from dawn to daydown, and only sweat and a day older to divide dawn from daydown. He was the South, washing out to sea with the land, the strength flowing away. To Cuba where men died. And Indian Territory, the treeless land. To Chicago where the pot was melting.

To New York where they begged for men they could not breed. The South's blood was draining away with her land, thinking with her trees.

The mill was quiet, a wisp of smoke bending from its stack. Sans stared at the mill, at its sleeping bigness. Mingo looked past the mill, watching the road.

They were at the south cut.

"Well," Sans said, reining his horse and swinging down. "You made it this far."

Mingo did not dismount.

The pale vault under the moon was streaked black by the arms of the naked oaks and shadowed by the tops of the pines. The wind was gone and the trees were silent, and there was no sound in the forest. On such nights, in the silver mist under the moon, nothing is real and the hearts of men cry out.

Sans reached up, bending down a pine sapling. He pulled free a cluster of needles and began weaving them, plaiting them together. "Just one thing more, Lebuba. Will you be coming back?"

"No." It was a whisper.

"You are closing the door forever?" Sans finished plaiting the needles.

"Yes." It was still a whisper.

"Then close it softly." He put his hand on his brother's stirrup strap, feeling for the strap in the quick darkness that enveloped him, dark though the moon was bright. "Do you remember what Brother Eubanks said? Some men ride a white horse, but only the dedicated deserve the plume." He handed him the woven needles. "It's from the pines of Lebanon."

Mingo held the pine needles and unfolded his purse and put the plume away. He said not a word. Sans stroked the white horse once, and slapped him on the flank: and Shannon lunged, leaping away into the south cut.

The elder brother did not hear the door close; it was closing so softly, and Mingo was through the cut and down the road to Mobile. The night swallowed him, and he was gone, the hoofs pounding an echo. Then the echo was gone.

Sans looked at the sapling where the needles had grown, and swung quickly into his saddle. It was a good saddle and a good horse.

A bay horse, Lebanon bred, and his hoofs sank in the sand of the valley, soundless as he walked away from the south cut.

The boilers of Peninsula's big mill pulsed their slow breath, the slow, even breathing of the sleeping mill. The steam hissed, seeping into the night, a lull in the stillness before the shrill cry of morning.

Bogue Homa was black and brooding, but there was a light, a small, steady light in the cabin of Gar Rivers. Sans rode that way and paused in the shelter of the water oaks. He dropped his reins and cupped his hands, calling, crying soft the old catamount cry of the Dabneys, "Cre-e-e—o-o-o-o!"

The light in the cabin went out and Gar Rivers slept.

Sans turned his horse back to the pike. He, too, was the South, the one who stayed at home, the South riding a bay horse up the sandy road in Dabney's Hollow.

The family was waiting, a light still burning in the big room. They would want to know about Mingo, to live again each moment of his going. How did he look? What did he say? Did he weep? Did he look handsome on his white horse? When did he say he was aiming to come back?

A light was burning, too, in the Thrumbull mansion, burning brighter than the light in The House.

Let the family wait. Let the old ones wait.

It was past midnight and he turned his horse toward the Thrumbull place. His heart was low, and Ruth alone could lift it up.

High on the ridge above the valley, the hounds bayed. They were running a fox. Old Sooner was leading the pack.